The High Priest
and
The Idol

Visit us at www.boldstrokesbooks.com

What Reviewers Say About
The Lyremouth Chronicles

"Jane Fletcher once again has written an exciting fantasy story for everyone. Though she sets her stories in foreign worlds where the traditional role of women are reversed, her characters (are) all too familiar in their inner lives and thoughts. Unlike the Celaeno series (which I highly recommend) where there are no men, this series incorporates male characters that help round out the story nicely...Fletcher has a way of balancing the fantasy with the human drama in a precise way. She never gets caught up in the minor details of the environment and forgets to tell the story, which happens too often in fantasy fiction...With Fletcher writing such strong work, readers of fantasy will continue to grow."—*Lambda Book Report*

"*The Exile and the Sorcerer* is a mesmerizing read, a tour-de-force packed with adventure, ordeals, complex twists and turns, and the internal introspection of appealing characters. The author writes effortlessly, handling the size and scope of the book with ease. Not since the fantasy works of Elizabeth Moon and Lynn Flewelling have I been so thoroughly engrossed in a tale. This is knockout fiction, tantalizingly told, and beautifully packaged."—*Midwest Book Review*

What Reviewers Say About Jane Fletcher's Celaeno Series

"...captivating, well-written stories in the fantasy genre that are built around women's struggles against themselves, one another, society, and nature."—*WomanSpace* Magazine

"In *Rangers at Roadsend* Fletcher not only gives us powerful characters, but she surprises us with an unexpected ending to the murder conspiracy plot, pushing the story in one direction only to have that direction reversed more than once. This is one thrill ride the reader will not want to get off."—*Independent Gay Writer*

"*The Walls of Westernfort* is not only a highly engaging and fast-paced adventure novel, it provides the reader with an interesting framework for examining the same questions of loyalty, faith, family and love."—*Midwest Book Review*

"*The Walls of Westernfort* is...a true delight. Bold, well-developed characters hold your interest from the beginning and keep you turning the pages. The main plot twists and turns until the very end. The subplot involves likeable women who seem destined not to be together."—*MegaScene*

By the Author

THE LYREMOUTH CHRONICLES

The Exile and the Sorcerer

The Traitor and the Chalice

The Empress and the Acolyte

The High Priest and the Idol

THE CELAENO SERIES

The Temple at Landfall

The Walls of Westernfort

Rangers at Roadsend

Dynasty of Rogues

Shadow of the Knife

The High Priest and The Idol

Lyremouth Chronicles
Book Four

by

Jane Fletcher

2009

THE HIGH PRIEST AND THE IDOL

ISBN 10: 1-60282-085-6
ISBN 13: 978-1-60282-085-2

This Trade Paperback Original Is Published By
Bold Strokes Books, Inc.
P.O. Box 249
Valley Falls, NY 12185

First Edition: July 2009

CREDITS
EDITOR: STACIA SEAMAN
PRODUCTION DESIGN: STACIA SEAMAN
COVER ART BY BARB KIWAK (WWW.KIWAK.COM)
COVER DESIGN BY SHERI (GRAPHICARTIST2020@HOTMAIL.COM)

Acknowledgments

To the usual suspects.

Dedication

To Joanie
for making it all fun again

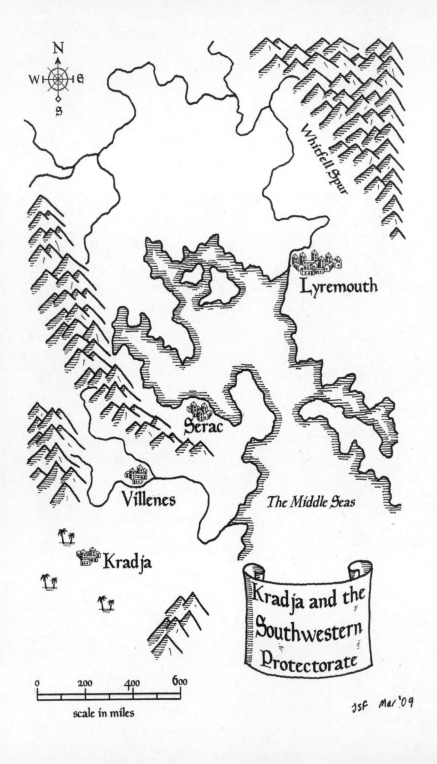

N

W   E

S

Whitfell Spur

Lyremouth

Serac

Villenes

The Middle Seas

Kradja

Kradja and the
Southwestern
Protectorate

0   200   400   600

scale in miles

JSF Mar '09

FOREWORD: THE RULE OF SORCERY

Magic changes everything

The rare individuals who could directly access the higher dimensions had dictated the history of the world. These workers of magic perceived more than the four normal dimensions of time and space known by the ungifted majority, and thus could manipulate their surroundings in ways that seemed as mystical and unstoppable to the rest of the population as a sighted archer might seem in the world of the blind.

A witch was someone who was aware of just one or two paranormal dimensions. Many could claim this title. Far more uncommon were sorcerers, who could perceive all three paranormal dimensions, including the paradoxical second aspect of time—the realm of soothsayers and oracles.

Nobody knew why some were born with these gifts. Whatever the cause, it did not lie in heredity. Children of the most powerful sorcerer were no more likely to be gifted with magic than those of a common shepherd, and therein lay the source of the chaos that sorcerers had inflicted on the world.

Their powers were vast. One sorcerer, acting alone, could carve out an empire, sweeping aside whatever embryonic culture the ungifted had painstakingly built. Cities and civilisations were created by sorcerers' paranormal abilities, and all fell back to anarchy on their deaths. No empire lasted longer than one generation.

Only the founding of the Coven at Lyremouth broke this cycle of empire and anarchy, and only for the lands under its control, the

Protectorate. On the death of the great philosopher-sorcerer Keovan of Lyremouth, his acolytes formed their alliance under an elected leader, the Guardian. Calling themselves the Coven, they invited other sorcerers and witches to join them. To the ordinary folk of the surrounding region they offered protection in return for the payment of taxes.

For four and a half centuries, the Coven grew in size and power. The territory that it controlled expanded also, by consent rather than invasion. The order and security offered by the Coven was an attractive lure, and bordering territories petitioned to join. In time, the Protectorate of Lyremouth came to dwarf the overnight empires of lone sorcerers.

Like any human institution, the Protectorate was not perfect, but it was generally benign and dependable. Guilds could manage their own affairs. Ungifted citizens had rights under the law. Folk might grumble at the taxes and distrust the autocratic sorcerers, yet—uniquely in the history of the world—they lived their lives in peace and prosperity, with the hope that their children and grandchildren might do the same.

It was a society where the circumstances of one's birth counted for nothing, compared to one's abilities. What did it matter who someone's parents were, or where they came from, if that person was a sorcerer? Rich or poor, male or female, dark skinned or pale, nothing counted in comparison to the ability to work magic.

However, there was no pretence at equality. The sorcerers were the unchallenged ruling elite. The social divide was an unbridgeable gulf, marked by distrust, bordering on outright hostility. For all the benefits the Coven brought, the common population viewed the sorcerers with resentment, and were in turn the subject of disdain.

The Coven sorcerer Jemeryl was a product of her civilisation and had never worried herself over the rights and wrongs of her status in society. Her goal in life was to study magic and rise up the Coven hierarchy. The ungifted subjects of the Protectorate were of as much concern to her as the sheep and cattle in the fields.

Meeting Tevi and falling in love changed Jemeryl's outlook more than she would have thought possible. Suddenly she found herself at odds with the leaders of the Coven, forced to justify and defend her relationship. The issue upsetting her fellow sorcerers was not that Tevi was also a woman—in the bisexual Protectorate this was viewed as commonplace—but because Jemeryl's lover was a common mercenary warrior. For Jemeryl this came as something of a revelation, forcing her to reconsider her place in the world she knew.

Whereas for Tevi, it came as no surprise at all. She had faced far worse condemnation on the islands of her birth, far outside the Protectorate. At least nobody on the mainland was going to kill her over the issue.

Part One

The High Priest

CHAPTER ONE—SUMMONED TO LYREMOUTH

Before much longer, the progression of the equinoxes was going to progress off the edge of the paper. Jemeryl sat back and ruefully studied the diagram. Despite her careful planning, with hindsight she could see that she should have positioned the first astral alignment point further from the centre of the page. Was the situation retrievable if she shifted the dates on by twelve years so she could fit the earlier bits in on the left? Jemeryl nodded thoughtfully. That should work well enough.

Her satisfaction lasted less than a second. The new section would then take up the space allocated for the table of the lunar eclipses she had yet to add. In fact, the more Jemeryl looked at the half-completed work, the more she reached the conclusion that her whole approach had been wrong to start with. The figures should have been broken up by planetary conjunction, rather than year. Briefly, Jemeryl considered erasing part of the diagram and amending what was left, maybe even turning the sheet widthways, but then she picked up the paper, scrunched it into a ball, and tossed it into the fire. The paper burned with an agreeable finality. Jemeryl smiled and pulled a clean sheet towards her.

"What makes you think you're going to do any better this time?"

The raucous voice was inhumanly devoid of inflection, but this did not stop Jemeryl catching the undertone of ridicule. She answered without looking up. "Because now I know what I'm doing."

"Excuse me? Haven't I heard that before? Paper doesn't grow on trees, you know."

"Your point being?"

Klara II landed on the desk in a blur of black and white feathers. She strutted forward to stand on the paper and stared up at Jemeryl. Her bead-like eyes glittered in the firelight. "My point being that you've wasted a lot of paper. Why do you have to start from scratch each time you make a mistake? It would be quicker to edit what you already have."

"I want to get it right."

"What is so important about this diagram?"

"Elthon, the idiot. He's spent two years trying to demonstrate that lunar conjunctions can be used to underpin oracles."

"So you're going to waste three years and half a forest proving him wrong."

"It won't take me that long."

"But you can't comment on the forest? Look, the Protectorate isn't going to collapse just because a weasel-faced, ginger-haired sorcerer produced a stupid diagram."

"Elthon has black hair."

"I wasn't talking about him."

"My hair's too dark to count as ginger." Jemeryl was grinning, knowing her familiar was merely trying to get a rise out of her. She pushed Klara off the paper.

"Check out a mirror sometime. Anyway, by the time you finish this diagram, it'll be grey. I suppose next you'll be telling me you're not a pedantically over-obsessive crank?"

"No. That's Elthon."

"You know the thing about turning into whatever you most dislike?"

"Can't see it applies, because I'm not about to turn into an annoying magpie."

Wings flapped. For an instant, Jemeryl assumed Klara had flown off in disgust, before the sound registered as coming from behind. Jemeryl turned her head in time to catch sight of a carrier pigeon swooping in through the half-open study window.

"Oh look. It's grey and gormless." Klara latched on to the fresh target for her sarcasm.

"Don't taunt the pigeon. It's rude of you."

"Why not? It's too dense to notice."

"It's not nice."

"Now who's being rude? I think it's a perfectly nice pigeon—just a bit on the stupid side."

For its part, the carrier pigeon bobbed its head up and down, cooing, as if agreeing with Klara.

Jemeryl shook her head at her familiar. "You're incorrigible."

"Who'd want a corriged magpie?"

Jemeryl chose to ignore Klara's question in favour of retrieving the note from the pigeon's leg. However, reading the contents turned her expression and mood progressively less cheerful. She read it a second time and then started on a third pass, but broke off. The words on the paper were not going to change, no matter how many times she read them. On the surface, the summons was straightforward, but what lay behind it? Jemeryl glanced at the fire, tempted to let the note follow her failed diagram, but regrettably, the letter could not be dismissed so easily. She rang a small bell and a few seconds later the head of a servant appeared around the door.

"Yes, ma'am?"

"I want to talk to Captain Teverik. Can you find her for me? Er…" Jemeryl frowned at the sheet of paper in her hand. "Tell her I'd like to talk to her fairly soon, but it isn't so urgent she needs to dash over if she's busy."

"Yes, ma'am." The head withdrew.

Jemeryl wandered to the window. Her residence at the apex of the hill commanded a view over the densely packed streets of Horzt and the surrounding farmlands. A sky of washed blue hung over the scene. The air was heavy with the weight of spring. To her nose it was the scent of rich soil and pollen. To her extended sorcerer senses it was a riot of auras, about to erupt now that winter was fading. Her eyes focused on the line of mountains to the south. Beyond them was the city of Lyremouth, the home of the Coven. The pigeon had flown all the way from there with the letter—a personal summons from Alendy, the Guardian.

Seven months had passed since Alendy had been elected to the position, making him the leader of the Coven. For Jemeryl, these had been seven months of wondering what he would do, while trying to persuade herself that most likely he would do nothing. Now a message had come. Was it what it seemed? Was she reading too much into it? Jemeryl chewed her lip. Would Alendy really be so blatant?

The door of the study opened again. "I got your message. Has something happened?"

The new arrival was Tevi, town guildmaster for the Mercenaries. Judging by the reinforced leather armour covering Tevi's tall frame, and the sweat plastering her dark hair to her forehead, she had been drilling the town guard when the servant found her. Regardless of how the message had been phrased, Tevi had obviously rushed over, not taking the time to shed the protective wear.

Jemeryl took a moment to study her lover. Although Tevi cleaned up well, the active warrior style definitely suited her. In fact, no matter how Tevi dressed—or undressed—she was well worth looking at. Jemeryl smiled. Whatever Alendy was planning, separating them was one thing he would never succeed at.

Jemeryl nodded towards the pigeon. "I've just had a letter."

"Is there a problem?"

"I assume so, though I don't know what it is."

"What?" Tevi's face wrinkled in confusion.

Klara piped up. "Don't worry. It's not you. She's been progressing equinoxes all morning. It always makes her turn cryptic."

Tevi ignored the magpie and came close enough to put her hand on Jemeryl's arm. "What is it?"

"In detail I don't know but..." Jemeryl indicated the letter on her desk. "It's a summons to go to Lyremouth immediately."

"No other information?"

"None. Not even a hint. They're sending an interim sorcerer to stand in for me. He should be here in a few days." Jemeryl slipped her arm around Tevi's waist for a quick hug before sinking back down in her chair. She picked up the paper but, rather than read, merely stared at it. The words were telling her nothing. The paper they were written on was just as informative. "And I'm to go alone."

The air left Tevi's lungs in a sigh and she dropped into a chair on the other side of the desk. For a while she sat glaring, before saying, "So. Alendy has decided to play games with us."

"I don't know. I can't believe he'd be so blatant about it."

"I can. It's no secret he disapproves of us. Gilliart was on our side, so there was nothing he could do while she was Guardian. But it's what now…seven, eight months since she died? I'd say that was the right sort of time-frame for him to get a feel for being Guardian and want to see what sort of power he has."

"Well, one thing he very definitely doesn't have the power to do, is to say who I share my bed with."

"Not directly. But he can order you to one end of the Protectorate and leave me at the other. We're perfectly free to be lovers, but not to get within a thousand miles of each other."

This was all familiar territory that they had covered often before. Jemeryl shook her head. "I've told you, there's no way he could get away with it. Wherever he sends me, you can join me. And if he keeps mucking around, what he's doing will be obvious to every other sorcerer in the Coven."

"Will they care? You know most are on his side."

"Oh true. My consorting with an ordinary citizen shows no regard for the status of sorcerer, and therefore demeans them as well." Jemeryl knew her ironic grin was a half shade away from being a grimace.

"Exactly. They aren't going to get upset about us."

"Not about us as such, but they will get upset. We sorcerers are very tetchy about our rights. We get irked enough by the rules we have to obey. We don't want to concede anything more. And we certainly don't want rules about our private lives. If I lose the right to pick my lover, then they do too."

Tevi started to speak, but Jemeryl held up her hand and went on. "As a member of the Coven, I'm sworn to obey the Guardian. But on the flip side, Alendy has sworn to vouchsafe the rights of Coven members. He's so obsessive about the pre-eminence of sorcerers. He can't have it both ways and decide I don't have the same sort of freedoms a farm hand would take for granted."

Tevi slumped back in her chair. "So what are you going to do?"

"I've got to obey the summons. Maybe, just maybe, Alendy has a good reason for it."

"And if not?"

"Then I'll pull out the Coven rule book and give him more grief than he'll know what to do with."

"I can go with you anyway. I'll help you turn the book's pages."

"If I obey his orders to the letter it'll make me an irreproachable victim of an abuse of power, and my case will be all the stronger. Don't worry. I can guarantee we'll be back together again soon."

"If you don't come back, you know I'll follow you. Wherever you are."

"Yes. I'll be counting on it."

Tevi pursed her lips, clearly not mollified. "When will you go, and for how long?"

"I'll leave tomorrow, but I can't say when I'll be back. I'll leave Klara with you. I can use her to pass on messages."

"And a damn sight more effective than the grey gimp over there." Klara fluffed up her feathers.

Jemeryl reached out and stroked Klara with her forefinger. The magpie was her familiar. The bond between them was so close that, effectively, she was doing some of her thinking in Klara's head. "By the time I get to Lyremouth, it will be too tiring to mind ride her for long. But no matter how far away I am, I'll be able to make contact, if only for a few minutes a day. I'll be able to let you know where I am, and what's happening. The rest of the time, she'll be quiet."

"That'll be no bad thing." Despite her manifest discontent with the plan, Tevi gave a half grin.

Klara hopped onto Tevi's wrist. "And I love you too, sweetie."

❖

The anteroom to the Guardian's quarters had not changed since the first time Jemeryl had seen it, more than two decades before. Dark wood panelling peeked between the same hanging tapestries. The row of ornate chairs at one side would not have needed replacing. They were so uncomfortable that most visitors chose to stand, ensuring a lack of wear on the seats. Heavy leaded windows gave a view over Lyremouth harbour—a scene blurred by a haze of sea-mist, as it had been on the day of Jemeryl's first visit.

Back then, she had been an eleven-year-old child, recently confirmed as being able to perceive and control all three paranormal dimensions, and sent to Lyremouth to study as an apprentice sorcerer.

Jemeryl had felt few regrets in leaving the village of her birth, and none at leaving the family, who had shunned her from the day it become apparent that she was able to work magic. Growing up had not been easy. The other children in the village had known she was different, and had shown it in various spiteful ways, until Jemeryl's growing power made provoking her too dangerous. Even then, some children had always been ready to see just how far she could be pushed. The memories of rejection and ridicule still hurt. Looking back, the main cause for surprise was that nobody had been killed, or turned into a frog.

Loneliness had been the worst of it. Coming to the Coven at Lyremouth had been the start of a wonderful time in Jemeryl's life, surrounded by people who saw the world with all the same multidimensional complexity that she did. For the first time, Jemeryl felt she belonged. She had friends. She had not wanted to leave. Meeting Tevi had changed that—had changed her outlook in many ways.

Jemeryl knew her childhood did not count as unusual among sorcerers. They were all born into families that were not like them. They grew up, through their formative years, surrounded by people who appeared weak and stupid, unable to see the obvious. In return, they were feared and ostracised. Was it any wonder that so many sorcerers were emotionally scarred by their childhoods and held the ungifted in disregard, bordering on contempt?

The laws of the Protectorate granted rights to all its citizens. Members of the Coven were sworn to defend those rights, with their lives if need be. They were supposed to watch over and lead the citizens in their care, like shepherds watching their flocks. For many sorcerers this analogy was all too apt and they viewed the ungifted masses as no better than sheep. So when it came to her and Tevi? Jemeryl's lips twisted in a wry smile. Yes, the analogy fitted pretty closely there as well.

The door to Alendy's rooms opened and a junior witch appeared. "The Guardian can see you now."

Send in the sheep-shagger. Jemeryl tried to dismiss the thought from her head. The meeting carried enough potential to get awkward, without any undue flippancy on her part.

Alendy was a portly man, a few years shy of seventy. His bald head made his face seem all the rounder. Jemeryl had always thought that he took himself too seriously and being elected as Guardian was unlikely to have softened this trait. When she entered, he was seated in a high-backed chair beside a window. His pose gave the impression that he was working a little too hard at appearing relaxed.

Alendy waited until she was also seated before speaking. "Thank you for coming. I was wondering how things are going in the borderlands near you."

The topic was not what she had expected and Jemeryl took a few seconds to consider her answer. "It's getting calmer. With Revozik's new empire expanding from the east, the dragons are retreating. Trade is picking up. Nine caravans had already passed through when I left, which is up two from this time last year."

"How do you judge Revozik?"

Regimes outside the Protectorate were always in a state of flux. In the case of the lands north of Horzt it had been a period of exceptional turbulence. For the common population, the dragons had been no more deadly than the wars between aspiring sorcerers, seeking to step into the void left by Bykoda's death and the collapse of her empire. So far, Revozik was showing no sign of being more despotic than the former empress, and regardless of what he was like, most folk would welcome his rule, if it could provide a measure of security.

"He's young, but learning. I think he's someone the Coven can work with. I'd been toying with the idea of visiting him in person this summer."

"And in Horzt itself?"

Jemeryl continued to answer the questions, sure they were not the real reason she had been summoned. Much of the information, Alendy must have already known. The rest could have been answered in a written report. Possibly, Alendy wanted time to gauge her mood before getting to his real objective. Jemeryl forced herself to stay calm, to wait and be patient, but it was a bad sign if the Guardian felt he needed to sidle into the discussion.

At last Alendy leaned back in his chair and steepled his fingers. "You must be wondering why I summoned you."

Such an obvious statement needed no reply. Jemeryl tilted her head to the side, surprised at how tense she felt. Alendy had finished prevaricating.

"When you were here as an apprentice, there was one of your fellows, Ciamon. You remember him?"

"Yes."

"You got on well together and parted on good terms?"

"Yes."

"That's what I thought. I don't suppose you're still in contact with him."

Jemeryl's previous tension solidified in a knot of anger. Alendy was still sidling around the subject. The waste of time would be bad enough, even if the end goal was legitimate—which it was not. Already, she could guess where the trail was heading, and it was all the more insulting if Alendy thought he could string her into going along with it. Why could the man not come straight out and say what he meant?

"Is this about my relationship with Tevi?"

"No. Why should it be?" Alendy's denial came a little too quickly.

"Because, as I'm sure you know, Ci and I were lovers for a while. And no. I don't want to give up Tevi in favour of another sorcerer. Not him, or anyone else." Jemeryl knew her tone was not as deferential as it should be when addressing the Guardian, but he had no right to meddle in her personal affairs.

Alendy's face darkened, either in anger or embarrassment. "All right. If that's the way you want to deal with this. You know how I feel about your liaison with a common mercenary. It's highly undesirable, as one day you'll realise. However, I accept you're not going to take my advice, and there's nothing I can do about it." He took a deep breath. "I'm asking you about Ciamon because he's had an accident."

"Accident? How serious is it?"

"Serious enough that he needs help. Unfortunately, it's left him disturbed and he's not going to accept this help from someone he doesn't trust."

And he doesn't trust you. That's two of us. The thought shot through Jemeryl's head, although all she said was, "What sort of help?"

"That will be for the healers to gauge, when they see him. I want you to talk him into returning to Lyremouth."

"Where's he now?"

"Outside the Protectorate. The desert town of Kradja, you know of it?"

"It's got a big temple, that specialises in..." Jemeryl frowned, probing her memory. "Oracles?"

"Yes. That's it."

"Why has he gone there? Is he after a prophecy?"

Alendy shook his head. "I don't think the temple has anything to do with it. He was working in Serac. Kradja lay on the quickest route out of the Protectorate."

So Ciamon was fleeing, but from what? Jemeryl bowed her head, thinking. She was sure that Alendy was not telling her everything. What approach would have the best hope of producing worthwhile answers?

"Why send me after him? Surely he has friends in Serac who could get to him quicker."

Alendy took a moment before replying, clearly picking his words. "Ciamon has not had a happy record since finishing his apprenticeship. He has strong views which put him at odds with most other sorcerers. He's held a number of posts, but I regret to say he's had trouble fitting in wherever he's been. You shared a close bond in the past. There's a better chance he'll listen to you than anyone in Serac."

Ciamon had been idealistic, a passionate dreamer. He had been compassionate to the extent that Jemeryl was sure some latent telepathy was involved. He had been quick to make judgements about right and wrong, and had not been afraid to challenge the Coven leaders when he found something he thought was wrong. He annoyed a lot of people. It sounded as if he had not changed much.

"You said he'd had an accident. What happened?"

"I don't have all the details."

And you don't want to tell me the ones you do have, Jemeryl thought in frustration. That much was clear.

Alendy continued. "Just over a year ago, Gilliart sent him to Serac as assistant to an elderly sorcerer. Ralieu is brilliant, but she's also a little eccentric, as some very talented sorcerers are. I think Gilliart hoped the two nonconformists would get along together. He joined Ralieu just before Gilliart died and what with my election and the transition period, I regret I wasn't able to keep as close an eye on things as I'd have liked."

Why would the appointment of an assistant require the personal attention of the Guardian? There had to be something more to it, and whatever that something more was, Alendy's admission provided one obvious conclusion and a partial answer in explaining his unease. *It was a dangerous situation that you knew required monitoring, and you let it slip.*

"What state is Ciamon likely to be in? I'd appreciate any preparation before I meet him."

"There was no physical damage to him, although regrettably, a few other people lost their lives. At first, Ciamon seemed unharmed, but a short while later his behaviour became increasingly erratic. After making a series of wild threats he vanished. We traced him to Kradja, but I'm afraid I don't know anything else. I've recalled Ralieu to Lyremouth, to find out more."

"When is Ralieu due to arrive? Can I speak to her?"

"Ralieu is hard to predict. She's assured me she's on the way but…" Alendy shrugged. "I'm certain nothing she has to say will help you."

You don't want me to talk to her. Was she being too suspicious? Jemeryl chewed her lip, but then another niggling thought wormed its way into her head. "You said Ciamon had been making threats?"

If so, then something had definitely changed him. Ciamon was always willing to argue his case with passion and persistence, but he had never been violent. He had never let his battle against perceived injustice become a vindictive attack, even on those he believed guilty.

"Not against anyone in particular. To be honest, they were nothing but mad ravings. They only show how badly disturbed he is. The only person he's likely to hurt is himself. Which is why I want him here. Ciamon was injured as a result of his assignment from the Coven. This explains something of the grudge he now clearly carries. As Guardian, I owe it to him, to see that he is cared for and receives treatment. You are one of the few people I think he might listen to."

I'm also too junior to challenge you if I dig up anything. And if I start making noise, since everyone knows you and I are in conflict over Tevi, you can try to pass my report off as biased. I ought to think up an excuse to say no, head back to Horzt and leave you to stew. It was what common sense told her. But common sense was not the only voice in Jemeryl's head.

She closed her eyes. Without effort, she recalled Ciamon, running down a street while laughing at a shared joke, playing with a puppy they found, kissing in a doorway at dawn. She remembered his face, artless and innocent, sleeping beside her. She remembered him, ardent and unswerving, wanting to set the world to rights, and believing that he could. Dreams rarely came true. Ciamon's had clearly evaporated more than most.

Alendy was not telling the whole truth. Of that, Jemeryl was sure. And she was equally sure that, whatever he might say, separating her and Tevi played some part in his motives. Yet Ciamon was in trouble and she could not abandon him. Not because he had been her lover, but because he had been her friend, and because she knew, despite all the years separating them, that if their positions were reversed, he would not desert her.

Jemeryl raised her head. "When do you want me to leave?"

❖

Iralin had aged in the eight years since they last met, to an extent that shocked Jemeryl. The old tutor had lost so much weight that she was little more than a skeleton sitting hunched in a chair. Her hair had been white for as long as Jemeryl could remember. Now it was thinning as well, looking like a halo around her head where the sunlight hit. Despite her frailty, she got quickly to her feet when she saw Jemeryl and her eyes were as sharp as ever.

"Jemeryl. I wasn't expecting to see you here. Have you been recalled from Horzt?"

If Alendy had not discussed the matter with Iralin, it was unlikely that he would have spoken to anyone else. Iralin's former role as tutor meant she was familiar with all that had gone on regarding Ciamon, and she would thus be the obvious person to seek out for advice. However, Iralin also had the seniority to ask probing questions. Was Alendy really so keen to avoid scrutiny? Regardless of his intention, he had neglected to give instructions about confidentiality, so there was no reason for Jemeryl to keep silent. After guiding Iralin back to her seat, she proceeded to recount the details of her meeting with the Guardian earlier that day.

"I've said I'll do it, but I don't trust Alendy. I wish you'd become Guardian instead of him." Jemeryl concluded.

"Please! Don't wish that on me. I have enough trouble keeping my room in order. I wouldn't want to be responsible for the whole Protectorate."

"You didn't always feel that way."

"I wasn't always this old." Iralin sighed and settled back in her chair.

"Then if not you, someone else. I know he'd been deputy for years, but that's no reason to..." Jemeryl finished in a contemptuous pout.

"Alendy's not that bad. He's not dishonest, stupid, or weak-willed. And he'll always do what he thinks is right for the Protectorate."

"I guess that's my big problem with him. He thinks the future of the Protectorate depends on splitting up me and Tevi."

"I think you're overstating the situation. Alendy has strong views about maintaining the status of sorcerers."

"And my relationship with Tevi debases the whole Coven."

"Maybe it does, in his eyes."

"There's no maybe about it. He's a narrow-minded bigot."

"Bigot?"

"He thinks sorcerers are better than everyone else."

"And you don't?"

"No."

Iralin smiled. "You answered that too quickly. Take a moment and think. Are you sure you don't feel just a little bit superior to the person who washes your clothes?"

Jemeryl paused, poking around at her conscience. Admittedly, she could spark a few reactions she was not so pleased with, but on one point she was certain. "I don't feel superior to Tevi."

"I'm pleased to hear it. But Alendy isn't having an affair with her and has no desire to start one."

"He better not have."

Iralin laughed. "It's all right. I think you're safe. But you have to allow his attitude towards her won't be the same as yours."

"True. And that's one thing I worry about. He sees her as a worthless pawn who's upsetting his vision of how the world ought to be. I'm scared he might do something to her while I'm away."

"Alendy won't step outside the law."

"There's enough he can do from inside it."

"Such as?"

"He could get her guild to send her on a very dangerous mission." Jemeryl could feel her stomach tightening at the thought. She swallowed, wishing she could also swallow her fears. "I want her to be here when I get back."

"You're worrying too much. And being unfair on him."

"I've left Klara with Tevi, so we can keep in contact. But it's becoming more of an effort to mind ride. Once I've crossed the Middle Seas, it's going to get harder still." Jemeryl bit her lip. "Can you keep an eye out for Tevi and make sure she's all right?"

"I'm not exactly in the thick of things anymore. Even if Alendy did do something—not that I can imagine he would—but I wouldn't know anything until it was too late."

The words were not comforting and it was not something Jemeryl wanted to discuss at length. She met Iralin's eyes and held them until the elderly woman sighed and said, "All right. I promise to do what I can."

"Thanks."

"When do you leave Lyremouth?"

"As soon as they can get me passage on a ship bound for Serac. I'll have a couple of witches in attendance, but it shouldn't take more than a day or two to sort out."

"So you've got time to see what I've been working on?"

"Of course."

Jemeryl smiled. Some things would never change. She was not surprised that the old woman was still actively pursuing her research. Iralin might be ancient, but she shared with Jemeryl a love of learning. Only death or senility was going to stop either of them from studying magic.

❖

Tevi's face and voice were distorted by Klara's senses, but recognisable, once Jemeryl allowed for the softened bass and weird colours. "You're going to Kradja?"

"Yes. You've been there, haven't you?"

"Just the once. Make sure you visit the temple. It's impressive. And camels—you ought to see them in the market. They're weird. Desert sunsets, though. They beat the lot. They're…" Tevi smiled wistfully. "I wish I was going with you."

"So do I."

"I miss you."

"I miss you too."

"Talking is nice, but it's no substitute for holding you close."

The conversation was revisiting familiar, painful ground. The journey to Lyremouth had taken Jemeryl a month. Kradja was as far away again. No matter how quickly she concluded her mission with Ciamon, she would not be back in Tevi's arms until midsummer. Jemeryl was trying hard not to nurse her anger, since it could do no good, but there was no reason at all why Tevi could not have gone with her—no reason except for Alendy's aversion to them being together. Jemeryl clamped down on the thought.

"You know I'm not going to be able to contact you so often in future. The elemental forces in the sea will be hard to balance for more than a few minutes at a time." As it was, Jemeryl could feel the strain of projecting her mind over the hundreds of miles. She would not be able to keep it up much longer, and the residual awareness of her body, back in the room at Lyremouth, was trying to claim her attention. She was required to deal with something. "I've got to go."

"All right." Tevi looked sad. "Contact me whenever you can. I love you."

"I love you too, and I will. I promise."

Tevi blew a kiss, a gesture Jemeryl could not reciprocate as a magpie.

"Bye."

Jemeryl loosened the bonds tying her mind in Klara's body. The world bucked and surged. Her stomach contorted as if trying to turn itself inside out. After a few seconds the nausea retreated, only to be replaced by the pounding of a headache at the back of her skull.

The pain faded although the pounding remained. Jemeryl clapped her hands over her ears. Her head felt far too big, then it shrank to the size of a pinhead before finally regaining its proper size and relationship to her neck. The world was back in place, and her body was again her own, with nothing worse than a tingle over her left eyebrow.

Someone was at her door. This was the noise that had intruded on her awareness while she had been mind riding Klara. Filtered through the magpie senses, it had sounded like a mob trying to smash their way in, but was now only a polite tapping.

Jemeryl took a last deep breath to steady herself and called, "Enter."

Both visitors wore a green amulet on their left wrist, inscribed with a pattern of oak leaves, marking them as middle-ranking witches. In style, the amulets were the same as the one on Jemeryl's own wrist, although hers was black, as befitting a sorcerer. At the front was a blond man. His face had a firm jaw, full lips, and startling blue eyes. The woman behind him was taller, dark-haired, with high, chiselled cheekbones. They looked to be in their late twenties.

The man spoke for them. "Madam Jemeryl?"

"Yes?"

"My name in Taedias, I'm adept in the sixth dimension. This is Gante"—the woman nodded in acknowledgement—"adept in the fifth. We will be accompanying you to Kradja. We've been sent to introduce ourselves and to tell you that passage to Serac has been arranged on a merchant ship, leaving at high tide tomorrow evening."

Gante nodded again, as if confirming that the information was correct, and then both witches stood rigidly in the doorway.

"Thank you. That's great."

"Is there anything you need us to do before then?" Taedias's voice was without modulation. If he were an actor, describing his performance as wooden would be an insult to trees.

"No. I'm all set to go." Jemeryl gave a wide smile, hoping to put her new companions at their ease. It showed no sign of working.

"We've arranged for a porter to carry your bags to the harbour."

"I can carry them my—" Jemeryl broke off. It did not matter. "Fine."

"We'll be here after dinner tomorrow to escort you to the docks."

"Thanks."

"Is there anything else?"

"No. See you then." By now, Jemeryl's smile was masking her clenched teeth.

Taedias gave a formal bow, Gante nodded for a third time, and then the pair shuffled a retreat. After they had gone, Jemeryl sat, staring at the closed door in bemusement. Judging the two witches on such a brief first meeting would be unfair, although neither had impressed her with their intellect. However, it was impossible to miss that they were two of the most physically attractive people Jemeryl had seen around the Coven.

She frowned. Surely Alendy had not handpicked them, in the hope she would fall for their good looks, start an affair with one or the other, and abandon Tevi. The idea was insulting. Alendy could not be that crass, could he?

❖

Long before completing the journey, Jemeryl had formed the opinion that if Alendy had truly thought she might lose her heart to either witch, it went far beyond the realms of mere insult. Neither was someone she would want as a close friend, let alone anything else. If she combined their best personality traits together, between them they had the charm, wit, and incisiveness generally associated with a bowl of cold porridge.

At least Gante was easy to ignore. Jemeryl had only once heard her string more than five words together, and this had been to explain that she did not like being rained on. Taedias went to the other extreme and said everything twice—three times if he himself was the subject of the remark. Jemeryl had come to think of him as Tedious, and was dreading that she would call him it by mistake.

They were halfway across the desert, and he was complaining about the heat and the flies, in the same way he had complained about seasickness and the rough manners of sailors on the voyage, the price of beer when they landed in Serac, the poor state of the road over the Merlieu hills, and the inadequate plumbing at their lodging in Villenes. All of these were, needless to say, targeted solely at him, by a vindictive fate.

He also had a headache. "It's behind my eyes, you know, and flares out towards my ears."

"Um." Jemeryl had one too. Could headaches be infectious?

A shout rang out, far more interesting than Taedias moaning, even though Jemeryl had no idea what was said. In Serac, she had hired a team consisting of a couple of guides and a wagon crew, all of whom were from the district around Kradja. As a consequence of their work, the entire team could make themselves understood in a range of languages, including several dwarven dialects. Among themselves, the hired hands usually spoke in a sibilant language that Jemeryl thought belonged to the desert nomads.

The shout had come from a guide who was scouting ahead and had stopped at the top of a low ridge. Jemeryl slowed her horse to get a translation from the driver of the supply wagon.

"What is it?"

The driver smiled broadly. "She can see the oasis we camp by tonight. We have made good time."

Before Jemeryl could say anything, Taedias piped up. "Great. I'm sure all the bouncing around is making my head worse. It's starting to upset my eyes, though I wasn't going to say anything. You know I don't like to complain."

Jemeryl bit back a string of replies. She knew of no such thing. Moreover, the power of suggestion was clearly at work. Her own headache was getting worse, and the light was behaving strangely, twisting in the sixth dimension and breaking into rainbows where it glinted off mica in the sand. In fact, the whole world seemed out of kilter, partly leaden, partly chaotic. Jemeryl had hoped to contact Tevi when they camped that evening, but it was not going to happen until she felt better.

While they approached the oasis, Taedias continued to describe his symptoms in unwanted detail. Jemeryl just wished he would shut up. Apart from anything else, the commentary was unnecessary, since she was feeling exactly the same. Had they eaten something bad at lunch? In which case, why did the wagon driver look so cheery? Surely he would also be suffering, since he, and the rest of the team, had shared the meal.

As an adept of the fifth dimension, Gante ought to have some skill as a healer. Currently she was at the rear of the group. Possibly she felt that being unable to see people's faces relieved her of any obligation to communicate.

Jemeryl dropped back to join her. "How are you feeling?"

Gante wrinkled her nose. "Not good."

"Do you have a headache?"

"Yes."

"How about the light? Does it seem odd?"

Gante tried out several different shrugs, the medium in which she was at her most eloquent. "The light's all right. But…"

Jemeryl waited, yet nothing was forthcoming. Talking to the woman was like getting blood out of a miserly vampire. "But?"

"My horse feels dead."

Jemeryl caught her lower lip in her teeth. It would make some sort of sense, if there were such a thing as a magical illness. The ungifted wagon driver was not bothered at all. Taedias was adept in the sixth dimension, which held the physical energies that bound the world together. Hence he was experiencing the malady in terms of light. Gante was adept in the fifth dimension, which held life forces, so she was noticing an effect in the animals around her. As a sorcerer, Jemeryl was able to perceive all dimensions, and was not only seeing changes in light and the horse she was riding, but time was also acting oddly. The minutes were tripping over themselves. But what sort of illness only targeted paranormal perception?

Abruptly, they were at the oasis, then a hundred yards away, and finally back at the waterside. Time was definitely not running in a nice steady way. Jemeryl shook her head, hoping to clear it, and tried to focus on her surroundings, not that this helped. The palm trees lining the water were bleached of life. The still pool reflected the sky in a smeared kaleidoscope of colour. The sound of the wind over the sand was broken into a staccato rhythm as the seconds disintegrated.

Jemeryl got down from her horse and stumbled to one of the palm trees. She sat with her back against the trunk, head held in her hands. What was wrong with her? She no longer felt so bad physically; even her headache had faded. But it was as if the illness now infected her surroundings rather than her body.

Again, a shout claimed her attention, this time in a language she understood. Jemeryl took a deep breath and shoved herself to her feet. She was overreacting. She was not in pain, nor was she about to throw up or pass out. She needed to get a grip on herself.

"Madam sorcerer," one of the guides called again.

"Yes?"

"There are people approaching."

"So?" The oasis was a common campsite. It was not surprising if others wanted to stop there.

"They have weapons."

"Ah."

This was more ominous. A group with drawn swards was unlikely to be honest traders, wanting to make camp for the night. The well-used oasis might be an obvious place for bandits to lie in wait.

The ambushers were in for a surprise. Even in her current state, Jemeryl was sure she could cope with a gang of sword-wielding thugs. She hobbled over to the guide and squinted at the desert, struggling with the broken light. The approaching group must have numbered about twenty. If they were bandits, they were being very brazen about it, marching forward in a line, with no attempt to conceal themselves. Just for the sake of style, surely bandits would make some effort to skulk. The group clearly felt they had the right to claim the oasis, which might mean that they represented some legitimate power.

Then Jemeryl's vision cleared enough to see the red cloaks and gold helmets. The uniformed soldiers were now only a few dozen yards away. Abruptly, Jemeryl's headache re-erupted in white-hot fury, imploding and sucking the world inside it. Her legs gave way. From a long way off, she heard someone scream. She did not think it was herself, although she could not be sure. And then, between one breath and the next, the headache vanished. The world snapped back into place—or parts of it did.

Jemeryl found herself on her knees in the sand, surrounded by the new arrivals. One of them grasped her sleeve and yanked her left arm up, displaying the black sorcerer's amulet on her wrist. Judging by the man's manner, he was an officer, relaxed and confident, the only one not carrying a drawn sword.

He let Jemeryl's arm drop. "Our High Priest said the Coven would send someone soon. He was right. They've sent us a sorcerer. Or to be precise, someone who used to be a sorcerer."

Jemeryl stared up into the officer's face. What he said was true. Already she had identified the bits of the world that had not returned. The universe had shrunk to four dimensions. Energy and life were contained only by height, depth, and length. Time was a simple linear progression. She could not grasp the energy tensors. She could not massage the auras of the bodies around her. She could not probe into the future. She was less than half what she had been. The world was devoid of magic.

The officer's triumphant smile broadened. "How does it feel to be a normal person?"

CHAPTER TWO—EQUALITUS IN ASCENDANCY

The town of Kradja grew from the desert. From a distance, only the huge dome of the temple carried the unmistakable stamp of a craftsman's handiwork. The mud brick walls of the smaller buildings around it were the same colour as the sand, so that they might have been natural rock formations, sculpted by the wind. In the barren wilderness, the bright green fronds of palm trees seemed more out of place than the houses.

The illusion of environmental harmony did not last once the party reached the busy streets. On the outskirts, the structures were crumbling hovels, patched with whatever the owners could scavenge. Nearer to the centre, the roads were lined with mansions, protected by iron gates and guards. Everywhere the acrid air was full of shouting and an overpowering medley of scents—spice and smoke, food and leather, unwashed bodies and refuse. The sounds and smells of humanity assaulted the senses.

Or such senses as one had. After three days in her ungifted state, Jemeryl was still struggling to cope. She knew the horse she rode was alive because she could see it move and feel its warmth, but she could not trace its aura. She could not manipulate the life essence within it. Heat and light washed over her, gravity held her down, yet she could not reach into the sixth dimension and mould the forces to her will. The seconds flowed by, without complexity or option.

Jemeryl looked up at the dome of the temple, getting ever nearer—the home of the famous oracle. Of all her paranormal senses, prophecy was the one she valued the least. In her opinion, it was too haphazard to be useful. The information it gave could only be trusted when nothing could alter the outcome. Knowing the inevitable was pointless. It never made anything any easier.

Yet, perversely, worrying about the future was the thing that currently occupied Jemeryl's thoughts the most. She did not know what had happened to her senses, but she so desperately wanted to believe that it was a question of when, not if, she would get them back.

The worst of it was knowing that the other dimensions were still there. Everyone's body extended across all seven dimensions. The ungifted were merely insensible to the higher three. They blundered through them, blind and deaf, unable to manipulate what was in front of them. Now Jemeryl knew that she too was stumbling blind. She felt so utterly powerless. And yet, she was merely experiencing the world exactly the same way Tevi did, every day. How did Tevi bear it?

The attitude of her captors only underlined her vulnerability. After the initial confrontation, they had made a conspicuous point of ignoring her. Even when giving directions, the words were directed at Jemeryl's horse, rather than her. She had been told the High Priest would talk to her, but nothing else.

The group clearly belonged to a military force. They referred to themselves as sentinels and gave their leader the title of sergeant. The High Priest featured in their conversations, as did the names Equalitus and Sefriall, but the little Jemeryl overheard added nothing to her knowledge beyond this.

The two witches and Jemeryl had not been bound, as if to emphasise that they were not taken seriously as a threat, but they were watched closely enough to prevent any attempt at escape. Not that Jemeryl had any desire to. She needed to know more, and currently, the High Priest topped the list of people she wanted to talk to. His sentinels had expected the loss of magic. The High Priest was surely the one who could best explain the how and why of it.

Jemeryl's musing ended when her captors shepherded her and the others into a courtyard lined by stables. They were now so close to the temple that its shadow fell on them, a blessed relief from the burning sun. Most people in sight were soldiers, with helmets, swords, and long red cloaks.

News of their arrival had been sent ahead when they reached the outskirts of Kradja, and more troops were awaiting them just outside the courtyard. The officer was distinguished by gold epaulettes on his shoulders and a plume on his helmet. Did this make him a captain?

Once the prisoners were lined up, the new officer conferred briefly with the sergeant before raising his voice to a bark. "The local hirelings. They're of no interest. They can go."

The wagon crew and guides needed no second telling. They hurried away, before anyone had a chance for a change of mind.

The red-cloaked soldiers formed a curved phalanx behind Jemeryl and the two witches, hemming them in. Then a rough shove on her shoulder propelled Jemeryl forward, a few steps clear of Gante and Taedias.

After days of being ignored, Jemeryl was now the focus of attention. The captain slowly scanned her up and down, and then sneered. "So. It's a glorious, almighty sorcerer. Do you want me to kiss your arse?"

Behind her, Jemeryl heard Taedias draw breath, about to say something. She glanced back in time to see Gante nudge him in the ribs to shut him up. For all her reticence, Gante had the more common sense of the two, although this was no great feat.

When nobody spoke, the captain went on. "I used to live in the Protectorate, slogging my guts out to pay taxes so you could swan around, doing nothing and playing at being god. Well, we've got a new god now." He laughed. "You're not saying much. Is being a mere mortal all a bit of a shock to you?"

"There doesn't seem much to say." Jemeryl paused. "But I'll concede that losing access to the higher dimensions was a surprise."

"A surprise? You have no idea. We're all going to be equal, and you won't like that, will you? It's going to be the end of the Coven."

"That's ridiculous." Taedias would keep silent no longer.

The captain glared at him. "Who asked you to speak, sonny-boy?"

Thankfully, Taedias shut up, which could only have been due to surprise. Jemeryl was sure he lacked the intuition to realise the captain was deliberately trying to provoke a response.

After a few more seconds of silence, the captain turned to his troops. "Take them away." He glanced back at Jemeryl. "We've got a nice dark room ready for you."

The dark room turned out to be a cellar under the temple.

Judging by the boxes to one side it was normally used as a stockroom. Presumably, the temple did not have much call for a purpose-built dungeon.

"You can't keep us here!" Taedias had got over his surprise. Jemeryl knew it had been too good to last.

"Can't we?" the captain threw back.

"There are no windows."

The captain peered around, feigning deliberation. "You know, I think you're right. There aren't."

Taedias stomped up to stand toe to toe with him. "I demand you take us to whoever's in command."

"You demand?" Any veneer of humour had vanished from the captain's tone.

"This has gone on long enough."

"Believe me, it's only just started."

"Listen, you oaf—"

"Taedias!" Jemeryl had to intervene before things got out of hand. She grabbed Taedias's shoulder and pulled him away, then faced the captain. "I'm sorry for my assistant. He's…" *a pompous little ass with the brains of a cabbage.* Although true, this was not something Jemeryl felt she should say aloud. She hunted through her head for something placatory.

She did not get the chance. Without warning, the captain backhanded her across the face. Jemeryl staggered away and stumbled to her knees. Of course, the insulting *oaf* was the opening the captain had been looking for, the sort of defiance he had sought as an excuse for some rough treatment. And although Taedias had been the one to rise to the bait, there was no doubt that she, as a sorcerer, was the one the captain wanted to go after.

Flanked by two soldiers, the captain moved in close, his eyes glinting in the torchlight, both hands balled into fists. "Things are changing and you're going to learn the new rules."

The soldiers hoisted Jemeryl back to her feet and held her, arms locked behind her back. The captain raised his fist for another blow. Jemeryl tried to cower away, but pinioned as she was, she could not shield herself from the attack.

"What's going on?" A new voice rang out.

The captain jerked around and faced the woman standing in the doorway. "The prisoners are…"

"Yes?"

"I…um…felt…"

Under the woman's stern gaze, the captain straightened his back, standing blankly to attention. The soldiers released their grip and edged away. Gently, Jemeryl probed her injuries. Her shoulders tingled from the strain they had been under and her face throbbed, but she knew things could have been so much worse.

When it was clear there was going to be no further answer, the woman continued. "Unless I missed something significant that happened before I arrived, I really can't see why any violence is necessary." She looked around. "And I don't think this is suitable accommodation for our guests."

With a sharp gesture, she dismissed the soldiers. They hurried from the room. At last, the woman's attention turned to Jemeryl. "Let me apologise. The world is changing. Great times are coming and it can go to people's heads. I'm afraid our sentinels can sometimes be a little too zealous in their duties."

"That's all right."

If *all right* was a tad overgenerous, the improved situation was enough that Jemeryl was not going to quibble over semantics. She considered the new arrival. The woman was in her forties. Despite being short and a little on the plump side, she had a commanding presence and an expression that said she was not to be trifled with.

The woman spoke. "Let me introduce myself. My name is Sefriall. I'm deputy to the High Priest. I know you've come from Lyremouth, but you are…?"

"Jemeryl, oath-bound sorcerer of the Coven."—*or I used to be*—"These are Gante and Taedias, my assistants."

Sefriall nodded her head in acknowledgement. "Please, follow me." She continued talking as she led them from the cellar and into a clearly residential section of the temple complex. "We had expected a delegation from the Coven, although not so soon. It was mere chance that our routine patrol found you. We had thought it would take longer for word about the ascendancy of Equalitus to reach Lyremouth."

"Equalitus is the name of the High Priest?" Jemeryl guessed.

Sefriall glanced at her. "Equalitus is the god he serves—the only god worshipped in this temple."

"I thought the temple was dedicated to a god of prophecy."

"This temple used to house many creeds, the followers of Harretha among them. But no longer. Some months ago, the High Priest arrived, and taught us about Equalitus, and showed us his power—the power to rid the world of corruption and injustice. I was a priest of Koneath, the Cyclian builder, until I was shown that Equalitus was more deserving of my devotion."

"All the priests changed their allegiance?" From what Jemeryl knew about the hold religion could exert on its followers, this seemed surprising.

"Alas. Not all. Some could not see their error." Sefriall looked regretful. "They have left the temple."

Jemeryl could think of only one way to stage that sort of coup. "The High Priest, he's a sorcerer?"

"There are no sorcerers in Kradja anymore. The god Equalitus removes the iniquitous gifts from all under his emanation."

"So he's behind my inability to reach the higher dimensions…to work magic?"

"But of course."

"Why?"

Sefriall frowned. "Why what?"

"Why does the High Priest want to stop people using magic?"

"Because magic is a curse. Because it's unfair. It allows the few to subjugate the many. It is the root of all the evil and hardships that beset the world. This is what the High Priest has shown us. At the moment the blessing of Equalitus covers just one town, but as the number of his followers grows so does his strength. Equalitus will remove the blight of magic from the entire world and usher in a new age of freedom and equality."

Jemeryl stopped, head spinning. "The entire world? You mean it? Not just Kradja? The High Priest wants to destroy the Coven?"

Sefriall shook her head. "Please don't think of it as destruction. The High Priest only wishes good for all humanity. He will bring about the Coven's downfall, and I understand that you'll oppose this. But your opposition will be fruitless. Please, try to understand, we don't wish you harm. But the time of empires and sorcerers is over. The time of liberty and equality is here."

The room they finally reached was sleeping quarters, presumably either for guests or priests. A row of four beds and footlockers lined one wall. A wide window provided a view over the gardens that bounded the temple on three sides.

Sefriall indicated a table against the wall with wine, fruit, and a wash bowl laid out. "Relax. Refresh yourselves. The High Priest will see you as soon as he's available."

After a last bow, Sefriall left. Once the door was shut, Taedias shuffled over, head down, shoulders hunched. His manner was more subdued than Jemeryl had seen before. The assault in the cellar had clearly shaken him. If Jemeryl had known the threat of violence would have such a strong effect, she might have been tempted to use it before.

He made a couple of aborted attempts to speak before whispering, "Now we're here, do you think there's any chance of us finding Ciamon?"

Jemeryl stared through the open window at the gardens while her thoughts churned over what scraps of information she had. Was she reading too much into what Sefriall had told her? However, the guesswork was building up into a picture. Alendy had not revealed everything he knew about Ciamon. Even if he had, Jemeryl was getting the increasing suspicion that Alendy himself did not have more than a fraction of the full story.

When she did not reply, Taedias went on. "Do you think there's any point in us asking Sefriall about Ciamon?"

Jemeryl took a deep breath. "I have the sneaky suspicion we're about to meet him."

❖

Evening was at hand when a temple servant arrived to escort Jemeryl and the two witches to the promised meeting. They were shown into a large audience chamber. The setting was clearly designed to impress. The vaulted ceiling was decorated with gold leaf motifs. Mosaic tiles covered the floor. The low sun shone horizontally through ornate arched windows and glinted off walls of polished pink marble. At either side stood a row of silent, unmoving sentinels in their red cloaks.

At the end of the room, the High Priest sat on a raised dais, although not on a throne. His ordinary chair seemed all the more modest by comparison with its surroundings, as if to make the point that he was merely a humble servant of his god. His robes were plain, unadorned white. A small group of attendant priests was gathered behind him, Sefriall among them.

The servant who had escorted Jemeryl indicated a spot for her to stand on, suitably removed from the notables to show proper deference. Jemeryl ignored the guidance and advanced to just before the dais. The priests behind the chair glared at her in agitation, but did nothing, leaving it to their leader to deal with the show of impertinence.

Jemeryl looked up at the High Priest. Apart from a receding hairline, he had not changed much. "Hello, Ci. It's been a long time."

"Jem!" Ciamon looked first surprised, then annoyed. "So they roped you in to talk me round. It's not going to work. And to be honest, I'm disappointed in you."

"Alendy did talk me into coming, but I only said yes because I wanted to help you."

"Help me?"

"As far as you're willing to be helped."

"Great. Because the help I want is in putting an end to the Coven and the Protectorate. Was this what you had in mind?"

"I can't believe you mean that."

"Why?"

"Because the Ciamon I knew cared about people, and wouldn't have killed millions, for any reason—good or bad."

"You're here to lecture me about killing people?" Ciamon sounded outraged.

"I'm here because I'm your friend."

"The Jemeryl who was my friend wouldn't have helped cover up murder."

"Who's been murdered?"

"You don't know?"

Jemeryl paused, scouring her memory. "Alendy said some

people were killed in an accident. The same accident where you were injured."

"It was no accident."

"Whatever happened, it—"

"You don't brick people up in a room to starve by accident."

"Starve? When did that happen?"

"You really don't know?" Ciamon's expression softened and he leaned back in his chair. "They hid the truth from you as well? I'm relieved. I wouldn't like to think you'd lost all your—" He broke off and looked around. "I want to talk to Jemeryl in private. You may leave us."

The faces of the attendant priests showed a mixture of curiosity and resentment, but they obediently filed from the room. Predictably, Taedias needed additional prompting from the soldiers before he also left. The doors closed after the last one. Ciamon pushed himself from his chair and approached Jemeryl. His expression was hesitant, wary, but then it eased into a true smile and he grasped her by both shoulders.

"As you said, it's been a long time." His smile warmed still more. "I'm pleased to see you. I'd wondered how you were doing."

Jemeryl took a step closer and wrapped him in a quick hug before moving away. "I've always been meaning to write to you but..." She shrugged. "You know how it goes. Time slips by."

"Where have you been?"

"Last eight years, I've been town sorcerer in Horzt. Before that I was way up north in Bykoda's empire, as it was then. She's dead now. How about you?"

"Oh. I've been here and there. Mainly there. People keep sending me somewhere else." He pulled a wry smile. "You remember how good I was at making myself popular?"

Jemeryl studied him, refreshing her memory. Ciamon was definitely her type, tall and dark-haired, with a relaxed manner and self-deprecating humour, but he lacked Tevi's calm, inner toughness. Tevi knew who she was. Though he might deny it, Ciamon would always be searching for someone else to tell him the answer.

"Alendy said you'd not had an easy time."

"Alendy!" Ciamon spat the name as if it was an obscenity.

"I don't like him either."

"Now he's Guardian. What does that say about the Protectorate? I wouldn't trust him to protect a hen house. He—" Ciamon broke off, pinching the bridge of his nose. "Do you know what he did?"

"You said he murdered someone."

"No. Not him, but he let it happen. Then he tried to cover it up."

"How?" Jemeryl did not trust Alendy, but deliberate murder was hard to believe.

Ciamon dropped his hand and wandered back to his chair, although he did not sit. "My last posting for the Coven. I was sent to work with an ancient harpy called Ralieu. She wouldn't tell me what she was doing, just got me running around, tidying up after her." His shoulders twitched. "It was pretty much all I'd been doing since leaving Lyremouth. You'd be surprised at the tricks I've picked up. I'm really handy with a broom now."

Jemeryl pursed her lips, trying to keep her expression neutral. Ciamon would be the first to admit that he was not a very good sorcerer. Jemeryl hoped she was not unduly arrogant in believing his abilities to fall far below her own. However, he was able to perceive and control all seven dimensions, and he was not stupid. The Coven had clearly been wasting his talents.

Then more memories slotted into place. Back when they were apprentices, Ciamon had been a poor student, lacking dedication. He had compounded his shortcomings by neglecting to develop what ability he had. While she had been ambitious, Ciamon had been cynical about the power structure of the Coven, knowing he would never rise up its ladder. At times he had been deliberately perverse, revelling in failure. The lack of rivalry between them might have helped the start of the relationship, but had the incompatibility ultimately put an end to it?

"You resented being treated as a lackey?" Jemeryl certainly would have, in his place.

"I didn't mind. I just did what I was told. I didn't know what Ralieu was up to. To be honest, I didn't much care." His expression grew troubled. "At the bottom of it, I guess I feel guilty about that. Because if I'd known…"

"What was she doing?"

"Trying to enslave people. Taking over their minds. And I was helping her." He gave a sigh. "That would be bad enough. But then she ran her experiment."

Ciamon leaned forward against the chair, shoulders slumped, eyes closed. "Two convicts from the town were brought over. I don't know what they'd done, but they'd both been condemned to death, so it meant they lost any rights as human beings." His voice dripped scorn. "We had an underground test room. Ralieu got everyone to assemble—her, me, a witch, the convicts, a couple of warders, and three people who worked for her." He shook his head. "The cook and the gardener. A stable hand. Ordinary innocent people."

"Why the cook?"

"Ralieu needed the numbers. I'll explain later. She'd built this device in the centre of the room. The witch was in charge of making the final adjustments. I was by the door with Ralieu. She was monitoring. I was twiddling my thumbs. Then the witch dropped the last crystal into place and my head imploded."

"That was when you got injured?"

"I'm not injured. No more than you are. It was just the shock of having my senses in the upper dimension ripped away."

"Right. That's what happened to me at the oasis." Jemeryl frowned. "But I don't remember seeing any device. Were the soldiers carrying one?"

"No. It's not portable And anyway, there's no need. The range of the emanation is suff—"

"Hang on a moment." Jemeryl's thoughts had backtracked a step. "You're telling me you've brought this device to Kradja?"

"No. I made my own copy when I got here."

"Why? What is it?" *And are the effects permanent?* Jemeryl could not bring herself to voice the last question.

"It's just a harmonic array emanator. It imposes a morphology on the skein. The tricky bit is getting the morphology right. That's what Ralieu was working on."

"Why did she want to do that? I thought you said she was…" Jemeryl trailed off in confusion as she tried to work out the implications. The morphology would not do any permanent damage, would it?

"I don't think it's what she intended." Ciamon shrugged, diffidently. "Shall I carry on with the story?"

"Oh...yes."

"In the cellar, being engulfed by the effects of the morphology, I missed what happened next. The first thing I knew..." He grimaced. "The convicts had seized their chance. They'd got the sword off one warder and stabbed him. I got my eyes open in time to see them finish off the witch, who was still on his knees by the emanator. I tried to stop them, but the upper dimensions were gone. Then Ralieu grabbed my arm and told me to get her out. She's too old to move fast on her own. We escaped before the convicts noticed, and then Ralieu locked the door."

Ciamon paced to the other side of the room and back, in obvious agitation. "The stable hand—a nice girl, and the cook..." He stopped pacing and met Jemeryl's eyes. "And I'd just helped lock them in a room with a couple of armed murderers."

"Without magic, there was nothing else you could have done."

"Except, once we'd gone a hundred yards, all our senses returned. We could have unlocked the door and dealt with the convicts when they came out. That's what we should have done. When Ralieu sent me to get helpers, I thought she wanted to send them in, but Ralieu ordered them to brick up the door. I tried to stop them." Ciamon's face twisted in pain. "But I was just a gofer. She was a revered elder. Nobody paid me any attention. I couldn't fight her. You know what sort of sorcerer I am. Ralieu had me beat on every paranormal plane. And all I could think about was the people in the cellar."

"It's..." Jemeryl could not find any words.

Tears formed in Ciamon's eyes. "The Coven is foul from top to bottom."

"No." That much Jemeryl could deny. "Ralieu is just one corrupt sorcerer."

"From top to bottom. I wanted Ralieu to pay for what she'd done. I contacted the Coven. I sent a message to Alendy himself. And he ordered me to shut up. He said if I spread the story, he'd have me recalled to Lyremouth and set me cleaning the Coven latrines. That's when I started doing what I should have done from the start."

"What?"

"I found out exactly what Ralieu was up to. I started reading her notes, probing around in her study when she wasn't there. The morphology she'd designed. It puts a perceptual bar on the upper dimensions. The emanator draws its power from auras. That's why she'd needed the cook and the others, so there were enough to draw on."

"Why would Ralieu want to do such a thing?"

"Like I said, I think it was a mistake. She was playing around with mind control, but her morphology was wrong."

"But you've done it on purpose, right? You read Ralieu's notes and made a stronger emanator, so it projects its morphology on the skein for miles rather than yards. Why? What next?"

"I didn't have to make it stronger. Like I said, the emanator draws its strength from people. The more people integrated in its morphology, the stronger it is, so the boundary expands, which in turn draws in more people."

Jemeryl paused, juggling the sums in her head. At last she asked quietly, dreading the answer, "How far can it go?"

"Eventually, it will cover the entire world. I'm going to put an end to magic and the Coven."

Jemeryl turned her head and stared out the window. The sun was touching the horizon, turning the sky to fire. Red and purple flared across the heavens. Tevi was right. The desert sunset was awe-inspiring. The same sun was also setting over Lyremouth, miles to the north. Was it also setting figuratively? Were the Coven's days numbered?

❖

Two others were watching the sunset from a temple balcony.

The taller figure, a man, spoke first. "The woman who arrived today, what do you make of her?"

"I think she proves what we've suspected all along. Ciamon is a renegade Coven sorcerer."

"He's certainly no priest."

"That much is obvious." The woman paused thoughtfully. "No… he's a sorcerer sure enough. And the Coven sent an old friend to talk to him."

"If he's a sorcerer, why would he want to rid the world of magic?"

"Who knows? I used to think his goal was to be the only sorcerer left."

The man looked startled. "You think he can still work magic?"

"Yes. Remember his idol."

The man pondered this for a while. "He plans to rule the world?"

"I'm not sure. I sometimes wonder if he truly believes what he spouts about equality and justice. Perhaps he's telling the truth about his aims."

"Or maybe he has a really big grudge against the Coven," the man suggested.

"Maybe. Home-grown enemies are always the most vengeful."

"Like our own home-grown enemies?"

"Darjain and his followers?" The woman laughed. "Darjain doesn't understand the concept of vengeful. Alkoan is more of a threat."

"I'm watching him."

"Good. And though Darjain is too indecisive to pose a threat, he's still the figurehead for the old priests. Anything that happens will start near him. Don't let your guard slip."

"This new arrival doesn't change anything?"

"I don't think so. Ciamon and his sham god have broken the old order. We need to be ready to seize our chance and build a new one." The woman spoke confidently.

"I still can't get over the brazen sacrilege. How dare he desecrate our temple? Does he think we can't tell the difference between the work of divinity and cheap magic tricks?"

"He's a sorcerer. For all his vilification of the Coven, he's just as bad. Sorcerers' powers make them think they're on a par with the gods."

"He'll learn of his error."

"Oh yes. You may count on it. Ciamon used his magic to tamper with things he had no right to touch. He has mocked the gods. The gods will not be mocked."

❖

The central hall of the temple at Kradja was a huge, echoing space, filled with the undulating rumble of early morning worshippers. From a balcony at the rear, Jemeryl looked down on the scene. Places where shrines to older gods had been removed were obvious, even to someone who had never seen the temple before. The outer circle of alcoves stood empty, lacking a focus. Yet nobody seemed to care about the vacant plinths and unadorned altars. All attention was centred on the middle of the floor, where stood a golden idol. A circle of armed guards held back the eager crowd.

"Why set yourself up as a High Priest? Why the new religion?"

Ciamon leaned on the balustrade beside her. "Why not? Somehow it seems appropriate. Isn't the idea of equality worth worshipping?"

"You're deceiving people."

"It's for their own good." Ciamon looked awkward for a moment, but then shrugged. "The area of the skein affected by the morphology depends on the population it can draw on. I had to set the emanator up in a large town. I thought about Villenes, but whoever picked Kradja for the temple wasn't working by chance. This is the centre of a convergence of ley lines. They concentrate power in the skein, making the morphology all the more effective."

"That doesn't mean you had to take over the temple."

Ciamon sighed. "I needed to make sure the emanator was safe. I encased it in the idol as the first step, to stop accidental damage, but it won't do much more than that. I'm affected by the morphology the same as everyone else, so there's nothing I could do if anyone attacked it. I needed help. And I needed to give people a reason to help me."

Jemeryl indicated the guards in their red cloaks. "Did you instigate them, or were they here before?"

"My deputy, Sefriall, set them up. She calls them the sentinels."

"They're ready to fight and die for a story you've made up?"

Ciamon flinched at the word *die*. "I'm hoping it won't come to that. But if the sentinels are called on to fight, it will be for the sake of creating a better world. Isn't that worth dying for?"

"You've still got them believing a lie."

"It's a story, not a lie."

"Those worshippers down there, do they appreciate the difference?"

Jemeryl watched Ciamon struggling with his conscience. He had been the most honest person she had ever known. He had also been the most compassionate. Had shock at what he witnessed in Serac let his compassion overwhelm his honesty? Had his ethics been taken beyond the breaking point? Jemeryl wanted to understand.

"It's no different to how it was before. Kradja is built on religion.

Every weird cult you can think of comes here. If you go back far enough, somebody made them all up. They're all stories. I've just created one more. People can carry on praying and making offerings, but now it's for something real. Once the morphology has encompassed the entire..."

Ciamon broke off and then continued, his voice more confident, alight with passion. "Can you imagine what it will mean? What the world will be like when everyone is equal? When people like Alendy and Ralieu have to answer for what they do, the same as everyone else? They won't be able to get away with murder just because they can see other dimensions. And outside the Protectorate, there'll be no more sorcerers setting up empires and enslaving people. With true equality there'll be freedom for all, and justice, and an end to bigotry. You must see that. The Coven is corrupt and has to go. We can make the world better. We have to."

Jemeryl stared at the idol. The Coven was not perfect. Too many sorcerers thought they were better than ordinary people. Undoubtedly the abuse of power went on, but was getting rid of magic the answer? What would Tevi say? At the thought of her lover, Jemeryl felt her expression soften. Would life be easier if they were equal in the eyes of everyone?

"I don't know," she said at last.

"Really? That's a more reasoned answer than I'd hoped for, but I'm betting Alendy won't be so ready to start thinking." Ciamon turned away and wandered to a small window. "You asked about my justification for taking over the temple. I know the Coven will try to destroy the emanator and stop the morphology. The sentinels are here if Alendy hires a band of mercenaries to attack it. And beyond that..." Ciamon smiled, staring into the distance.

"What?"

"Let's just say I have other defences in place."

"What are they?"

He glanced back at Jemeryl. "The other dimensions are still there, you know. Magical artefacts still work, like the emanator itself. So I put some spells in place before the morphology was activated."

"What sort of spells?"

"It'd be best if I don't tell you in detail, but take it from me, no matter what sort of attack the Coven launches against this temple and the idol, it won't harm the emanator."

Jemeryl frowned. Ciamon had been a weak sorcerer and a poor student. What sort of spells could he have set in place? "Are you sure? I wouldn't like to guarantee any sort of defence against all the Coven resources."

"I can." Ciamon smiled, his eyes fixed on something outside the window. "The emanator is absolutely secure inside the idol. You can tell Alendy to save himself the trouble of trying to destroy it." He paused. "That's if you go back to Lyremouth."

"You want to keep me here?"

"I'd like to. But you're free to go if you want." A boyish grin lit his face, replacing his former earnestness. "Come and see my idol close up. See if you can spot one of my protective spells."

A flight of stairs led down to the main floor of the temple. The worshippers shifted respectfully out of the High Priest's way. Initially, Jemeryl's attention was on the faces around her, noting the happy expressions, bordering on rapturous. Abruptly, she became aware of a shift in her own feelings, although, once spotted, she recognised it had been building up, step by step, as she crossed the floor. She stopped and stared at the idol, still a few dozen yards away.

From the balcony, it had been an aesthetically pleasing likeness of a naked man, sitting cross-legged. Now it was beautiful, displaying a perfection of form that seemed to be expressing some profound truth about the nature of life. More than this, she felt a wave of love engulf her. Tears of joy formed in her eyes.

"It's projecting a glamour."

Ciamon's grin broadened. "Yep. And the closer you get, the stronger it is. I'm betting most people won't be able to bring themselves to hurt it, long before they get close enough to try."

"It's effective. But..."

"But?"

"Coven rules forbid casting a glamour on people without their consent."

"It's not hurting anyone."

"It's an abuse of magic."

"It's a non-violent way of protecting the idol. And I needed to do something to get people to believe my new religion was real." Ciamon indicated the crowds jostling to get nearer to the idol. "Look at how happy they are. You can't tell me they'd refuse their consent, even if I told them the truth." He sighed. "But I have to go. Sefriall wants to talk to me about something. Think about what I said. I'd really like it if you stayed here with me. Even a High Priest needs friends."

Jemeryl watched Ciamon leave and then turned back to the idol. The glamour it cast was seductive. She could happily have stood, basking in its love all day—except that she knew it was a simple exercise of magic, and her helplessness to resist it was frightening. She was vulnerable to spells in a way she had never been before. Fear overwhelmed the love.

Was this how ordinary people felt every day, back in the Protectorate? No wonder so many of them resented sorcerers. The imbalance of power was bad enough, even if the power was exercised for the good of all, with justice and humility—but when the sorcerers displayed nothing but arrogance? When they got away with murder?

Jemeryl had sworn loyalty to the Coven. She was oath-bound to obey the Guardian. But was Ciamon right? Should she stay with him?

Jemeryl and the two witches were shown into the same audience chamber as before. The same group of attendants were gathered behind Ciamon's chair. For all Jemeryl could tell, they might even be the same sentinels lining the walls.

Ciamon stood at their approach, although he waited for them to stop before speaking. "I'm sending you back to Lyremouth with a message for your Guardian. When you speak to him, tell him what you have seen here and tell him that the days of the Coven's tyranny are over. The god Equalitus is in the ascendancy and will usher in an age of peace, justice, and liberty for all. Tell Alendy to accept the inevitable, and bow to the will of Equalitus. I do not wish strife, but the Coven will be undone and nothing can stop it. The Guardian cannot prevail against a god, and only misery will come of any attempt he might make. Finally, although dealings between us have not gone well in the past, assure Alendy that I do not seek vengeance. The time of Equalitus will begin with forgiveness for all who ask." Ciamon sat down. "You may go now as my messengers."

Jemeryl wondered whether Gante and Taedias would remember all that. Not that it mattered. Repeating Ciamon's words would be a waste of breath. There was no way Alendy would sit back and do nothing.

Equally, Jemeryl knew exactly what she had to do. She stepped closer to the dais. "Actually, I've changed my mind. I want to stay here and support you."

CHAPTER THREE—THE TEARS OF YALAISH

As far as Tevi could work out, someone on the town watch, or maybe two people, had innocently mistaken another watchman's lover for a whore, and had offered him money for sex. However, whoever it was had only offered a tenth of the standard going rate in Horzt, due to a mathematical error, rather than any thought to compound the insult. A third watchman had accidentally used the resulting brawl to pay back a fourth watchman for definitely not cheating at cards the month before. Nobody, including the people in question, had any idea why the other three had got involved, if in fact they had. The only thing everyone was agreed on was that none of them had thrown the first punch.

Tevi sighed and rubbed the back of her head. Getting a straight story out of them was going to be impossible, partly because everyone had been too drunk at the time to be credible witnesses, but mainly because you never ratted on your comrades to a senior officer, no matter what they had done to you.

Civilians who had not been in charge of an army might think that the high pressure of commanding a battle was the worst part. Others might pick the logistic headache of getting enough food and shelter to soldiers in remote terrain whenever it was needed. From Tevi's point of view, although both presented nightmarish problems, they were part of the job she was paid to do. The bit that really annoyed her was this—sorting out off-duty disciplinary issues, firmly enough and fairly enough to maintain respect, when everyone was acting as if she was the enemy.

She was reasonably sure some members of the watch before her were comparatively innocent. On the other hand, she also had a hefty bill for compensation from the tavern owner for the damage caused in the fight. She had to take some action, and somebody was going to have to pay up. So, with no better information to work on, she split the bill evenly between the seven as a fine, and then added on a chunk to show how irritated she was by it all.

Inevitably, she was treating some people more harshly than they deserved, and they would resent it, as would the rest of the watch. Tevi took comfort from knowing that the unofficial justice of the barracks would square things out. While her subordinates filed from the room, Tevi made a private bet with herself as to which of them would be sporting more black eyes and bruises by sunset.

She also caught some muttered comments which she chose to ignore, but the sibilant hiss of *the sorcerer's slut* was unmistakable. Tevi clenched her jaw. Of course, they were angry at the fine she had just imposed. The avenue the anger had taken was both predictable and galling. Tevi knew the watchmen had been even less willing to speak than might have been the case with another officer, because she was further from being *one of us* than mere rank accounted for.

No matter how well she fulfilled her role as guildmaster, no matter how hard she worked, no matter what her abilities, some would always be convinced that she had only reached her current position because she was Jemeryl's lover. The slur was all the more annoying because the senior mercenary guildmasters were just as untrusting of the Coven as everyone else. Tevi knew that a significant faction in the guild had tried to block her appointment in Horzt purely because of her link with Jemeryl.

Her link with Jemeryl.

As the words slipped into her head, the irritation with her subordinates was shunted aside. Currently, something was wrong with the link, and she did not know what or why. Tevi went to the window and leaned against the frame, staring south towards Kradja—not that she could see anything of note, and certainly nothing that might give her the answers she needed. What was happening to Jemeryl?

A knock roused her from the brooding. Without turning her head she called, "Yes?"

She heard the door open. "Please, ma'am, Thaldo wants to see you right away."

"I'm coming." Tevi pushed away from the wall and marched from the room. She could only hope that the deputising town sorcerer had something new to tell her.

Thaldo was in Jemeryl's study—his study, until her return. He seemed nervous and disorganised, but this was his normal state. "Tevirik, I think I…er…thanks for coming…um, yes."

Tevi got to the point. "Have you worked out what's wrong with Klara?"

Five days before, when Tevi had returned to her room, she had found the magpie unconscious on the floor. Despite the absence of any detectable injury or illness, Klara had shown no sign of waking. Tevi's only comfort was that Jemeryl was definitely alive, and not under the influence of something strong enough to break the bond between sorcerer and familiar. If all contact was lost, Klara would act like a wild magpie, rather than lie comatose.

Thaldo sidled over to where Klara lay on a cushion, surrounded by a circle of crystals. "Um…The familiar is completely healthy, and the link to Jemeryl appears strong. There's no distortion of the sort I'd expect if Jemeryl was wearing an iron collar or…something like that. And if she was seriously ill, I ought to be able to pick up a taint in the ether."

Tevi sighed. As sorcerers went, Thaldo was easy enough to get along with. From the start, he had treated Tevi with a politeness verging on deference, very unlike the autocratic disdain she had anticipated. Tevi guessed he was in his early twenties, and although juvenile sorcerers could be the most conceited of the lot, in Thaldo, inexperience translated into a lack of confidence. He was also manifestly well meaning. Tevi knew the crystals around Klara were to promote healing, but she was fairly sure the small silver balls on the cushion had no magical function, but were Thaldo's idea of a nice get well soon present for a magpie. He might be surprised if he ever got to hear Klara's opinion of them.

However, Thaldo's agitated dithering was a strain on Tevi's patience. A show of confidence would have helped ease her fears, even if it was an act. His habit of telling her things she already knew was also irritating. The report on Klara was identical to the one he had been giving her for the previous three days.

"What's happened? Why did you send for me?"

"Oh, I..." Thaldo jerked his head towards a bookcase where a carrier pigeon was perched. "I've just received a reply from Lyremouth."

"And? Do they know anything?"

"I don't think so. But they, um...didn't say much."

"No one has seen anything like it before?"

Thaldo shook his head. "They didn't say."

"And there's no news about Jem?"

"I don't know. Er...They wouldn't..."

Tevi turned away, until she had got her anger under control. It was not Thaldo's fault. "Let me guess. They said it was totally inappropriate for Jem to be in contact with an ungifted warrior, and they weren't going to do anything to encourage her sordid behaviour. If they had any information about Jem, they wouldn't dream of giving it to you to pass on. And in future, you and most definitely me should not stick our noses into places they have no right to be."

Thaldo swallowed audibly. "They weren't quite that...um..."

"I gave the unedited version. They may have been a bit less blunt in the wording, but it's what they meant." Tevi walked to the cushion and stared down at the unconscious magpie.

The last time Tevi had spoken to Jemeryl was nine days ago, just after she had left Villenes. Assuming the journey had gone to plan, Jemeryl should now be in Kradja. Over twenty days would be needed to get from Horzt to Lyremouth and the journey on to Kradja would be at least as long again. Allowing for delays on the road, she was unlikely to be in Kradja in much under fifty days. She would be far too late to help with any crisis—even if whatever had caused Klara to collapse was something an ungifted warrior might be the slightest help with. Anything that could overcome a sorcerer was unlikely to be vulnerable to swords and arrows. Yet there was no way that Tevi could stay where she was and do nothing.

"I'm going after her."

"Are you sure? I'd..."

Tevi glanced up. Thaldo appeared to be on the point of tears. "What?"

"I'd rather you didn't."

"I can't just sit here waiting."

"I understand. But the...d-d-dragons." On the last word, his composure failed completely.

"They've never been anywhere near Horzt, and now Revozik has them moving even further away."

"I know, but I...I mean, I can't. And you..." Thaldo was clearly terrified of dragons. Did this explain his bashfulness towards her?

"I'd be no use if they came here anyway."

"But you've flown on one."

"Only because it wanted me to do it a favour." Tevi's words were not helping. She could see it in Thaldo's eyes. Anyone who dragons called on for help was clearly formidable. "It was a one-off thing. If it met me now it would eat me, just like it would anyone else." Another bad choice of words. "I'm no more useful to you than any other mercenary. Jem and I have been partners for twelve years. I have to go after her."

Thaldo nodded, clearly unconvinced. "I suppose so."

"I'll want to be off as soon as—" Tevi stopped. Her contract with the town council to lead the watch still had months to run. Yet breaking a contract was one of the worst offences a member of the Guild of Mercenary Warriors could commit. "I'll need to sort out about the town watch. Maybe I can..." Tevi bit her lip. Would they let her buy herself out? What other options did she have?

Thaldo cleared his throat. "If you're really sure about going, and um...I could give you a dispensation, since I'm leader of the council... as it were. And I'll take care of Klara for you." Thaldo still looked sick, but he managed a weak smile.

"Thanks."

For a neurotic sorcerer, Thaldo was not a bad man.

❖

There were no two ways about it, the gatekeeper was sneering at her as he said, "I'll pass your message on to the relevant people."

Judging by the man's manner, the message might get passed on late next year, if he felt like it, and the relevant person would be someone writing a book titled *Stupid grunts who've shown up at the Coven*.

Tevi took a step back and looked up. She knew the tallest tower was where the Guardian could be found. She also knew that her chances of getting in were slightly worse than non-existent. This was her third attempt to find out information about Jemeryl, and it was going no better than the previous two.

The buildings that housed the central administration of the Coven were on the edge of the city of Lyremouth. The complex had clearly grown without planning. A jumble of size and scale meant it was nothing to look at, but as someone had once said to her, "When you're as important as the Coven, you don't have to resort to fancy brickwork to impress people."

Even the name *gatekeeper* was more of a traditional title than a factual one. There were no gates, and no wall for them to sit in. The Coven did not need them to keep out the unwanted, and Tevi knew better than to attempt to force her way in.

She tried one last appeal, to see if a hint of a threat would work. "Look, I know I'm just an ordinary citizen, and you think I've got no right to claim any sort of bond with a sorcerer like Jemeryl. That's your opinion, and you've got as much right to it as anyone else. But it's only your opinion, and the person who really counts here is Jemeryl. Because she's not going to be pleased at you trying to impose your views onto her life. Judging by the orange amulet I see on your arm, you're just a junior witch. Do you seriously want to upset a sorcerer?"

The gatekeeper flushed, clearly annoyed at having an ungifted citizen belittle his status, but the set of his jaw did not change. "Maybe Jemeryl is a sorcerer. But she's not the Guardian, is she?"

His words confirmed what Tevi had suspected. She doubted Alendy would have demeaned himself by giving specific instructions about someone as insignificant as herself. Admitting that he was aware of who she was would make her seem far too important. However, the gatekeeper clearly knew he would have Alendy's approval in denying her entrance, or any sort of assistance.

Tevi gave the gatekeeper one last angry glare and then stalked away between the avenue of trees to join the main road into Lyremouth. She would have to try something different.

Before Jemeryl left Lyremouth, she had told Tevi that her old mentor was the person to rely on in any difficulty. Tevi suspected that a request from her to meet Iralin would get no more favourable a response from the gatekeeper. But it would be a different matter if Iralin was the one doing the asking. Nobody with any sense would dare say no. Tevi looked back over her shoulder and smiled. In fact, she half hoped the gatekeeper would defy Iralin. It would be fun to see what sort of state he ended up in.

After her previous two failed attempts, Tevi had come prepared. Once on the road and out of sight of the gatekeeper she pulled the folded sheet of paper from her pocket.

Madam Iralin

> *Some years ago you kindly helped me with problems caused by the inadequate disposal of a basilisk's head. Although your intervention at the time resolved the matter, I am still bothered by the longer term issues, particularly those relating to separation of the elements that had been combined following your instructions.*

> *I wonder if you could be so good as to render further assistance. If you are willing, please send word to my normal residence in Lyremouth.*

Yours gratefully
Wess Tanaislanda

Tevi smiled. She was sure Iralin would understand, and she was equally sure the gatekeeper would not, even if he should chance to see the letter. All she needed was a courier. Luckily, a suitable candidate appeared within minutes.

The emblem on the girl's cloak marked her as a Coven apprentice. She was sauntering into the grounds and clearly in no hurry, therefore more likely to listen to an appeal.

Tevi adopted a stoop before hailing her, half hiding behind a tree. "Excuse me, ma'am."

"What is it?"

Tevi shuffled forward, casting nervous glances towards the buildings. "I've got a letter to deliver."

"And?"

"I'm scared."

"Of what?"

"The...the...in the Coven." Tevi ducked her head. Irrational fear of sorcerers was not uncommon and could cause people to act in odd ways. The rational fear was bad enough. "This letter's from my mistress. She sent me with it, but please, ma'am, I don't want to go in there."

The girl delivered a scornful look. "I shouldn't think you'd be let in if you asked. You can pass your letter to the gatekeeper. He'll see it's delivered."

"I don't want to go no closer. Please, ma'am, could you help me?" Tevi held out the sheet, taking care to keep her palm upward so that the girl would not see the mercenary tattoo on the back.

The girl sighed dramatically and took the note. She cast her eyes over it. "It's for Iralin?"

"Yes, ma'am."

"I'll see that she gets it."

"Thank you, ma'am. You're so kind."

❖

Eight years had passed since Tevi last walked the streets of Lyremouth. It had not changed. The city fascinated and repelled her in equal amounts, much as it had when she first arrived, an exile from the Western Isles. So much was alien to her, although less than it had been back then. Yet despite everything that still jarred, the lure was strong, to find an anonymous corner where she felt safe and call it home, as thousands had done before her.

The hub of the Protectorate was a study in contrasts. Both wealth and poverty were conspicuous in their blatant crassness. The dense maze of narrow alleys was cut by wide, tree-lined thoroughfares converging on a hundred squares and plazas. One moment Tevi was battling through the throng while a cacophony of street vendors competed to sell every conceivable produce. A dozen steps later and an unexpected public garden appeared around a corner, a handkerchief-sized space of calm, greenery, and birdsong. Workmen swarmed over new buildings, monuments to rising fortunes, while graffiti-covered statues of forgotten notables stood neglected in once fashionable neighbourhoods.

As she wandered, Tevi mulled over her options. Enough clues were in her letter to let Iralin work out who Wess Tanaislanda was. Who else from the small group of islands had ever set foot in the Protectorate? Iralin would also know where to find her. Tevi hoped that the next day would bring a summons to the Coven, with a letter of authorisation the gatekeeper would have to obey.

But if not? Tevi chewed on her lip. She was not going to get any other help from the Coven, so she would have to continue on to Kradja and hope she did not miss Jemeryl on the way, coming back. In fact, for all she knew, Jemeryl might already be in Lyremouth, lying in the Coven infirmary. Tevi sighed. She would give Iralin three days to reply and then she would start asking at the docks for passage to Serac, the first leg in the journey.

Dusk was drawing in when Tevi's aimless meandering brought her back to the main square, where the guildhall for the Mercenary Warriors was sited. Like the Coven, the guildhall was a collection of buildings, some old, some new. More than just administration, the guildhall provided accommodation, training, and medical facilities for its members, in return for the tithe of their income.

The tattoos on Tevi's hands, crossed swords in red and gold, marked her as a vouchsafed guild warrior and she had been allocated a private room in the block assigned to senior mercenaries, rather than a place in a dormitory such as a junior might expect. The thought struck Tevi that, in the guildhall, she had indeed found a corner of Lyremouth she might be happy to call home, were it not that her home would always be with Jemeryl.

Tevi pushed open the door to her room. The evening was advanced and darkness was thickening. A candle stood ready in its holder on the table. Was it too early to light it? Before she had time to take a step, the decision was made for her.

The candle burst spontaneously into life and a voice from the corner said, "I've been waiting for you."

Tevi spun towards the speaker, although years of living with Jemeryl made her less startled by the self-lighting candle than might otherwise have been the case.

Iralin levered herself to her feet. "Where have you been?"

"I've—"

"On second thoughts, don't answer that. We don't have time. When can you be ready to leave?"

Tevi took a breath. When she sent the note, she had not expected Iralin to come to her room in person. The urgency of the response was also surprising, and unsettling. But what was the point of asking for help if you did not accept it when it came?

"As soon as I've thrown some things in a bag."

"Throw them quickly."

Tevi shoved open the lid on her footlocker and started ramming the contents into her backpack. "Why the rush?"

"I've arranged passage for you on a boat to Serac that leaves on this evening's tide. I was worried you'd be too late to catch it."

"Sorry. If I'd known, I'd have come back sooner."

Iralin gave an amused snort. "It's all right. Even sorcerers have trouble with mind reading. I wouldn't expect it from you."

Tevi stood up. "I'm ready."

"Good. I've got a carriage waiting in the rear yard."

The elderly sorcerer needed what breath she had for walking. Tevi waited until they were seated in the carriage before asking, "You've got me passage to Serac, you say. Is Jem there, or is she still in Kradja?"

"How much do you know about what she's been doing?"

"I know that Alendy sent her to Kradja, allegedly to track down an old friend."

"Allegedly?"

"I think he mainly wanted to get her as far from me as possible."

"That might be part of his motive, I guess. What else do you know?"

"Not much. We were talking every few days, but then Klara collapsed. She hasn't moved since. When the stand-in sorcerer couldn't help, I came to Lyremouth in search of answers."

"Her familiar? Ah, yes. That explains how you knew something was wrong."

An ice fist clenched Tevi's gut. "Is Jemeryl hurt?"

"No. At least not as far as I know."

"You said that something was wrong."

"Indeed. The sorcerer who Jemeryl went to find has turned renegade on the Coven."

"Ciamon?"

"Yes. He and Jemeryl were apprentices together."

"I know. Jem's told me all about him." Tevi put a slight emphasis on the word *all*.

Iralin nodded approvingly, presumably happy that she did not have to explain more. "He's set himself up as High Priest in the temple and constructed a device that removes the ability to work magic from everyone who gets inside its field of influence."

"Is that's why Klara went into a coma? Jem got close to the device."

"She needn't be that close."

"How far does the effect reach?"

"We don't know. Its creator claims it will eventually spread out and cover the entire world."

Iralin's answer left Tevi temporarily lost for words. "Why would he want to do that?"

"Who knows? I'm afraid the witches who've reported back to us aren't of the highest calibre."

From the remarks Jemeryl had made about her companions, Tevi recognised the description. "He kept Jem prisoner and sent her assistants back?"

Iralin's expression was sombre. "The story we have is that she agreed to stay of her own free will. She's gone over to his side."

"I don't believe it."

"Nor do I. The witches only arrived back in Lyremouth a few hours ago. They're tired and even less informative than normal. Tomorrow might bring a clearer picture, but in the meantime, I thought it best to get you on your way to Jemeryl"—Iralin paused—"and out of Alendy's reach."

"You think he might want to harm me, in revenge for what Jem has supposedly done?"

"Not revenge. Although I admit I was surprised at how quickly he accepted the witch's story."

"He doesn't trust her. A sorcerer who'll pick someone like me as a lover is capable of anything." Tevi spoke with raw irony.

"Perhaps he does think that way. Whatever his reasons, I fear he might want to use you as a hostage. He'll certainly try to stop you joining Jemeryl. Speaking for myself, I'm sure Jemeryl has stayed in Kradja as part of a plan. And I'm equally sure she'll appreciate your help with it."

The carriage drew onto the docks and stopped by the gangplank to a merchant ship, riding high in the water. In the light of the setting sun, the crew were visible on deck, making ready to cast off.

Iralin handed a purse to Tevi. "Here's money and a warrant to help you on your way. It's made out for a Wess Tanaislanda. Keep your real name secret until you're outside the Protectorate. I think that would be a good idea."

Tevi took the purse and stepped down from the carriage. "Thank you."

"Safe journey and good luck. Tell Jemeryl I'm counting on her."

❖

Tevi reined in her horse at the top of a crest and considered the town of Kradja, several miles distant. The huge dome of the temple dominated the smaller buildings around it. Midday sun shimmered on the sand-filled air, casting a golden haze over the scene. The dome seemed to be floating on a sea of light.

The guide stopped beside her. Siashe belonged to the desert nomads although he had abandoned his people's traditional way of life for the more lucrative trade of escorting pilgrims and traders across the desert. He had confided in Tevi that herding people and goats both presented problems, but the people were harder to feed, watch, control, and keep together. They were also less appreciative. The plus side for people was that once they got to their destination, you could say good-bye and never set eyes on them again. The goats, you were stuck with for life—with the plus side being that if you got sick of the sight of one, you could eat it.

Tevi surveyed the whole panoramic scene. The ground was covered with dust, sand, and rock. The scant vegetation was coarse knotted shrubs and stubby cactus, more brown than yellow. The only greenery was the tops of palm trees in Kradja. A line of broken cliffs filled the horizon. Far in the distance to the east, Tevi could see a hazy smear on the sand. She pointed to it. "Another oasis?"

"Liaraja Yalaish deh," Siashe said in the sibilant desert language.

Tevi gave her best attempt at repeating the sounds.

Siashe laughed and patted her shoulder. "Close, my friend."

"What does it mean?"

"The tears of Yalaish."

"Who's Yalaish?"

"The great mother of all." Siashe glanced over his shoulder. The rest of the caravan had caught up. He urged his horse on. "For my people, she's the first god who gave birth to the world. When she saw what she had brought forth, she wept. The oases are where her tears fell to earth. As long as the world exists, they will never run dry."

"You built the temple for her?"

"My people do not build temples. But since the temple is there, some of her worshippers make use of it. You will find a shrine to Yalaish inside. She's the very fat woman."

"Who did build the temple?"

"The followers of Harretha."

"Harretha?"

"God of prophecy. Centuries ago, a band of travellers camped at the oasis. Among them was a priest of Harretha. He came from…" Siashe waved his hand vaguely. "Somewhere else. That night, in his sleep, the priest was bitten by a snake. While he lay at the point of death he had many visions of the future." Siashe shrugged. "He recovered and built his temple, dedicated to Harretha's incarnation as a snake."

"They just took over your oasis."

"It wasn't the most important one." Siashe pointed. "There. To the north. Do you see that peak? At the foot of it is where the first of Yalaish's tears fell. That's the most sacred oasis. No temples are there." He grinned. "And never will be."

"Never is a long time. There's a new god in Kradja. Stirring things up. Getting people excited. There's no saying what might happen."

"A new god blows into Kradja every time the wind changes. They come. They go. It makes no difference. Yalaish was the first. When the temple has crumbled into dust she will still be here. The last. This new god will be forgotten when the next one arrives."

Tevi jerked her thumb back at the pilgrims on the wagons behind. "Do you want to tell them that?"

"No. Because they wouldn't believe me. Besides, I don't want to talk people out of travelling to Kradja. Otherwise, I'd have to go back to herding goats."

"And getting fat on the ones that looked at you sideways."

Siashe laughed. "Ah yes. Those ones are always the troublemakers."

"Nothing wrong with troublemakers. They're good for business." Tevi held out her hands with their tattoos. Siashe had seen them before, but it emphasised her point. "I'm betting there's going to be a shake-up in Kradja. And where there's change, there's trouble. I'm betting, before long, there's going to be plenty of work for a hired sword. Besides, I don't have a trade like goat herding to fall back on."

"I don't think you need to worry, my friend. No matter how things go in Kradja, you'll never be short of work. People will still be following your calling when they've forgotten what goats are."

Tevi smiled. She and the guide had got on well, the only two in the caravan who were not on fire with talk of the new god, but she had not revealed her true reason for going to Kradja. The rest were only too eager. On the journey across the desert, Tevi had heard enough to make her seriously question everyone's sanity. All were convinced that by removing magic, the new god would bring about a paradise of peace and prosperity. However, this was the only thing they were agreed on and none had any concrete ideas about what real difference it would make to their lives, let alone be able to explain why it would be such a huge improvement on what they already had.

By the time the caravan reached the outskirts of the town, the pilgrims were hysterical with excitement. Most jumped down and vanished into the crowd, long before Siashe called a halt in the central market square. The few who waited were the old and infirm with enough common sense to know their days of jumping from moving vehicles were over—a couple lacking this common sense had been left in the street behind, lying in the dust.

Tevi looked around. She had been in Kradja many years before. The buildings were the same as she remembered, but the mood of the market was not. Fewer goods were on sale, and the biggest crowds were gathered around street preachers haranguing the assembled masses from any available vantage point. Waves of people ebbed and flowed across the space. The air was crackling with tension. The eyes of passers by were jittery, half crazed.

"So here we are, my friend." Siashe had manœuvred his horse next to Tevi's.

"Yes. You did well. We made good time."

"Do you know where you'll be staying in town?"

Tevi frowned. She wanted to go straight to the temple and search for Jemeryl, but getting herself established in suitable lodgings would be sensible. After her long journey from Horzt, a few more hours would not matter.

"No. Can you recommend somewhere?"

"That's why I asked. I'll be staying at the Four Winds House. It's cheap, safe, and the owner is an old friend of mine. I'll show you the way, if you want."

"Thanks."

When they reached it, Tevi discovered the Four Winds House was in a poorer district of town, but the area was quiet, peaceful after the fervour of the market. Like all the buildings around it, the inn was constructed from mud bricks. It was arranged in the form of three dirt courtyards, surrounded by single-storey rooms.

Tevi and Siashe stabled their horses at the rear and went in search of the owner.

"Raf," Siashe called out, spotting a portly, middle-aged woman backing out of a doorway.

The woman turned round. "Ah, Siashe, my friend. It's good to see you back. And you've got company."

Siashe made the introductions. "Tevi's a mercenary who's just come in with me, from Serac. Raf's a total scoundrel, but you can trust her, because the only thing she cares for is money. Pay her and all is well."

"And Siashe is a lying turd who can't be believed." Raf laughed as she spoke, clearly not in the least offended. Like Siashe, copper-coloured skin and fair hair revealed her nomad origins, although the softened vowels of her accent were less pronounced.

Siashe was not deflected. "No, I mean it. Money can be counted and added up. It always makes sense. Someone who's motivated by money can be understood. Predictable. But Kradja attracts madmen, like a dung heap attracts flies. They think their god is sitting on their shoulder and wants them to do whatever wild idea gets into their head. They do not make sense and you never know where you are with them from one second to the next."

"Will you listen to him." Raf was still laughing, but then she became more serious. "But maybe there is something in what you say."

"The new god?" Tevi asked.

Raf nodded. "I don't like it. This High Priest is—"

Siashe interrupted. "This new god will be just like all the others. Remember the fuss when the Cyclians first arrived?" He turned to Tevi. "The Cyclians believe the world repeats the same cycle endlessly. They have three gods. Koneath the builder, Toqwani the destroyer, and Rashem the reclaimer. Continually, Koneath builds, only to have her work destroyed by Toqwani, and then Rashem gathers up the debris, extracts the raw materials, and gives them to Koneath to use over again. It's a spectacularly pointless religion."

"What does Koneath build?"

"God-type things—stars, mountains, people," Siashe replied. "The Cyclians arrived here a couple of decades ago. At first, some people let it go to their heads, and decided that if they worshipped Toqwani, it gave them the right to smash anything they wanted. I was a child then, so it all seemed like fun. Then a few people were murdered and everyone got upset. But the Cyclians calmed down, and the next god arrived, and it all went back to how it had been before." He turned back to Raf. "This new god will be exactly the same."

"I'm not so sure. This isn't just a few hotheads getting excited. There's new force in the land. All the witches have lost their power— the healers and the soothsayers."

"I've heard the High Priest claims he's going to destroy the Coven." Tevi was interested to see what response she got to this.

"Yes. That's what worries me," Raf said.

"You don't want to see an end to sorcerers?"

"The sorcerers, I'm not bothered about. I won't waste tears, either way. It's not going to happen, though, is it? The Coven is too powerful. But this High Priest might do enough to provoke a war. If a swarm of Coven sorcerers attack us, there'll be nothing left of Kradja but dust."

"You seriously think the people would follow him into a war with the Coven? Everyone's gone mad?" Siashe's scepticism was clear.

Raf poked a finger into his shoulder. "Don't scoff. There's something at work in the temple. Go see for yourself. The idol is taking over people's minds. It has the town buzzing like a hornets' nest, and that's not something to laugh at."

"Very well. We'll get ourselves settled and then go to the temple." Siashe looked at Tevi. "What do you say? Do you want to come with me?"

"Sure."

❖

A flood of people was pouring into the main hall of the temple. Tevi overheard excited mutterings.

"Hurry. He'll be here soon."

"The High Priest. Is it true?"

"Yes. Soon. Hurry."

She wormed her way closer to Siashe. "It looks like we picked the wrong time. With all these people, we aren't going to get anywhere near the idol."

"True, but we might as well listen to what this High Priest has to say for himself."

"Fine by me."

The temple walls were made of thick, ancient stone that swallowed some sounds and amplified others. A circle of high windows allowed in a soft light. The dim, cavernous space of the main hall would have been cool after the desert sun, were it not for the heat generated by hundreds of bodies. In the centre, a golden idol was seated on a raised plinth. A circle of red-cloaked soldiers held the masses back from the immediate vicinity, but there was still competition among the worshippers to get as close as possible. They stood tightly packed together, staring up at the idol.

Tevi and Siashe found a spot with a little more breathing room at one side. The atmosphere was excited, volatile—dangerously so. Although the crowd was currently jubilant, Tevi sensed its mood could shift in an instant.

The sudden burst of angry voices came as no surprise. "I know you! You're one of those damned Nolians. What are you doing here?"

Tevi looked around. A few yards away, two people had a third backed up against a pillar. The man singled out was trying to edge away while babbling. "No, I'm not. I've renounced Nolius. I saw I was wrong."

His accusers were not placated. "Filthy scum."

More heads turned, attracted by the aggressive tone. Already a ring was forming, hemming the man in. Even if he evaded the first two, he would not get far. A woman shoved him back roughly against the pillar.

"No. Please. I'm not a Nolian anymore. Not now." His expression slipped into panic.

The man's pleas were ignored. The crowd had turned feral, feeding off the overcharged atmosphere in the hall. Another onlooker swung at him, a full-force punch that connected with his head, and then the ring of people closed in, blocking their victim from Tevi's view. His voice sounded again, this time as a scream. The level of violence was escalating and he would be lucky to escape with his life.

Tevi took a step forward. What should she do? Going to his aid would risk her mission to find Jemeryl, and she would be hopelessly outnumbered. Yet Tevi could not stand back and do nothing. Fortunately, she was spared the need to intervene. Before Tevi could act, three red-cloaked soldiers appeared, barging their way through the crowd.

"What's going on?"

"Nolian bastard," were the only words Tevi picked from the various responses.

The soldiers manhandled the last couple of attackers away and reached the victim. He looked dishevelled and terrified, but not yet badly hurt.

"I'm not a Nolian. I'm not."

"Yeah, well. It don't matter what you are. The High Priest has said he doesn't want any Nolians hurt." Judging by the soldier's tone, she was not in complete agreement with the High Priest on this matter, but regardless of her personal opinion, she was still going to see the ruling enforced.

Under the harsh gaze of the soldiers, the mob shuffled back and the ex-Nolian made his escape.

"What's going on?" Siashe whispered in Tevi's ear. "The Nolians are harmless. Nice people mostly. Why pick on them?"

"I guess their beliefs don't fit with the new religion."

"I can't see what makes them worse than anyone else. Nolius is a god of reincarnation. His followers believe he bestows magical ability as a reward for good deeds in past lives. Sorcerers are people who were very virtuous in their previous existence."

Tevi laughed. "Do you think they've met many real sorcerers?"

"Have you?" Siashe's tone was rhetorical. He clearly assumed the answer would be no. Many people never encountered even one sorcerer, face-to-face, in their entire lives.

"Well, you know…" Tevi hedged. She had been close to making a slip.

Fortunately, Siashe moved on. "If they want to pick on a religion, why not one of the sex cults?"

"Kradja has sex cults?"

"Of course. Everything ends up here. They're a real pest, accosting you in the street. Trying to get you to go to their orgies."

"I'd have thought that would make them popular."

Siashe grinned. "Think about it. What does it say if you have to join a cult in order to get anyone to knock boots with you?"

Tevi opened her mouth, but at that moment a wave of sighs swept across the temple floor. A man dressed in white robes now stood partway down the stairs at the rear of the hall. Tevi did not need the muttered comment to know this was the High Priest.

She studied Ciamon—Jemeryl's adolescent lover—surprised by the rise of uncomfortable emotions. She had not expected such a strong and immediate antipathy. Yet Jemeryl had spoken of him warmly. Tevi frowned. Was she jealous? Should she not trust Jemeryl's judgement and give him the chance to prove himself? Of course, it was possible he was holding Jemeryl in Kradja against her will, in which case she could feel free to dislike him as much as she wanted.

Ciamon raised his voice. "Thousands of years ago, the great god Equalitus was imprisoned by his enemy—Nolius the deceiver, the usurper, the perverter. Now Equalitus is free and a battle is raging in the heavens that is reflected here on earth. Great days are ahead, that will require great feats. But rest assured, with the strength of our faith, victory will be his. Equalitus will overcome his enemy and Nolius will be cast out of the overworld. All his evil work will be undone and the curse of magic will become a memory. Those who Nolius has corrupted will be made ordinary mortals again, no longer able to oppress their fellows. Then we will have peace and justice. All will live in harmony and none will claim domination over another. All will be united in love. Who now can imagine the wonder that will be ours?"

Ciamon carried on spouting ever more effusive words, describing the paradise that was to come, but Tevi's attention was not on him. The stairs where Ciamon stood led up to a balcony, running around the rear of the hall. A row of watchers were lined along it—priests supporting their leader, to judge by their clothes. Standing close to the centre, and dressed in a similar white robe to the High Priest, was Jemeryl.

CHAPTER FOUR—SECRET PASSAGES

Tevi much preferred the temple without the fanatical hordes. The huge hall was not deserted the next morning, but she could walk freely, and the temperature was bearable. The atmosphere the previous evening had been smouldering, in many different ways. Or more accurately, it had been like a pot over the fire, with its lid wedged on. The pressure was building up, and soon it would explode. Somebody was going to get very badly scalded.

Even now, the temple was not as Tevi remembered from her first visit, over a dozen years before. Back then, the main hall of the temple had exuded a party mood. The priests had performed their rites; seers had chanted; pilgrims had tottered from idol to idol, awe in their eyes. The temple had been chaotic and outrageous, but it had embraced a happy diversity. Now it was possessed of a far too serious single-mindedness. Then there had been devotion, and exhilaration and anticipation, but beneath it all was a sense of fun. That had gone.

Tevi stopped and looked around, certain her memory was not at fault. Of course, she was not the same person as she had been. On her first visit to Kradja, she had been twenty years old, naïve and unsure, newly exiled from her island home for the crime of wanting another woman as a lover. In this, she was fortunate that she was the queen's granddaughter. Someone of lower rank would more likely have been executed than exiled. The irony was that she had done no more than want—not as much as a kiss. The woman she had wanted was the one who had betrayed her.

With hindsight, events had not worked out badly. Tevi knew she was far more content on the mainland than she could ever have been on the Western Isles. In the Protectorate, nobody was the least bit bothered that her lover was female. They might think her a little perverse for only being interested in women, much as they would if she only wanted a lover whose favourite colour was blue, but since she was not in the process of seeking a new one, the issue was never raised.

The real problem upsetting so many was that her lover was a sorcerer. But Tevi was not about to change. People would just have to deal with being upset. Their problem, not hers. Tevi's heart was fixed on Jemeryl, in a way that only deepened and strengthened with each passing year. Nothing but death was going to separate them for long, whatever Alendy might intend. Tevi glanced up at the spot on the balcony where she had seen Jemeryl the night before, and then carried on pacing the perimeter of the hall.

How best to proceed? Jemeryl was unharmed, but was she free to do as she wished? How safe was her position? In thinking it through, Tevi had come up with three scenarios. The first, and to Tevi's mind, least likely, was that Jemeryl really had become a follower of Ciamon's new religion. In this case, Jemeryl was perfectly happy and safe and in no need of rescuing. Urgent action was not called for. Once Tevi was sure of the situation, she could send an open message, and trust that when they met and talked, Jemeryl would be able to explain her reasons.

The second option was that Jemeryl was being forced to act in the way she was. In this case, charging in wildly would be very dangerous, regardless of whether it was physical threats or magical ensnarement that was dictating her behaviour. Before making a move, Tevi had to find out exactly what she was up against and how to get Jemeryl free, safely and without risk. Jemeryl was currently unhurt, and as long as Ciamon thought his hold on her was secure, she was in no immediate danger. Slow and cautious was the way to proceed.

The final option was that Jemeryl was pretending to support Ciamon as part of a plan. Tevi did not want to do anything to spoil the plan, which would certainly be the case if she tried to rescue Jemeryl, whether or not she succeeded. And, as with the previous two scenarios, if Jemeryl had hoodwinked Ciamon into believing her story, she was currently safe and in no need of a quick exit.

Tevi sighed. No matter what was going on, the first step had to be making contact with Jemeryl and finding what her situation was. This was where things got difficult. In fact, even slow, cautious progress might be a bit much to hope for.

Where would Ciamon be keeping Jemeryl? Certainly inside the temple complex. A Coven sorcerer was always an important guest and even as a prisoner, Ciamon would want Jemeryl near at hand. But how secure would it be? Tevi hoped her partner was not chained in a dungeon between main hall appearances, and not just because it would make getting to her harder. Thankfully, on the evidence of the night before, it looked as if Jemeryl was being numbered among Ciamon's priests, and as such would get ordinary accommodation, albeit with a squad of guards outside the door and bars on the window.

Tevi stopped her pacing and again looked at the balcony where Jemeryl had stood. When Ciamon had finished describing the paradise Equalitus would bring about, blaming the Nolians for every ill that beset the world, and appealing for everyone to be nice to each other, he had returned to the balcony and left via a doorway at the end. The other priests, Jemeryl among them, had waited for Ciamon to pass and then followed him out. Tevi stared at the doorway, wondering what lay on the other side. However, she was sure she would not be allowed to wander through, and did not wish to draw attention to herself by trying.

Apart from the circle of guards ringing the idol, more were dotted around the main hall. Tevi had learnt that these red-cloaked soldiers were known as sentinels and had a reputation for piety, loyalty, and ruthlessness. They were the High Priest's personal holy army. Two were standing sentry at the bottom of the stairs to the balcony. Getting into any sort of conflict with them would not be a good move.

Tevi continued pacing until she had completed her circuit of the main hall. From the doorway, she looked back across the floor. The golden idol in the middle dominated the space. Admittedly it was large, yet the effect was more than mere size could account for. Tevi frowned, realising that while her thoughts had been centred on Jemeryl, the idol had been scratching at the edges of her mind, calling to her. Raf claimed a force was at work in the temple. Was the idol more than just a symbol of the High Priest's new god? What part did it play in his plan?

Tevi walked forward. With each step, the lure of the idol grew, first peace, then delight. Tevi stopped a stride away from ecstasy. Around her, worshippers stared at the idol in rapture. None were immune. Tevi was now close enough to see tears of joy running down the faces of the sentinels on guard. The idol was beautiful beyond words, filling her soul with love.

Tevi bowed her head, battling with conflicting emotions. It was insane to hold any idea of resisting the happiness, the fulfilment, the sense of being cared for. Who could do such a thing? Who would want to? And yet, Tevi had been subjected to magical entrapment before, enough to recognise the signs. Ciamon had cast a magical glamour on his idol, of that Tevi was sure. Anger at the barefaced manipulation drove back Tevi's joy. Ciamon was a renegade from the Coven. If he had been caught indulging in tricks like this, no wonder he had needed to flee the Protectorate.

His device prevented others from working magic, but not him. Was this his plan—to block all other sorcerers so he could take over the world, unchallenged? It made it all the more inconceivable that Jemeryl had voluntarily joined his side. So, was she pretending to support him, or was Ciamon forcing her? Because if he was willing and able to use magic like this, then it confirmed he could have taken over Jemeryl's mind. Would she recognise Tevi when they met or would she be his puppet? Progress might have to be even slower and more cautious than expected.

The thought loosened the last of the idol's hold on her. Tevi backed away. Halfway to the door, she collided with another worshipper, a tall, heavily built young man.

"I'm sorry. I wasn't looking where..." Even before Tevi had completed speaking, the man had wandered off.

Tevi turned to the door and then stopped, perplexed. Admittedly, the accident had been minor, but the man had not taken the few seconds required to accept her customary apology. He must be in a rush, yet he was not hurrying away. She watched him plod unswervingly across the floor.

Tevi frowned. Reading body language was something she was good at, and this man's was all wrong. If he was heading for a specific destination, he should be striding with more determination; and if he was idly strolling through the temple, he should be more distracted by things around him. Moving in a straight line was completely at odds with his dawdle.

The main implication was that he had somewhere he wanted to

go, but he did not want to make it obvious. It was also a safe deduction that he was an amateur when it came to subterfuge. Luckily for him, no one else appeared to have picked up on him. None of the red-cloaked sentinels were looking in his direction. So who was he, where was he going, and why was he trying to avoid detection? Displaying what she hoped was a higher degree of stealth, Tevi followed after.

A row of alcoves that had once housed shrines lined the rear of the temple under the balcony. One of these, deeper than the rest, was his goal. Tevi could see the tension in the man's neck as he battled the temptation to look over his shoulder before disappearing into it. He was definitely up to something.

Tevi stopped by the adjacent opening, allowing enough time so it would not be apparent that she was in pursuit, although spending too long meditating on the empty altar, vacant niches and absence of offerings would in itself be suspicious. She had already noted how symbols of the previous plethora of gods had been removed. Why had it been necessary? Had Ciamon really needed to claim the entire temple? Did he know the sort of trouble he was stirring up? Sorcerer or not, would he be able to control the trouble, when it burst out?

The man had not re-emerged from the alcove after a full minute. What was he doing? Tevi moved on, and discovered that the opening was actually a corridor, which eventually broadened out into a round chamber. This room was also empty—even more so than Tevi had expected. The man she had followed was missing, and there were no doors or windows for him to have left by.

Tevi knew the man had not come out the same way he entered. Either he, like Ciamon, was still able to use magic, or there was a concealed exit. Logic said that if the man was capable of the magic needed to disappear, he could have become invisible before entering the temple and jogged across the main hall waving his hands, so a secret door was far more likely.

The temptation was strong to tap the walls, trying to detect a hollow spot, but Tevi had no way of knowing how far her quarry had gone. He might still be within hearing range. A secret way into the temple was exactly what she needed and she did not want to scare him off.

Tevi went back to the main hall. She picked a spot with a clear view of the alcove entrance and joined the adoring ring of worshippers around the idol. All she had to do was wait until she saw the man again, if not today, then tomorrow, or the day after. Despite her feeling of impatience, time was not critical.

Slow and cautious.

❖

Midday had passed before the man reappeared. Fortunately, standing by the idol for so long did not count as unusual behaviour. The glamour was addictive. Tevi suspected the sentinels would have to forcibly eject people from the temple each night, sending them away to eat and sleep. The unpleasant image rose in Tevi's mind of the idol in years to come, surrounded by the white bones of its entranced worshippers. She hoped the sentinels had the discipline to combat the lure. Did Ciamon know what he created? Did he care?

Tevi had spent much of the time speculating about the man she was waiting for. It was not safe to assume he was a potential ally. In the normal run of things, enough bad reasons existed to explain his actions. Thieves, assassins, and spies came to mind. Given the fanatical hothouse of Kradja, who knew what his motives were?

The man left the temple in the same ineptly mock-casual way he had entered. Tevi tailed him through the market with its rabid preachers and into the surrounding streets, where the façade of normality still held, but cracks were showing. Shops were open for business, craftsmen hammered, wove, and sharpened, customers haggled and hawkers called, but too many people sat idle in doorways, waiting for paradise to start. Tevi skirted around a disorderly procession of chanting, dancing believers. A couple caught her hands, urging her to join in. Tevi shrugged them off, but at least they were happy and well meaning. The small groups gathering on corners with the air of wild dogs were not so reassuring.

The man's route took him to the poorer side of Kradja, not far from the Four Winds House. His visit to the temple had clearly been a strain on him, and now he was out, the relief caused him to act, ironically, in a more blatantly furtive way, repeatedly glancing back over his shoulder. However, his lack of focus and discipline meant that Tevi would have needed to be jumping up and down for him to have much chance of spotting her. He was clearly an amateur at spying, but this did not mean much. Thieves also start out as amateurs.

He looked three times up and down the street before ducking into a side alley. To judge from the way his anxiety had ratcheted up still higher, he was near his final goal. Tevi slipped from the doorway she had hidden in and reached the junction in time to see him knock on the door to a cellar and talk to whoever answered. He peered around frantically once more before disappearing from view.

Tevi carried on at a casual stroll while taking in the neighbourhood. The area was poor but reputable, the homes of labourers rather than lowlifes. The shops were grocers and butchers, not brothels. The building her quarry had entered looked to be the back of one such business. Tevi walked around to the front to see what she could learn.

A flour sack hung over the doorway, denoting a baker. The man had certainly not been delivering cakes to the priests, but was he a legitimate worker—the owner or an employee? As she passed the doorway, Tevi glanced in to see a conventional array of bread and pies on sale; everything seeming normal, but might the shop be a front for something more sinister?

Further along the road, a few old folk stood gossiping in a doorway, and a gang of young children were playing football at a point where the street widened out. At the sight of them, Tevi smiled—the best informants she could hope for.

Most children stopped playing as she approached, although two at the rear continued kicking the ball back and forth.

Tevi crouched and held up a couple of coins. "I wonder if you can tell me who owns that baker's shop there."

One child started to answer, before a friend pulled him back and whispered something in his ear. The words Tevi caught were in the language of the desert nomads. Her knowledge was too limited to understand what was said, even had the girl spoken loudly, but it was not necessary. From the way she was acting, the girl was obviously proposing that they trick the stranger.

"Tashde rah." As far as Tevi could tell, the phrase was a forceful version of something like *stop that.* She had heard Siashe use it a dozen times on his horse, or anything else that annoyed him.

The effect on the children was immediate. The boy glared at the others behind him and then grinned contritely at Tevi. "It belongs to Aslie. She's the baker. It used to be her uncle's, but he's got a new place near the market."

"Do you know what she keeps in the cellar at the back?"

The boy wrinkled his nose. "Flour, I guess."

The coins made a ringing sound as Tevi rubbed them together. "So, who would it be I saw going in there?"

"Her brother."

"No, it's not. It's the ratman." One of the children disagreed.

"Yes, it is. Aslie's brother hides there 'cause he's frightened of the idol in the temple." The boy looked back at Tevi. "Him and his friends."

"My dad said it was the ratman. Aslie's got rats."

"Your dad don't know nothing." A fight looked likely to break out.

Tevi intervened. "You said they're frightened of the new idol."

"Yeah."

"No, they aren't." More dissent from another child. "They left 'cause they wouldn't quit the old gods."

Tevi again jumped in. "The old gods. Do Aslie's brother and his friends still worship them?"

"I 'spect so." The girl rubbed the side of her nose. "They used to be priests."

Tevi smiled and tossed the coins into the air for the children to scramble after. They had not seemed utterly reliable, but what they said made sense. It stood to reason that the cast-out priests would not be happy, and who would be more likely to know about secret passages in the temple?

Tevi strolled back to the alleyway at the rear of the shop while considering her options. How best to make contact with the ousted priests? Listening at the door was unlikely to reveal much, and would not help gain their trust if she was caught. Sneaking in stood an even smaller chance of success. In fact, no form of subterfuge was likely to yield worthwhile results, which left her with just one option. Tevi knocked on the cellar door.

After a long silence, Tevi was about to knock again when a voice on the other side asked, uncertainly, "What's the word?"

"I assume you mean the password. I'm sorry. I don't know it. I've come to talk to you about getting into the temple."

An even longer silence greeted this. At last, the voice asked, "Who are you?"

"Potentially, a friend. Would you be willing to talk about it?"

The door opened. Inside was dark, but not so much that Tevi could not see the drawn bow pointed in her direction. She raised her hands in surrender. When nothing else happened for a while, she asked, "Shall I come in? I feel a bit conspicuous standing out here like this."

The door opened wider, and a hand beckoned her forward. As soon as she was through, more hands grabbed her, shoved her face first against the wall, and patted her down. The long knife was removed from her belt and the short one from her boot, but the attempt at a search was laughable. Tevi could have got a small arsenal past it, had she wished.

Tevi was then released, allowing her to face the room. Her eyes had adjusted to the weak light, enough to see a dozen people staring at her, including the man she had tailed from the temple. She could well believe they were priests. Their age and physical condition made it very clear they were not warriors. Even though the arrow was still pointing vaguely in her direction, and two others held drawn blades, if it came to a fight, the outcome was not a forgone conclusion. Quite apart from her martial training, Tevi had one other advantage.

The women of the Western Isles brewed a potion they gave to girls that affected the child's development. The result was that Tevi, like all her female kin, had grown up vastly stronger than normal. The strength potion was the only one known to the Coven, and in fact, until Tevi had arrived on the mainland, most sorcerers had declared such a thing to be impossible. Since leaving Lyremouth, Tevi had taken care not to display her potion-enhanced strength, mainly so as not to attract attention. The element of surprise was an added bonus in situation like this.

"Who are you?" The question was repeated in a voice quavering with both age and anxiety.

"My name's Tevi. I'm a mercenary, from the Protectorate." She held up the backs of her hands to show the tattoos.

"What are you doing here?" The speaker was an elderly man, with a nervous expression and indecisive posture. Despite his lack of forcefulness, the others in the cellar were clearly deferring to him. If things turned nasty, Tevi was comforted that the leader would choose to flee rather than fight.

"Here as in Kradja, or here in your cellar?"

"What do you want with us?"

"I want to talk to someone inside the temple, and I think you might be able to help me."

"You're working for that fraudster—Ciamon." The new speaker was far more aggressive than his leader, as well as being a couple of decades younger. He was one of the people holding a knife.

"No."

"Then how come you found us? How did you know about our meeting?" He took a step forward, raising his knife.

"Please, Alkoan. Let her speak first."

At the elderly man's appeal, the aggressive one, presumably called Alkoan, scowled but moved back. "Speak quickly then."

"I saw him"—Tevi pointed—"in the temple, acting suspiciously. So I followed. He went into a side chamber and vanished. I waited until he came out and tailed him here."

"Why?"

"I guessed he went into a secret passage. As I said before, I want to talk to someone. A secret passage is exactly what I need."

"Who do you want to talk to?"

Tevi hesitated for a second, but no made-up story was likely to be received any more favourably than the truth. "A senior sorcerer at Lyremouth sent me to find her former pupil, who's supposedly gone over to Ciamon's side. But the person who sent me doesn't believe it. She thinks it's all part of a plan. I'm to give what help I can."

"The Coven sent you, on your own, rather than a troop of sorcerers?"

"If you know anything about what Ciamon's doing, you'll know he's made a device that stops anyone working magic near it. Sorcerers would be slightly less use than ordinary folk, since they'd have no experience of how to do anything without spells. And a large group arriving here would be too easy for the sentinels to spot. Hence just me. My skills are unaffected by the device. I'm still as deadly as before."

The old man nodded. "A Coven sorcerer did arrive two months ago, Ciamon's lover."

"She's not—" Tevi stopped.

When Jemeryl had spoken of her past relationship with Ciamon, Tevi had been surprised by the twinge of jealousy, but that was all it had been, a brief twinge. Even her reaction when she saw him was due more to his current activities than anything that had gone before. Tevi had no doubts about the strength of Jemeryl's commitment to her. But supposing Ciamon had taken over Jemeryl's mind. What might he have forced her to do? Tevi felt her hands tighten into fists. In that case, there would be blood spilt.

However, this was conjecture, and she did not want to confuse these potential allies. "Jemeryl won't have really gone over to his side."

"How can you know? Are you familiar with this sorcerer?" Alkoan's scepticism was clear.

"Yes. She's close kin of mine." It was true in spirit, and should not upset the priests' sense of propriety, should they have strong feelings about what was appropriate between sorcerers and the ungifted. "That's why I was picked for this, and why I said yes."

"A mercenary?" Alkoan looked thoughtful, and a little less hostile. "Are you an assassin?"

"I'm—"

Before Tevi could finish her answer, another priest jumped in. "Can you kill Ciamon for us?"

The cellar erupted. "And that traitor, Sefriall."

"We must have patience."

"It's not your followers being hunted by mobs."

"Let Yalaish guide us."

"It's time to follow the path of Toqwani."

"Silence!" For the first time, the old man had raised his voice. He was still lacking vigour, but the other priests subsided at his command. He turned to Tevi. "My name is Darjain. I'm a priest of Yalaish, and leader of those assembled here, as long as they'll follow me." The last part was delivered with a sideways glance at Alkoan. "We were banished from the temple when Ciamon arrived, with his sham religion."

"Which is why we have to kill him." Alkoan addressed Tevi. "Will you help us?"

"We haven't yet decided that." Darjain's words were no surprise. Tevi had seen enough of him already to know that he was the well-meaning sort who never decided anything.

She replied to Alkoan. "It's not that simple."

"Why not?"

"Ciamon's a sorcerer, and his magic is still working. Have you felt the glamour his idol is kicking out?"

Another priest interjected. "So it is a spell."

"Of course." Alkoan looked exasperated. "What else could it be?" He turned back to Tevi. "What do you think we should do?"

"What I said. Help me talk to Jemeryl. She's a Coven sorcerer. Even without her magic, she'll have more idea about how to deal with Ciamon than anyone here has. We need her advice."

"How do we know you're not a follower of Ciamon? How do we know you won't pass on what you've found out about us?"

"The only things I've found out is you meet in this cellar and you use secret passages in the temple. I knew that much before I knocked on the door. If I was working for Ciamon, I could have told him already and he'd have sent a dozen sentinels here."

Several priests glanced at the door, while a couple looked nauseous at the idea.

"Yalaish will protect us." Darjain spoke with more confidence than before. "This is a trial we must endure."

Another priest nodded. "The cycle will continue. All things will pass."

"But the great cycle has its phases. I say this is time for Toqwani the destroyer. We must fight." Alkoan's position was predictable.

"Before we get hunted down like rats."

"All this has been foretold." A new priest joined in. She had been sitting on the floor to the side, with her arms wrapped around her knees, playing no part in the debate until now. "The holy fool will die amid fire and destruction. The despised idol will fall. The blasphemer will be consumed by the dessert."

"How about getting your god to give us some prophecies we can make use of?" Alkoan snapped.

"Please. Stop bickering. We have enough trouble, without fighting each other." Darjain held up his hands. When silence had returned, he looked at Tevi. "We must proceed carefully. Your kinswoman, this Jemeryl, might be useful. Tomorrow afternoon, Parrash is due to return to the temple." He indicated the man who Tevi had followed. "This cellar belongs to his sister. She's the baker. Meet him here at noon and he will guide you."

Tevi was a little surprised. Darjain could make decisions, after all—although a decision to get more information before doing anything was maybe one he could handle.

❖

The afternoon sun was at its hottest when Tevi returned to Four Winds House. She found Siashe sitting in the shade outside the room she shared with him. Raf was also there and carved wooden pieces were laid out on a grid scored in the dust before them, although the game was clearly over. They indicated for Tevi to join them.

"I was telling Raf you were curious about the sex cults here," Siashe said, smiling as he passed her a bottle.

"I'm always interested in local customs." Tevi sipped cautiously. She had already discovered that items considered delicacies in Kradja were not always to her liking. This time, the spiced wine turned out to be good, if a little pungent.

"Your interest goes no further than talk?" Raf was teasing.

"Certainly. Especially since the healers are out of action."

"You show great wisdom. But health isn't the only reason to be cautious." Raf laughed and looked at Siashe. "You remember Daole?"

"Yes. Wasn't she living with a partner by the south gate?"

"She was. And note the word *was*." Raf launched into a tale. The story got progressively more absurd until Tevi was sure it had to be partly made up, but it was funny.

"…and Daole's chickens were never seen again." Raf reached the outrageous conclusion, and levered herself to her feet. "But I've got things to do." She gestured at Siashe. "If I don't see you tomorrow morning, safe journey and speedy return, my friend."

"I'll keep you in my thoughts. Stay safe."

"I'll do my best." Raf toddled away

"You're leaving tomorrow?" Tevi asked, still wiping tears from her eyes.

"Yes. A new caravan. Traders to Lijoni. Should be saner than pilgrims. You'll have the room to yourself for a while." Siashe grinned. "But what about you? Have you found work yet?"

"Maybe. Have you heard of a priest called Darjain?"

Siashe looked surprised. "Of course. But you're not going to tell me he's hired your services."

"Why? Is there something wrong with him?"

"Hardly. He's the kindest man in Kradja. Not only wouldn't he hurt a fly, he'd give it food and water and send it on its way with prayers for its well-being. He's not the sort of man to employ a hired sword."

"He's not exactly offered to pay for my work, but do you know he has been kicked out of the temple by the new High Priest?"

Siashe sucked his breath through his teeth. "The man is mad—the High Priest, not Darjain, he's just a bit soft in the head. Darjain is an old man. He's done much good in his life, and very little harm. He should be left to worship his god in peace. But he'd never resort to violence, or pay others to do it on his behalf."

"He's leader of the cast-out priests. Some of them aren't quite as forgiving." Tevi had debated whether to discuss the situation with Siashe, but his knowledge of the town and its inhabitants might prove useful.

Siashe turned his head and stared over the rooftops, although there was nothing obvious to see in the cloudless blue sky. "Did I ever tell you about the strange thing I saw recently, when I was guiding a party across the desert from Serac?"

Tevi frowned at the change of topic. "No."

"In this party was a mercenary, a member of the Protectorate guild. She seemed ordinary enough. Then one night when we made camp, I couldn't sleep, so I sat a while, watching the stars. This mercenary appeared, but she didn't see me sitting alone in the dark. The night was chill. I think she wanted a blanket from her pack. But do you know what had happened?"

"What?"

"When a driver had unhitched the mules, the wagon must have rolled onto the mercenary's pack. It was wedged under the wheel. So the mercenary caught hold of the wheel, lifted it, and pulled her pack free. Can you see why I was so surprised?"

"Yes. I think so." Tevi now understood where the story was headed.

"Four strong men would struggle to lift the wagon, yet this one woman had done it on her own. I saw it myself. After she'd gone, I sat and thought, because sleep was even further from me than before. The mercenary's strength had to be magical. She was from the Protectorate, and she was headed to Kradja, where a new High Priest had sworn to overthrow the Coven. The sums weren't hard, and the conclusion I reached was that this mercenary's business in Kradja was something I had no wish to get mixed up in. Better if I could deny all knowledge. So I decided to say nothing."

"You're telling me now."

Siashe turned back to face her. "Because I liked this mercenary. I think she was a good person. And now I wish I'd given her some advice. I think she's walking a dangerous path. If ever she needs a place to hide, to the north of here is a mountain which I'd pointed out to her. Below it is another oasis."

Tevi nodded.

"This oasis is sacred to my people. It has no temple or town, but there are caves in the cliffs overlooking it. Those caves are a refuge. In time of trouble, someone could go there and be safe, if they said they were a friend of Siashe, son of Jeqwai."

"Thank you."

"My people worship Yalaish. They will not follow this High Priest." Siashe smiled. "Stay safe, my friend."

❖

Parrash was the only one waiting in the cellar when Tevi arrived the next day. He peered at her, clearly ill at ease, but then squared his shoulders. "What was I doing yesterday that made you suspicious?"

"The way you moved. You were too purposeful for the speed you were going."

"Just that?"

"Enough to get my attention."

"I'm the only one with the nerve to do it…to go into the temple," Parrash said defensively. "Well, Alkoan would, but his face is too well known. I'm just a neophyte."

Tevi considered saying something flattering about his courage, but it might sound patronising. Instead she smiled in a friendly fashion. "Shall we go?"

Parrash nodded and led the way out. Tevi fell into step beside him. As she had already noted, Parrash was carrying excess weight, and from the way he moved it was fat, not muscle, as might be expected in a priest. She judged him to be in his late twenties, young enough still to be agile, and his weight was not nearly excessive enough to count as obese, but Tevi predicted that by middle age he would be round and waddling.

Midday was siesta time and the streets around the bakery were empty. Tevi had some questions to ask while there was no risk of being overheard.

"You'd be in trouble if you were caught in the temple. But I guess it's easy for them to sit back and let you take the risks."

"You're telling me."

"So why are you doing it? What's the point?"

"Darjain wants more information before we do anything. He'll always want more information. He's…" Parrash kicked at a pebble. His expression was troubled. "I was training to be an initiate of Yalaish when Ciamon arrived. Darjain was our senior priest. I used to think he was wonderful but he…" Parrash ran out of words.

"Darjain doesn't seem well suited to be a leader in a time of crisis."

"You can say that again."

"So why is he? Why does everyone follow him?"

"He was speaker for the convocation."

"Which is?"

"The assembly that ran the temple. It used to meet in the basilica. All the religions had representatives. The speaker's job was to call the meeting to order and see it stuck to the agenda, and tell people to be polite. Darjain got to be speaker because he was the only priest who nobody hated."

"He wasn't the High Priest?"

"We never used to have one before Ciamon. All the faiths were independent. Now we need to work together and Darjain's the only one with any sort of authority over everyone." Parrash grimaced. "Except we're not working. We've been meeting in my sister's cellar for months, and we've done nothing but talk. I think Alkoan's right."

Tevi had wondered if Parrash would be too suspicious of her motives to talk. Luckily, it seemed as if he had a lot he wanted to get off his chest. "Alkoan wants to kill Ciamon."

"Yes. He's a Cyclian. He used to favour Rashem, but since we've been expelled, he's tending more to Toqwani."

"Does he have much support from the other priests?"

"He does from Botha. You can't blame her. She's a Nolian. The new religion has painted her god as the source of all evil. Her followers get attacked all the time. Some have been killed, though the sentinels deny it."

"I saw one nearly lynched in the temple."

"It's getting worse. I'm surprised Sefriall has gone along with it. Botha and her used to be close."

"Sefriall?"

"She was one of the Cyclians. When Ciamon showed up, she switched to him. Sold us all out. Now she's his deputy and in charge of the sentinels. She talked a few other priests into swapping allegiance as well. But some are just pretending. They're still on our side really. They're the ones I meet in the temple." He sighed heavily. "It's still getting us nowhere, though."

The streets were getting busier as they neared the centre of town. Parrash glanced around theatrically, as if to check that no one was in earshot. Fortunately for him, theatrical behaviour was not unusual in Kradja. He stared up at the dome of the temple, set against a brilliant blue sky.

"Yalaish is the all-mother. She gave birth to the world. All life is hers. I used to think if I was one of her priests, I'd be…" Parrash shrugged. "I don't know. Maybe when this is all over I'll switch to the Cyclians." Parrash clearly admired Alkoan, but Tevi could tell that his words owed more to cynicism.

The growing crowds made talking freely dangerous and they walked the rest of the way in silence. Once in the temple hall, Tevi led the way, a leisurely stroll, taking in a detour or two to nowhere in particular. She might as well give Parrash a few pointers in deception, but she was not sure if the lesson was absorbed. She could sense his impatience. He was clearly desperate to be out of sight of the sentinels and even gave an audible sigh of relief when they finally reached the small rear chamber. For his sake, Tevi hoped she and Jemeryl could take care of Ciamon and his device soon. Parrash's long-term future as an undercover agent did not look good.

The neophyte priest immediately hurried to a region of the wall and hunched close, using his back as a shield.

Tevi was having none of it. She tugged on his shoulder. "Show me."

"You don't need to—"

"If anything happens, I want to be able to find my way in and out. Show me."

Parrash frowned, but his hand was on an embossed head, wreathed in plants. Tevi would know where to start looking anyway. "There, feel under the flower. The catch."

Tevi slid her fingers under the stone rose. A petal shifted at her touch.

"Pull it up."

Tevi did so and heard a bolt snap back.

"Now, here. This panel. Push down and to the side."

A hatch swung open, two feet square. Parrash crawled through, grunting faintly.

Tevi followed. "Do you have a lantern?"

"Don't need it. Give it a few seconds. Anyway, a lantern in here would shine through the cracks and be visible outside."

Tevi waited until her eyes adapted. Sure enough, a series of small holes let in enough light to see by even after Parrash had slid the panel back in place. She found they were standing in a narrow irregular walkway, squeezed between one wall and another. Parrash started to sidle along, his size making swift movement impossible, but even Tevi could not walk normally in the cramped space.

"Why was this passage made?" Tevi asked.

"The followers of Harretha. They're the ones who built the temple. The place is riddled with their secret passages."

"But why?"

"They used to spy on people, and then pretend they learnt the stuff in a vision from their god. Complete bunch of frauds. They were the only ones who knew about it. Kel finally let us in on the secret."

"Kel's one of the priests?"

"A seer. She was there yesterday, sitting on the floor, spouting the same old nonsense."

"Does—"

Parrash stopped her with a hand on her arm and whispered, "We ought to keep the noise down."

"Right."

They carried on in as close to silence as the awkward manœuvring allowed. On their route, Tevi passed many spots where a larger hole gave a clear view of a temple room or corridor. Several times she heard voices, amplified by the acoustics of the tunnel. The builders who had constructed the maze for spying had known what they were doing.

After an age of squeezing through the cramped space, Parrash stopped. He leaned his mouth close to Tevi's ear. "There's another exit here. It's easy to open from inside. When you want to return, the catch is on the roof of the lion's mouth. You'll see what I mean. Your kinswoman's room is opposite. About twenty feet to the left. You should take your time and make sure the coast is clear before you get out. I'm going to meet with my contact."

"Thanks."

"Good luck."

"You too."

Parrash edged away. Tevi waited, listening. Despite her best effort, she could hear nothing. At last she reached out, found a handle, and pulled. A hatch opened at knee height.

After the dim passage, the corridor outside was bright enough to make Tevi's eyes water, but she did not want to hang around. Squinting, Tevi shut the hatch, then scuttled across the corridor and through the door Parrash had indicated.

No one was currently in the sparsely furnished room. A bed was against one wall with a footlocker at the end. Tevi pulled the lid open and smiled, recognising the belongings. Judging by the absence of other items, Jemeryl was the sole occupant of the room, but she might have company with her when she returned. Tevi ought to get out of sight, and here lay a problem. Hiding places were regrettably limited. The space under the bed was too small and the footlocker was full. There were no bars on the window, but Tevi did not like the idea of dangling outside for an indefinite period. The curtain over the entrance to the garderobe was thin with a foot gap at the bottom, but with no better option, Tevi slipped into the confined space and took a seat. She might as well rest while waiting.

Time passed slowly. The square of sunlight through the window inched up the bedroom wall. Tevi was almost falling asleep when at last, the door handle rattled and turned. Taking care not to disturb the curtain, Tevi raised her feet, then tilted her head and peered around the gap at the side. Jemeryl walked in, accompanied by someone who looked and acted like a servant, carrying a pile of clothes. The servant laid the clothes on the footlocker, bowed, and left.

Jemeryl was alone. But was her mind her own? There was one way to find out. Tevi opened the curtain and stepped out. "Hello, Jem."

Jemeryl spun around, surprise turning quickly to relief. She crossed the space between them and flung her arms around Tevi.

"I was wondering when you'd get here."

CHAPTER FIVE—A CAUSE TO DOUBT

After months on her own, the comfort of Tevi's physical presence was overwhelming for Jemeryl. She sat beside Tevi on the edge of the bed, her head resting on Tevi's shoulder and Tevi's arm around her waist. Could she ever get tired of this? Simply being with her lover, hearing her voice, holding her hand, and looking at her. Of course there was much more that Jemeryl wanted to do, but it would not be wise. She was not due anywhere, and although she was normally left alone, it was possible that someone might walk in on them at any moment.

If they were disturbed, Tevi would need to act the part of a servant. With luck, the ploy would work. Surely nobody could recognise every genuine temple employee on sight. A half-second warning from the sound of the door handle would be enough for Tevi to pick up a fistful of cleaning rags, but not to readjust her clothing. Even so, Jemeryl knew it would be safer to conclude this meeting quickly. Until they had more time, with guaranteed privacy, the limited contact would have to suffice.

Jemeryl raised their joined hands to her lips, pressed a kiss on Tevi's knuckles, and then sat staring at the familiar mercenary tattoos, mulling over what Tevi had told her. "Do you know what sort of resources these deposed priests can call on? How many are there?"

"I get the feeling there's only a few. But they might have a role in stopping Ciamon."

"If we decide to do it."

"Do what?"

Jemeryl squeezed Tevi's hand, realising just how desperately she needed to talk things over. "You don't think he might be right? That the world would be better without magic? I've been talking to him, and I'm not so sure anymore."

"Jem?" Tevi swivelled around to face her. "Are you serious? Have you really gone over to his side?"

"No. I don't know. I haven't known since I got here." Jemeryl gave a wry smile. "I'm hoping you can help sort me out."

"Is that why you chose to stay?"

"Not exactly, but I knew whatever way I decided, in the end, I needed to be close."

"I don't understand your doubts."

"Ci's right when he says it's not fair that some people, like me, are born able to see into all the dimensions, and we get to run everything as if we own the Protectorate. I'm a sorcerer, but I'm no better than anyone else. What right have I to lord it over people?"

"How will getting rid of magic make things any better?"

Jemeryl frowned, confused. "Because then everyone will be the same."

"But they won't, will they? Some will be stronger, or richer, or born into the right family. And then they'll get to lord it over everyone else, and it won't be the slightest bit different."

"Magic is so"—Jemeryl waved her hand, searching for the right word—"powerful. It's not like all the other differences that separate people."

"I can't say I noticed, when I was growing up. Since we didn't have sorcerers, it meant my grandmother got to rule everything, just because of who her mother was. And the men, the way their lives were...nobody in the Protectorate has it that bad, believe me. It was as if they were slaves or children all their lives."

"That's because of your magic potion."

"No. Before we had the potion, it was exactly the same, except it was the men who got to do what they wanted and the women who were treated like children."

Jemeryl could not agree. "The difference between men and women is insignificant. Do you honestly think if there were no sorcerers, then the whole world would start acting as if gender was some great division between people?"

"Maybe. Or maybe they'd think of some other trait to pick on, like what their skin was."

"Nobody is going to enslave or kill somebody else over something daft like that."

"Don't you believe it."

"Magic makes a massive difference to the amount of power somebody has."

"And if the difference wasn't so marked, maybe the people on the top would have to work that much harder to stay in their place, and be that much more brutal in keeping the rest down. Ciamon's device isn't going to change what people are like, and it isn't going to make everyone equal."

"It can make everyone equal under the law. I know the Coven has rules and things, but the rules get broken. Some bad things get done, and the culprits get away with it, because of what they are."

"My grandmother could do what she liked and get away with it, because her word was the law. I was exiled. If it had suited her, I'd be dead. I agree the Protectorate isn't perfect, but it's a good starting point. If that story Ciamon told you is true, you need to go back to Lyremouth, start making a fuss, and challenge Alendy and the other sorcerer."

"It's not just the Protectorate. Ci will put an end to people like Bykoda. I know how much you hated her empire."

"Part of what I hated about Bykoda was the way she reminded me of my grandmother. The pair of them were cut from the same cloth."

"So your objections boil down to how you felt about your grandmother?"

"She's a genuine practical example. All Ciamon has are naïve pipe dreams."

Jemeryl chewed her lip, trying to get to the core of her doubts. "Ci's a good man. He wants to make the world a better place."

"Don't we all? But he's going the wrong way about it."

"He means well."

"They're the most dangerous sort."

Jemeryl closed her eyes. Was Tevi right? Over the previous months, her opinion had swung back and forth, until she was no longer sure what she thought. Ciamon's idealism was infectious. Whether or not events worked out the way he intended, Jemeryl wanted to believe it was possible to build a better world.

"You don't think ideals are worth striving for, even if you fail?"

"I'll leave you to explain it to the first pile of corpses we come across."

"I'm talking about freedom and fairness."

"I'm talking about massacres."

Jemeryl opened her eyes and studied Tevi's face. "You're serious?"

"Yes."

"You think it will come to that?"

"I know it will. I was worried before I came here. But now..." Tevi shook her head. "There's going to be a bloodbath."

"Why?"

"Because he's an idiot. He doesn't know what he's stirring up. This new religion has got the whole town simmering—his stupid god and blaming the Nolians for everything."

"That's just a story he made up."

"Perhaps to him. But doesn't he expect people to believe it? The first night I was here, I saw somebody almost beaten to death because of it." Tevi held both of Jemeryl's hands. "Look. Ciamon thinks that getting rid of magic will make the world perfect. I think it will mean that a different group of bastards end up on top. Maybe he's right and I'm wrong. But if I'm the one who's right, millions could die. It's too big a risk to take on the chance that all bad behaviour is due to sorcerers. We have to stop him."

Jemeryl leaned forward and rested her head on Tevi's shoulder. Part of her still agreed with Ciamon, but she trusted Tevi's judgement. "If you're sure."

"I am."

The sudden surge of relief surprised Jemeryl. Was it because sharing the decision had shared the responsibility? Was she pleased not to have to make a moral judgement on the issue? Or was it that she now had an excuse to try and get back all her special abilities? Now she could tell herself that she was doing it for the sake of others. "Tevi, I..."

"What?"

"Thanks."

"For what?"

"Being here when I need you." Jemeryl kissed Tevi softly. The issue was still not fully resolved for her, but it could wait. "Stoping Ci isn't going to be easy."

"Seeing he's able to work magic and you can't."

"No. He's affected the same as me."

"His idol still projects its glamour."

"That's because the seven dimensions are still there. The forces in them work the same as ever. All the morphology does is to stop us being able to perceive them."

"Morphology?"

"It's what his emanator projects. It imposes a morphology, a pattern, on the skein."

"And the skein is?"

"The web that interconnects all life forces in the fifth dimension. It's called the skein because it's such a tangled mess." Jemeryl paused. "Except I guess, with the morphology, it isn't as tangled as before."

"His device is an untangler?"

"It's a harmonic array emanator. But I guess that won't make a lot of sense to you."

"It's all right. Haven't you noticed I've got pretty good at bluffing?" Tevi grinned. "His device has put a pattern on the skein, and that stops magic working?"

"It puts a perceptual bar on the higher dimensions, so I'm blind to them, like you. But the dimensions themselves are unaffected. Magic that was set up before the morphology was imposed will carry on working. Even more than before, because nobody can now see how to dispel it. Hence the glamour on the idol is still going."

Tevi nodded. "Right. That explains Klara. Your bond to her was still there, but you could no longer pull the strings."

"She's not a puppet. But the analogy isn't too far off."

"So there's no reason why the priests can't kill Ciamon?"

Jemeryl shook her head sharply. "They mustn't."

"You still care about him?"

Jemeryl was aware of Tevi, studying her face. "It's not that. Yes, I do care about him. We were very close friends."

"You were lovers."

"Does that bother you?"

"Not as long as it stays in the past tense."

Jemeryl laughed. "You don't need to worry. It was over, long before we finished as apprentices. Ci is a kind, caring person, but he's far too much emotional hard work. There are only so many times a day I can cope with my lover bursting into tears."

"Now you tell me. Could you let me know what my limit is, so I don't go over by accident?"

"Don't worry, you've never come close." Jemeryl smiled, and then became more serious. "I don't want to see him killed, but that's not why I said no. Killing him won't do any good, because the emanator will carry on projecting its morphology, and that's what we need to stop. I was always a much stronger sorcerer than Ci. Once we get the magic back, I'll be able to overcome him. Then we can take him to Lyremouth." Jemeryl frowned. She did not like the scenario, but what other option was there? "He can tell his story. If nothing else, he'll see his old superior punished for what she did."

"Then we have to destroy the idol."

"Yes. But that's where we hit the problem. Before he activated the emanator, Ci put some protective spells on it. The glamour was one. I don't know what the others are. I doubt these priests will be able to get through the protection, and it would be dangerous for them to try."

"What can we do?"

"I need Ci to tell me what protective spells he used. Then, maybe, I can think of a way round them. If Ci is murdered, we'll never find out how to destroy the idol."

"So, you need to work on him, and I need to talk the priests into attacking the idol rather than killing Ciamon."

"That sums it up." Jemeryl leaned forward and kissed Tevi again, their lips moulding together. She had missed this contact so much, but then she broke away. "And now you need to go, before someone turns up and you have to act like a housemaid."

"You don't think I'd be good at the part?"

"I'm sure you would. I just don't think I'd be able to watch you do it without laughing."

❖

Finding the lever in the lion's mouth was easy. Finding her way back down the branching passage was less so. Before she had gone half the distance to the exit, Tevi resolved to coerce Parrash into drawing a map for her. More by luck than anything else, she got to the exit without getting lost.

Just before she reached the final corner, she heard a click, like the sound of the bolt on the hatch. Either it was Parrash or it was bad news. Did the sentinels know about the tunnels? Tevi had spent a long time in Jemeryl's room, waiting for her to arrive, and had assumed that Parrash would have concluded his business ages ago. Was he coming back for a second time? Or was she about to be caught?

Yet when Tevi turned the corner, the last few yards of passageway were empty, as was the chamber outside. Not until Tevi reached the main hall of the temple did she spot the neophyte priest. Parrash was crossing the floor, showing even less discretion and more haste than normal.

Tevi made her own circuitous exit, but broke into a jog once she was in the street, with the result that she overtook Parrash well before he reached the baker's shop.

"Hey. Did you get delayed? You were only a few seconds in front of me."

Parrash stopped and turned, looking disoriented. "Er...yes. I had to wait for my contact. Then I...I thought I'd wait for you, so you didn't get lost on the way out."

"You mean you gave up on me just a minute too soon?" Tevi smiled as she spoke, to show she was not seriously bothered.

"You were such a long time. I thought maybe you'd finished before me, and left. So, er...you were just behind me?"

"That's what I said."

"Right." Parrash stared down at his feet. "How did your business go?"

"I've got some information I need to pass on to Darjain and the rest. When's the next meeting?"

"I could tell them it for you."

"That's all right. Some people might need a bit of persuading. I'll argue the case myself."

"If you're sure." Parrash looked even more unhappy. "Er...the next meeting. It's tomorrow evening. At dusk."

"Fine. I'll see you there."

Parrash nodded and scurried away. Tevi watched him go. Parrash was not only inept at clandestine activities, he was a lousy liar as well. So what had he been doing in the tunnels?

❖

The same faces were gathered in the cellar when Tevi arrived. Were these the chosen representatives of their different religions, or was this the total sum of ousted priests? Tevi frowned. How many would it take to destroy the idol? And should she try to find more allies, ready for when Jemeryl had the information she needed? It was something she ought to think about. Better to plan now than to be caught out when the time came to act.

Tevi took her place in the circle. The person on her right passed her an engraved silver flask, shaped like a teardrop and smelling strongly of alcohol. Tevi took a careful sip, expecting the worst. To her surprise, it was fine brandy, not rough spirits or a highly scented concoction. The deposed priests must have a rich benefactor. She took a second sip and then the flask continued its circuit, back to Darjain, from whom it apparently had originated.

The cellar was clearly used primarily as a storeroom. Sacks of grain were piled in one corner and a fine dusting of flour covered the tops of three crates, one of which Darjain was using as a table. Bedrolls stacked against the wall showed that some, if not all, of the priests were living in these makeshift quarters.

"Did your kinswoman have anything to say?" Darjain opened the questions as soon as everyone was settled.

"Could she tell us how to defeat a sorcerer?" Alkoan was more direct in his question.

"Ciamon isn't a sorcerer at the moment. I asked Jem. She said he's affected by the device he made just like everyone else."

"So we can get rid of him easily?"

"Yes. But she said killing him wasn't a good idea."

"She would, wouldn't she? She wants to protect her lover."

"They aren't lovers."

"The temple will be loveless when four stars combine." The seer, Kel, had joined the circle but was no more in tune with her fellow conspirators.

"Parrash has overheard them talking." Alkoan was more focused. "They were lovers, years ago, but not now."

"So she says."

Tevi waved her hand dismissively. "It doesn't matter."

She was not going to argue the point, but she noted the meaningful look Parrash directed her way. He dropped his head, but not before Tevi had seen the faint blush on his face. He clearly knew something about her relationship with Jemeryl. Guessing how he had found out was easy. The web of secret passages in the temple had been designed for eavesdropping. How much had he listened in on her conversation with Jemeryl? It would explain why he had been only a short way ahead of her, and would also explain his manner when she had caught up with him afterwards.

The idea was not pleasant, but now Tevi thought about it, neither was it surprising. She was a stranger who had tracked down the conspirators. Of course she would not have their trust and they would want to find out more about her. Checking that her meeting with Jemeryl matched the story she had spun was an obvious step. Yet Alkoan had no idea about how things truly stood between her and Jemeryl. Had Parrash not shared the information with him? This seemed odd, given Parrash's obvious admiration for the Cyclian priest. But if not Alkoan, then who? Had Parrash reported back to someone else or was he purely satisfying his own curiosity?

Whatever was going on, the answers would have to wait. Tevi continued. "Jem's past relationship with Ciamon isn't why she's saying it. She wants to stop him as much as you do but she can't do it while her magic is blocked."

"So she's no help."

"She can be. The idol is the problem, for both of you. The glamour on it is what has let Ciamon build up his following, and the magical device that stops Jem working magic is inside it. If the idol goes, so does his power."

"If we destroy it, Ciamon could make another." Alkoan was predictably hard to convince.

Darjain was more positive. "But his religion would be shown up for the sham it is. The people would return to the true gods."

"Our gods are—"

Tevi interrupted before the meeting got sidetracked. "Ciamon is a renegade sorcerer from the Coven. That's why Jem came here. She was supposed to talk him into going back. After his plans to destroy the Coven, they'll be even keener to see him in Lyremouth. Once the idol is destroyed, Jem will be able to take care of him. She's far more adept at magic. Then you'll have no idol, no High Priest, and everything can go back to how it was."

"The idol…yes." Darjain smiled as he spoke. "It's an affront to the temple. A mock god, that in turn mocks the very stones around it. It has no sanctity. No virtue. It would have to go anyway. Destroying it is an act of piety."

Tevi guessed the lack of blood spilt also found favour with the elderly priest.

Alkoan was not so happy. "I've got an alternate plan. We kill Ciamon. We dump his idol in a dungheap, as it deserves, but we leave it intact, so it can continue ridding the world of sorcerers and their denigration of our faith. We know they laugh at us. We'll do the laughing when they're gone, and we can spread the word across all the land."

Admittedly, every sorcerer Tevi had met had been sceptical about religion. This was mainly due to the sorcerer's ability to see the paranormal forces the priests talked about and know the claims were hopelessly, and often comically, wrong. However, this would not be a good argument to put to her audience. Tevi was trying to think of a better one, when another priest spoke.

"No. Magic is the blessing of Nolius. If this accused idol continues to exist, how will our god reward the virtuous? I say we destroy the idol. Then we deal with this false priest. I'll enjoy paying him back for the pain he has caused to the faithful."

Tevi guessed the speaker was Botha. Her words sparked a flurry of disagreement.

"Once we destroy the idol, Ciamon will be a sorcerer again. How will you deal with him then?"

"An iron collar stops a sorcerer working magic. If we put a collar on Ciamon before we destroy the idol we could—"

"Well, I nominate you to walk into the temple and put the collar on him. I'll stand outside and applaud when you come out."

"The last word before the darkness. The dead child cries for vengeance. How many will pay the price?"

"What do you say that we kill Ciamon first and then destroy the idol?"

"Please, please be calm." Darjain stood, holding his arms out. "These spats do credit to no one. We are priests. We are the visible face of our gods. We owe them better representation." The noise subsided. Darjain turned back to Tevi. "Was there anything else?"

"Personally, I'm not bothered what you decide to do with Ciamon, once the idol is gone." Tevi did not want to get involved in the issue. If she had to be honest, she lacked Jemeryl's concern for the man. Besides, once Jemeryl could use her magical ability again, the priests' chances of inflicting any sort of revenge on Ciamon were slight.

Possibly, the same idea had occurred to Alkoan. "We have to kill him before the magic returns. The sooner, the better."

"No. Ciamon has put protective spells on the idol."

"You said he was no longer a sorcerer."

"A people seek revenge for a poisoned tear."

Tevi ignored Kel's contribution. "Old spells still work, like the glamour. If you attack the idol now, you won't succeed, and you'll most likely be killed in the attempt. We need to wait until Jemeryl has found out how to get around the spells. She needs information from him. That's why she doesn't want him hurt."

Darjain nodded. "This sounds good to me."

It would, Tevi thought. *You don't have to kill anyone, and now you have a reason to spend even more time doing nothing at all.*

Yet she recognised that Darjain was a good man, out of his depth. By all accounts, he truly cared for others. He could not be blamed for ending up in a situation where he could not cope. He had loved his peaceful god and he did not know why she had deserted him. And of all faults, surely the most forgivable was being too slow to inflict harm on others, even when it was necessary. If only more people suffered from the same shortcoming, the world truly would be a better place.

❖

Ciamon sat sprawled on a couch, with his heels resting on a low table. He had abandoned his robes and was dressed casually, in loose knee breeches and a light blue shirt, open at the neck. His feet were bare. Jemeryl was struck by the memory of him as an apprentice in Lyremouth, sitting in the same pose, with the same boyish grin on his face, explaining how to set the world to rights. It had seemed so simple, back then.

He swirled the red wine around in his glass. "Do you remember Hallum and the refectory table?" Ciamon's thoughts were also clearly in the past.

"The love charm we gave him?"

"Yeah. With hindsight, don't you think we could have thought it through a bit better? I mean, be honest, after what he did to the table, did you ever feel comfy eating breakfast there again?"

"Now you put it like that…" Jemeryl took a sip of her wine. "Do you know what happened to Hallum?"

"He was up in Denbury when I was there. He'd found himself the perfect partner—a well-padded chaise longue."

"I guess it's a good lay," Jemeryl said, laughing.

"Actually, his partner is a witch. But I tell you, if you could see the guy, I'd pick the chaise longue any day. If you're going to settle down, you might as well be comfy."

"I've got no complaints." Jemeryl had already told him about Tevi. "But what about you? Have you never settled down with anyone?"

"Or item of furniture?" Ciamon grinned. "No. I've had a few flings, but they usually come to grief at about the time I get demoted to floor-sweeping duties. Nobody wants to be seen with an incompetent sorcerer."

"I wouldn't call you incompetent."

"Would you like a list of people who have? I don't mind. They're right. I can't be bothered with all the swotting and scribbling, trying to prove some trivial point that nobody with any real sense would give a rat's arse about."

Jemeryl leaned back in her chair and sipped her wine, trying not to look as if she was thinking too hard. Ciamon had obviously not changed. He would still happily admit to being a poor scholar with no enthusiasm for studying magic. She had been a stronger sorcerer than Ciamon to start with and since finishing her apprenticeship, she had spent many years advancing her studies. Despite this, Jemeryl knew of no set of spells that might bestow absolute invulnerability against the full might of the Coven. How could Ciamon be so sure nothing could overcome the defences he had put on the idol? Somewhere, Ciamon must have picked up a truly amazing spell, and surely the ordinance at Denbury would be the most likely place.

Jemeryl tried fishing. "You must have found something that caught your interest in Denbury."

"You know me. The elemental forces were always more your sort of thing. I'd have been happier at the hospital in Ekranos."

"If you want some irony, I did get sent to Ekranos for a while."

"Really?"

"Just for six months."

"I wished I'd gone there. The magic side of it wouldn't have done much for me, but saving peoples' lives, I could have put some commitment into it…believed in what I was doing."

Jemeryl paused as an idea struck her. Had Ciamon realised it too? "You know the morphology will put an end to the hospital?"

"Yes. I know. I've given some thought to it."

"And?"

"We're talking about equality, and freedom and justice. They're worth making sacrifices for."

His own words were failing to convince Ciamon. Jemeryl could see it in his face. "What's happened in Kradja? There must have been a hospital or infirmary here. What are people doing now when they're ill?"

The frown on his face deepened. "I, er…don't know."

Jemeryl tried to cover her irritation at another example of Ciamon letting things slide. If he was going to take charge then he ought to make more effort to know what was happening. But immediately her irritation was swamped by shame. In her first appointment after becoming a sorcerer, she had been guilty of exactly the same failing. It was the reason she had been removed from her post and ordered to accompany Tevi. And if she had not fallen in love with an ordinary ungifted citizen, would her attitude have changed? Would age automatically have made her behave more responsibly? She had no right to criticise Ciamon.

"Perhaps you could find out about the infirmary. Somebody must know."

"Yeah. I'll—" The door opened to admit Sefriall. Immediately, Ciamon latched on to his deputy. "Ah. Just the person. Is there a hospital in Kradja?"

If the line of questioning surprised Sefriall, she did not show it. "There was an infirmary attached to the temple. It was run by followers of Perithalma, god of healing."

"And now?"

"They would not switch allegiance to Equalitus, so the infirmary was closed."

Ciamon bounced to his feet. "I didn't mean that to happen. Why did nobody tell me?"

"You gave orders that no god but Equalitus could be worshipped in the temple."

"But healing! The—" He bowed his head, pinching the bridge of his nose. From their time as lovers, Jemeryl recognised the action as Ciamon fighting to keep a lid on his anger. His mood shifts could make lightning look sluggish. "I want you to find the healers and tell them they can come back."

"The witches can no longer work their magic. What use will they be?"

"They've got knowledge about how bodies work. Herbs and compounds will still be effective. We have to—" Ciamon stopped, doubt to the point of panic written on his face.

"Oh yes. Of course. I see where you're going." Sefriall spoke in sudden enlightenment. "Even under the dominion of Equalitus, people will still become sick and injured. Before now, the healer witches kept their knowledge secret, hoarding it like misers. Now they must share what they know and train everyone. The new healers will not have the same privileged magical insight, but bones will still set straight in a splint, potions will still cure."

"Yes." Ciamon grabbed her words like a lifeline.

Jemeryl shook her head. "It's not that simple. I worked in Ekranos for a while."

Sefriall nodded. "Even in Kradja we have heard of the great hospital, and of its library. Once the knowledge in there is set free, who knows what miracles may be realised?"

"You're right." Ciamon's face cleared. His anger evaporated as quickly as it had come and he dropped back onto the couch. "If we all work together, we can defeat illness, just as we can defeat injustice and tyranny."

Jemeryl also sank back in her seat. Arguing was pointless. This was not the first occasion where she had witnessed Sefriall's ability to manipulate Ciamon, telling him what he wanted to hear, but slanting it to her own agenda. The situation was worrying. Ciamon was a bad politician, and Sefriall had ambitions. Jemeryl knew that he was playing no part in running the town. All practical matters were left in Sefriall's hands, and Jemeryl did not trust her. She was not someone who Jemeryl would have chosen to run the world. Would Sefriall also remind Tevi of her grandmother?

Ciamon picked up his wineglass. "So. What was it you wanted?"

Sefriall sighed, sorrowfully. "There was trouble in town last night. Nothing serious. A few hotheads drinking too much. Some people were hurt and a couple of houses and a shop were burnt down."

"Do you have any idea who did it?"

"I have suspicions. But the most important thing is to stop it happening again. We don't want violence in Kradja."

"Certainly not."

"I'd like to expand the sentinels. More soldiers. More patrols."

Ciamon nodded. "Yes. Sure. Whatever you think necessary."

"I'll see to it. And I'll give orders to trace the healers and get them to reopen the infirmary." Sefriall paused as if thinking. "Shall I also ask for volunteers to be instructed in medicine?"

"Yes." Ciamon beamed at his deputy. "That sounds great."

"I'll see to it at once." Sefriall bowed and left the room.

Ciamon leaned forward to refill his glass, then settled back on the couch. "Do you remember the day we persuaded Riko that the goose was really her tutor, checking up on her?"

Jemeryl nodded and also lifted her glass, but her mood for reminiscing had faded.

❖

Tevi sketched in another few lines, adding to the map that Parrash had given to her. With each day, the diagram was becoming more convoluted, especially since it had to work in three dimensions. Describing the secret passages as a maze was no exaggeration, and mapping every section would take ages. However, the ability to move wherever she wanted, unseen and unhindered, gave Tevi a nice feeling of reassurance, and the work might deliver some practical benefit, once

Jemeryl had sorted out how to attack the idol. Besides, Tevi had nothing better to do with her time. As a bonus, just possibly she would overhear something of note—or not.

"My feet are killing me, and I've got a blister." The amplified voice drifted through the passageway.

"I had a blister last week."

"Which foot?"

"Left."

"Mine's on the right."

"Oh."

All of which was a fair example of what Tevi had overheard to date. The sentinels and priests did not lead the most exciting of lives. Then Tevi heard another voice that immediately caught her attention— Jemeryl's.

"I'll join you for dinner."

Tevi backtracked a few steps to a spyhole that provided a view of a tiled hallway. Midway along it, Jemeryl stood talking to Ciamon outside an open doorway. Presumably they had just emerged from the room behind them.

"Great. I'll send someone to let you know when we're ready to eat."

"Thanks. See you later." Jemeryl patted his arm and then turned away.

The stab of jealousy was more than a twinge. Not that Tevi thought of Ciamon as any sort of rival over Jemeryl. Their body language was of old friends, and nothing more. But she would so much like to be the one having dinner with Jemeryl that night. Months had gone by since the last time they had been able to share food and idle conversation— chatting about what they had done during the day, funny stories and plans. Tevi missed the simple domestic routines, a casual touch in passing, waking with Jemeryl's face beside her, knowing at the end of a hard day that someone could be counted on to sympathise.

Tevi's eyes turned to Ciamon, as she tried yet again to work out how she felt. Imagining him and Jemeryl as adolescent sweethearts was odd. Despite Jemeryl's assertion that he was a good man, Tevi did not feel any warmth towards him. Was it jealousy? He was a touch overdramatic, hopelessly naïve, and weirdly insipid, but there was nothing Tevi could pick out to condemn in him, apart from the fact that he was planing on destroying all known civilisation.

Ciamon returned to the room and shut the door. Jemeryl reached the end of the hall and vanished around the corner. Tevi sighed. The brief exchange put an end to any idea of sneaking into Jemeryl's room, even for a few moments. She had no idea when dinner might be and dared not risk being caught by whoever Ciamon sent with the summons. Feeling more than a little despondent, Tevi made her way out of the tunnels.

Late afternoon sunlight washed over the streets of Kradja when she emerged from the temple, dusting the scene with gold. For once, the town seemed safe and unremarkable. Street traders shouted, a wagon piled with sacks rumbled by, and dogs sniffed at piles of refuse while a lazy cat watched from a window ledge. Only the mud brick walls and sand on the road marked Kradja as in any way different from dozens of other towns Tevi knew.

But Kradja was not the same, not at the moment, and the differences went deeper than details of mud brick and sand. Tevi turned a corner. Ahead of her, a hysterical preacher stood on a rickety chair, screeching at a growing crowd. Behind him were burnt-out houses. The listeners were silent in a way that was more frightening than a riot. Stains on the ground at their feet could only be blood, and half buried in the debris were the unmistakable shapes of corpses with blackened, peeling skin. Why had nobody taken them away for burial? Did no one care?

Like a shape-shifting parasite from legend, a monster had infested Kradja, absorbed and usurped the town. Now it wore the face of Kradja—but beneath the façade? How long before the monster fully revealed itself? And what would happen then? Tevi shivered, cold, despite the desert sun.

It was with a feeling of relief that Tevi reached her room in the Four Winds House, but the second she stepped through the door the tension returned. Someone had been in her room, and it was not just an innocent visit by inn staff. The signs were small, but unmistakable. Her bedding was neater than she had left it. The belt hanging from her sword, propped in the corner, was twisted. The corner of her cloak was peeking from her footlocker. Tevi lifted the lid to push it back in, and froze. Inside the chest, the signs were even more obvious. From what

Tevi could see, most of the items had been taken out and then dumped back in, haphazardly.

Why? Simple theft did not seem likely. Her sword was valuable—far more so than might be thought at a simple examination. It was a rune-sword, crafted to harmonise with temporal currents. Yet even without knowing this, a thief would surely have taken the weapon. Well-made swords were easy-to-sell items.

The rooms at Four Winds House were all unlocked, but the inn was never empty, and the layout made it difficult for an intruder to sneak in, unseen. Someone had to know something about who had been there, and Tevi had a good idea who that someone was. She went in search of Raf.

The innkeeper was shovelling refuse in the stable when Tevi found her. Raf glanced up sharply at her approach but then went back to her work. "Can I help you?"

"Someone's been in my room."

"Have they?" Raf sounded nonchalantly indifferent.

"They searched it."

"Oh. Anything stolen?"

Tevi folded her arms. "Not that I can see. Who was it?"

"How should I know?"

Tevi put her foot on the head of the broom. "Who was it?"

"I…" Raf's voice died at the sight of the expression on Tevi's face. "Er…yeah. It was your friend."

"My friend?"

"He said he wanted to talk to you. Asked to wait in your room."

"And you let him?"

"He looked honest."

Tevi remembered how Siashe had introduced the innkeeper. "How much did he pay you?"

Raf hesitated, as if debating whether she should deny the implication, but then gave a weak smile. "Just a small tip."

"If I double it, will you describe him to me?"

Raf grinned. "Of course. A tall guy, bit overweight. Thirty or so. Used to be a priest at the temple. I think his sister owns a baker's shop near here."

CHAPTER SIX—CONSPIRACIES

A series of questions skittered around in Tevi's head as she jogged through the streets, bound for the bakery. What had Parrash been looking for? And what, if anything, had he found? Had someone told him to do it, or had he been acting of his own volition? If the priests had searched her room the day after she made contact, Tevi would have understood it. But why wait until now? Had something changed? Was Parrash putting a plan into action that had not been discussed at the meeting?

The last question was the one prompting Tevi to challenge Parrash immediately rather than wait and see what came next. Under Darjain's leadership, the ousted priests were utterly ineffectual. While Tevi understood Alkoan's frustration, she did not want him and his faction doing anything rash.

Tevi needed the answers quickly, which should not prove too difficult once she found Parrash. He struck her as someone who would buckle when threatened, and in the circumstances, Tevi felt a show of anger was justified. With luck, she would catch him at his sister's bakery without Alkoan or other supporters on hand to back him up.

As it turned out, Tevi reached the final corner just in time to see Parrash shoot from the door and scuttle off in the opposite direction, head down and shoulders hunched, as if afraid that retribution was about to fall on him from the sky. He had taken no time to look around and Tevi was sure he had not spotted her on the busy street. Parrash was not fleeing from her approach and he was definitely up to something. After allowing him a little more of a lead, Tevi followed.

Parrash headed back towards the centre of Kradja and the main town square. The sun was low on the horizon and the market was starting to wind down for the day when they arrived. The crowds around the wild preachers were thinning, but most traders still had their wares set out. Tevi had assumed that Parrash would bypass the stalls and go straight to the temple, but instead he stopped at one—a herbalist, fully stocked with bundles of dried leafs and bottles of liquid. Tevi attached herself to a nearby audience around a preacher to observe.

"What can I do for you?" the trader called from the rear of her stall, where she was measuring powder into a jar.

Parrash mumbled in reply, his voice too low for Tevi to make out. The trader promptly put down the jar and beckoned him to a strongbox behind her stall. Although the box was clearly designed for security, it was not locked. The trader tugged open the lid and pulled out a couple of items for inspection. Parrash pointed to the one he wanted.

But what was it?

Parrash was manifestly nervous and trying to hide it. Tevi could see his shoulders shaking with the effort to not look behind every few seconds. His feet were twitching in his boots. His back was as stiff as a plank. He was having to haggle over the cost, and anyone could see he did not want to. He would rather have paid the asking price and been off, but that would be too blatantly suspicious. The minutes he was forced to stand must have been agony, although Tevi could not bring herself to feel much in the way of sympathy. At last, he paid the money, received a small pouch, and hurried off, his route heading straight for the main temple gates.

Tevi had not been close enough to hear what he asked for. Now she was torn. Should she follow him, or should she question the trader? The quick, common sense answer was that if Parrash was going to the temple, then the secret passages were surely his goal. Following him without being seen and heard would be difficult, and the chances were that she would lose him in the dark. Much easier to wait for him to come out, which gave her plenty of time for the trader.

Tevi trotted up to the stall. "Did he buy the cinnamon?"

The trader looked confused. "Pardon?"

"Parrash. He was here just now. I work for his sister. I'm supposed to get an ounce of cinnamon. But stupid me has gone and left the money behind. Then I spotted him here. I don't want to go all the way to the bakery and back if he's already got it."

"No. He was buying the dog button extract."

Tevi frowned. "I didn't think we used that in the bread."

"I'd hope not. It's to poison the rats in your cellar."

"Oh. Right. About time someone dealt with the little buggers." Tevi tried not to look shocked. "Fine. I'll be back with the money shortly, then."

"You better hurry. I'm about to shut up shop."

Tevi raced for the temple. Undoubtedly there were rats in the cellar from time to time. What grain store did not suffer from them? And Parrash's sister might well want to poison any there were. However, Tevi was sure that Parrash had not bought the dog button extract to deal with any vermin infestation, and certainly not one in the temple. His true plans for the poison were very easy to work out. She had to stop him.

Alkoan wanted to kill Ciamon, and despite what had been agreed with the others, he was not willing to wait any longer. He must have talked Parrash into buying and planting the poison. The neophyte priest would never have the initiative to do it on his own. Parrash was clearly nervous and unhappy, but from what he had already said, he admired Alkoan and was out of patience with Darjain. Tevi still had no idea how searching her room fitted into the plot, but she suspected she would not like the answer when she found out.

The sentinels on duty meant that Tevi dared not run in the main hall, but neither could Parrash. Although she saw no sign of him, he should not be too far ahead. Tevi stopped and listened as soon as she was inside the secret passage. The sounds of someone moving away were faint and hard to pinpoint, but surely Parrash would be heading for Ciamon's quarters. Tevi made what haste she could in pursuit. The narrow, twisted passages were not designed for speed, though she should do better than the heavily built man. She ought to overtake him—providing she did not get lost.

Tevi reached a junction where she had to make a decision. Left or right? Despite hopes to have gained on Parrash, when she listened she could hear no footsteps or scuffing to guide her. Had he realised that he was being followed? Might it frighten him into abandoning the assassination attempt? Tevi certainly could not rely on it.

Two exits from the tunnels were near the High Priest's rooms. One was in a corridor leading to his study. The other was directly into his bedchamber. The bedchamber had to be the safer bet. In the early evening, the room was most likely unoccupied, and any fare laid out would be for Ciamon's consumption alone.

However, when Tevi reached the spyhole for the bedchamber, the room was empty. It was also devoid of any food or drink the poison could have been added to. She closed her eyes, concentrating all her attention on her ears, but could hear nothing to indicate that Parrash was either soon to arrive or had recently left the room.

Urgently, Tevi backtracked along the passage, going from spyhole to spyhole, searching for Parrash, Jemeryl, or Ciamon himself. If she could not stop Parrash putting the poison into something, at least she could give a warning.

The sixth spyhole gave a view of a small chamber next to Ciamon's study. Two lamps hung from the ceiling, lighting the room softly. A meal was laid out on a knee-high table, surrounded by multicoloured silk cushions. Causal low-level dining was traditional in Kradja. Tevi peeked through just in time to see Parrash emptying the pouch's contents into a wine carafe.

"Parrash. Don't!" Tevi shouted and thumped on the wall.

The stone must have muffled the sound, but Parrash clearly heard something. He flinched and glanced towards the spyhole.

"Stop!"

If Parrash heard and recognised the command, he chose to ignore it. His initial expression of fear eased into one that was more satisfied than guilty. Even though his hands were shaking, he continued resolutely, repositioning the carafe in the middle of the table, and tossing the empty pouch away.

"It won't do any good." Tevi might as well have not spoken.

Parrash pulled something else from his pocket, threw it with the pouch under the table and then scurried from the room.

Tevi felt as if her blood had turned to ice. Jemeryl was due to join Ciamon for dinner and would also drink the wine. The memory of the brief conversation Tevi had overheard kept playing through her head. How long did she have? How long before Jemeryl arrived? She had to warn them. The exit by Ciamon's study was a long way off, through the circuitous maze of tunnels. Tevi set off, taking three steps in an awkward sideways lope, and then stopped. She did not have to be in the room. Once Jemeryl and Ciamon appeared she could shout to them.

Tevi shuffled back to the spyhole. Minutes trickled by before the door again opened. Tevi opened her mouth, only to close it when, instead of Jemeryl and Ciamon, three musicians entered, carrying flute, lute, and bodhrán. They sat to one side and started tuning their instruments. The sound barely permeated the thick stone. Tevi had to press her ear against the wall to hear the practice notes. Her shouts and thumps got no response. Once the musicians started playing in earnest, nobody in the room stood any chance of hearing her.

Jemeryl might arrive at any second. Tevi scrambled along the passage, banging her knees and elbows in her haste. Her frantic footwork stirred up the dust of centuries, making her cough. At one point she cracked her head on a protruding joist, hidden in the darkness. Her shirt tore on a nail in passing.

She reached the exit and felt for the lever, but nothing happened when she tugged. More frantic yanking was also fruitless. The hatch did not open. Tevi crouched and felt around. Was there another catch? Or had Parrash sabotaged this one in some way? The light was too weak to see and Tevi did not have another second to waste.

The wooden hatch was made of heavy timber. Most people would need an axe to get through it. However, Tevi's body had been permanently modified by the potion she had taken as a girl. She stood, turned sideways, and kicked with as much force as the cramped space allowed. On the third thump she heard splintering. On the fifth, the wood gave way completely. A sixth final shove and the panel fell out, allowing in more light. Tevi dived through.

The sound of her demolishing the hatch had already attracted attention. Tevi heard shouts as she emerged into the corridor. Two elderly priests stood at the end, pointing at her and screeching. A servant's head was sticking from a doorway, also looking in her direction. Of more concern were the two armed sentinels outside the door to the room where dinner had been laid out. They were advancing towards her, drawing their swords. Tevi was outnumbered and outarmed. The small dagger she carried would be no use, but her own risk counted for nothing. The only thought in Tevi's head was that if guards were outside the room, it could only mean that Ciamon, and possibly Jemeryl, were inside. She did not have time for explanations.

"You. Stop right there," one of the sentinels shouted.

Tevi grabbed the broken panel and leapt to her feet. The sentinels clearly expected her to flee and broke into a run. Their surprise when Tevi charged towards them was evident and they faltered. Tevi pulled back her arm and hurled the panel, spinning it as if she was skimming a stone across a pond.

The panel arched through the air, tracing a lazy curve into the stomach of one sentinel. The man was rocked backwards by the force and slipped to his knees, dropping his sword. His comrade skidded to a stop, shock on her face. She took a half step back, reaching out, and then her expression hardened. She turned to Tevi, but she was out of time.

Tevi crashed into the sentinel, straight-arming her in the chest and sending her flying off her feet. The woman slammed into the wall and slid to the ground. Tevi hurdled over her crumpled form and charged on. She wrenched open the door of the dining room.

At opposite ends of the table, Ciamon and Jemeryl were seated on cushions. Sefriall knelt to one side with the wine carafe in her hand and three goblets before her on the table. Everyone jerked around as Tevi burst in. The gentle sounds of music cut off abruptly.

Tevi pointed at the carafe. "Don't drink the wine. It's been poisoned."

❖

Jemeryl had barely got over her shock at Tevi's entrance when the door was shoved open even wider and two sentinels lurched in. Judging by the dazed look in their eyes and the blood on the face of one, they had already had a run-in with Tevi. Undeterred, they closed in on her again.

"No. It's all right. She's a friend."

"She is?" Ciamon was clearly still struggling with surprise.

"If she's right about the wine then she's just saved your life. How much show of friendship do you want?"

"But do you know her?"

Jemeryl hesitated. Ciamon was not going to like the truth, but the risks of lying to him were too great. Without knowing more about how Tevi got to be there and why she thought the wine was poisoned, any made-up story stood a high chance of unravelling. Getting caught out in a lie would go down even worse than the truth.

"Yes. She's my partner. You remember the one I told you about?"

"What's she doing here?"

"To be honest, I'm not completely sure. Maybe you should ask her."

Ciamon looked at the two sentinels who were still standing in the doorway, swords drawn. "It's all right. You can wait outside. But call for reinforcements. And you can go as well." His gesture encompassed the musicians. They hurried from the room. When the door was shut, Ciamon turned back to Tevi. "What makes you think the wine is poisoned?"

Jemeryl had no way to pass on the message that only something close to the truth would work, but Tevi clearly reached the same conclusion for herself. "I saw the person do it."

"You did what? When? Where were you?"

She pointed to the wall. "This temple is riddled with secret passages. I was watching this room through the spyhole over there."

Ciamon stared at the wall, looking dumbfounded. "How do you know about the passages?"

"I met some priests who used to live here. They told me."

"Darjain and his accomplices." Sefriall spoke for the first time.

Ciamon turned to her. "What do you know about this? Did you know there were secret passages?"

"No."

"The temple was built by followers of Harretha," Tevi said. "They made the passages, and they hadn't been sharing the knowledge."

Ciamon had been standing. Now he sank onto the cushions, hands over his eyes, obviously thinking. Jemeryl watched him anxiously. He had always been prone to go to extremes of naïve credulity when he liked someone and obsessive suspicion when he did not. Which way was he going to go now?

Eventually he raised his head. "Right. You found out about the passages from the priests. But why are you in Kradja?"

"I'm looking out for Jem. When she didn't come home, I followed her here."

Ciamon's eyes jumped back to Jemeryl. "You knew she was here?"

"Yes."

"Why the secrecy? Why didn't you tell me?"

"Tevi thought she'd be more effective watching from the background. Obviously she was right. If she'd been here in the open, she'd have been drinking poison with us."

"You could have explained that to me. What else have you been hiding?" Ciamon glowered at Jemeryl, his doubt and distrust plain. He returned to Tevi. "You saw someone pour something into the wine?"

"Yes."

"What makes you sure it was poison?"

"I'd followed him from the herbalist where he'd bought it."

"Do you know his name?"

Before Tevi could reply, Sefriall cut in. "Do you think you can believe a word she says?"

"Test the wine on rats, if you don't believe me."

Sefriall was not deflected. "Oh, I don't doubt there's poison in it. But how did it get there? It's an odd coincidence you just happened to be looking through the right spyhole at exactly the right time. How do we know you didn't put the poison in yourself?"

"Why would I do that?"

"To gain the High Priest's trust."

"But we already have that, don't we?" Jemeryl said, determined to counteract Sefriall's manipulation. Ciamon had always been quick to see a conspiracy. The more complex and convoluted the motives you ascribed to someone, the more ready Ciamon was to believe it.

Worryingly, he did not answer, but continued questioning Tevi. "Who do you accuse of being the poisoner?"

"One of the priests. I don't know all their names."

Sefriall gave a snort of contempt. "I must admit they'd be my second guess at the culprits. I've warned you about cracking down on Darjain and his accomplices. They're plotting against you."

"It was nothing to do with Darjain," Tevi said.

"How can you know that?" Sefriall went back on the offensive. "These seditious priests told you about the secret tunnels, you say. Why? What part do you play in their schemes? Are you working for them?"

"I'm here solely to look after Jem."

"So she's in on it too?"

"Jem isn't—"

Ciamon cut Tevi off. "We'll deal with the conjecture after we have your full story. Start at the beginning. You saw the priest buying poison and followed him to the temple?"

"Yes."

"Why didn't you try to stop him before he could administer the poison?"

"I lost track of him in the passages. It's a maze. I was trying to find him when I saw him through the spyhole. He was pouring the poison he had bought into the carafe. Then he threw the empty pouch under the table and left."

Sefriall bent down. "The pouch is here. And so is this." She stood up, holding a piece of paper. She glanced at it and then passed it to Ciamon. "I think you might want to read it."

Ciamon spent a full minute studying the sheet. "Who is Wess Tanaislanda?"

Jemeryl saw Tevi react. This person was clearly known to her, and hearing the name was equally clearly not good news. For Jemeryl's part, the question was easy to answer. Hoping to distract attention, Jemeryl said, "I've never heard the name before."

Ciamon's smile was not encouraging. "Really? It's got her description here. A female vouchsafed mercenary. Tall. Dark-haired. Aged thirty or thereabouts. Does it remind you of anyone? This is a writ for safe passage. Apparently Wess is travelling on Coven business. And it's signed by your old tutor, Iralin." Ciamon's eyes bored into her. "Are you sure you don't know her?"

"Er…" Jemeryl was confused.

Tevi sighed. "That writ is mine."

"From Iralin, a senior Coven sorcerer?"

"Yes. She was worried about Jem as well. That's why she helped me get here."

"So, what's your name Wess or Tevi?"

"I'm Tevi. Wess Tanaislanda is the name I was travelling under."

"Why the deception?"

"Because Alendy would have stopped me coming."

"Any idea how the writ ended up under the table?" Ciamon's tone made the question a taunting challenge.

"I saw the poisoner put it there."

"You didn't mention that before."

"I didn't know what it was." Tevi's shoulders slumped, as

if suspecting that she would not be believed. "But the reason I was following him to start with, was he'd just searched my room at the inn where I'm staying."

Sefriall joined in again. "I think both the High Priest and myself can think of an alternate explanation. You dropped the paper after you had put the poison in the wine."

"Oh come on. It's a blatant and very clumsy attempt to frame me. Think. What reason would I even have carry the writ around with me? It's no use in Kradja. And of all the things I might have dropped, I was careless enough to lose the one thing that could be traced back to me."

Jemeryl was pleased to see Sefriall's haughty expression change to a frown. Tevi had won that one, but it might not be enough. Ciamon was subdued, rubbing the paper between thumb and forefinger while he made an obvious attempt to marshal his thoughts. "Regardless. It's a very useful thing for me to have seen. It tells me you're a mercenary in the pay of the Coven. Which ties in with the way you and Jemeryl have been secretly working together behind my back." The eyes Ciamon turned on Jemeryl were full of pain and regret. "I thought you were my..."

He looked down sharply and concentrated on putting the writ down very carefully, lining the bottom edge with the table. The silence in the room drew out. Jemeryl wanted to say "I'm sorry," but that would be an admission of guilt. At the moment, Ciamon only had conjecture. "I am your friend, Ci." That much was true, and always would be.

"What do you want to do with them?" Sefriall asked.

"Do? Nothing. Jemeryl is my guest and I extend the same hospitality to her partner. They can stay in the same room. But I want a guard kept outside, watching them at all times." The eyes Ciamon raised glinted with tears in the light of the lanterns. "I'm sorry Jem, I just can't..."

"It's all right. With assassins around, it would be a good idea anyway. You might want to think about it too."

He gave the ghost of a smile. "I want to trust you. But it..." He took a deep breath. "We'll talk more tomorrow, when we've had time to think things over. Perhaps your partner's story will sound better then."

"Fine. Tomorrow."

Sefriall was not finished. "And the dissident priests who tried to murder you, if we believe this mercenary's story? Are you going to leave them until tomorrow as well?"

"They're not important."

"Your mercy and kindness do you credit. But too much leniency will be misunderstood. If you let this go, they'll try again. We cannot expect fortune to forever smile on us."

"We don't know which, if any, of them was involved."

"If the sentinels brought them all in for questioning, I'm sure we could get to the truth."

"No." Ciamon's voice was firmer. "I'm not interested in retribution. When they see the wonders Equalitus will bring to the world, they'll realise they've been misguided in their opposition. Give it time, and all foes will become friends. That's the true victory we are after."

Sefriall bowed her head. "Very well. But I fear some hearts are so soaked in evil they'll never change. I fear for you. Supposing the next attempt on your life succeeds?"

"We don't know there will be another. But there's one thing we can do." Ciamon looked at Tevi. "Tomorrow, I want you to show Sefriall the entrance to the tunnels, and anything else you know about them."

Tevi nodded. "I've got a map."

❖

As soon as the bedroom door closed, Tevi crossed the small space between them and wrapped Jemeryl in a fierce hug. "I'm so pleased I got to you before you touched the wine."

"I'm sort of happy about it too."

"I was terrified I wasn't going to make it in time."

Tevi bowed her head and placed a soft, nuzzling kiss on Jemeryl's neck. She let her mouth work slowly up to Jemeryl's ear, catching the lobe gently in her teeth and then running her tongue around the rim. Jemeryl shook in her arms, gasping.

Tevi opened her mouth and breathed into Jemeryl's ear. "There's a spyhole in here. Be careful what you say."

"Where?" Jemeryl whispered the word so softly it sounded like a sigh.

"Behind my right shoulder. I doubt anyone will be there, but we can't be sure."

"Have you been watching me?"

"What do you think?"

At the moment, although the sentinels had the map, their only way in was through the hatch Tevi had kicked down. She was due to show Sefriall the other entrances in daylight the next morning. The route to Jemeryl's room was not straightforward and the network of passages was tricky enough to deal with during the day. In total darkness it would be impossible to navigate, except that the sentinels did not need to worry about detection and could carry lanterns, dousing them only when they were in position.

Would the sentinels be taking advantage of the secret passages so soon? Tevi suspected they would want to thoroughly explore the maze first before deciding what use they could make of it. But if they did decide to experiment with the eavesdropping capability, without doubt she and Jemeryl would be at the top of the list for surveillance.

Jemeryl took her time, first planting a series of small kisses across Tevi's eyes and cheeks, and then continuing the journey until her mouth touched Tevi's ear. "We can find somewhere to talk tomorrow. There's no rush. For now we can just sleep."

"I want to make love to you." Tevi spoke the words aloud, not caring if she was overheard. After all, surely it was what any eavesdropper would be expecting her to say.

"Supposing we have an audience?" Jemeryl whispered her response.

Tevi picked Jemeryl up, carried her to the bed, and then lay down beside her. Again she brought her mouth close to Jemeryl's ear. "Then I hope they go blind."

"Blow out the candles."

Once the room was in darkness, Tevi heard Jemeryl removing her clothing and pulling back the sheets and blankets. Tevi felt her way to the bed, stripping off her own clothes on the way. She slipped in beside Jemeryl, who was naked under the covers. The touch of her lover was so familiar, and yet so special. Tevi felt her own body come alight, from the tingling that rippled over her skin, to the slow fire smouldering between her legs.

Separation from Jemeryl had been a torment for far too long. Before the events of that evening, Tevi had planned to enter the secret passages during the day, wait until night by the exit nearest to Jemeryl's room, and then sneak into bed with her when it was dark. She was delaying only until the night of the next meeting in the cellar, which she would not attend, so she could be confident no one was at the spyhole. Despite the unwelcome potential audience, the big advantage now was that she need not worry about oversleeping and being caught in Jemeryl's bed the next morning.

Tevi's hands roamed over Jemeryl as she reacquainted herself with her lover's body—not that she had forgotten a single detail. She traced the hard ridge of Jemeryl's collarbone. She had remembered the texture of Jemeryl's skin, its touch, how it smelled, how it tasted, how it looked. Tevi could recall exactly the constellation of freckles scattered between collarbone and Jemeryl's right breast. She could have drawn it from memory. But she could not see it, and the absence bothered her.

Making love in the dark was not something they ever did. Jemeryl's body was the most beautiful thing Tevi had ever seen. She could look forever at the wavy auburn hair, narrow impish face, full round breasts, and the soft cushion of Jemeryl's stomach. Tevi liked to watch Jemeryl respond to her touch, to read the visual clues as to what Jemeryl wanted and needed. She liked to watch Jemeryl's face contort in ecstasy as she climaxed.

Tevi pushed Jemeryl onto her back and rolled on top of her. Their lips met in a long slow kiss. Jemeryl's hands stroked her back, her sides, and lightly tickled the back of her neck. Tevi never ceased to be surprised that something so exciting could yet fill her with a deep sense of peace. Passion was rising, soon it would overwhelm her, and yet—

Tevi slid her mouth to Jemeryl's ear. "I wish I could see you."

"I wish I could sense you in all seven dimensions. I'm afraid you're a little bit flat at the moment, darling." Jemeryl's arms tightened, squashing Tevi against her, as if to make the point. "But I still love you madly."

Of course, Tevi thought. *Jem is even more sensory deprived.* Despite the fact they were in the same state, for Jemeryl it was a level of blindness she was not used to. Tevi was without one of her senses. Jemeryl was missing half her world. If for no other reason, Tevi would want to destroy the idol to give back to Jemeryl everything she had lost.

Tevi raised her hand and stroked the side of Jemeryl's face, concentrating on the texture and detail that her sense of touch could reveal. A light fuzz of hair lined Jemeryl's jaw beneath her ear. A mole on her cheekbone was a small raised bump. The first faint wrinkles of age were in the laugh lines around her lips. Tevi felt muscles contract as Jemeryl kissed her fingertips, leaving the merest hint of moisture behind.

Jemeryl's breath was a soft dry rasp, catching at the back of her throat in the middle. Tevi had heard that sound before, but had she noticed how it synchronised with a slight tensing of Jemeryl's stomach? Had she picked out the high note at the end, the beginnings of a groan of passion? How much had she really concentrated on the sounds her lover made? Tevi would have said without question that she loved the taste of Jemeryl, but even in this, had she blurred the fine detail of the experience? How much had she missed by concentrating on sight?

Maybe this novelty was something she should take advantage of, and see what she could learn. She was going to make love to Jemeryl very carefully and slowly, and let touch, taste, and hearing compensate for what neither of them could see.

Jemeryl sat beside the small circular fountain in an enclosed courtyard, surrounded by birdsong and the undulating splatter of falling water. Morning sunlight glittered in a rainbow on the spray. Jemeryl ran her hand through the rippling pool, enjoying the coolness between her fingers. Voices and the sound of footsteps made her look up. Tevi was arriving at their prearranged rendezvous, after showing Sefriall and the sentinels as much as she could about the network of secret tunnels.

"How did it go?"

"Fine."

Tevi's smile was forced, so presumably she was being diplomatic in her answer, but she did not appear angry, so Sefriall must have been demanding rather than belligerent in her pursuit of information. But then, without Ciamon around, there was no point trying to inflame suspicion. From what Jemeryl had seen, the woman was never vindictive for the fun of it. She was always in control of herself, always had a motive. Jemeryl was not sure if this made things better or worse from an ethical standpoint, but it did make Sefriall easier to predict.

Tevi planted a quick greeting kiss on Jemeryl's lips and then sat on the fountain wall beside her. In the background, the escort of sentinels took up position beside their three comrades already in the courtyard. The sentinels were keeping a close eye on them, but were not standing near enough to overhear what was said, as long as she and Tevi kept their voices down. When they had picked the place to talk, Tevi had been sure that the secret passages did not extend beyond the temple building, so the surrounding gardens were safe, and even if someone was secreted near at hand, the background noise from the pool should make eavesdropping difficult.

"Did you recognise who put the poison in the wine?" Jemeryl had noticed Tevi dodging the question when asked the previous night.

"Parrash. But I'll bet anything you want Alkoan was the one who gave the instructions. He's at the root of it, I know."

"Was that why you didn't name him?"

"There's nasty things happening in town. I didn't want his death on my conscience."

"Death?"

"Yes. But if I'd known he was going to frame me like that…" Tevi pouted.

"How did he get the writ?"

"Like I said, Parrash had been through my room. I was tailing him to find out why. But when he bought the poison I rather lost sight of it."

"How did he know the writ was there?"

"I'd guess he just got lucky. He was looking for anything that could be tied to me."

"Why?"

Tevi wrinkled her nose. "A scapegoat, in case Sefriall wanted to avenge Ciamon's death. Alkoan's very keen on an end to all sorcerers. I guess he hoped to pin it on you and the Coven through me. He wouldn't have known you were going to drink the wine as well."

"He knows we're partners?"

"Parrash does. So the writ was perfect for him. It even had a brief description of me. But a glove would have done. After Ciamon was dead, he could have sent in an anonymous tip. The sentinels would have searched my room and found the matching glove."

Jemeryl grimaced. "The awkward thing about the writ is now Ci's convinced you're working for the Coven."

"I'm sorry. I should have dumped it once I was outside the Protectorate. I had no use for it."

"A glove wouldn't have caused the same problems. But..." Jemeryl paused, thinking. "How far do Alkoan's plans go?"

"I think he hopes his Cyclian religion will spread across the whole world. That's why he doesn't want the idol destroyed. He wants the Coven to go." Tevi smiled at her. "You sorcerers are far too sceptical about religion."

"It's hard to take seriously. Not when you can see what's really going on."

Tevi's expression became more thoughtful. "That's the big problem, you know. Even though Ciamon is using religion to stir things up, he can't quite believe people will be ready to commit mass murder over silly made-up stories. At heart, he—" Tevi broke off at a servant's approach.

"Excuse me." The man bowed politely.

"What is it?"

"Your belongings have been collected from Four Winds House. They're in your room." The servant bowed and backed away.

Tevi waited until he was out of earshot. "And no doubt searched."

"Was there anything in them you wouldn't want found?"

"No. The only incriminating thing was the writ with Iralin's signature on it." Tevi gave a wry smile. "Shall we go and check it's all there? And I'd like to change my shirt." She twisted her shoulder to show the large slash across the back of the one she had on.

"Why not? And even though it's caused problems, I'm pleased Iralin did help you with the writ." Jemeryl slipped her hand through to link arms with Tevi. She had taken three steps before another memory surfaced. "Wess Tanaislanda? You didn't really pass yourself off as that, did you?"

Tevi shrugged. "It seemed like a cute idea at the time."

CHAPTER SEVEN—BEYOND REASON

Ciamon was not hostile, and he clearly wanted to trust her, but he had equally clearly put Jemeryl back on the list of people in need of converting.

"You have to admit the Coven is corrupt."

Jemeryl rubbed her forehead, thinking what to say. How should she play this? If she pretended complete agreement, would it only make him more suspicious? If she opposed him, what chance she might change his mind? More likely he would see her as the enemy, and might even send her back to Lyremouth. Could she manage to come over as someone with enough doubts to want to keep Tevi's presence in Kradja secret, while still not seeming like a lost cause, from his point of view? It was a thin line to walk.

"I agree the Coven is less than perfect."

"The world will be a better, fairer place without it."

Jemeryl twisted her face in an uncertain frown. "Maybe, but the Protectorate provides safety and a living for millions of ordinary people. We need to make sure they are still provided for."

"Protectorate? The only thing the Coven really protects is itself. It doesn't protect ordinary people, it enslaves them."

"No." Jemeryl shook her head. "I told you I spent some time up in Bykoda's empire, before she died. That was enslavement. The Protectorate is nothing like as bad."

"So tyranny is all right as long as there's a worse example to be found?"

"Of course not. But I don't believe the Protectorate is as bad as you say."

"You really think Alendy is going to put himself out to protect ungifted citizens?"

This was definitely one area where she was in genuine and complete agreement with Ciamon. "Only if he saw it as being for the good of the Coven."

"Exactly. As far as he's concerned, sorcerers are the only people who matter."

Jemeryl relaxed in her chair, more than happy to hear her own views expressed by someone else. She and Ciamon were sitting in the shade of a flower-covered arbour, in the part of the temple gardens reserved for the High Priest. Not far away, Tevi stood in full sun, throwing a stick for a lumbering half-grown puppy. The stray dogs around the temple had little regard for either the High Priest's status or his privacy, and one had found its way in. To Sefriall's evident dismay, not only had Ciamon refused to have it driven out, but he had sent to the kitchens for food and water. Now it was happily playing with its new friend.

"Alendy certainly disapproves of my relationship with Tevi. I'm sure part of the reason he picked me to come here was so he could split us up."

"Yes, well, that's…" Ciamon's voice trailed away, sounding uncharacteristically vague.

Jemeryl stared at him. Ciamon could be imprecise and uncertain but never vague. She would have been hard-pressed to explain the difference, but she knew it when she heard it in his voice.

"What?"

"It can't be…" Ciamon's expression was pained.

Jemeryl stared at him, surprised. She had questioned Tevi about whether she was jealous. Maybe Ciamon was the one she should have asked. "What is it?"

"You know your relationship with her is going to change?"

"In what way?"

"It needn't be a bad thing. In fact it won't, as long as you're willing to accept it."

Jemeryl could only frown in reply.

"And if you work at it, one day you and Tevi could share what we had."

"Pardon?"

"You know—a completely equal, reciprocal relationship."

Jemeryl was aware her jaw was hanging open. It took her several attempts to find her voice. "What do you think we have at the moment?"

"Oh, I know you'd try to treat her well, and she does seem genuinely fond of you, but…"

"But?" Jemeryl could feel anger rising inside her.

"But up until now, you've not been on an equal footing. It's going to change, for both of you. She'll have to learn to see you as an ordinary person. And you'll have to give up your—"

Jemeryl could take no more. "You think I call all the shots while Tevi looks up to me and just does what she's told? I don't know who you're insulting more."

At first Ciamon was taken aback, then he went on the offensive. "You're not going to tell me she doesn't defer to your judgement. And you take it for granted that she will."

"That's exactly what I'm going to tell you."

Now Ciamon was the one looking bewildered. "But she doesn't have the complexity of your world view. She won't be able to understand things the way you do."

"She isn't an idiot." Jemeryl was pleased that Tevi was not close enough to hear.

"Of course not. I wasn't saying she was."

"It sounded like it."

Ciamon waved his hands, as if it would help sum up what he meant. "The way we sorcerers see things gives us an unfair advantage. No matter what we intend, an ungifted person's opinion can never carry the same weight with us, because they can't see the whole pic—"

"You think we have a better grasp on reality?"

"No. Not exactly. We overanalyse and dissect knowledge. The straightforward approach the ungifted have to life is much cleaner, more honest. We need to learn to value that."

"They're like children?"

"I didn't say that."

"But ungifted people have a simpler view of life?"

"Yes. And they have some of the same innocence and—"

"That's an absolute load of crap."

Ciamon's face flushed with anger. "You need to reconsider the way you view the ungifted."

"No. You do. You're the one who doesn't think they're our equals." Jemeryl leaned back and stared at him in contempt. "You're just as arrogant as Alendy. Worse in some ways, because at least he's up front about it. I've just seen it. You think you're being noble in voluntarily sinking down to their level."

"No. I'm on their side."

"And you're kind to animals."

"Where do you get the—" Ciamon was too furious to continue. Jemeryl recognised the signs, but she was far from being calm herself. For once she was happy to see Sefriall approach, if only for a space to regather her self-control.

Tevi left off playing with the puppy to join them. Judging by Sefriall's expression, she had important, but mixed, news.

"What is it?" Ciamon snapped.

"We've just received word that the emanation of Equalitus has reached the town of Villenes. The sway of our god has advanced to the very borders of the Protectorate."

Ciamon ran his hand through his hair, clearly trying to get a grip on his anger. "That's great."

"There are, regrettably, a few problems."

"What?"

"Villenes is controlled by a cartel of master merchants."

"Yes. I know. So?" Ciamon looked confused.

Jemeryl was a step ahead of him, based on her experience in Horzt, which had only recently joined the Protectorate. Villenes, like the other towns just outside the border, had grown rich on trade with its wealthy neighbour, while the presence of the Coven, so close by, kept rival sorcerers away. Power in these towns was therefore based on money rather than magic. The merchants of Villenes would be unaffected by the morphology, and unwilling to surrender their rule to the representative of a previously unknown and rather dubious religion.

The next words from Sefriall proved Jemeryl right. "The ruling cartel have refused to worship Equalitus. They've rebuffed your envoy and expelled the sentinels from the town. They say they'll not allow as much as a small shrine to be erected."

"What? Why?"

"Greed. Selfishness. They value money more than righteousness."

"We need to get them to see sense…er…to see that Equalitus will bring prosperity exceeding anything they've known so far."

"They're an affront to the faithful."

"They're just misguided."

"But they might lead others astray."

"Yes." Ciamon sighed. "They might hamper the spreading of the word. Which might slow the arrival of new converts in Kradja."

Which will slow the rate of expansion of the morphology, and you want it to put an end to the Coven as quickly as possible, just in case they think of a way to destroy the idol. Jemeryl provided the motive that Ciamon would not say aloud.

"Perhaps if you went in person you'd be able to persuade the non-believers." Sefriall suggested.

Ciamon's forehead furrowed as he mulled it over. "Maybe."

"With an army of sentinels at your back, I'm certain they'd listen to you very carefully."

"No." Ciamon's rejection was immediate. "I want to reason with them, not intimidate them."

"Fear provides good ears."

"I'll just take a dozen servants and a couple of guards, but not enough to frighten anyone."

"You need a show of strength. It's the only thing the master merchants will respect. You have to meet them on their own terms and play their game."

"No." Ciamon drew a deep breath. "My message is about freedom and friendship. Threats undermine that."

"Remember there's been an attempt on your life. Surely concern for your safety is reasonable."

"Six sentinels. No more." Ciamon glanced angrily at Jemeryl. "I'll also take Jem and her partner. I'm going to send them back to Lyremouth when we reach Villenes. They can take a message to Alendy for me."

❖

Tevi and Jemeryl stood at the edge of the oasis, looking out over the sand. The last of the sunset burned red on the horizon. Tevi looked up. Stars shone unblinking in the dark blue sky.

"I was standing right here when I got swamped by the morphology." Jemeryl said. "This must have been right on the edge of its range. It's taken two months to expand as far as Villenes."

"It's six days' travel. One hundred and fifty miles." Tevi did the sums. "So we have a fair bit of time before it reaches Lyremouth."

"Depends on whether the rate of expansion speeds up. Up to now, it's been feeding off sparse desert populations. Once it gets to the large towns around the Middle Seas"—Jemeryl shrugged—"who knows?"

Tevi glanced over her shoulder. The servants had finished erecting the tents and had started preparing dinner. Sparks from a campfire were spiralling up into the night. The party was even smaller than originally planed. Repeated appeals from Sefriall had only annoyed Ciamon into halving the amount of protection he was prepared to take. The resulting three sentinels had the duty of guarding Tevi and Jemeryl. However, it took more than a sword and a uniform to make a soldier. The trio in their red cloaks were sloppy and manifestly out of condition. Currently they were some way off, playing dice beneath a clump of palm trees.

"What are we going to do?" Tevi indicated the sentinels. "I can handle them if we want to get away and head back to Kradja."

"I'm not sure. What I really want is for Ci to tell me how he's protected the idol, but I don't think he's going to. I'm wondering if we might as well go back to Lyremouth and get advice. The sorcerer who made the first device ought to be there by now. Perhaps she knows something."

"How about I overpower the sentinels and the servants and we take Ciamon with us?"

"Isn't that a bit—"

Footsteps crunched softly in the sand. Ciamon was strolling in their direction. As usual, he gave Tevi a extra-friendly smile, and then ignored her.

"Jem. I've been thinking. I shouldn't have made assumptions about your relationship with Tevi. I'm sorry. It stands to reason you wouldn't spend twelve years with someone you didn't take seriously.

I know you'd be very careful to take Tevi's wishes into account when you make decisions. I'm sure she doesn't feel intimidated by you."

Are you just as sure she doesn't talk about me as if I'm not here? Tevi bit back the words. Jemeryl seemed equally unwilling to comment.

Ciamon continued. "But what you said about me being as arrogant as Alendy. You're wrong. I don't think I'm better than anyone else, and I don't think being able to work magic gives me the right to run other people's lives."

"You do," Jemeryl said. "You've decided what's best for everyone, and you've used your magic to make an emanator that'll impose your view on the world, regardless of what anyone else wants."

"I could hardly put it to a vote. Apart from anything else, the Coven wouldn't let me. And you know that's true. The Coven would never let the population decide to get rid of it."

"But would you let people vote on whether to get rid of the morphology?"

"Yes. Once the Coven is gone, if the people come to me and say they want things to go back to how they were, I'll destroy the emanator."

"It'll be too late then to rebuild the Coven."

"If people want the Coven back, I'm sure we'll be able to sort it out. I promise. I'll abide by the wishes of the people."

Tevi could tell that Ciamon was not seriously considering the possibility of people preferring the Coven to his paradise on earth. Talking to him was pointless. However, Jemeryl still kept going. "How about now? If the master merchants of Villenes won't agree to embrace your new order, will you abide by their decision?"

"They don't have the right to decide on behalf of the whole town."

"And you do?"

Ciamon shook his head sorrowfully. "Jem, I don't understand why you can't see that I only want what's best for the world."

"I understand that. It's your judgement, not your motives I..." Jemeryl sighed and took a step back. "I'm wasting my breath, aren't I? Excuse me, I'm going to wash before dinner."

Jemeryl strode away towards the tents. Ciamon dithered for a few steps, as if considering going after her, but then turned to Tevi. "Would she listen to you? Can't you try to talk her round?"

"I'm sure she'd listen to me, but as it happens, I agree with her."

"Why? You're ungifted. Don't you see what you have to gain?"

"I've got a better idea than most. I know what society is like without magic. I come from islands out in the Western Ocean. We're surrounded by hundreds of miles of water, and the rocks are full of iron. It means we don't get sorcerers or witches on the islands. We're in the state you want to impose on the rest of the world."

"Why did you leave?"

"I'd have been executed if I'd stayed."

"What had you done?"

"It was more a case of what I am."

Ciamon frowned. "What are you?"

"I'm a woman who prefers other women as lovers."

"And?"

"That's it."

"What?" Ciamon looked bewildered.

"For you, the big difference is between sorcerers and the ungifted. On the islands, the big difference was between women and men. You were only supposed to take lovers from the other sex to your own—the opposite sex, as we referred to it. Having a same-sex lover was a crime you could be executed for. I was merely exiled."

"Who told you to do this?"

"The queen was the one who exiled me."

"No. Your people. Who told them same-sex lovers were a crime?"

"Nobody. Ordinary people can think up things for themselves, you know. They don't need sorcerers to do everything for them."

Ciamon ignored the jibe. "It must have come from somewhere."

"They picked it up centuries ago, before they fled the mainland."

"Fled?"

"Didn't like sorcerers, I think. But believe me, they'd have been better off staying."

"At least they were free."

"No. Everyone was constrained by what sex they were. I wasn't free to pick a lover, and the men weren't free to do just about anything."

"But everyone was equal."

"Men were treated as inferior to women."

"That's nonsense."

Tevi laughed. "Of course, but that's the way it was. When it comes to equality, magic actually provides a weird equaliser. You can't tell which baby is going to be a sorcerer. It cuts down on the assumptions people make. You daren't dismiss a baby boy as inferior, because he just might grow up to be someone who can turn you to ash with a wave of his hand. Nobody gets their life planned out for them on the day they're born."

"What can you possibly plan for a baby?"

"On my islands it was easy. The women were going to be warriors, and spend their time looting and killing people on other islands. The men were going to be possessions. It's because of a magic potion we have that makes women strong. Before we got it, men were the warriors and the women were possessions. And this is what the whole world will be like, because of you."

"No. It won't."

"How do you know?"

Ciamon cast around irritably. "Because your people were culturally unbalanced by the sorcerers they'd fled from. Without the background of oppression, they'd never have developed their odd ideas."

"That's a big guess, and even if it's true, won't the society people develop now be just as unbalanced by the background of the Protectorate?"

"No. Because I won't let it." Ciamon turned and stalked away.

Tevi watched him go. Despite having spent time in Ciamon's company, Tevi still could not imagine what Jemeryl had ever seen in him. Had they been very young at the time? Had it been a phase Jemeryl went through? Tevi frowned. Was she being unfair? Perhaps her judgement was tainted by jealousy. Or maybe the man really was an idiot.

❖

Tevi opened her eyes. A noise had woken her, a noise she knew very well—the metallic rasp of a sword being drawn. She lay still, concentrating on her ears, trying to locate the source. Nothing in her immediate surroundings was moving. The only breathing in the tent, apart from her own, came from Jemeryl, sleeping beside her. Then she heard footsteps and soft voices, the sounds of people creeping through the campsite.

Tevi slipped silently from her bedding and pulled back the tent flap a fraction. The moon was half full and low in the sky, but its light was sufficient to see eight or more figures moving between the tents, swords in hand. The loose robes were the same as those worn by the nomads, but the scarves around their faces spoke of bandits.

Gangs of thieves were uncommon in the desert. Travellers to prey upon were hard to find, and usually travelled in large, well-defended caravans. The terrain was inhospitable, giving the bandits limited options to rest up between raids. More than this, the nomads took a dim view of theft, and were very capable of defending their home ground. Still, the risk of attack was real enough that guards should have been set around the camp. Why had the alarm not been raised?

Her movement had woken Jemeryl, who now started to stir. Tevi slid her hand over Jemeryl's mouth. It was too dark to see in the tent, but fortunately, Jemeryl did not struggle. Either from familiarity with the touch, or the empty space beside her, she must have worked out whose hand it was. She joined Tevi at the tent flap.

All Tevi's weapons were locked in a strongbox on one of the wagons. Ciamon had promised to return them to her in Villenes—which was no use now—and nothing in the tent offered much in the way of a weapon. Only the sentinels had swords, and the three soldiers were nowhere in sight. The servants had cooking utensils. Tevi would have settled for a cook's knife and frying pan club, but the raiders were closing in on Ciamon's tent, leaving no time to hunt around. She had to act quickly.

Tevi grabbed a short woollen riding cape and burst through the tent flap, hoping that enough noise would bring the sentinels to her side. "Wake up. Thieves! To arms!"

Yelps and groans came from the surrounding tents. At least some of the party had woken. The raiders also jerked around at the sound of Tevi's voice. A few of them froze, caught for a moment in indecision, but the one nearest Ciamon's tent, clearly the gang leader, pointed at Tevi. "Jaz, Kali, deal with her. We'll take care of the false priest."

Tevi took a firm grip on the cape and whirled it around in a spiral, turning the material into a heavy twisted cosh. It was not much of a weapon, but it was the best she had. Two raiders separated away from their comrades and closed in on her. Their careless, relaxed posture denoted overconfidence. Would this be their fatal mistake? Tevi kept her hand moving in small circles to stop the cloak unwinding. Where were the sentinels?

Both opponents rushed her simultaneously. Tevi dropped beneath their swords and dived to the side, tucking into a roll. As she regained her feet she swung the cape up with all her strength in a diagonal slice, catching one raider across his cheek. The man's head was snapped aside with a distinct crack. Had she broken his neck? Tevi pounded her foot into his stomach as he fell for added reassurance.

White fire erupted in Tevi's side. Where had that come from? For an instant Tevi was stunned with surprise, before realising the other raider had stabbed her, but it was only a glancing blow. Tevi twirled around. Her elbow made sharp contact with the woman's nose. The raider fell back, screaming. A spray of warm blood splattered Tevi's face.

Tevi counter-spun the cape to loosen it and then flapped it over the woman's right arm, snaring her sword in its thick folds. Still dazed, the raider tried to pull away, her attention for the moment diverted. Tevi moved in, chopping the edge of her hand hard into her opponent's throat. The raider dropped vertically, making gurgling sounds like someone being strangled. Tevi stamped on the woman's wrist to loosen her grip and claimed the sword for herself.

Both opponents were now on the ground, but still breathing, still moving. Although she hated to do it, Tevi sliced at the backs of their knees, hamstringing them—the coward's blow. Outnumbered as she was, Tevi dared not let them regain their feet and attack her again. The sentinels had still not arrived. However, Jemeryl had scrambled from their tent and picked up the other raider's dropped sword.

Tevi shook her head urgently. "Stay back."

Jemeryl frowned, but then slipped into the shadows behind the tent. Tevi was relieved—they did not have the time to argue. The remaining raiders were now encircling Ciamon's tent. None of them were looking around. Undoubtedly, they assumed the groans and screams had been Tevi's, not their comrades'.

The flap of Ciamon's tent opened and his face appeared, bleary eyed and still partially asleep. "What's going on? Who's making..."

Ciamon's voice died at the sight of the armed raiders. His eyes widened in fear, glinting white in the moonlight.

"If you know any prayers to your mock god you better start saying them. Or would you like to hear about a true faith before you die?" The jeering voice belonged to the leader who had spoken before.

"What do you want?" Ciamon's voice broke, the high pitch betrayed his terror.

"We want to kill you, of course."

"Why? What have I done to you?"

"You've violated our temple. You've stopped us worshipping our gods and stolen from their shrines. You've tried to take over things you had no right to touch. You have scorned that which is sacred."

"I haven't—"

"You most certainly have. And your heart is going to be a special offering on Toqwani's altar. I'm going to cut it out and put it there myself."

"But..."

"But. But. But?" The raider taunted. She was clearly enjoying herself, secure in the knowledge that she was in control and had no need to rush or worry. She should have looked behind her.

Tevi charged forward. She cannoned into the nearest raider, sending him crashing onto two of his comrades and bowling them all over like skittles. Whatever qualities the leader had been chosen for, quick reflexes was not one of them. She was absorbed in goading Ciamon, unwilling to break off. By the time she started to turn it was too late—for her. Tevi drove the sword into the woman's stomach, impaling her. Tevi's free arm wrapped around her in a deadly parody of a hug, holding her steady while levering the sword upward, slicing through muscle and bone.

Tevi released her hold on the gang leader, who fell to the ground, lifeless, and turned to face the others. Those she had knocked down were scrambling up again. Six raiders in total, and now they were fully aware of the threat she posed. The odds were not good. After a second of hesitation, two led the attack with the others close behind.

Suddenly, Jemeryl stepped from the shadows, also holding out a sword. She called over her shoulder. "Come on. We've got them."

Tevi took advantage of the momentary confusion to lash out at the nearest raider. The injury she inflicted was at most a flesh wound, but it was enough. The raider was hurt and did not want to see who else might be on the way. He turned and ran, and with that, the rest gave up the fight. Some halted briefly by the pair who Tevi had hamstrung, but neither could stand. Neither would ever walk unaided again. The unwounded raiders were evidently not willing to carry their comrades, so they abandoned them and fled the campsite. The sound of hoofbeats faded into the night. With the leader dead and two of their number prisoner, Tevi was sure the raiders would not be back.

The servants had been hiding in their tents, waiting until it was safe to come out. Now they emerged. Most dithered in a confused mass, whispering among themselves, but a few were more focused. One knelt to light torches from the remains of the campfire and two approached Tevi.

"Is the High Priest all right? Has he been hurt?"

"No, he's, um…"

Tevi was aware of sobbing from behind her. It had been going on since she tackled the gang leader. She turned round

Ciamon was on his knees, crying hysterically. He had his arms wrapped around himself. Even by the dim moonlight, Tevi could see that he was racked by convulsive shudders. The raider's threats had clearly unhinged him. Jemeryl was already at his side with her arm across his shoulders. Tevi went to join them.

"No. Keep away from me," Ciamon screeched.

To her surprise, Tevi realised she was the target for his comments.

Jemeryl murmured reassurance. "It's all right. It's Tevi. She's just saved you."

"She's got blood on her. I can see it. She killed them."

"They were going to kill you." It was the wrong thing to say.

"She's got…she's got a s-s-sword. Keep her away. Keep…" Ciamon was out of his mind with terror.

More servants came to assist the panic-stricken High Priest. Tevi left him to their care. He was not her problem. The remaining servants were still flapping around, asking inane questions. To Tevi's mind, the only valid ones were, who were the raiders? And what had happened to the sentinels?

The leader was dead at her feet, but the other two might provide some answers. Tevi started to walk to where they lay but stopped after the first step, hissing between her teeth. Pain flared up her side. She was indeed covered in blood, and not all of it had come from her opponents. The wound in her side was deeper than she had thought, and now the excitement was over, it was making itself felt. But it was not critical. Tending to it could wait a while. Tevi grabbed a torch from a servant and hobbled across the campsite.

The fallen raiders were both silent and unmoving. Not as much as a moan or a twitch came from either. Even before she reached their side, Tevi was sure they were dead. But why? She had deliberately hamstrung them, cutting the tendons in the backs of their legs. Neither would ever walk without crutches, but it should not have been fatal. Ignoring the pain in her side, Tevi knelt and rolled one onto his back. The man's throat had been slit. Their comrades had stopped by them briefly, before fleeing the oasis. Evidently the raiders did not want any of their number captured alive.

"Ma'am, I thought you might want to know. I've found two of the sentinels."

Tevi looked up. The speaker was the servant who had lit torches while the others flapped around aimlessly.

"Just two?"

"Yes. They're dead." He nodded at the corpse on the ground. "Like that. No sign of the third one. I guess there's not much point looking for her."

"Thanks. And I think you're right." Tevi tried to stand, but the world swam around her head and she sank back down, gasping.

"Are you hurt?"

"Just blood loss. I've got a cut. Not serious. Could you help me to the tent and then tell Jem?"

The servant did as requested and left. Tevi lay on her back, concentrating on breathing evenly. Within seconds the tent flap opened and Jemeryl ducked through. She dropped to her knees.

"Tevi. Are you all right?"

"I've got a slice on my side. It's not deep but—"

Already, Jemeryl was gently pulling Tevi shirt up and examining the wound. "Oh, darling, it's nasty."

"It's not hit anything vital. Could you press on it? Try to stop the bleeding."

"I worked in the hospital at Ekranos, remember?" Jemeryl groaned. "But then I could use all seven dimensions. This would be so easy to fix in the fifth. I feel helpless."

Tevi reached her arm over and squeezed Jemeryl's hand. "I think, maybe, I have the slightest inkling about how you feel. In the fight just now, my prescience wasn't there. It felt like I was fighting with a blindfold on."

Long ago, Jemeryl had explained how many apparently ungifted people had weak traces of a paranormal sense. Tevi's prescience was the faintest foreshadowing, working no more than a second into the future and providing information only about life-threatening events, but there could hardly be a more useful gift for a warrior to have.

"You did well without it."

"But with it, I'm sure I wouldn't have been stabbed. It would have warned me." Tevi grimaced, from frustration rather than pain. "And being injured means we have to forget any idea of kidnapping Ciamon. We don't have the sentinels to deal with, but I'm not up to racing across the desert with a prisoner in tow."

"We may get another chance. For now, we're all heading back to Kradja."

"Ciamon's decision?"

"Yes."

"Is he any calmer?"

"Still blubbering. I can't believe how he's gone to pieces."

"A gang of masked assassins trying to kill you can have that effect on some people."

"You dealt with them. Have I told you how pleased I am that you're my partner now, not him? I think Alendy was hoping if I met Ci again I'd want to swap back." Jemeryl gave a half laugh. "No damned chance at all."

"Good."

Jemeryl peeled back her hand and examined the cut, adjusting the position of the torch for better lighting. "The bleeding has eased, but it could do with a couple of stitches."

"I thought as much."

"I'll see if anyone has a kit I can borrow. I stitched up wounds a few times in Ekranos." Jemeryl grimaced. "But not on a fully conscious patient."

"It's all right. It won't be the first time for me. As long as you feel up to doing it."

Jemeryl nodded. "I just wish I had more experience."

"You didn't let lack of experience stop you waving the sword at the raiders. I told you to stay back."

"I couldn't leave you alone."

"But you don't know how to use it properly."

"It's simple. I worked it out for myself. You stick the pointy bit in people."

Tevi laughed weakly. "Who were you calling to? There wasn't anyone behind you."

"My imaginary army." Jemeryl shrugged. "The gang didn't want to call my bluff."

"You know, I wouldn't swap you for Ciamon either."

❖

"I did warn you." If Sefriall was making an effort not to gloat, she was failing.

"You were right." Ciamon sat hunched miserably in a window seat, looking out over Kradja.

Jemeryl was the only other person present. On the journey back, Ciamon had frequently requested her company, as if needing the reassurance of a link to his former life, but he had persisted in his irrational aversion to Tevi. They had arrived in Kradja less than an hour earlier, and Tevi was currently having her wound seen to by such healers as were available. Yet even if she had been free, Ciamon would not have allowed Tevi in the room. Jemeryl had no backup in challenging Sefriall's manipulation of the facts. Not that it mattered. Experience told her she had no chance of success.

Yet, Jemeryl felt she had to try. "As I recall, you didn't warn about an ambush. The sentinels you wanted Ci to take were to intimidate the master merchants of Villenes."

"They still would have kept the High Priest safe from attack."

"As long as too many of them didn't decide to slit their comrades' throats."

"Yes." Sefriall drew the word out, looking pensive. "I regret that one of the sentinels turned out to be in the pay of the master merchants."

"Why are you so sure it was the master merchants?"

"Who else would it be? Their aim was certainly not simple theft."

"I heard one say the name Toqwani. Doesn't that make it more likely the dissident priests were the ones behind it again?"

Sefriall shook her head. "I know my old associates. They were clerics, not soldiers. If you gave them a sword, they'd only cut their fingers on it. That's if they could muster the strength to pick it up."

Ciamon had been playing no part in the debate. At the use of the word *sword*, he cowered even further into the seat. The conversation was clearly painful to him. Now he stepped in. "It doesn't matter who was behind the attack. Sefriall was right. I should have had an army with me. Next time, I will."

Sefriall beamed. "If I might make a suggestion, why not make it a people's army? Rather than just soldiers, take along a host of ordinary people. When the folk of Villenes are able to talk to people like themselves and see their joy, surely it will sway their hearts."

"Yes. That's a great idea." Something of Ciamon's old smile returned.

"The logistics will be horrendous. How will you feed that many in the desert?" Jemeryl objected.

"It will require planning. But I feel I'm up to the task. If you're agreed, I'll set affairs in motion. In fifteen days we'll be ready to leave." Sefriall bowed and backed out.

Jemeryl dropped onto the seat opposite Ciamon. "Are you sure about this, Ci?"

"Yes. What happened at the oasis has made me see even more how important it is. Do you realise what we've done to the world?"

"We...What?"

"That evening, just before the attack, I was talking to...T...your partner." Ciamon was clearly having trouble with her name.

"Tevi."

"Yes. She told me about her home islands. Their whole culture, corrupted by us."

"Us? How?"

"Yes. Don't you see? Fighting. Killing people."

"There aren't any sorcerers on the islands. I've been there. It's a sixth-dimensional sinkhole."

"War is a consequence of magic. Throughout history, it's always been sorcerers who start them."

"That's because it's only been sorcerers with the power to do it."

Ciamon was not listening. "How many millions have died? When we value the life of an ungifted person so little, is it surprising if they don't value it themself?"

"I don't think your logic follows." Jemeryl might as well have spoken to the wall.

"Your partner's people, in permanent warfare, mimicking us and the way we act. Making artificial distinctions between people and pretending they're as important as magic. When I saw her, covered in blood and the sword in her hand, I realised what an awful thing we've unleashed on the world. That's why the Coven has to go."

Jemeryl sank back in her chair, realising that arguing with him would be an utter waste of breath. For Ciamon, his mission had become more important than the truth. It had become the truth. No matter what she said, he would start with what he already believed, use those beliefs to interpret any information he received, and then cite the resulting twisted facts to prove he had been right all along.

Ciamon was beyond reason.

CHAPTER EIGHT—SUNSET IN VILLENES

Villenes lay half a mile distant, at the confluence of two rivers. Ciamon's army lined the hilltops where the ground rose to the south, overlooking the town. Far to the north, the rolling Merlieu Hills crossed the horizon, marking the end of the Aldrak mountain chain. The late afternoon sun was obscured by a haze of cloud, the first Jemeryl had seen for months. Despite the reduced light, the green fields and orchards surrounding the town seemed strangely lurid after days spent crossing the parched desert.

In the centre of the army, Jemeryl stood a little behind Ciamon and his chosen elite—or rather the inner circle Sefriall had chosen for him. Facing them was a delegation of master merchants, a dozen middle-aged traders, their faces showing a mixture of fear and anger. At Ciamon's order, everyone was on foot, a symbol of the new equality. He had even left off his white robes.

Jemeryl glanced over her shoulder. A few feet away, Tevi was flanked by a squad of red-cloaked sentinels. The holy warriors stood in loosely formed ranks. Even to Jemeryl's untrained eyes they lacked proper martial discipline and order. Away from the centre, the people's army lost all military overtones and degenerated into an agitated mob.

She sidled closer to Tevi and whispered, "How do you think it's going to go?"

"Badly."

"Who for?"

"Everyone."

Jemeryl chewed her lip, wishing Tevi's judgement did not so closely match her own.

Ciamon advanced a few steps clear of his supporters. "People of Villenes, we have come to share the good news about the overthrow of tyranny. By the power of Equalitus the world will enter a new age of peace, love, and justice for all."

The merchants exchanged hard looks with each other, but said nothing.

"This is a glorious day for you. This is the day when you will enter the embrace of Equalitus and learn of the joy of true freedom and fraternity."

At the forefront of the merchant delegation was a heavily built elderly man. Judging by the encouraging nods the others were giving him, Jemeryl guessed he was their chosen spokesman. Now, he took a half step forward. "What if we said we weren't buying?"

Ciamon frowned. "Pardon?"

"We're happy with the way things are now. We're not interested in your fancy rhetoric."

"You don't understand what you're saying. What you have now is only a shadow of what will be yours. I've come to open your eyes to the truth."

"I think our eyes are open wide enough. We can see what you're offering, and we don't want it."

"You have no option. The emanation of Equalitus has washed over you. The world is changing. Accept it and join us."

"We know it's changing. The witches in town have lost their powers."

"So rejoice."

The merchant spokesman looked outraged. "Rejoice? What are we going to do if blight hits in spring? Supposing we have a drought. What'll we do without weather witches?"

Another merchant could stay quiet no longer. "What about the healers? My cousin's newborn died ten days ago, and the healers could do nothing to save her."

Ciamon held up his hands. "I know the transition period will have problems, but believe me, when the curse of magic is gone from the world, we can solve these issues. Nothing is impossible if we all work together."

"Well, before you get us to sign up for your wonderful new world, how about if you give some practical ideas for how to make it rain?" Anger was clearly displacing fear in the merchants.

Sefriall moved up to Ciamon's shoulder. "Of course, drought might affect your profits, and that's all you care about. You value money more than your souls."

"Money buys food. You can't eat idealistic claptrap."

"Money buys power. That's what worries you, isn't it? You don't want to give up your power over this town."

"In the embrace of Equalitus, no one will have power over another." Ciamon was ignored by both Sefriall and the merchants.

The spokesman squared up to Sefriall. "Don't act so noble. You're the one who's after power. You don't last in business as long as I have without learning how to spot people like you. Don't think we can't see through all the rubbish about gods."

"The power is not for myself but for the glory of my god."

"We've heard all that before as well. It's never for yourself, is it? Never because you're a ruthless, self-serving bastard."

"There will be an end to strife. Don't ape the intolerance of—" Ciamon was drowned out.

"I'm a faithful servant of my god. You are false unbelievers, corrupters of the truth." Sefriall's voice was rising in ardour and volume.

"Servant of your god? You're just a damned bunch of crooks. Your god's complete bullshit."

A crossbow bolt hissed through the air and embedded itself in the spokesman's chest.

Shouts rose on both sides as the man crumpled over and hit the ground. Loudest of all was Sefriall. "They insult Equalitus and the High Priest. They have turned their back on righteousness. They have condemned themselves."

Bellows from the sentinels reached a crescendo. Few would have heard Ciamon's moan. "No. Don't. It's not supposed to…" Jemeryl only caught it because she was close and knew his voice so well.

The remaining merchants were staring in horror at their fallen associate. A couple still shouted at Sefriall, but then a woman at the rear took a backwards step, turned, and ran. It was like pulling the stopper from a barrel. In an escalating rush, the other merchants streamed after her. The torrent did not end there. The sight of the merchants' backs as they ran away sucked in the army. With a roar, the sentinels surged forward, dogs after a hare.

Jemeryl was buffeted aside as the soldiers pounded past, their eyes locked on their prey, the fleeing merchants and the town of Villenes beyond. She fought to maintain her footing. If she fell she would get trampled. A harder shove sent her reeling but then a firm hand grasped her arm, holding her steady.

"You all right?" Tevi's shout was almost inaudible over the bedlam.

Jemeryl just nodded in reply.

Within minutes, the crowd around them thinned, allowing a clear view across the hillside. Everywhere, the people's army was pouring down the slope, descending on Villenes. The bodies of the delegation lay where they had been cut down, scattered on the grass in a ragged line leading to the town. The elderly master merchants had not been able to outrun the soldiers.

A confused cluster of sentinels and priests huddled nearby, the only ones apart from Jemeryl and Tevi who were not charging towards the town. Ciamon's voice came indistinctly from somewhere in the middle of the knot. Jemeryl squeezed her way through to his side.

Ciamon knelt on the ground, sobbing over the body of the spokesman. "It's magic. It has to be. It's the Coven. They've done this somehow."

Jemeryl crouched beside him. "No. It's not."

"That's what you would say. Was this why they sent you? To make this happen?"

"Of course not." Jemeryl caught his hand. "Come on, Ci. You know me and you know I wouldn't do it, even if I could."

"Sefriall. She was provoking them. Making it worse. Is she working for the Coven?"

"The Coven has nothing to do with this."

"But why did they kill him? There was no reason."

"He insulted your god." Tevi's voice was implacable at Jemeryl's shoulder.

"That's just…just a story. Nobody would kill someone over it."

"Nolians have already been murdered in Kradja."

Ciamon shook his head frantically. "No. I ordered them not to.

They weren't supposed to take it that way. Nolius is playing such an important role for me. When I saw his shrine and heard what his followers believed, it just seemed like...like..."

"Like it wouldn't matter if you blamed them for all the evil in the world?"

"You're saying it's my fault? I'm responsible for their deaths?"

"The people who did the killing are the ones responsible. You just gave them an excuse."

"No—no. It is all my fault." Ciamon looked as if he had been hit by a sudden revelation. "I should have realised the ungifted would be more susceptible to emotion. I simply didn't think they'd react so strongly. But I should have known their minds aren't as capable of reason as ours."

Tevi looked sick with disgust, and clearly could not bring herself to say more.

Ciamon brushed the hair back from the spokesman's forehead and then stared at the town. "What do we do?"

Was Ciamon finally ready to listen? Jemeryl gripped his shoulder. "We can put a stop to it. Go back to Kradja and destroy the emanator that creates the morphology."

"What will happen here?"

"There's nothing you can do."

"No. There has to be something. I'll take my share of the blame." Ciamon's expression hardened. "I'll stop it here and now. I'll tell them Equalitus doesn't want them to fight."

Ciamon lurched to his feet, but before he could move, Tevi grabbed his arm. "Jem's right. It's too late for that. There's nothing you can do here."

"You've been corrupted. It's not your fault, but you don't see how awful violence is. I have to do something." He looked at the sentinels. "Keep these two here. Don't let them stop me."

Immediately, hands grabbed Jemeryl from behind, pulling her back and pinning her arms to her side. At first she struggled, but then the cold touch of metal at her throat made her freeze. "Tevi!"

His followers had managed to free Ciamon from Tevi's grip but she was still fighting them. At Jemeryl's shout she looked over and immediately raised her hands in surrender. Ciamon was already a dozen yards away, sprinting down the hillside.

Tevi and Jemeryl were released once Ciamon was nearly at the town and it was clear that they were going to offer no further resistance. They settled down side by side on the grass to watch, helplessly. The priests had also departed for Villenes, leaving just the eight sentinel guards. Apart from this group, the entire army had entered the town. Already smoke was rising from a dozen locations.

"Looks like the divinely sanctioned looting has started."

"The people here will lose everything." Jemeryl was horrified at what was happening before her.

"Well, those with any sense will have packed their bags and fled before the army got here. But some will have hung on, so there'll still be plenty to loot—except by people who are standing on the hillside watching."

Tevi's words had an immediate impact on the sentinels. They muttered among themselves and became more animated.

"Captain. How long we gonna stand here?" One finally asked the question.

"You heard the High Priest's order."

"Yeah, but he said we had to make sure they didn't stop him. But he got to town ages ago, so they can't stop him now, can they?"

More mumbling indicated a high level of agreement with the speaker. Already, three sentinels were detaching themselves from the squad, edging down the hillside. The captain would soon be facing a mutiny and he wisely decided to give in. "Right. You can all go now." He nodded at Jemeryl and Tevi. "You too."

Half of the squad had already gone, racing towards the town. The rest were not far behind. The captain himself was not hanging around.

Jemeryl scrambled to her feet and was about to follow, but then stopped, realising Tevi had stayed sitting. "Aren't you coming?"

"What are we going to do?"

"We have to find Ci."

"Why?"

"He might get hurt."

"Then he'll have plenty of company in the infirmary, if he's lucky enough to end up there rather than the graveyard."

"Tevi, we need him to tell us how to destroy the emanator."

"That's if he knows."

"He does. Remember by the oasis, before the bandit attack. I asked if he'd destroy the emanator if everyone asked him and he said yes. Therefore he knows its weakness."

Tevi sighed and pushed herself to her feet. "All right. But watch out. It's going to be dangerous in there, and it might already be too late to help him."

Even before they reached the first buildings, the acrid smell of smoke was rasping at Jemeryl's throat. Heavy plumes of brown and grey trailed across the streets. The crackling of fire came from all around, a constant undertone to the shouts and screams filling the air.

Dense smoke from a burning house blanketed the main road. Ash rained down. When they entered the rolling black clouds, Jemeryl pulled the neck of her shirt up to cover her mouth and nose, not that it helped much, or stopped her eyes watering. She ploughed on, following Tevi blindly, trusting that her partner knew where they were going. A swirl of breeze created eddies in the smoke as they passed through. In a sudden clearing, Jemeryl looked down and saw a child's body under her foot. She had been about to tread on it. The smoke rolled back, hiding the young victim. Nausea heaved in Jemeryl's stomach.

What else might she tread on? This was not just about lost vision. Horror was hiding in the smoke-filled street. Jemeryl could not move, and then Tevi grasped her hand and dragged her on, around a corner into a clearer patch of road. Jemeryl leaned against a wall, gasping in the marginally fresher air and fighting with her stomach.

More bodies lay here, among them a red-cloaked sentinel. Dispassionately, Tevi made a quick search. "Someone's taken his sword, but..." She stood up with a long dagger in her hand. "This will be better than nothing."

At sudden loud shouts, Tevi glanced around, then took Jemeryl's arm, pressing her back into the cover of a doorway. A raucous gang stumbled by, their arms full of goods. The most prized were the bottles that several looters had in their hands. The contents were obviously alcoholic, which might account for the rabble's cheerfulness. To Jemeryl's disgust, a few were even singing.

"Someone always finds the wine shop first," Tevi muttered.

Jemeryl rested her forehead on Tevi's shoulder, trying to draw strength from her. This was an arena that Tevi knew. How to survive in a world of violence and bloodshed. The split-second judgements that would determine whether you saw sunrise the next day. How to dismiss the fate of the dead from your mind, so that you could focus on the threats of the living.

If Tevi wasn't here, would I be able to cope with it, Jemeryl wondered. *Would I survive, even if I had my magic?*

"As I thought. It's a nightmare," Tevi said.

"How are we going to find Ci in all this?" Jemeryl tried to focus on the practical issue.

"If we see anyone who looks like they could give a reasonable answer, we could ask. Failing that, I'd guess he'll have headed towards the centre of town."

"Right." Jemeryl took a deep breath and then coughed. "Shall we go on?"

"Sure. But keep alert. No one around here is going to waste time asking, 'friend or foe?'"

Progress was slow through the town, avoiding burning houses and looters, although most of Ciamon's army were too busy rifling through the wreckage to bother them. By the time they reached the civic centre of Villenes, the sun was low in the sky. Soon it would be dark. Already the burning buildings were showing up like beacons, lighting the streets.

"Stop! Please stop. Equalitus wants you to stop."

Jemeryl recognised Ciamon's voice. He had to be less than a hundred yards away. She tapped Tevi's shoulder and pointed in the direction of the plea. Tevi nodded and led the way under an archway which brought them out in a cobbled square. At the far end were steps leading up to the town hall. The doors had been smashed off their hinges and now hung awry across the entrance. Ciamon stood at the top of the stairs, with the wrecked doors as a backdrop, shouting at the gangs of looters who shambled by. Few gave him a second glance. Either they did not recognise him without the robes, or they were too drunk to care.

"Come on. Let's get him," Tevi said.

Piles of debris littered the ground. Jemeryl followed Tevi on a zigzagging route, skirting the obstructions and keeping out of Ciamon's direct line of sight. Now they had tracked him down, they did not want him to evade them again.

Eventually they reached an alcove in deep shadow at the side of the stairs, directly beneath where Ciamon stood. He still showed no sign of seeing them. Tevi took a step forward and then retreated, pushing Jemeryl back under cover of a stack of smashed crates. One of the more troublesome-looking gangs sauntered past. Several had acquired swords which they brandished at Ciamon, although none did more than jeer.

The echoes of their whooping had barely faded when Jemeryl heard another sound—hoofbeats and marching feet. Judging by her expression. Tevi had recognised it too. In all the chaos, somebody was exerting control over a disciplined group.

"Who do you think that is?" Jemeryl asked.

"Sentinels under a halfway decent officer would be my guess."

"They're coming this way."

"Sounds like it." Tevi looked up. "We may have missed our chance to snag Ciamon."

"Whoever it is might be on our side, the town watch or something."

"That would be nice, but I doubt it. We'll wait to see, before we step out and say hello."

The sounds of hoof and foot got louder, and then a troop of red-cloaked sentinels marched into the square, some carrying torches against the thickening darkness. They were following three people on horseback. Jemeryl was not surprised to see Sefriall in the lead. However, Tevi gasped.

"What is it?" Jemeryl whispered.

"On Sefriall's right. That man. It's Parrash."

Jemeryl had no time to think it through. Already the riders had halted before the town hall steps.

"Sefriall. You've got to stop them. They're killing people. They mustn't," Ciamon shouted.

Sefriall ignored him. She turned to the rider on her left. "Clear the square and make sure we aren't disturbed. I have some private business to conduct."

The man was wearing a red cloak and high-crested helmet, with enough gold trim and embellishments to mark him as a senior officer. He barked a series of orders at his subordinates. The column of sentinels broke into groups that marched across the square, scattering any looters before them. The soldiers then took up positions across the roads and alleys leading in, blocking all access to the square.

Jemeryl froze, her heart pounding, but no one had thought to investigate the dark alcove under the stairs, so she and Tevi were left undiscovered. She looked up. Sefriall was now within arm's reach of Ciamon. The man Tevi had identified as Parrash stood at her side.

"Sefriall, I told you. You have to stop the killing." Ciamon was more insistent.

"Why?"

"Because people are being killed. They're—"

"And your problem with this is…?"

"Hundreds of people are dying."

"Precisely. News of what has happened here will spread. What town will dare defy us now? All will open their gates to our armies."

"You're not upset?" Ciamon sounded incredulous.

"No. It's what I wanted."

"Wanted? You meant this to happen?"

"Of course. I planned it."

"You meant for all this death?"

"It's distasteful but necessary."

"No. It isn't. Equalitus is a god of peace."

Sefriall laughed. "Equalitus is a god of fools. Your god is a sad joke. Only the Cyclians have the true faith."

"You're…" Ciamon's voice died, his bewilderment plain.

"Did you think I'd forsake my gods for your pathetic child's fantasy? Especially when I saw so clearly that you were an unwitting tool of Toqwani, the destroyer. You've set in motion the destruction of the Coven and the sorcerers who mock us. Now it's my turn to do the will of Rashem, the reclaimer. From the ruins of the Protectorate we will build a new empire. A holy empire. It will dwarf all that has gone before. The word of the gods will be law."

"I'll have no part in this." Ciamon had got over his surprise and was turning to anger.

"True. You won't. You've fulfilled your purpose, and your job is over."

"If you think I'm just going to walk away from this and leave you to it, you're wrong."

"No. I've never thought that. Which is why I've been trying to have you killed. I'm hoping third time lucky."

"You what?"

Sefriall stepped forward. In the last of the daylight, Jemeryl saw the glint of a long blade, thrust out. Ciamon gasped, a strange, high-pitched noise like the air leaking from an inflated bladder. His face contorted in pain, and then eased, losing all expression in the serenity of death. His eyes rolled back, showing white as his body crashed onto the steps.

Jemeryl felt a scream die, strangled in her throat. The memory of every hopeless nightmare taunted her, but for this there would be no waking to relief tomorrow. This was real and forever. Her stomach and bowels kicked in synchronised spasms, both threatening to empty. Tears trickled down her face. Ciamon was gone and, with all his faults, he had deserved better.

Sefriall stepped away. Blood dripped from the edge of the dagger in her hand. She cast a reproachful look at Parrash. "You know what they say about when you want a job done."

"I followed your orders."

"I don't remember ordering you to alert the mercenary to the plan."

Parrash scowled, evidently deciding not to argue his case any further. He kicked at the body by his feet. "What are we going to do about him?"

"We'll have him disposed of." Sefriall turned and called out, "Belshaleid, I need some assistance. Send me four strong sentinels."

"Yes, my lady." The other horse rider was currently patrolling the outskirts of the square.

The requested sentinels arrived in short order.

"Take this carcass away," Sefriall ordered. "Find the hottest fire in town to dump it in. I don't want any chance of it being recognised. Get something to wrap him in so no one will spot him on the way. Understood?"

"Yes, lady."

Once the sentinels had left with Ciamon's body, Sefriall turned to Parrash. "So far it's all going well."

"Do you really think people will believe the story about Ciamon ascending into the sky on a beam of light?"

Sefriall gave a bark of laughter. "Of course. By morning they'll all have a hangover and a bad conscience, and ought to be malleable enough. The amount some of the rabble are drinking, there'll be a couple dozen witnesses who'll be sure they saw it with their own eyes. They ought to convince any doubters." She patted Parrash on the shoulder. "Come. We have things to organise before we return to Kradja."

The two priests walked down the steps and back to their horses. The sentinels formed up in columns and marched away behind them, leaving the square empty in the fading light. The shroud of smoke over Villenes was turning red and amber in the sunset.

Jemeryl knew she was shaking. Tevi must have been able to feel it as well. "Jem? Are you all right?"

"Yes."

Tevi's arms tightened around her in a hug. "I'm sorry about Ciamon. I know you liked him."

Jemeryl caught her lower lip in her teeth and could only nod.

"We might as well go."

Jemeryl squirmed free of Tevi's embrace and staggered uncertainly up the steps to the spot where Ciamon had died. The streak of red blood was soaking into the porous stone. She sank down beside it. Tevi joined her, but made no attempt to intervene or hurry her along.

Memories kept running through Jemeryl's head. The first time she'd seen him, a boy of twelve, standing in a corridor in Lyremouth on a rainy day, joking about the state of his shirt, then turning to her with an open smile, inviting her to join in the laughter.

The last time they had made love. They had both known it was over. It had been a gentle good-bye, for old times' sake. A soft warm memory, to hold over the years ahead. Jemeryl closed her eyes, remembering again his face—his forehead creased, his mouth opened, his face contorting just like it had when Sefriall had sunk the knife into his heart. Now she would never recall one event without the other.

Jemeryl's tears fell on the stone and were also absorbed.

❖

Fires still burned, lighting the night, but the mayhem on the streets was quietening down, due partly to the patrols of sentinels. Now that Sefriall's goals had been met, her soldiers were curbing the excesses of violence and taking weapons off anyone not wearing a red cloak. The other main reason for the decline in anarchy was that all the worst offenders were too drunk to stand, let alone cause trouble.

The sound of marching boots alerted Tevi to another patrol, coming in their direction. She and Jemeryl dived into a doorway and huddled there, trying to look like looters, sleeping off a hard day's pillaging. The patrol passed by without a second glance. The footsteps faded down the street. In the following silence, Tevi heard distant singing, and one long drawn-out scream. Pockets of disorder still existed. Closer by, she heard the sound of sobbing. Villenes was in ruins. Would it ever be rebuilt?

Once the patrol was out of sight, Tevi stood and scanned up and down the street. Midnight was long past and they had to be away by dawn. Regardless of whether Sefriall saw Jemeryl as a threat, the Cyclian priest had no love of sorcerers and might want a bargaining chip with the Coven. With luck, Sefriall currently had other things on her mind, but surely the word would soon go out to capture them, if it had not already.

In order to get away, she and Jemeryl needed transport. Unfortunately, the horses were in the main encampment, at the other side of the ridge where Ciamon's army had been assembled that afternoon. Tevi had a dim view of the professionalism and competence of the sentinels, but even so, they would have sentries set. Trying to sneak into the centre of their camp would be very risky and only to be considered as a last resort, but if they did not get lucky in another hour or so, they would be out of options.

A hefty snort and the jangle of a bridle came from close by. Tevi exchanged a quick look with Jemeryl and together they crept in the direction of the sound, keeping to the shadows. Another jangle and the shuffle of hooves carried cleanly on the night air. By now, Tevi was close enough to tell that it was coming from a yard behind what had once been a blacksmith's forge, although the building had been reduced to a burnt-out shell.

Tevi tried to keep her optimism in check. Two similar alerts had turned out to be an officer, surrounded by a dozen sentinels, and a couple of donkeys. However, when she slipped around the final corner, she saw a situation better than she had dared hope for.

Two sentinels were huddled in a corner, arms locked around each other in an embrace. By the looks of it, the soldiers were either scouts or couriers. Their horses were tethered nearby—fast, strong animals with well-stocked packs behind their saddles. The sentinels had also chosen a secluded spot for their encounter. This was understandable on their part. No matter how lax the army discipline, their officers would not be pleased if the two sentinels were caught at their current activity while on duty.

Tevi weighed up her options. Currently, the sentinels' attention was entirely given to each other. Were they so intent that they would not notice her sneak up on them? Or might another tactic be better? She dared not let them raise the alarm. There was no guarantee that none of their comrades were in earshot.

Her mind made up, Tevi pushed away from the wall and stumbled forward into the moonlight. By the time she was halfway across the yard, her uneven footsteps had caught the sentinels' notice. They broke off from their kiss.

"Hey. What are you doing here?"

Tevi faltered, reeled to the left, and then lurched onward, acting like a drunken looter.

"Clear off."

Tevi paid no notice. She staggered to a pillar a little to their left and leaned her hands against it, arms locked and head sagging, retching as if about to throw up.

"If you don't fucking shove off, I'm going to kick your arse right across Villenes."

The sentinels levered themselves out of the corner and approached Tevi, hastily adjusting their clothing. The nearest one threw a swinging punch at her, but it was a gesture more than an attack, intended to get her attention and unbalance her rather than cause harm.

Tevi ducked and caught hold of his arm. She pulled him sharply towards her and rammed the top of her head into his face. At the same time, her free hand pounded into his stomach. The sentinel fell back, dazed and groaning, onto his comrade, who was standing behind him. The second sentinel was clearly surprised to have his lover back in his arms so soon. Before he had worked out what to do with the dead weight he was holding, Tevi's fist smashed into his jaw, sending both crashing to the ground.

Earlier in the night, Tevi had picked up several lengths of cord. She had one sentinel's hands tied behind his back before either had started to move. The second was making an effort to squirm out from under his comrade, but a few more blows kept him down long enough to bind his hands as well.

"Neat." Jemeryl was at the horses, examining their packs, but she broke off long enough for a word of approval.

"Thanks."

"It looks like we have several days' provisions here."

"Couldn't be better."

Tevi stripped the red cloaks from the sentinels and then tore strips from their shirts to make gags. Jemeryl joined her as she tied the last knot.

"Is it all right to leave them?"

Tevi frowned. Both sentinels had their eyes open, although one was clearly having trouble focusing. "Knocks to the head are hard to predict. If one has a concussion and starts to be sick, I guess he might—"

"I meant, won't they set the pursuit onto us when they're found?"

"Oh, I shouldn't think so." Tevi crouched down. "Because they were riding on patrol when someone called to them. They followed the voice and got jumped by six horse thieves. They certainly weren't so busy making out that one lone woman got the drop on them."

The sentinels could only glare back at her. Tevi was pleased to note that both were now looking alert. Choking on vomit was not something she would wish on anyone, not even incompetent enemies.

The sentinels had discarded their helmets before getting into their amorous embrace. Tevi tossed one to Jemeryl, keeping the other for herself. "With these and the cloaks, we shouldn't get stopped on our way out of town."

They untethered the horses and led them onto the street. A quarter moon was rising, although its light was too weak for anything other than walking. However, the first hint of grey was on the eastern horizon. In less than an hour, the light would be strong enough to ride by. The only thing to decide was the direction.

"Where now?" Tevi asked.

"Lyremouth. We have to find a way to overcome whatever protection Ciamon put on the idol."

Tevi had heard the catch in Jemeryl's voice at her ex-lover's name.

She hesitated. What words should she say? Balancing support with sincerity would be tricky, yet surely silence was the worst response.

"Jem, I wasn't keen on Ciamon. You know that. But I'm truly sorry about what happened. I would have saved him if I could. He was a good person at heart."

"At heart he was too good. He…" Jemeryl sighed. "I know he's made a mess here. But he did it for the right reasons. He cared about other people, not just himself. He wanted to make the world better for everyone. That's the tragedy."

Tevi bit her lip. To her mind, the tragedy was all the people who had wanted nothing more than to spend the next day with their families and would now never see them again. "Ideals are worthless if they aren't practical. And other people are paying for his mistakes."

"Oh, I know. Don't get me wrong. But with all the things he did wrong, the human race would be worse if there weren't people like him in it. And I really want to think that…"

"What?"

"That it's possible to make a difference."

They reached a crossroads. While the light grew on the horizon, Tevi led the way north, towards the Merlieu Hills and the Protectorate.

Part Two

The Idol

CHAPTER NINE—THE NATURE OF GUILT

A t the sight of two horses, riding along the tree-lined avenue leading to the Coven, the gatekeeper stepped into the middle of the road and held up his hand. "Who seeks admission to the Coven?"

"I do. I'm—" Jemeryl got no further. Now he had got a closer look at her, the gatekeeper recognised her face.

"You're Jemeryl. You've turned traitor to the Coven. You're…you can't…" The man's eyes were stretched wide in panic.

"Yes. Of course I'm a traitor. That's why I've come here to make a report to Alendy."

"Don't think you can force your way through. I'm going to send for backup."

"Why don't you just tell Alendy I'm here and want to talk to him?" Jemeryl was starting to feel irritated.

"We've got defences, you know." The gatekeeper was backing away as he spoke.

At Jemeryl's side, Tevi leaned forward, resting her arms on the saddle horn. "You're wasting your time talking to him, Jem. Listening isn't his strong suit."

The gatekeeper fled through an archway. Jemeryl jumped down from her horse and advanced to within a few feet of the spot where he had been standing. Was the man acting like an idiot or was he genuinely that stupid? Regardless, Jemeryl did not want to hang around waiting for somebody to turn up who was willing to behave in a more sensible manner. However, his words about the defences had been the truth.

Ahead of her, power tensors in the ether barred the road, invisible to those who could not perceive the sixth dimension but quite deadly to anyone who blundered through uninvited. As a sorcerer, Jemeryl had the ability to nullify them from the outside, but it would not be easy or quick. She was just about to start untying the sixth dimension when a new voice rang out.

"Really, Jemeryl. Scaring the gatekeeper like that. It's quite shameful of you." Iralin stood on the other side of the tensors.

"I told you she was here." The gatekeeper was cowering behind the elderly sorcerer, and thus unable to see the amused glint in her eyes. He was evidently also unable to detect the ironic edge to her voice and leapt back in surprise when Iralin clapped her hands and the tensors vanished. "You can't let her in, she's—"

Iralin turned on him. "Why is it that the only brain cell you have in full working order is the one connected to your mouth?"

"But—"

"Traitors don't wander up to the gates without an army behind them."

"I was—"

"Can you see an army?"

As he had already demonstrated, the gatekeeper was deaf to irony. He went as far as to peer around before answering. "No, ma'am."

"So tell Alendy that Jemeryl is here and wants to talk to him." Iralin glanced over. "Can I take it that's your first priority?"

"Yes." Jemeryl smiled. As an apprentice, she had dreaded Iralin's sarcasm, but it was gratifying now to have it exercised on her behalf.

The gatekeeper again scuttled away towards the main buildings. Iralin followed on at a more sedate pace and Jemeryl fell in beside her.

"Is the situation in Kradja resolved?" Iralin asked.

"No. Far from it."

"Why have you come back?"

"I need help. I think it's going to take the whole Coven to sort it out."

"It's that serious?"

"I fear so. But thanks for helping Tevi get to me. Without her there, it would have gone a lot worse. For starters, I'd be dead." Jemeryl threw a quick smile over her shoulder at Tevi, who was behind them, leading both horses.

"Make sure you tell that to Alendy."

"He was angry with you?"

"Nothing I couldn't shrug off."

"We need to be ready to deal with him now." Jemeryl lowered her voice, talking quickly. "I think he might try to cover up some things that need to be out in the open."

"What?"

"I haven't got time now. When Alendy takes me off for a private briefing, why don't you keep hold of Tevi and let her tell you the full story?"

"I'm sure—"

Sounds of a disturbance interrupted Iralin. Alendy was arriving with a dozen other sorcerers and witches in support. Judging by his expression, he was not as pleased to see Jemeryl as Iralin had been, nor as convinced that a battle was not about to erupt. Iralin looked his direction and then patted Jemeryl's arm reassuringly.

Alendy planted his feet squarely on the cobblestones. "Jemeryl. I hadn't expected to see you here after the reports I received about your actions in Kradja."

"What reports were they?"

"That you'd joined forces with the renegade you'd been sent you bring back." Alendy frowned. "Are you here as his emissary?"

"No. I'm still loyal to the Coven. But I saw how serious the situation was. I only said what I did about joining him because I needed an excuse to stay in Kradja and get more information."

"Why didn't you explain your reasons to the others in your party?"

"I didn't get a chance to talk to them in private. If I'd announced my true reasons when everyone was there, I doubt I'd have been allowed to remain."

Alendy relaxed his posture. "So. Do you have anything to report?"

"Oh, yes."

"Do you know what Ciamon is up to?"

Jemeryl took a deep breath, making sure she had control of her voice. "He's not up to anything much now, or ever will be again. He's dead. Murdered."

Alendy looked startled. "Not by you?"

"No. Of course not."

The rigidity in the set of Alendy's shoulders eased and an expression of relief flooded his face. "So the problem is resolved."

"Far from it. In fact, it's got an awful lot worse."

"But—"

"The morphology is still spreading. The woman who murdered Ciamon has taken control in Kradja. She arranged the destruction of Villenes. There was just a smoking ruin when her army left. Unless we stop her, the entire Protectorate will follow."

A flurry of incredulous comments broke out from the listeners. Alendy silenced them with an angry glare and a cutting gesture before turning back to Jemeryl. "I'll need a full report from you. We'll go to my study."

"If you wish. But it would be quicker to call a meeting of all the senior sorcerers so I only have to go through the details once."

"I'll be the judge of what resources are needed, once I know the true situation."

As she had expected, Jemeryl could tell that Alendy was hoping to keep as much hidden as possible. She glanced over her shoulder, to where Tevi was minding the horses. Iralin had shifted back and now stood beside her. Alendy's eyes had once flicked in Tevi's direction, and thereafter he had made a conspicuous point of ignoring her. Jemeryl pursed her lips. One of these days, Alendy would realise that Tevi was not somebody you could safely ignore.

The group of sorcerers were dismissed, no doubt to start speculating wildly. Jemeryl smiled, imagining what sort of rumours would be spreading by nightfall. Gossip always had been the favourite pastime in the Coven. Iralin hobbled off with her arm linked through Tevi's, to get some far more accurate information.

In the Guardian's quarters, Alendy listened to the first part of Jemeryl's report impassively. More than anything else, his lack of surprise confirmed the suspicions that he had known far more than he had previously admitted. But how deeply was he implicated? Jemeryl wished she could demand answers, but their relative positions in the Coven hierarchy did not allow it. However, her report ought to include Ciamon's story in full, including the background reasons for his actions. If she phrased the accusations to make it clear she was merely repeating what Ciamon had said, she could see what sort of explanation Alendy would volunteer.

"Ciamon told me Ralieu's experiment went wrong. Instead of whatever the emanator was supposed to do, it projected a morphology on the skein that prevented everyone affected by it from accessing the higher dimensions. He and Ralieu escaped, but then she locked the door and had the emanator bricked in, despite there being several innocent citizens still inside. He claimed that they were left to starve to death."

Alendy's jaw tightened visibly. "The situation was not so clear cut."

Jemeryl took a breath, trying to make her tone not sound accusatory. "You knew about it?"

"Not when I spoke to you before. But I told you I'd recalled Ralieu to Lyremouth. I've since questioned her and learned of the regrettable events."

Regrettable? Cold-blooded murder seemed a better description to Jemeryl. "She admitted her actions?"

"Yes."

"People were bricked in to starve on her orders?"

"The innocent ones were already dead."

"How could she be sure?"

"She studied the auras in the fifth dimension."

"Didn't the morphology prevent—" Jemeryl stopped in confusion.

"The morphology stops those within it from accessing the higher dimensions. From the outside, Ralieu was able to detect that only two people were alive in the cellar. She made the assumption that they were the criminals."

Why had Ralieu not told Ciamon this? Why had he not checked for himself? Jemeryl's head sank as she battled to control the tears that threatened. Of course, Ciamon always was a weak sorcerer. His first instinct had never been to rely on magic. But if he had known, would it have made a difference? Would he have cared about the murderers enough to recreate the morphology?

Jemeryl raised her head. She knew what Ciamon would have said. "Surely Ralieu could have sent in a squad of soldiers to arrest the criminals and put them on trial. It's what the laws of the Protectorate demand. If guilty, they should have been hanged, not starved."

"I agree her judgement wasn't good. I can't condone what she did."

"Ciamon was convinced you covered for her when he told you about it. This was his motivation for wanting to destroy the Coven. He thought you were—"

"Ciamon was a—" Alendy broke off with an sharp sigh. "He had no regard for the reputation of the Coven."

He didn't think sorcerers had more rights than anyone else. Jemeryl closed her mouth and let her expression speak for her.

Alendy flushed, either in anger or embarrassment. "Ciamon was prone to causing trouble with his superiors. I assumed this was just one more example. You have to understand that Ralieu is brilliant but unconventional. She's pushed forward our knowledge in so many fields. I assumed Ciamon misunderstood something. The level Ralieu was working on went far beyond his abilities to comprehend."

He was pretty good at understanding morality. Jemeryl wished she dared say it aloud. Instead she continued with the story. "After the events in the cellar, Ciamon started investigating what Ralieu had been doing. So he wasn't completely in the dark about what she'd been up to. He claimed Ralieu had been working on a method of mind control, and her aim had been to enslave people."

"That wasn't her intention. But yes, mind control was involved."

The admission was astounding. "Was her work sanctioned?" Jemeryl could not help blurting out the question.

"No. Not as such." Alendy paced to the window and stood with his back to Jemeryl. "Gilliart always closely monitored what Ralieu was doing, but with everything involved with taking over as Guardian, it wasn't my top priority. Ralieu has been an inspired innovator. I felt that strict supervision was…"

You were so in awe of her magical abilities that you thought it degrading to treat a great sorcerer like a child. Jemeryl mentally tacked on his full reasons. *You let an eccentric mastermind follow whatever wild idea drifted through her head. I bet you ignored Gilliart's specific advice in doing so. And now you're wondering how much of the blame is going to end up on your shoulders.*

"Go on with your report." Alendy threw the order over his shoulder, clearly unwilling to justify himself further.

Pushing the issue was unnecessary, Jemeryl told herself. Others, more senior, would make the accusations. With the fate of the Protectorate at stake, even the Guardian would not be able to keep the story secret or hide his mistakes.

Alendy neither moved nor said anything else until she had finished her account. Even then he stayed staring through the window as he asked, "This morphology. Do you think it could cover the entire Protectorate?"

"I've no idea."

"You've seen the emanator."

"No, just the idol it's inside, and I was blind to the higher dimensions at the time. I could tell nothing about its construction. Ciamon knew how it worked and he thought it could. The only person who could give a better answer would be Ralieu."

"I've spoken to her. She agrees with Ciamon's assessment. But I hoped…" Alendy sighed and turned away from the window, shoulders sagging. His face was drained of colour. He walked slowly across the room, with the air of a man going to the gallows. "Yes. You were correct. I'll need to call a meeting of all the senior sorcerers. You need to be there too."

"And Tevi."

"She isn't…" Alendy's voice died, as if he lacked the will to argue.

"She has useful knowledge of the situation in Kradja. Maybe Ralieu can tell us something as well."

"Ralieu wouldn't be helpful at the meeting. She won't be there."

"We can't afford to dismiss any source of information. You haven't—" Jemeryl stopped herself. She was at risk of stepping over the line. She could not give orders to the Guardian.

Alendy's head shot up and he met her gaze angrily, and then the expression on his face shifted, revealing the fear and worry beneath. When he spoke, it sounded like a plea for understanding. "No matter what you think of me, I'm not playing games. Ralieu can't cope in groups. If she gets stressed, she might refuse to speak for a month. She'd only confuse the issue, anyway. You have my permission to talk to her afterwards and pass on what she says to anyone you choose."

Alendy stood up straighter, and his voice softened, yet sounding both more determined and more sincere. "I may end up being known as a poor Guardian. It's not what I hope for and I'll do everything I can to see that history remembers me more favourably. But if that's how it goes…" He sighed. "The one thing I don't want to be remembered as is the last Guardian."

❖

The main council chamber of the Coven was circular, with the speaker's raised lectern facing the arched doorway. The seats rose in tiers on all sides, and currently not a single one was vacant. Some people were even sitting in the aisles. Rarely had Jemeryl been the focus of so much attention. As her account progressed, she was aware of the mood in the chamber shifting from curiosity, to surprise, to dismay. Several times she had to break off and wait for silence to return.

Jemeryl reached the end of her report and sat down between Iralin and Tevi, leaving the lectern vacant. The debate that followed was predictable, starting with a flurry of questions. Of these, at least a third were from people who had not understood what she had said and were therefore either misconceived or had already been answered. On top of this, a couple of sorcerers seemed deliberately perverse in trying to steer the debate onto their own particular field of interest. The seers' attempts to project omnipotence were even more strained than normal. Jemeryl also noted the steadily growing blatancy in pointed comments, from people who obviously disliked Alendy, sharpening their knives ready for his back.

Alendy let it continue until any pretence of genuine inquiry was gone and then he stood, claiming the floor of the chamber. "This meeting has more pressing matters to deal with than assigning blame. There are things that with hindsight, I wish I'd done differently. Of course there are. But debating them now isn't going to help. When the crisis is over, I promise a full investigation. No one's actions, including my own, will be exempt. What this meeting needs to concentrate on is working out our response."

Alendy's words were greeted with scowls from some. However, from what Jemeryl could tell, these were due more to disappointment at having the fun postponed rather than disagreement with the way the Guardian had set priorities.

"We need to destroy the idol," someone behind Jemeryl said. She turned her head, but not in time to identify the speaker.

"Yes. Obviously." Alendy's voice held a note of exasperation. "The problem is Ciamon placed magical defences on it, and we don't know what these are. But Ciamon asserted that they're very potent."

"In his dreams." This time the speaker was an elderly sorcerer, named Weilan, who was sat on the front row. He had followed Jemeryl's report intently, with an expression of scepticism bordering on incredulity, although he had not spoken before.

"Ciamon was sure we wouldn't be able to overcome them," Jemeryl said.

"Given that Ciamon couldn't put out a candle except by blowing at it, I wouldn't get too worried over what he thought was possible. Believe me, I knew the man, and I know what he was capable of. It didn't amount to much."

"Yes, of course, Weilan. He was your assistant for a while, wasn't he?" Alendy's tone had perked up.

"Supposedly. I mean, he was assigned to me, but the only thing he was any good at was sweeping the floor. We have janitors to do that. I expect more from a sorcerer."

"If I remember correctly, protective shields have been a special interest to you. Were you working on them when Ciamon was with you?"

"Yes. I'd almost like to think he has put some serious defences on the idol, because that might mean he'd paid attention to me rather than floating around in a daze, which was all he ever seemed to do."

While not completely unfounded, Jemeryl felt the criticism underestimated Ciamon's talent. "He wasn't incapable."

"True. That was the annoying bit. He simply had no interest and wasn't prepared to exert himself."

"This was something he cared about. It might have motivated him."

"If I understand the timescale correctly, he'd have needed to put a decade of work into two months."

The image of Ciamon on the balcony ran through Jemeryl's head. "He sounded so confident when he told me about it."

"Then he was bluffing."

Jemeryl sat back, frowning. Bluffing had never been Ciamon's style. He had been an atrocious card player. His face always gave his hand away. Jemeryl felt her throat constrict at the memory.

Alendy looked at Weilan thoughtfully. "You're an expert in protective shields, and you worked with Ciamon. How long would you need to make a portable device to destroy the idol, even if the person using it couldn't perceive the higher dimensions?"

"For any spell Ciamon might have used?" Weilan snorted dismissively. "Ten minutes."

"This is serious. Remember what rides on it."

"You mean absolutely, definitely, stake the future of the world on it, certain?"

"Yes."

Weilan pursed his lips, clearly running options through his head. "Give me three days."

"You got them. And any assistance you require. Just ask." Alendy turned to address the whole meeting. "Does anyone else have any suggestions—practical ones?"

"I do." To many people's evident surprise, it was Tevi who had spoken.

Alendy stared at her. "What?"

"I was a captain in Bykoda's army for three years. All the officers apart from me were either witches or sorcerers, but the ordinary soldiers weren't. Her armoury made all sorts of magical weapons that anyone could use. They were"—Tevi grimaced—"very effective at killing people. With the resources of the Coven, you could produce a similar arsenal. Make the weapons and the Guild of Mercenaries will provide the warriors to use them. They'll clear the way through to Kradja. Sefriall's sentinels won't stand a chance. Then you can walk in and take your time dismantling the idol."

"We can't give that sort of power to ordinary citizens," a voice shouted from the back.

"Bykoda did."

"Supposing the mercenaries hang on to the weapons? Can we trust them?"

Tevi looked angry, but her voice stayed level. "Guild warriors will stand by their word. It's what our livelihood depends on."

"Will they risk their lives for the Coven?"

"Sefriall hoped the destruction of Villenes would cause so much fear nobody would dare oppose her. My guess is it'll have the opposite effect. The thought of the same thing happening here…" Tevi did not need to finish.

"But they can't—"

Alendy interrupted. "We cannot reject the idea out of hand." He directed a long, hard look at Tevi. "If it's the only way to save the Protectorate from destruction, then we'll do it. But it must be a last resort."

"I agree. The loss of life would be appalling."

Alendy nodded. Jemeryl suspected his reluctance was for reasons more in common with those of the other speakers than with Tevi's.

"Hopefully, these weapons will be unnecessary. But we'll make them in readiness, while a small team return to Kradja with Weilan's device." Alendy stopped in front of Jemeryl. "If you're willing, I'd like you to lead the team since you have some familiarity with the town and this Sefriall."

"Of course." Jemeryl had half expected the assignment.

"You'll have a couple of volunteers with you."

"I'll go." Tevi spoke immediately.

"You would be more use here, sharing your knowledge of Bykoda's weapons."

Tevi shrugged. "I've got three days. That'll be more than enough to tell everything I know."

"You—"

Jemeryl spoke up. "As team leader, I'd like Tevi with me. My knowledge was restricted to inside the temple. Tevi has contacts in town, including a group of dissident priests, who might be valuable."

For a moment, Alendy looked ready to argue, but then he nodded. "Very well. It's your decision."

❖

Ralieu was at least eighty years old, although still in sound health physically. Unfortunately, the same could not be said for her wits. She had a disconcerting habit of talking about herself in the third person, and a tendency to break off mid-sentence to examine some minor detail of the room. After watching her spend a whole minute tracing the grain in her chair's wooden armrest as if it was remarkable, Tevi had reached the conclusion they were wasting their time. They were not going to learn anything worthwhile from the old woman.

She muttered to Jemeryl, who was standing beside her, "Age has got to her."

"I'm not so sure."

"Her mind has gone walkies."

"She might always have been like this."

"I thought she was a great inventor."

"The two can go hand in hand. Some sorcerers have an odd set of senses. They see and link up things in remarkable ways, but they're out of step with the rest of the human race. You don't know how lucky you are that I'm normal."

"If you'd been acting like this when we met, I'd still be running."

"She's not so bad, and underneath it all, I think she's quite sane."

"I'll take your word for it."

"I just need to get the hang of how she's thinking."

"It's up to you, then. I'll just stand here and watch." Tevi leaned her shoulder against the wall.

"Thanks." Jemeryl gave an ironic grin and then sat in the chair opposite Ralieu's. She repeated the question she had asked before. "Why did you design the morphology?"

"The gardener was upset."

"What was he upset about?"

"Lots of things. The cabbages. His daughter. The slugs."

"Did the morphology have anything to do with something upsetting the gardener?"

"Yes, of course. His daughter was murdered, you know. Ralieu had to do something about it."

"The morphology was going to help the gardener deal with his daughter's murder?"

Ralieu looked sad. "No. Nothing could be done. She was dead, and he is too."

Tevi could sense Jemeryl's frustration, although her face stayed placid. "Why design the morphology? What was it going to achieve?"

"The gardener was a good man. Ralieu wanted to help."

"You were trying to stop him being upset?"

"I was trying to upset the murderer. He needed it. The murderer had something missing in his mind." Ralieu traced the outline of her

The High Priest and the Idol

own skull with both hands, as if to illustrate. "Ralieu knows she doesn't think the same as other people, but she cares when her friends are unhappy. She feels guilt."

Is she guilty about the people she bricked up? Tevi wondered.

"The morphology was going to make people feel guilty?"

Ralieu relaxed back in her chair, smiling broadly. "Yes. That's it precisely." She drew a pattern in the air. "You see it there in the skein? The confluence in the fifth dimension that ties us all together? The murderer wasn't attached. He couldn't feel other people's unhappiness."

Tevi pushed away from the wall. Maybe Jemeryl was right and there was some sort of sense to be found in the ancient sorcerer. "Jem, is she saying regret and sympathy are caused by magic?"

Jemeryl was frowning as she watched Ralieu's fingers weave shapes. Maybe to a sorcerer there was some significance in the gesture.

"Jem?"

"Not exactly. It's empathy rather than sympathy, and I've never quite thought of it as a by-product of the skein, but..." Jemeryl's face twisted in a grimace of deep concentration. "She might have a point if she's subsuming it with the tangential sixth-dimensional persona."

Tevi assumed that was some sort of a yes. She moved into Ralieu's line of sight. "That was the mind control you were working on? You wanted everyone to feel empathy for others?"

Ralieu scrambled eagerly from her chair, hurried over, and then bent down to examine the stitching on Tevi's waistband. Tevi met Jemeryl's eyes, raising both hands in a gesture of helplessness. Talking about the elderly woman as if she were not there seemed impolite, but addressing her directly obviously required some special sorcerer talent.

"Jem, do you know if that's what she was doing?"

"I think so."

"Was she allowed to?"

"No. Any sort of mental manipulation requires the subject's informed consent."

"Stupid. Stupid. Stupid." Ralieu spoke angrily. At first Tevi assumed the outburst was criticising some aspect of her clothing. However, Ralieu was now glaring at Jemeryl. "Stupid rules. Being cured of unkindness, nobody has the right to refuse consent for that.

Ralieu isn't talking about freedom of thought. People can think what they want, but they need the right alignment in their head to do the thinking with. People can't think with a defective mind."

"Who gets to say what's defective?" Tevi asked. To her surprise, this time, she was answered.

"It's a defect when you murder a child and feel no guilt."

"People like to think they're responsible for what they do. They can choose whether they're a good or a bad person."

Ralieu plonked herself back in her chair, and stared at Tevi. "When they were born, they didn't get to choose whether they fit in the skein like this"—Ralieu stabbed at the air at if pointing something out—"or like this. So where does choice come into it?"

"They have the right to say no to you changing them."

"People would only say no because they're misaligned. With the morphology they would want to say yes. Then we'd have their consent."

"You can't backdate consent."

"Yes, I can. The girl didn't consent to be murdered. I'll backdate that. Like the backstitching on your belt."

Tevi shook her head, giving up. Ralieu was half making sense, but it was never going to be a coherent discussion.

Jemeryl took over. "The morphology didn't work as you wanted, did it?"

"Yes, it did."

"It affects magic, not morality."

"Only after Ralieu modified it."

Jemeryl frowned. "It was affecting empathy, but you changed it to affect magic?"

"I had to."

"Why?"

"The morphology affected everyone."

"What was the problem?"

"The empathy was overwhelming. Even sorcerers were affected. That was the problem."

"In what way?"

"Sometimes a leader has to make decisions that hurt people. Once the morphology covered the entire Protectorate, Coven sorcerers wouldn't be able to make independent judgements. How would the

Guardian rule? Ralieu tried to modify the morphology so it wouldn't affect people who could access the higher dimensions. But she got the aural conjunction transposed. Instead of using associations on the upper dimensions as neutral nodes, it severed them, and the empathic confluence was lost in the cross-stream."

The second half of Ralieu's explanation was gobbledegook to Tevi, but the first half she understood very clearly. "What you mean is that although you expect ungifted people to be quite happy to lose their freedom of thought, you won't stand for it as a sorcerer."

"We have responsibility."

"And you want to be responsible for what you do." Tevi felt anger bubbling inside her.

"Want is not the issue. We are responsible."

"And people like me aren't?"

"Not as much, and there aren't the same benefits for us."

"Benefits?"

"We aren't so vulnerable. We can choose not to be murdered. If Ralieu was an ordinary person, at the mercy of all the dangers the ungifted face, she'd be happy for the morphology to shield her."

"You're sure about that?"

"Of course."

Tevi gave up. She had met enough sorcerers, of sounder mind than Ralieu, who could not be persuaded that the ungifted valued their freedom as much as any member of the Coven.

"Ralieu made a stupid mistake in her modification, and when she tested it…" The old sorcerer went back to tracing the wood grain on her armrest, but continued talking, her voice soft, sorrowful. "Ralieu saw the convicts kill Eli. He was still stunned by the morphology enveloping him. Hirn was on the far side of the room. Ralieu beckoned to him, but the convicts had him cornered. He looked at Ralieu. Hirn had been her gardener for years. He loved flowers and his daughter was dead. But there was nothing Ralieu could do. She bustled Ciamon from the room. He was standing there, useless." Tears filled her eyes.

"Alendy said you checked the fifth dimension for life signs."

"Only two left. But then…but…maybe Hirn was one of them."

Jemeryl looked surprised. "If you thought of that, why didn't you send for guards? If nothing else they could have arrested his killers."

"A silly, silly mistake."

"Which bit?"

"The morphology. How could Ralieu have been so careless? She'd got it all wrong. The empathy was snared in the second harmonic. In the aftermath, for a while, Ralieu lost her alignment with the skein. She was so angry. All she could think about was revenge. That's why she ordered the door bricked up. She didn't know what she was doing until it was too late. Now she looks back, it was awful, to not have her own mind."

Except if you were one of the ungifted, in which case you'd have welcomed it. Tevi made enough sense of Ralieu's explanation to spot the hypocrisy.

"But Ralieu now knows exactly what she did wrong with the morphology. She wanted to sort out the problem and try again, But Alendy won't let her." The old woman wiped her eyes. "The world would have been so much better and kinder, but it will never happen."

Tevi groaned. The worst of it was that Ralieu, like Ciamon, had meant well. She turned, about to go, but Jemeryl had more questions. "What sort of protection did the emanator have?"

"None. Who'd have harmed it?"

"Ciamon copied your work."

"Copied! The thief stole all Ralieu's notebooks. Ten years of research."

Jemeryl leaned forward. "Were there any powerful defensive spells in them?"

"Ralieu found a way to keep slugs off the cabbages. That made the gardener happy...before his daughter was murdered," Ralieu ended sadly.

"No. I mean a way to protect the emanator from harm, so nobody could attack it."

Ralieu shook her head. "No, that was never Ralieu's interest. You should talk to Weilan. He's made a great study of those sort of things."

❖

The main council chamber was less full than before, but even so, over four dozen people were present. The sorcerer who had questioned Ralieu about the construction of the emanator was concluding her report—or Tevi hoped this was the case. As far as she was concerned it had been a tedious hour filled with incomprehensible descriptions of tensors, fluxes, and ordinances.

Tevi leaned a little closer to Jemeryl and whispered, "I'm hoping all that made sense to you."

"Yes, it did. And it explained something that had puzzled me."

"What?"

"When I was captured at the oasis. The way the arrival of the sentinels coincided with me being suddenly overwhelmed. But the emanation is not only powered by auras, it constructs the morphology around them."

"And that tells you something interesting?"

"It tells me the patrol of sentinels formed a localised focus that strengthened the morphology around them."

"Oh yes. Silly of me not to have spotted it."

Grinning, Jemeryl barged Tevi gently with her shoulder. "You didn't have to be here, remember?"

Weilan approached the lectern. "I've constructed four Illaniam pentagrams, and infused them with a sixth-dimensional extinguishing sequence in a Basid array. I imagine some of you won't fully understand all this entails." He paused. "In which case you should look it up in the library, because I can't be bothered explaining it. I'll just show you how it works, then we can all go and do something useful."

Tevi could have applauded.

Weilan gestured impatiently to his assistant, a young woman, who scurried into the middle of the council chamber carrying a canvas sack as long as her arm but only a few inches across. The assistant opened the tie and emptied the contents on the floor. Tevi leaned forward for a better view, although this left her none the wiser. The sack had held five black wooden poles, inscribed with white runes; five orange crystals, each mounted on a strange claw-like fixture; five short silver rods; and a stone talisman.

Fumbling a little in haste, the woman arranged the poles in a star, using the crystal claw mountings as clasps where the poles crossed. To finish, she slipped the silver rods through holes in the middle of each pole and into the talisman, like spokes on a wheel fixing the stone in place. She stood up, holding the device out before her. The assembly process had taken just over three minutes and the resulting pentagram was two feet across.

Weilan had watched his assistant critically. Tevi imagined that he was not an easy person to work for. Now he carried on with his explanation. "As I said, there are four of these pentagrams. The team needs to surround the idol with them. I've allowed for mishap. As long as three pentagrams are in place, they'll be sufficient to propagate the Illaniam field. The Basid array will then extinguish any sixth-dimensional confluences."

"How close will we need to be to the idol?" Jemeryl asked.

"Within thirty yards would be fine."

Jemeryl frowned. "They'll never let us carry them that near the idol."

"Lucky if they let us through the temple door." Tevi voiced her own objection.

"As my assistant demonstrated, you can assemble the pentagrams when you're inside the temple. The sacks are small enough to conceal under your clothes."

"Shall we sing a few songs and wave flags while we're doing it?"

Weilan glared at Tevi. "I leave any additional artistic displays to your discretion."

Jemeryl patted Tevi's leg. "We'll sort something out when we're there. Maybe we can break in at night, or your priests might provide a distraction for the sentinels."

Tevi did not think it would be quite so easy, but she had faith in Jemeryl.

Alendy now took the lectern. "The last thing is to announce the remaining members of the party. Would Ashkinet and Larric stand up."

Like everyone else in the chamber, Tevi looked at the two named sorcerers, although she remembered them both. She and Jemeryl had conducted a series of meetings with the many volunteers. The pair chosen had been a joint decision, ratified by Alendy.

Ashkinet was in her mid thirties. She was originally from one of the nomad tribes, although she had moved to Lyremouth at a young age and joined the Coven. Presumably she had not left due to any serious disagreement or rejection, and still felt a connection to the region of her birth. In the meeting, she had made it clear she was keen to help for the sake of her family. She was quiet and serious, with none of the rough humour Tevi had come to associate with the nomads.

Larric was far more outgoing. He was also younger, barely into his twenties. It was obvious that he admired Jemeryl greatly and was familiar with the work she had done with Bykoda. He even made a conspicuous show of being friendly to Tevi, either due to innate amiability or a respect for someone who had ridden a dragon. It was also obvious that he was ambitious and hoped the mission to Kradja would boost his career in the Coven.

Once everyone had finished studying the party members, Alendy signalled for them to sit. "For the final arrangements, I've commandeered a fast ship and crew that will be ready to leave on the dawn tide tomorrow. Our hopes go with you."

CHAPTER TEN—GOD OF DESTRUCTION

After twenty days, Jemeryl was still unsettled by the sight of Tevi with blond hair, a thin face, and blue eyes that were level with her own, even though it was her own magic that had wrought the change. The risk of them being recognised in Kradja had made the disguise necessary. Jemeryl suspected that her partner was finding it no easier to adjust to the new appearance she had given herself.

Jemeryl had cast a transforming spell while they were on the ship to Serac, to give them a chance to get accustomed to their new forms before they re-entered the region affected by the morphology. To minimise the adjustment, she had left their gender and approximate ages unchanged, but the new bodies still required getting used to.

Tevi was currently sitting opposite her in the wagon. Jemeryl studied the set of Tevi's shoulders, the way her hands moved as she talked, a twitch of her eyebrows. The familiar mannerisms on the unfamiliar body were disconcerting. The disguise could not be undone until the idol was destroyed and the ability to work magic returned, but if everything went to plan, that would not be long. Kradja was less than a mile away. The caravan had nearly finished its journey across the desert.

She and Tevi were in the second to last wagon, with Larric and Ashkinet beside them. The rest of the seats were packed with zealous pilgrims and aspirant warriors, eager to join the new holy army. The floor well between the rows of seats was piled with baggage. As transport went, it had been one of the worst journeys Jemeryl had ever endured. Dust and heat had made the cramped conditions all the more unbearable.

However, what had really tested her was the incessant, inane babbling of her fellow travellers. The nearer they got to Kradja, the worse it had become. If Jemeryl still had the ability to access the higher dimensions, she would have been desperately tempted to cast a spell of silence on them, regardless of what Coven rules said about the treatment of the ungifted.

Suddenly, as if her wish had been answered, a hush fell on the wagon. Jemeryl broke from her contemplation of Tevi's appearance. The cause was easy to spot. The final few hundred yards of the road into Kradja were lined with a row of gibbets, each one exhibiting a rotting corpse. The bodies were sun blackened and pecked by birds, their desiccated lips pulled back into an obscene parody of a smile. Jemeryl felt her stomach make a dry heave. She clamped her hand to her mouth, fighting back the nausea. One of the other passengers was not so successful, although luckily he was able to get his head over the side of the wagon first.

"Unbelievers," a stony-faced pilgrim muttered.

The word was taken up by others, as if no other justification of the executions was needed.

Sentinels were stationed around the bases of the gibbets. Jemeryl did not need Tevi's professional opinion to know that the military quality of Sefriall's soldiers had fallen yet lower. They lounged around, jeering at onlookers, acting and sounding like a rabble. Nothing but the red cloaks marked them as a unified force, and even these were of varying style and hue. Sefriall must be recruiting anyone who volunteered to join her army and be running low on supplies to equip them. Any enterprising merchant with a stock of cloth and red dye would be doing a lively trade.

The wagons rolled on into Kradja, exchanging the last of the gibbets for crumbling terraces of mud brick houses. The streets were busy. The drone of chanting came from small groups clustered on corners. Not all chanters were concentrating on their prayers. Many directed anxious sideways glances around, while others, their eyes hard and hostile, tracked the new arrivals. More inhabitants scurried along, heads down, as if not wanting to attract attention.

Jemeryl had little previous experience of the town to make a comparison with, but surely the air of fear and watchfulness was new.

Tevi had spoken of a pot about to boil over. This was a plague house. The inhabitants were gripped by the same desperate hope and gnawing fear, while all the time waiting to see who would be the next to succumb. Underlying it all was the pall of sickness.

Nearer to the centre of town, the state of the buildings improved, but the mood of the population was unchanged. The passengers disgorged into the central market square as soon as the caravan stopped.

Tevi tapped Jemeryl's arm. "Come. Let's see the idol."

"Oh yes. I can't wait," Larric added.

Their voices aped the fervour of their fellow travellers. Jemeryl forced herself to smile and nod enthusiastically. They had to act like pilgrims, although she would have liked nothing better than to find a quiet room where she could shut out the insanity and the sickness.

Signs of Sefriall's takeover were obvious, even before they entered the temple. The number of sentinels on duty had trebled, and the walls were daubed with a design made up of three linked circles enclosed inside a larger one. Many of the pilgrims swarming over the temple grounds wore similar medallions. Jemeryl guessed it was a symbol of the Cyclian gods.

Banners carrying the same circular sign decorated the main hall. The once vacant alcoves around the perimeter now held statues. The repeated images were of a pregnant woman in green carrying a hammer, a man with a red cloak and a scythe, and someone of indeterminate gender dressed in blue, holding a burning torch. Doubtless these were representations of the three Cyclian gods.

The alcoves also held paintings and tapestries, silver incense burners, offering bowls, and other works of art. These ornaments were all of a far higher workmanship than the statues themselves which, once Jemeryl got close enough to examine, looked to have been roughly hacked into shape and slapped with paint.

Tevi, at her shoulder, asked softly, "Why didn't they bring back the original idols? There were enough of them when I was first here. These look like someone knocked them out in a rush."

"Ciamon must have destroyed all the other idols when he took over. Besides, nobody is looking at them. They can't compete with the glamour."

This was certainly the case. Ciamon's idol still claimed the centre of the floor, surrounded by the enraptured hordes. However, Sefriall had put the mark of her gods on this as well. Now a scythe lay across the idol's outstretched arms, and a red toga had been draped over its torso. Hung around its neck was a medallion in the form of the Cyclian symbol.

"Sefriall has turned Ciamon's god into Toqwani," Tevi whispered.

"Looks like it."

"I wonder what the pilgrims will make of it. This wasn't what they thought they were coming to."

"Do you think any of them had a clear enough idea to know what to expect? They just want something to get fanatical over. The glamour is all Sefriall needs."

Larric's eyes had also been fixed on the idol. He now sidled closer and spoke in an undertone. "So this is what magic feels like to the ungifted." He grimaced. "It's odd. I know it's just a projection, but I can't duck around it. And I sort of like the feeling, though I don't want to."

"I know what you mean." Even standing some way back, Jemeryl could feel the waves of love and joy washing over her. Surrendering to the happiness was so tempting.

Instead, Jemeryl retreated further and looked around. The main hall was full of people, both worshippers and sentinels, surging back and forth in constant flux. Despite the crowds, getting within thirty yards of the idol ought to be easy enough, although assembling the pentagrams without attracting attention would be impossible.

"What are you thinking?" Tevi asked.

"That breaking in at night is going to be our best bet."

"Maybe."

"My other thought is that I'd really like to get out of the crowds and find a nice quiet room somewhere." Jemeryl linked her arm through Tevi's. "Is there anywhere in town you'd recommend for lodgings?"

"Four Winds House would be fine." Tevi's lips formed the familiar smile, which looked so strange on her new face. "It's not as if Raf's going to recognise me."

❖

"I've sorted out a room for you."

"Thanks."

"This way."

Raf's eager expression gave Tevi a bad feeling as she and the others followed the innkeeper across the courtyard. The number of people flooding into Kradja had clearly put a strain on lodging houses, and Raf was making the most of it. Whereas before, the inn had been mostly empty during the day, now dozens of guests were loitering in the shade.

The room turned out to be what Tevi remembered as being a storage cupboard, with barely enough space for the two narrow mattresses on the ground. Tevi eyed them critically. It was good that Larric and Ashkinet got on well together, since they were about to get a lot closer, and while snuggling up to Jemeryl was nice, if they both breathed out at the same time, the one on the edge would end up on the floor.

"It's a bit cramped but you won't be sharing with anyone else and you'll be together."

Tevi nodded. Apparently, her former room was currently occupied by eight people. The accommodation Raf had first offered involved splitting the group up and squeezing them in wherever she could find space. Fortunately, Alendy had not stinted on resources, and the prospect of money had prompted Raf to be more creative.

"How much is this?" Tevi asked.

"Six pennies a day."

Tevi grimaced. That was four times the charge of her previous stay, and Raf had not finished.

"Each. Payment ten days in advance."

It was blatant extortion. Regardless, Tevi agreed. "Done."

They needed privacy to make their plans and could easily afford it. In fact, they could afford a whole suite in the best hotel in Kradja, but dared not risk the attention this would attract. As long as Raf got her money, she would not ask questions. Tevi fished the coins from her purse and Raf toddled away, happy.

Jemeryl dumped her bag in a corner, and considered each of the walls in turn. "All right. Forget what I said about relaxing in a quiet room. Is there somewhere else we can go?"

"There's a tavern across the way."

"What's the beer like?" Larric asked.

"Passable, when I went with Siashe. The food wasn't bad either."

"So we're set for dinner."

Jemeryl smiled. "If we're lucky, we might pick up some gossip as well."

The second Tevi entered the tavern, she knew that luck was not going to be with them. The hard, suspicious scowls said it all. Strangers were no longer welcome. The staff even seemed unwilling to take their order and when the food and drink eventually arrived, Tevi found that the quality had deteriorated atrociously. Was it a sign of the changes in Kradja, or intended to discourage them from returning?

If that was the aim, it was not going to work on any mercenary as hungry as Tevi after her journey, although she was the first by a large margin in finishing her meal. "Another drink?"

Larric was the only one to nod.

Tevi made her way back across the tavern. Her effect on the clientele was unmistakable. As she passed, people became less animated and the flow of words became more guarded, if it did not stop altogether.

While waiting to be served, Tevi leaned her elbow on the bar and scanned the room, trying to act relaxed and disinterested. No one would meet her eyes, although several of the faces she remembered. If she had kept her true form, Tevi wondered, would people have recognised her as Siashe's friend, and been more forthcoming? Or would someone have turned her over to the sentinels in exchange for a reward? Even if it were possible to reveal her identity, the risk was not worth taking.

"I've heard Darjain is…"

The familiar name caught Tevi's ear, coming from a group huddled at the end of the bar. She tried not to show any reaction as she edged closer, but the speaker spotted her and clammed up.

Tevi desperately wanted to discover what had happened to the ex-priests. Now that Ciamon was gone, had they returned to the temple? This did not seem too likely, given that Parrash had been a turncoat, working for Sefriall. He would not have been her spy if she did not view the ousted priests as enemies.

Was it worth confronting the speaker at the bar and asking what he knew? Tevi's head sagged. The answer had to be no. If Darjain and the others were back in the temple then locating them would be pointless, since they were no longer a potential source of allies. And if they were opposed to Sefriall, then they would be in hiding. In which case, the man would not blurt out their whereabouts to a total stranger, even if he knew it.

"Are you sure you want another drink?" Jemeryl joined her at the bar, with Ashkinet.

"It's all a bit irrelevant since the staff are ignoring me."

"That's what I thought. We might as well go."

Tevi nodded. "I'll tell Larric."

It took a second to spot him at the other side of the room. Tevi liked Larric. Anyone would, with his charm and easy humour. Already the group of locals he had joined were smiling, their postures more relaxed and expansive. Someone said something and Larric threw back his head, laughing. Tevi had no way of assessing Larric's magical abilities, but with his ambition and his ability to win folk around, she predicted he had a great future ahead in the Coven.

"Actually, I think we might leave him here," Tevi said, changing her mind.

"You sure?" Jemeryl looked across the room. Her face showed enlightenment. "Oh. He seems to have found some new friends."

"He's the sort who always does."

The next time Larric glanced her way, Tevi gave a thumbs-up sign and headed for the door. He would know where to find them. She followed Jemeryl and Ashkinet from the tavern.

Two hours passed before Larric also returned to the Four Winds House, seeming none the worse for wear. Either he had been careful to watch his drink, or he had a good head for alcohol. Tevi was relieved. The last thing they wanted was someone getting careless in public.

"Did you learn anything?" Jemeryl asked.

"Oh yes. Lots. But I assume you're not interested in whose partner is having an affair, or which trader has a secret store of cheap opium for sale."

"Nothing else?"

"A few things." Larric dropped onto a mattress and stretched out his legs. "From our point of view the most crucial was from a woman whose sister works in the temple. Apparently the sentinels stand vigil over the idol all night long. So it means breaking in after dark won't help. We'd be even more conspicuous than during the day. There won't even be crowds to merge into."

"Why do they do it?" Ashkinet asked.

"Piety?"

Tevi pursed her lips. "Or addiction. The way the glamour feels, they probably have to fight off the volunteers."

Beside her, Jemeryl sighed. "Right. Plan two. We get someone to create a diversion. Did you pick up anything of use there?"

"I think so. Two groups actually." Larric turned to Ashkinet. "Have you noticed there aren't many nomads in town?"

She nodded. "Yes. And I've been getting odd looks."

"There's been big trouble. Sefriall has forbidden the worship of any gods other than hers in the whole town, not just the temple."

"My people would never forsake Yalaish."

"Precisely. There were running battles in town between nomads and sentinels. The sentinels mostly won, so the nomads withdrew to the desert, where they've got the advantage."

Tevi eyed Ashkinet in concern. With her coppery skin and fair hair, she was clearly from the desert tribes. "Do you think it's safe for her to be in town? Does she need a disguise?"

Larric shook his head. "She should be all right. A few have stayed, like Raf. The ones who've given up on Yalaish. Maybe she could learn some Cyclian prayers to mutter when the sentinels are around."

"I'll do it."

Tevi suspected the suggestion had been light-hearted on Larric's part, although Ashkinet had taken it seriously. She resolved to pick up the makings of a disguise anyway, just in case it was needed.

Jemeryl looked thoughtful. "It sounds like the nomads would be keen to help us, if we can contact them."

"That's why I mentioned them." Larric smiled. "I've also found out a bit about the old priests."

"Are they safe?" Tevi asked.

"Some are. Some we saw on the way in, hanging from the gibbets."

"Have you heard about Darjain?"

"I didn't get names and if anyone knows where the ones who escaped are, they weren't saying." Larric frowned. "I don't blame them. It's got very nasty. That's most of what I heard. People being denounced. Rounded up. Getting a five-second trial before they're hanged, if they're lucky. Mostly, the sentinels don't bother and kill them on the spot. There were rumours about spies and paid informers—as in, if you don't pay them, they'll inform on you, regardless of whether you're an unbeliever or not."

"Anything else?" Jemeryl asked.

"Nothing that will help us."

"You've done well."

Larric smiled at the praise. "Thanks."

"Tomorrow." Jemeryl chewed her lip for a few seconds before continuing. "I'll spend the day in the temple, working out the schedule. When guards change. Details like that. Ashkinet will try to contact the nomads and Tevi will hunt for the ex-priests. Larric—you can just go from bar to bar. See what you can pick up."

"My dream assignment."

"But for now, we need more practice at the pentagrams. Speed will be vital."

Tevi nodded and reached for the bag in the corner. On the voyage, and any other chance since, they had taken turns to practise. All had grown proficient and could assemble the parts by the count of twenty, a fraction of the time it had taken Weilan's assistant. Tevi just hoped they would get that long. How good would the diversion be?

❖

Tevi sauntered along the street, acting like a pilgrim with time on her hands. From the outside, the bakery belonging to Parrash's sister looked the same as before, although the flow of customers through the door had dropped to nothing. Presumably, the sister had been involved in the plot, and so had not been accused of harbouring the deposed priests. However, word must have leaked and the association with Sefriall's spies was enough to scare customers away. Tevi felt that it fell short, as far as poetic justice went, but was better than nothing.

As she reached the open door, Tevi peered inside while trying not to appear too interested. Would she attract attention if she went in, given the way everyone else was avoiding the shop? Surely a stranger in town would not know the background, and might well see the lack of a queue as a bonus. Her mind made up, Tevi changed direction.

The shop owner was not around and the only person serving was a boy of about fourteen. Tevi guessed he was either Parrash's nephew or younger brother.

"Can I help?" The boy looked inordinately pleased to see her. If business did not improve soon, his family was going to be out of work.

"Yeah. Got any meat pies? Something I can take away for lunch?"

"Sure. The best in town."

If the pie that Tevi ended up with was the best, she could only dread the worst Kradja had to offer. The crust was stale and dry, easily two days old. Tevi decided not to put it to a taste test. If it had been sitting around for that long in the desert heat, the filling would be off. She could understand that, with slow sales, baking fresh food every day might be uneconomical, but poisoning the few remaining customers was a poor long-term sales strategy.

Tevi tossed the inedible pie onto a pile of refuse accumulating in the rear alleyway, while feeling a twinge of pity for any stray dog that might be desperate enough to scavenge it. Yet although her visit had failed to provide lunch, it had not been a waste of time. She had seen and heard enough to know that the bakery was not working normally. No voices or other sounds had came from the rear rooms and the temperature in the building made it clear that the ovens were cold. Sneaking into the cellar would not be without risk, but neither was it unacceptably dangerous.

Tevi looked around. The narrow alley was deserted. Several buildings overlooked the back of the bakery, but no faces peered through windows and with the evident unpopularity of the baker, the chances were good that anyone breaking in would not be reported, even if spotted. She pressed her ear against the cellar door. Judging by the total silence, nobody was on the other side. However, as expected, the door was locked. Anything else would have been too much to hope for.

The door itself and the wooden frame were of indifferent construction, and the state of repair was poor. With Tevi's potion-enhanced strength, kicking it down would be easy, but not without making enough noise to alert the shop assistant, as well as everyone else in the neighbourhood. She needed another way in.

Tevi took a step back. The bakery had no ground-floor windows, and those on the upper floor all had closed shutters. These would be hard to reach without a ladder, and most likely were bolted on the inside, anyway. Another step back and Tevi's gaze went still higher, to the top of the building. Like every other mud brick dwelling in Kradja, the roof was flat, surrounded by a low parapet. Tevi nodded. That was the place to start. She left the alley.

In under an hour, Tevi was back, carrying a small bag over her shoulder. The alley was as quiet and deserted as before. Tevi took a moment for a last quick look around and then pulled out a length of rope and a grappling iron. Within seconds, she was on the roof and the rope and iron were back in the bag. Anyone spotting her now would have no way of knowing that she was not supposed to be there.

As Tevi had hoped, the trapdoor in the corner was flung open, possibly out of habit. When the ovens were going, the rooftop exit would be used to vent heat from the building. A short ladder was in place, protruding slightly through the opening. Tevi crouched by the hatch, listening intently, but for all she could hear, the bakery might have been totally deserted.

Stealthily, Tevi climbed down the ladder to a landing at the top of a twisting flight of stairs. The three doorways around her were all closed. No sound of movement came from any of them. The stairs were old and warped, but she had no option. Descending them, Tevi transferred her weight from foot to foot as gradually as she could, keeping to the edge of the steps to avoid creaks. Twice the wood groaned under her, making her pulse race, but no challenge came.

At last, Tevi reached the ground floor. A short passageway provided a view straight through the shop to the street door, where the young shop assistant was leaning against the jamb, staring out, most likely in the hope of spotting customers. Two more doorways opened on either side of the passage. Voices rumbled indistinctly on the left, but luckily the entrance to the cellar was on the right of the building. Carefully, Tevi inched open the door, ready to flee. If it came to it, she was sure she would have no problem bowling over the boy in the doorway.

A pair of cold ovens filled the rear of the room, a bare table occupied the middle, and a huge mixing urn stood in a corner, but apart from this, the room was empty. The trapdoor to the cellar was closed but unlocked. Tevi descended the final flight of stairs.

The first thing was to secure her escape route. The door to the alley was bolted top and bottom. Tevi slid the blots back and pulled the door open wide. Not only could she be off the instant she heard anyone enter the room above, but the light in the cellar was greatly improved to conduct a search.

Unfortunately, the light did not help. After a wasted half hour of scouring the cellar, Tevi slumped on the floor, resting her back against the wall, and looked around despondently. Was there anything she had missed? The piles of bedrolls and other belongings had gone, along with any indication that the priests had ever been there. No notes, no papers, and no clues as to what had happened. Was it a good sign that there were also no blood stains? How many had escaped?

To Tevi's left, between her and the door, a wooden crate was shoved haphazardly away from the wall. The top was covered with a fine layer of flour, scuffed and scraped where it had been used as a table. Tevi had already checked it carefully, but now her eyes were level with the top, the oblique light picked up a previously missed imprint in the flour. Tevi shifted to her knees and got closer.

The overall outline was a soft-edged cone, about as long as her hand, with a small detailed design in the middle. Tevi twisted her neck to view it the right way up. The picture was a sunburst with a stylised antelope leaping over it. The heraldic nature made Tevi sure it was some sort of crest, and she was equally sure she knew what had caused it. At the meeting, Darjain had passed around a silver teardrop-shaped flask, filled with fine brandy, and had then had put the flask down on the crate.

Darjain was the leader of the group. He was also an old man, ill equipped to living in the cramped and primitive conditions of the cellar. If a devout supporter was offering better accommodation, surely Darjain would have had first claim on it. The fine brandy and silver flask certainly had not come from the bakery. It was more likely that Darjain had been staying with a wealthy benefactor. In which case, the flask would be from his supporter, and the symbol would be the family crest.

Tevi again squinted at the design. It was the nearest thing to a lead that she had, but was she reading too much into it? For completeness, she made one last circuit of the room, to be sure she had overlooked nothing, and then left, pulling the cellar door shut behind her.

The north of Kradja was the wealthy side of town, where mansions were enclosed in their own small estates. The families who lived there were rich, with high walls and armed guards outside their doors. Yet even they were not immune to the fear and sickness infecting Kradja. Tevi could sense it in the shuttered windows and edgy manner of the guards. While money gave the veneer of security, it might also make them a target. Presumably Sefriall was paying her sentinels with something. What would she do when the money ran out?

The midafternoon sun was high overhead, beating down and leaving little in the way of shade. Tevi walked along a wide street, lined on either side by heavy stone walls. No mud bricks here. She passed a wrought iron gateway, manned by more of the liveried guards bearing huge spiked halberds, twice as tall as themselves. Through the bars she caught a glimpse of palm trees, ferns, and exotic flowers. The guards eyed her suspiciously but made no other move. Their bearing and alertness was vastly more professional than that of the sentinels. Yet walls, halberds, and guards would be no defence against the hundreds who would attack, if Sefriall gave the order.

Tevi turned a corner. Midway along the street opposite was another iron gateway, but this was unguarded and open. As Tevi watched, two women dressed in the scruffy clothes of homeless pilgrims sauntered out and headed off down the road, arm in arm. It was hard to imagine what legitimate business they could have in the mansion. The pair were certainly not the owners, or their servants, or tradesfolk, but their manner was not that of thieves. Tevi walked up to the gateway.

The garden inside had been trampled and delicate plants uprooted. Wherever space allowed, crude shelters had been constructed from fronds stripped from the palm trees. A dozen or more people were in the ravaged garden, dressed similarly to the two women who had left. Most were sprawled in the shade, talking. One was cooking over a fire. An ornate fountain occupied the centre of the area. Water still cascaded from the mouths of twin lions, but the stone bodies had been daubed with the Cyclian symbol. A couple of young children were splashing in the pool, squealing as they ran through the spray.

On the opposite side of the garden was a manor house, graceful and prosperous, except the glass windows had been shattered and the doorway battered down. More Cyclian symbols were in evidence. Clearly this well-off family had already fallen foul of Sefriall. Her sentinels had attacked and pillaged the property and now it was home for the pilgrims flooding into Kradja. Even in its current state, it was better than sleeping on the street as many others were doing.

But who were the ousted family, and what had they done? Tevi could make a guess but she wanted proof—which did not take long to find, once she reached the house. Chiselled in the stonework over the entrance was a crest. Despite the Cyclian symbol painted over it, the antelope leaping over the rising sun was unmistakable.

Of course Parrash had known who was providing shelter and support for Darjain and his followers. The family and everyone else in the house would have been arrested within hours of Sefriall returning to Kradja. Tevi pouted. She had been wasting her time.

"The Calequirals." A voice spoke at Tevi's shoulder.

She glanced around. An elderly man had wandered over. Possibly he was one of Sefriall's informers checking her out, or maybe he just wanted someone to talk to. In either case, admitting ignorance ought to be safe.

"I'm new in town. The Calec…um. What did you say?"

"Calequirals."

"Did they used to live here?"

"Yes."

Tevi pointed at the design over the door. "Was that their family crest?"

"I suppose so."

"What happened to them?"

"They worshipped Yalaish. They'd been in Kradja for generations, but reckoned they had nomad roots. Wouldn't swap to the true faith."

"I hope the sentinels got them all." Tevi tried to put some vehemence into her voice.

The man spat at the ground. "Nah. Not with their money. They'd paid off someone, so they got word. Most escaped. Now they're out in the desert somewhere, with the other unbelievers."

"Their time will come. You'll see."

"Trust on it." The man patted her arm and wandered away.

Tevi again stared up at the leaping antelope. Maybe she had not been wasting her time after all.

❖

Jemeryl could count over twenty sentinels in the temple, and at least ten times that many worshippers, gathered around the idol in adoration. The eyes of those nearest to it were glazed over, lost in the rapture. Jemeryl could well understand it. The allure was overwhelming, even though she was keeping as far back as possible without seeming conspicuous.

The effect grew stronger the longer and closer the person stood by the idol, until all thought was washed away by the sea of love. None were immune, including the sentinels, as Jemeryl noted thoughtfully. This might prove useful to their plans. If she and the others timed their attack towards the end of a period of sentry duty, the sentinels nearest would be dazed and slow to react. Those around the edge of the main hall would be quicker, but they would also have further to travel, and they would have to plough through a field of worshippers.

From what Jemeryl had seen, the number of pilgrims increased throughout the day. Many would arrive intending only a quick visit, to pray or just gaze on the idol for a few minutes, but the weakest willed would be ensnared, and not leave until the sentinels bundled them out at dusk. Adding it all up, Jemeryl reckoned the best time to make their attack would be just before the end of the day, when the sentinels would be in a stupor and the largest number of entranced bodies would be in their way. She paused, chewing her lip. Or maybe just before the last changeover of sentries. Surely at the very end of the day, extra sentinels would be drafted in to help clear the mindless worshippers from the hall.

Mindless.

A shudder of revulsion gave Jemeryl gooseflesh as she looked at the people around her. The worst thing was that she could so easily give in and join them. She loved the idol. She could not help it. As with the first time she had come under the spell, the sense of helplessness was awful, but now there was an added edge. Before, the glamour had been the work of Ciamon, a good man, a friend, a sometime lover. Now it was bolstering the power of Sefriall, a murderer who wanted to impose her remorseless theocracy on the world.

Did the citizens of the Protectorate feel the same about magic? Did it all come down to trust? Did the citizens trust the Coven? And how much of her trust in Ciamon was purely personal, in defiance of the truth? For all his condemnation of the Coven, he had abused the power of magic in ways Protectorate laws utterly forbade. In his actions, he had shown contempt for the freedom he had espoused. Jemeryl bowed her head to hide the tears. But he had not deserved to die.

The sound of marching broke into Jemeryl's thoughts. Her head shot up. What time was it? How long had she been standing there? She turned her head, looking through the open doors. Judging by the length of the shadows, she had lost the better part of an hour. She had to move away.

The marching had been the arrival of a fresh deployment of sentries. The newly arrived sentinels were rousing their comrades, while one wearing more gold braid than the rest snapped orders. This must be the last change of the day. Another two hours would bring dusk and time for the temple to close. The crowds around her had thickened while she had been in her glamour-induced daze. Jemeryl backed away from the idol towards the exit. Regardless of whether she might learn more by staying, she could not bear the thought of falling under its spell again.

The air on the temple steps was dry and dusty, but blessedly free of cloying incense. Jemeryl took a deep breath, hoping to clear her head and inject some sharpness to her thoughts. The day had been moderately productive. Now it was time to return to Four Winds House and see what the others had discovered.

Only Ashkinet was in the tiny room when she arrived. "Anything to report?" Jemeryl asked.

"No, alas. Most nomads have left the city and those who remain are the ones who've renounced their faith in Yalaish, so they won't be ready recruits for us."

"Any idea where the rest might be?"

"Oases are dotted across the desert, some known only by my kin."

"Do you know how to find any?"

"I know an important one is nearby, but as for finding it…" Ashkinet shook her head regretfully. "I was only a child when I went to Lyremouth, no older than eight. My parents could see I had magical ability and thought I'd have a better life with the Coven."

"They sent you on your own?"

"No. They went with me, but my mother always missed the desert. They returned when I was old enough not to need them so much. I've only seen them once since. I visited just after I became a sorcerer. But I hope, once this business with the idol is done, to spend a while here." Ashkinet gave the broadest smile Jemeryl had yet seen from her. "We exchange letters and I understand my baby brother has made me an aunt."

"I'm sure you'll—" The door opening interrupted Jemeryl. Larric ambled in and collapsed on a mattress. She smiled at him. "How's your day gone?"

"I've discovered Kradja brews some of the worst beer I've ever had the misfortune to taste. I guess conditions here aren't ideal." He grinned. "But that isn't what you want to know."

"Not right now."

"I've picked up bits and pieces. The most interesting was from a blacksmith's apprentice. She and her master had been summoned to the temple by Sefriall."

"Why?"

"Some problem with a locked door. Anyway, they weren't able to open it, and mostly the apprentice was angling for sympathy over the threats they got. She thought they were going to end up decorating the road into town. But Sefriall got distracted by a messenger charging in with news about a battle with the nomads."

"Who won?"

"The nomads mostly. They'd holed up in some caves."

Ashkinet spoke up. "Yes. The oasis I told you about has caves behind it. Well defended."

Larric continued. "Apparently so. The report was about how many sentinels died trying to storm them. But then Sefriall remembered her audience and dismissed them, so the apprentice escaped the gibbet."

"The nomads are really going to hate Sefriall." Before Jemeryl could say more, the sound of footsteps outside caught her attention.

The door opened for Tevi. "I see I'm last."

"We haven't been back long. Have you learned anything?"

"I know where some priests are. They'd been sheltering with a family called the Calequirals."

"I've heard about them," Larric said, nodding. "They fled with the nomads."

"Great. If we find the nomads, we'll reach the priests as well."

"It's not that easy." Quickly, Jemeryl recapped what had been said so far. "Even if we find this oasis, it might be under siege," she finished.

Tevi shook her head. "With a well-trained army, I wouldn't rate my chances taking on the nomads in the desert, and the sentinels are a long way from well trained. If they set up camp, they'll be sitting targets for hit-and-run skirmishers. They'd lose a tenth of their number every night."

"So if only we knew where this oasis was, we'd be all set," Jemeryl said, sighing. "We can't really ask around."

Tevi smiled. "Would it cheer you up if I said I know how to get there?"

"How?"

"On the way here, the first time, my guide pointed it out."

CHAPTER ELEVEN—THE POISONED TEAR

From a distance, the oasis was an enticing patch of lush green amid the sand. This impression did not last. Before they had got within half a mile, Jemeryl could spot the mutilated trees and trampled bushes, and the closer they got, the more evident the destruction became. Short of chopping all the palms down, someone had inflicted as much damage as they could on the oasis.

Even so, Jemeryl was anxious to get there for a chance to rest. Either a lone wagon or four people riding out of town on horseback would have been too conspicuous and Tevi had been sure the distance was perfectly feasible to cover in two days on foot. In this Tevi had been technically correct, but Jemeryl was aware her shoulders were chafed by the straps of her backpack, blisters stung her heels where sand had leaked into her shoes, and her throat was rasped raw from gasping in hot air. At night, the temperature in the open desert had dropped so sharply that even when she was wrapped around Tevi, the chill had seeped into her bones. The wagon journey to Kradja had been idyllic by comparison.

At her side, Ashkinet's progress was getting noticeably uneven. At first, Jemeryl assumed it was due to fatigue. When the footsteps finally stopped, she turned, about to offer words of encouragement. However, the expression on Ashkinet's face was not exhaustion but outrage, verging on horror.

"Who…they…how dare they?" Ashkinet looked stunned.

Jemeryl walked back to her. "Are you all right?"

Ashkinet's eyes stared through Jemeryl, locked on the vandalised oasis. "This is where Yalaish's first tear fell to earth. It's a sacred site. A holy site. How dare anyone defile it?"

"It mightn't have been deliberate. A battle was fought here. Things get damaged if they're in the way."

"No. This was done on purpose. Look." Ashkinet held out an arm, pointing. "The lilies are dead. The water's been poisoned. That doesn't happen in a battle." Her tone hardened. "There will be blood spilt for this. You may count on it."

Ashkinet brushed past Jemeryl and marched the last hundred yards to the water's edge. The truth of her words was undeniable. The water stank and had a dull, oily surface. The bottom was obscured, but flashes of pallid silver showed where it was littered with the rotting bodies of dead fish. Reeds had been ripped up by the roots and cast aside. Their decomposing leaves added to the stench. On the far side of the pool, a rock face rose sheer from the water. Daubed on it in blood-red paint was a huge Cyclian symbol.

Tears were in Ashkinet's eyes as she knelt beside the water. "My parents brought me here before we left for Lyremouth. They wanted me to see it. I think they also wanted to say good-bye. It was beautiful, peaceful. The water was clear, like liquid light." She swallowed. "With all I've learned since, I know my people's beliefs are false. Yalaish is not real. Yet I remembered this place and it's always been…" She waved her hands, searching for words. "Home in my heart. To see it now…" Her hands tightened in fists. "Sefriall is insane to have done this. Insane. And she will pay. My people will see to it. Blood will fall."

Jemeryl knelt beside her. "When the idol's gone, we can put it right. We'll have our power back. It'll be simple."

Ashkinet met Jemeryl's eyes. "Not simple. Restored isn't the same as never defiled."

No easy words came to Jemeryl. She patted Ashkinet's shoulder and stood awkwardly.

The oasis was situated at the mouth of a valley. On either side, twin ridges of rock broke through the sand, getting higher, until they merged in a mountainous crest to the north. The old red stone was pockmarked and crisscrossed with ravines, evidence of countless sandstorms that had left the peak a scarred finger, pointing at the cloudless sky.

Tevi was standing a few yards away. Jemeryl joined her and pointed to the mountain. "That must be where the caves are."

"Yup."

"When Ashkinet is ready to move, we'll head there. See if we can find anyone."

"It won't be necessary. They're coming to find us."

"What?" Jemeryl dropped her gaze from the peak. The valley ahead was empty, but on either side, a score or more of figures now lined the ridges—warriors, judging by the weapons in their hands. "Oh. Right. Do you think they'll listen to us before they attack?"

"They should do. It's obvious we're not sentinels. If they get a good look at Ashkinet, they'll see she's one of them."

"Shall I tell her she's needed?"

"They aren't charging towards us, so there's no rush. And her gut reaction is probably going to sit well with them." Tevi grinned and whispered. "I can't judge what's an appropriate amount of grief to show at having your holy pool polluted."

"Don't you thi—" Jemeryl stopped, seeing movement on the right-hand side. Two older, unarmed nomads had left the line in the company of a half dozen warriors. "I think a delegation's coming to see us."

"Promising. They're sending a couple of elders to ask who we are. Much better than trying to work it out from our corpses."

Larric edged nearer. "What do we do?"

"Wait."

Ashkinet had also become aware of what was happening. She left the waterside. "Do you want me to talk to them?"

Tevi nodded. "That would be best. If you want, I'll come with you. I know some names that might help."

"Sure."

Jemeryl and Larric held back a few steps, watching Tevi and Ashkinet meet the approaching group. The atmosphere was initially tense, but within seconds it was clear that the introductions were going well. The warriors lowered their weapons. The elders, Tevi, and Ashkinet all adopted relaxed postures. Even so, Jemeryl was a little surprised when one of the elders wrapped Ashkinet in a hug. Was this a meeting of long-separated relatives?

Tevi beckoned Jemeryl and Larric forward.

"Shalista Jemeryl dehni," Ashkinet said.

Jemeryl assumed she was being introduced and bowed politely.

"Shalista Larric dehni."

Larric copied her action.

The elders bowed in reply, and then led the way towards a point on the right hand ridge, where a thicker, deeper crevice split the rock face. Ashkinet took a position between them, still talking excitedly, but Tevi dropped back to walk beside Jemeryl.

"Did they say what happen at the oasis?" Jemeryl asked.

"They might have. I don't understand enough of the language to tell." Tevi nodded at the people in front. "I think the woman is a friend of Ashkinet's grandfather, and at the moment they're catching up on relatives."

The warriors had formed a loose cordon around them, their manner making it clear they saw their function as protectors, not captors. The one walking on Jemeryl's left got closer. "You wish to know about the battle here?" He spoke the language of the Protectorate clearly, although with a heavy accent.

"Yes. Please."

"The red-cloaked demons, hundreds of them. They came here. Of course, we fought them. We would defend *Yalaish si liarajali* with the last drop of our blood. But so many, we had no hope and the elders ordered us to the caves. The demons could not overcome us there. So they took a coward's revenge on the sacred trees and water, while we hid in our holes, watching them." Judging by his expression of shame, the young man would have rather died.

The oasis will recover. Dead people don't get better. Remembering Ashkinet's reaction. Jemeryl kept the thought to herself. "While you're still breathing, you can hope to put right the wrong."

"That was what the elders said. If we had fought we would all have been killed, and there would be none left to hunt down Sefriall and rip her foul heart from her body. When she has paid for what she has done, then we will cleanse the oasis and beg forgiveness from Yalaish."

The response was rather more bloodthirsty than what Jemeryl had intended, but she chose to say nothing. Once the morphology was gone, Sefriall's hold on power would be weakened. If she could not keep the loyalty of her sentinels, she would be in grave danger. Jemeryl wondered if, despite the murder of Ciamon, she ought to offer a warning to the new High Priest. Although surely, if Sefriall had any sense, she would be able to work out for herself that she needed to run very fast and very far.

The elders reached the west flank of the valley and disappeared into the crevice. The rest of the party followed. Jemeryl saw that the split in the rock formed a gully, just wide enough for two to walk abreast. As they advanced further in, the walls rose high on either side, and the light filtered down, diffuse. Jemeryl heard voices from above. She looked up and finally spotted archers stationed in nooks in the rock face although in the weak light little more than their faces and the tips of their arrows were visible.

Tevi was studying the arrangement with a professional interest. "Nice."

"I'm not sure if that's the word I'd use."

"I guess my judgement might also depend on whether I was attacking or defending."

Eventually the walls joined overhead, forming a true cave. Just at the point where the darkness was too dense to walk in safely, the route turned a corner and opened into a wide space, thirty yards across, lit by burning torches around the sides. More people were assembled here, awaiting them.

"It's Darjain." The relief in Tevi's voice was evident. "And Botha standing behind him."

Jemeryl caught her arm. "Before you dash over, remember you'll need to tell them who you are."

"Oh. Yes. Right." Tevi looked at her hands, as if to remind herself of her changed appearance.

Jemeryl tagged on behind, listening. Up until now, she had only Tevi's description of the deposed priests' leader to work on, and had been interested to meet Darjain.

As a result of the strength potion, on the islands where Tevi had been born, while girls were raised as warriors, the boys grew up, weaker than their sisters and consigned to a life of tending house and childcare. Despite all the years Tevi had lived in the Protectorate, that had shown her the islands' gender based stereotypes were nonsense, the attitudes ingrained during her childhood were still there. Jemeryl knew that, somewhere deep inside, Tevi could not help seeing men as vulnerable and intrinsically gentler and more nurturing than women.

How much was this affecting Tevi's view of the elderly leader of the deposed priests?

However, Jemeryl soon reached the conclusion that, in this case, Tevi was right. Darjain really was a kind, harmless, and devout advocate of a loving god. The younger female priest, Botha, was far more strident. Her hand gripped the pendant hanging around her neck so tightly that when she released it, the design was imprinted on her palm, a crescent moon with an eye engraved on it, no doubt the symbol of her god.

Another person joined them, presumably another priest, since he was not a nomad, and Tevi's explanation had to go back to the beginning. She reached the point where Ciamon was murdered before this new priest spoke.

"You were certainly right that his death achieved nothing. Sefriall is a hundred times worse than he ever was. She has disgraced us all and made me ashamed to call myself a Cyclian."

Darjain took the speaker's hand. "No, Alkoan, you mustn't take it like that. Your gods are good. The sickness is only in Sefriall. Her crimes don't reflect on you."

"Only her death can expunge the stain from our faith."

Tevi interrupted. "Maybe, but it won't help any more than killing Ciamon. As I said before, it's the idol we need to get rid of. That's why we're here."

"A pity we didn't do it before."

"With Parrash as a spy for Sefriall, I'm not sure how much success we'd have had. But it's going to be different now." Tevi beckoned Jemeryl closer. "This is Jem, my partner. The other two with us are also Coven sorcerers."

"I thought magic doesn't work anymore."

Jemeryl nodded. "That's because there's a device inside the idol. It projects a morphology on the skein that puts a perceptual bar on the upper dimension. But we've got a weapon that will stop it. Then we'll be able to work magic again."

Tevi put an arm around her shoulders. "Exactly. Once we've got rid of the morphology, Jem and the others will be able to defeat Sefriall and the temple can return to how it was."

Jemeryl was about to object. Direct confrontation with Sefriall was not part of her plan, although possibly Tevi was right. Sefriall and her sentinels might still try to fight, even after the emanator was destroyed. Jemeryl closed her mouth. Regardless of how things went, this was not the time to argue the point.

Alkoan folded his arms, challenging. "So why are you here, rather than in Kradja where the idol is?"

"Because we need help. We need people to distract the sentinels so we have a chance to assemble the weapon."

"Then I predict you'll have very little trouble getting volunteers."

❖

Alkoan was right. Once the situation was explained, every nomad aged over fifteen and below fifty volunteered, as did most of the rest. Picking who to take was a challenge for Jemeryl, but not such a big challenge as persuading those not chosen to accept her decision.

Even after seeing Ashkinet's reaction to the despoiled oasis, Jemeryl had not been prepared for the strength of feeling among the nomads. Of course, Ashkinet had spent decades away from the desert and was no longer a believer. The committed followers of Yalaish were affected more deeply and on more levels.

Jemeryl soon came to realise how important the oasis was to the nomads. In damaging it, Sefriall had done more than show contempt for their god—she had attacked the core of their self-identity. She had made them feel undeserving of life, and their desire for revenge burned savage and uncontrollable. So much so, that it was her main reason for rejecting most applicants. Their ability to calmly work to a plan was in doubt.

Of those who seemed to have the most secure hold on their emotions, Jemeryl picked the three with the best command of the Protectorate language, thereby cutting down on the risk of misunderstandings. The disappointment of those not selected was immediate and vigorous in its expression. At several points, it looked as if violence might erupt, and only intervention from the elders calmed things down.

Other volunteers were even harder to dissuade. All three priests insisted on joining the distraction party, and since they were not subject to the rule of the elders, Jemeryl had no one to call on for backing. As it was, the offers from Alkoan and Botha she was happy to accept in place of more volatile nomads. Even though there was a risk their faces might be recognised, neither had the distinctive nomad looks. Surely the sentinels might be alerted if a group of people with copper skin and fair hair entered the temple at the same time.

Darjain was another matter. The old man was frail to the point of being unsteady on his feet. He certainly could not walk the distance back to Kradja and he might slow things down in the temple as well. Jemeryl tried to talk him out of it, without success.

Darjain was resolute. "The people here have mules. Someone will lend me one."

If anything, Tevi was even less happy than Jemeryl at the thought of the old man taking part. "You ought to stay here, safe among your friends."

"How can I count myself safe, when my god is under attack?"

"But you don't have to—"

"No buts. I do have to. For too long I've done nothing. I've been lax in my duty. I've let this evil grow. My god needs my help."

"Your god is immortal. You're not."

"Precisely. I'm an old man. Soon I'll leave this world. How will I stand before Yalaish if I have failed in my duty to her? It's not my life here that's at stake, but my soul."

Tevi appealed to the other priest. "Alkoan, Botha, can't you talk sense into him?"

Alkoan pursed his lips. "Personally, I think it's the most sense he's made since Ciamon took over the temple. I understand his outrage. He has to defend his god, in the same way that I have to expunge the shame Sefriall is inflicting on the name of all Cyclians."

Botha nodded. "Nolius teaches that this life is a test that will determine our fate in the next. Whatever happens, Darjain's life this time is nearly over. It's right that his mind is set on what's to come."

"Jem?" Tevi turned and held up her hands in appeal.

Jemeryl shook her head. "I agree with you, but I think, my love, this is one fight we're going to lose." She stopped, chewing her lip thoughtfully, and mulled over something else Darjain had said. "But you don't suppose someone might be willing to lend me a mule as well?"

❖

The mules had been a good idea, Tevi thought.

The nomads' helpfulness had not ended there. They had provided transport, food, and tents for everyone, as well as an escort until almost within sight of Kradja. The escort had then returned, leaving only the last few miles be to completed on foot, alone. The nomads had been generous, clearly providing the best they had. The meal in the tent on the previous night had been wonderful—choice cuts of meat, soft bread, wild honey, and goat cheese. There had also been wine. Surely grapes could not grow in the desert, so what had it been fermented from?

Tevi tried to concentrate on the problem. She tried to recall the flavour and aroma of the meal. How good it had tasted in her mouth and how full it had made her stomach feel. The warm, soft blurring of the wine. She tried to remember afterwards, making love to Jemeryl in the luxury and privacy of their tent. She tried to call on every delicious memory she could, as a shield against the glamour of the idol, washing over her with its seductive power. She had to stay focused and in control. The moment to act was almost upon them.

Her clothes were the loose robes worn by many in the desert. The bundle of rods and poles was small enough to be concealed underneath, but large enough that Tevi was aware of them every time she moved. She could not bend in the way she normally did, so extra caution was needed. She had to think about her actions and plan them in advance to make sure the rigidity in her posture would not be apparent, and in order to think, she must not give in to the glamour.

Tevi manœuvred her way into the middle of a cluster of pilgrims, trying to act like one of them, mimicking their languid shuffle. She could only hope her eyes were not too sharp. Those of everyone around her were glazed over.

The good thing was that the worshippers were too lost in their entranced state to react quickly to anything. The sentinels would have to physically shove bodies aside to get to her and the others. Admittedly, this would not take much doing. The worshippers would not have the coordination to resist, even if they wanted to, but the few extra seconds might be vital.

A short way to her left, Jemeryl was also imitating the spellbound pilgrims. Ashkinet was to her right, nearest the stairs to the upper balcony, and Larric was directly opposite, on the other side of the idol. All were in position. Now all they needed was the distraction.

Tevi's eyes returned to the idol. It was beautiful. Waves of love engulfed her and for a moment she was assailed by doubt. How could she plan on harming it? Desperately, Tevi dug through her memories. That morning, waking beside Jemeryl and knowing she was where she needed to be. Last night, Jemeryl's body, naked in her arms, how good it felt, how right. The taste and the smell and the touch of Jemeryl. Tevi recalled the softness of Jemeryl's breast under her hand, a hard nipple against her tongue, and the taut thigh muscles as Jemeryl's body arched. If Tevi closed her eyes she could see Jemeryl's face staring down at her. Even the change in appearance did not hide the emotion in her eyes. The memory filled Tevi with joy. This was love, pure and unshakeable. Compared to it, the glamour was no more than the crudest sham. For an instant, the spell was broken, and then it flowed back, but weaker and more transparent than before. Tevi smiled. She was in control.

"Destroy the false idol." The cry rang out from near the main door.

"Yalaish is the all-mother." The words were in a thick, nomad accent.

"This is no true god."

"Forgive me, Yalaish." Darjain's voice wavered with the effort to maintain volume.

The diversion had started.

As Tevi had suspected, nobody around her, neither pilgrims nor sentries, showed any reaction to the uproar. However, the sentinels who were positioned around the walls were already moving to counter the threats contained in the angry shouts. Tevi wasted no time watching them. With a sharp tug she released the bundle from beneath her clothes. The items clattered to the floor. Tevi knelt. Now she would be even harder to spot from the perimeter of the hall.

Within seconds, they had the poles laid out in a pentagram. The crystal clips snapped into place. Threading the rods through and into the stone talisman took a little more precision, and trying to rush was counterproductive. Somehow, the holes had been so much bigger and easier to locate when practising in the tent the night before. Tevi slapped her hand on her thigh as a spur to concentration and slid the last two rods into place. The device was complete.

Tevi leapt to her feet and held the pentagram out, towards the idol. On the other side, Larric was already in place. A few moments later, Ashkinet and Jemeryl also bobbed up into view, with assembled pentagrams in their hands.

Always before, when practising, they had never had more than one pentagram assembled at a time. Jemeryl explained that the devices needed to interact with each other to do their job of unravelling magic. One on its own would achieve nothing, and until they were in the temple, she did not want any other spells, such as their disguises, accidentally undone. This was thus the first time the devices had been tested. The sorcerers were all certain they would work. Tevi could only hope they were right, because very soon they were going to have a large number of angry sentinels to deal with.

Yet something was clearly happening. Tevi was holding the central talisman, as she had been instructed. The stone was warming in her hand while the pentagram was quivering to a rhythm like a heartbeat. Could she hear a faint whine? And surely she could smell summer lightning.

"Look! By the idol. Those people." The shout came from the stairs, followed by, "Get them! Stop them! Whatever they're doing."

Tevi grimaced but did not move. Time was running out. The pentagrams had better work quickly. She heard shouting and movement, coming her way. Some of the worshippers near her were stirring, staring around blearily like woken sleepers. The disturbance was getting closer. Mere seconds were left.

"You. Stop that!"

Tevi could not turn to look, but the sentinels must only be a step or two away.

Something snapped. The sensation was so strong that for a moment Tevi thought she had heard it, but the locus had been inside her. Something huge had vanished, leaving the world cold, bleak, and empty. Wails and screams rose up across the hall even as Tevi recognised what had gone. The idol was no longer projecting its glamour. She gaped at the statue, amazed at the change. The shape was the same but how ordinary it looked. How sad.

Another wave hit. The force this time was so strong it knocked Tevi to her knees. The pentagram fell from her grip. Her body felt wrenched and swollen. Like a kick in her stomach that radiated out through her bones, an instant of pain made her eyes blur and then it settled.

Tevi stared at her hands, braced against the floor. And they were her hands, her fingers, her skin. On the backs were the mercenary tattoos, twin crossed swords in red and gold. The magical disguise had gone. She was back in her true form.

"What have you done?"

Hands grabbed Tevi's shoulders and yanked her to her feet. Three sentinels surrounded her. Their faces were terrified and furious. One had a drawn sword. Beyond them, chaos was claiming the temple. Shrieking, sobbing pilgrims surged in a mass and more sentinels were charging into the main hall.

"What have y—" The sentinel was too enraged to complete the sentence a second time. She raised her sword, either to strike Tevi around the head with the pommel or to slash with the blade.

What was Jemeryl doing? Why was she not taking control of the situation? Tevi looked over her shoulder and saw Jemeryl, rooted in the same spot where she had been before. She also had reverted to her normal appearance. Her expression was shocked, and surprised, and confused. As Tevi watched, two sentinels reached her and grabbed her roughly. They started to drag her towards the stairs. The conclusion was obvious. The pentagrams had not worked.

The sound of sharp movement got Tevi's attention as the sword-wielding sentinel lashed out. Tevi's body reacted on instinct, ducking under the blow. The questions would have to wait. She had to move quickly. The sentinels would not expect her strength, which would give her the bonus of surprise. Not that Tevi felt she needed it, given the holy warriors' abysmally low standards.

She seized the sentinel on her right, hoisted him off his feet, and hurled him into his comrades. They went down in a jumble of arms and legs, taking a few dazed worshippers with them. Tevi darted around the pile of bodies and barged her way through the confused melee, cutting a line across the hall to intercept the pair who had captured Jemeryl. She overtook them midway to the staircase. Both went down with barely a groan.

"Tevi. It hasn't—" Jemeryl looked bewildered.

"I know. It hasn't worked. We can talk about it later. We need to get the others and go."

Tevi looked up. A sick knot formed in her stomach as she realised these two goals might prove impossible. Dozens more sentinels now lined the stairs in ranks. Already Larric, Alkoan, and two nomads were there, securely held prisoners. Knots of red-cloaked soldiers marked where Botha and Darjain were also being dragged away, and yet more sentinels were weaving through the crowd, homing in on where she and Jemeryl stood, surrounding them and blocking off their retreat.

Suddenly, a new crescendo of screams erupted. One of the nomads on the stairs had shaken free, snatched the sword from her captor, and stabbed him. In an instant she was also struck down, but the sight of blood was too much for the overwrought worshippers. With a deafening barrage of shrieks and roars the people surged towards the doors. Tevi and Jemeryl were carried along by the flow. The isolated sentinels who stood in the way of the mob were trampled underfoot. A two-deep line of the red-cloaked soldiers, blockading the exit, proved no more effective. The fleeing horde knocked them aside.

At first, Tevi tried to fight her way back to the stairs. The thought of abandoning the others was agony, but their case was hopeless. In the end, she simply hung on to Jemeryl and let the mob sweep them to the relative safety of the market square where the people dispersed, running off in ones and twos.

Tevi pulled Jemeryl into the shelter of an alleyway. "Are you all right, Jem?"

"I…" She shook her head. "It didn't work."

"Something did. The glamour has gone, and so have our disguises."

"But…" Jemeryl's eyes were fixed in disbelief on the temple. "What did Ciamon do? How could he—"

"That's tomorrow's problem. Right now, we need to hide."

"It's…right." Jemeryl shook her head, as if to clear it. "Where are the others?"

"Prisoners." The word stuck in Tevi's throat. "They're all prisoners except us."

"What'll happen to them?"

Tevi linked arms with Jemeryl and towed her down the alley. "The same as will happen to us if we don't start moving."

"Tevi?" Jemeryl's tone required more of an answer.

"The nomads were putting up a fight, so they're probably already dead. Larric said the priests captured before now have been hanged. I can't see why anything different should happen to Darjain and the other two." Tevi clenched her teeth, fighting to stay in control. Giving in to grief and guilt would help no one.

"Larric and Ashkinet?"

"I don't know. Sefriall may want them as bargaining chips with the Coven. Or she may not."

"What are we going to do?"

"We're going to make ourselves less conspicuous."

By the time they reached the Four Winds House, Jemeryl was showing signs of getting over her shock and thinking more clearly. "We can't stay here."

"True. As soon as Raf recognises me she'll be claiming her reward from Sefriall."

"She isn't the only one who can identify us."

"We need a new disguise." Tevi crouched beside her backpack in the corner and dug through the contents. Her fingers closed around the small bottle she had bought some days earlier. "I got this for Ashkinet. I thought she might need it."

"What is it?"

"Dye."

Jemeryl frowned. "For clothes?"

"For hair and skin. In case looking like a nomad became a bit too dangerous. But it will do for us. Maybe not my hair. It's that colour anyway." Tevi started pulling her clothes over her head. "But first we need to strip."

Deep brown skin softened some of the angular contours of Jemeryl's face while accentuating others, and with her wavy auburn hair hacked short and dyed black she looked very different, at least to a first glance. Tevi knew her own appearance would not have changed so much, but she was less well known to the sentinels.

For clothes, they stayed with the loose robes. Tevi kicked them around the floor to pick up as much dirt as possible, and mimic the look of someone sleeping rough on the streets. Fortunately, Raf had not swept the room before renting it out. The tattoos on Tevi's hands were less conspicuous under the dye. She further concealed them by tying strips of rags around her hands like a labourer.

Jemeryl held up her arm with the black sorcerer's amulet. Up until now, it had been hidden as part of her altered form. "Disguising this isn't going to be easy."

"Can you take it off?"

"Maybe, if I had my magical abilities and a month to do it in. It's one of the tests to show if an amulet is genuine. If you can get it off then it isn't genuine."

Tevi pursed her lips as a couple of ideas came to her. "I know what we can do." She looked around. Nothing in the room would help. "Wait here."

News about the events at the temple had clearly reached the inn. The dusty courtyards were buzzing with animated knots of people. Tevi could imagine the heights of invention the rumours were reaching, and luckily the stories were more interesting than the sight of a dark-haired, dark-skinned woman hurrying to the stable. Nobody spared her more than a quick glance.

Within a few minutes, Tevi was back in the room with what she needed—two thin lengths of wood. Tevi ripped strips from spare clothes and started to bind the slats on either side of Jemeryl's forearm.

"You know, it was really clumsy of you to break your arm like that."

Jemeryl gave a wry grin. "I guess I shouldn't have drunk so much."

"You said it."

"What do I do if some sentinels want to examine what's under the strapping?"

"Scream as loudly as you can and see if you can scare them off."

"Will that work?"

"It might."

With the slats bound in place, from Jemeryl's palm to her elbow, not even the outline of the amulet was noticeable. Tevi completed the fake splint by making a sling and tying it behind Jemeryl's neck. She stuffed food and other useful items into one of the backpacks, which she then swung over her shoulder.

"Time to go."

"Where?"

"We could try the mansion I told you about. There might be some free space. If not, Kradja has an extensive selection of doorways to chose from."

"Sounds wonderful."

Dusk was settling over the town. In the fading light, the mood on the streets was jittery. Groups were huddled everywhere, talking, their faces showing anger, disbelief and fear. Tevi and Jemeryl skirted the edge of a tense noisy crowd listening to a ranting preacher. The rhetoric was even more violent than normal—if anything in Kradja under Sefriall could count as normal. A chorus of shouts from a few streets away sounded like a riot. Tevi pitied whoever the bitter mob had picked on as its victim.

Patrols of sentinels were also in evidence, marching belligerently down the centre of roads, shoving the crowds aside. From time to time they would single out someone to be searched, beaten, or hauled away. Tevi could see no pattern to the individuals selected for this treatment; probably there was none. Sefriall's soldiers merely wanted to intimidate with a show of taking action.

Fortunately, the sentinels made no attempt to stop Tevi and Jemeryl as they shuffled across town, their pace deliberately slow and indecisive. If the sentinels were on the lookout for anything, it would be people fleeing, not those with time to kill.

When they got to the Calequiral mansion, they found a similar state of anxious upheaval. Tevi and Jemeryl slunk in through the open gateway. The people gathered in the garden looked ready to erupt without warning, and either a panicked stampede or a lynch mob was equally likely.

Just inside the door of the mansion, an elderly woman was standing alone, swaying back and forth as if in time to an unheard dirge.

"Excuse me."

The woman stared in Tevi's direction but her eyes did not focus. "What?"

"Is there any space in here? My sister and me. We got here yesterday. Spent last night by the market, but the idol...it's..." Tevi nervously looked back through the garden. "We don't want to stay out there. Especially after what happen to my sister's arm."

The woman went back to her swaying, but just when Tevi thought the request was to go unanswered, she said, "Second floor, at the end of the hall. The people there were weak in their faith. We dealt with them. Now it's free."

"Thank you."

The spot turned out to be a recess beneath a smashed window, the draught of cold night air making it less popular. However, it gave Tevi and Jemeryl the excuse to huddle together closely. The rest of the hall was a carpet of bodies. Darkness fell, but their fellow squatters were not about to sleep. Tevi and Jemeryl lay, listening to the ardent voices.

"They attacked the idol."

"It's sacrilege."

"How dare they defile a holy shrine?"

Jemeryl put her mouth close to Tevi's ear. "The nomads would agree with them there."

"Toqwani is angry." The speaker's voice held a sob.

"We've lost his love."

"Sefriall said if we work to please the gods, they may restore the blessing on the idol. She's going to tell us what we need to do to get back in the gods' favour."

"I bet she is," Jemeryl whispered again.

The voices down the hallway went on. "Sefriall has said the attackers were Nolians, working in the pay of the Coven. Sorcerers only get their powers by making blood sacrifices to Nolius."

"He's the god of evil."

Tevi wrapped her arms around Jemeryl and murmured, "Sefriall is getting as good at the religious bullshit as ever Ciamon was."

"Oh, I think she's far better at it. She's had longer to practice."

CHAPTER TWELVE—BEHIND THE TEMPLE

Even with Tevi's assistance, clambering onto the roof of the Calequiral mansion required a bit of effort and a good head for heights. Jemeryl found the manœuvre all the more awkward since she had to maintain the fiction of her broken arm. She was tempted to question Tevi's choice of location. However, when they finally reached a flatter spot, where she could sit comfortably and feel reasonably secure, Jemeryl had to admit the rooftop perch had three big points to recommend it. The view over the roofs of Kradja was impressive, showing off the huge dome of the temple to its best effect. The second was a delightful cool breeze rippling by, surprisingly clear of noise, dust, and the odour of the streets. The most important reason, though, was the complete absence of risk of them being overheard.

"I can't believe what Ci's done. I never thought he had it in him." Jemeryl's mind had been running into the same incredulous block all night, keeping her from sleep. "He wasn't that good a sorcerer."

Tevi frowned and rubbed her neck. "I don't understand magic—obviously. So in terms I do understand, if you compare their abilities, Weilan's pentagrams not being able to punch through Ciamon's defence is a bit like a strong, well-armed warrior getting into a fight with a three-year-old toddler and losing?"

"Precisely."

"So there's only one way Ciamon could have done it. He cheated."

"You can't cheat at magic."

"You can always cheat."

"Would you like to explain how?"

Tevi stared over the rooftops, clearly pondering the question. Jemeryl studied her lover's face in profile. The challenge had not been delivered cynically. Without magical ability or Coven training, Tevi could approach problems, unencumbered by preconceived ideas. Sometimes her fresh perspective could be very effective at providing a breakthrough. Jemeryl smiled. Even if Tevi could suggest nothing this time, looking at her was a pleasant way to spend a few minutes. The black hair and grey eyes really did suit her best.

Tevi's expression sharpened. Clearly she had thought of something. "The glamour went, so we know the pentagrams worked."

"Right."

"More than that, we know they overcame any defences Ciamon put on the idol."

"No. Because the emanator is still projecting the morphology."

"Surely whatever spells were protecting the emanator would have protected the glamour as well."

Jemeryl paused, mulling it over. "When you put it like that, yes. I'd have thought so. But—"

"So the only sensible conclusion is that the emanator isn't in the idol. Ciamon put it somewhere else."

"He said it was there."

"Then he lied."

Jemeryl shook her head. "Ci never liked lying."

"He may not have liked it, but he'd do it for what he believed in. Like all that stuff about his new god."

"I don't think he saw that as a lie. It was just an allegorical story."

"Then he was getting allegorical about the emanator being in the idol."

"I don't—" Jemeryl stopped as a memory slipped into her head.

"What is it, Jem? You're thinking. I can tell."

"Way back. When Ci was first telling me about the morphology. We were standing on the balcony at the back of the main hall, overlooking the worshippers and the idol. That was when he boasted the Coven wouldn't be able to destroy the emanator, no matter what they did to the idol."

"Which would make sense if the emanator wasn't in the idol."

"Right. And while he was speaking, he wandered away and stared out a window. His voice grew in confidence. He was so sure. That was what made the impression on me—why I remember it so clearly. Something about the way he stopped looking at the idol and went to the window, as if he was making a point."

"In what way?"

"At the time, I assumed it was defiance. Him looking towards Lyremouth. But now I think back, I'm sure we were on the south side of the temple. So it would have been the wrong direction." Jemeryl stopped, chewing her lip. Was she truly so sure?

"You think he was looking at wherever the emanator really was?"

"Maybe." Jemeryl sighed. "It's not a lot to go on."

"At the moment, it's the best lead we have."

"Where does it get us?"

"For starters, we can go to the temple, and see if we can work out what Ciamon was looking at."

Jemeryl sat, shoulders slumped, staring at the tiled roof between her feet while she pushed the memory around in her head. She knew at the time, the idea had not occurred to her that Ciamon might be looking at the real home of the emanator. How much faith could she put in the possibility now? Was she deluding herself, by imagining things with hindsight?

"It might be a waste of time."

Tevi slid closer and slipped her arm around Jemeryl's waist. "We don't have much in the way of options. We can check out the temple, or we can go back to Lyremouth." Tevi's arm tightened in a way that felt more like a spasm than a hug.

"What is it?"

"If we go, it means we've abandoned everyone. Maybe Sefriall will wait two days before she has Darjain and the others hanged, but she won't wait two months. For any hope of saving them, we need to do something now. And it won't just be them. If we can't stop the morphology, it will be down to the mercenaries and any magical weapons the Coven has made. Tens of thousands will die."

Tevi was right. The alternative was not good. "When you put it like that…"

"It's not as if we have anything to lose by checking out the idea."

Jemeryl nodded. "True. I guess we ought to call by the temple anyway and add our tears to the general outpouring."

Currently, every believer in Kradja was squeezing into the temple to beg for forgiveness and the return of the god's favour. Purely to keep up their cover, they ought to go.

Tevi grinned. "We'll have a wail of a time."

❖

If there should be a competition for histrionics in the temple, Jemeryl did not envy whoever got the job of judge. So many were putting so much effort into their entreaties. Did pulling out your hair by the roots rank above kneeling and banging your head on the stone floor? Did you get more points for screaming or knocking yourself out? Fortunately, merely standing dumbstruck with grief was acceptable form, so she and Tevi did not need to indulge in self-mutilation to preserve their disguise.

The main hall was crammed full, to the extent that finding a space to talk without being overheard was impossible. Jemeryl was wondering if they should wait until getting outside before swapping notes when Tevi sniffed, wiped her eyes, and then crumpled onto her shoulder. Jemeryl could feel Tevi's body shaking, as if with sobs. The posture meant Tevi's mouth was less than an inch from her ear when she whispered, "Can you remember where you were standing?"

"Yup." It was play-acting time. Jemeryl patted Tevi's back in a gesture of soft sympathy with her free arm. The other was in its sling. "More or less."

The image was clear in Jemeryl's mind, of standing on the balcony with Ciamon and looking down on the idol. She could envisage the angle it was at and its relation to the main doors. If only she could go back to the balcony, she would have no trouble pinpointing the exact spot where she had stood. Unfortunately, getting access to the balcony was the tricky bit. Six sentinels guarded the staircase leading to it, and asking if she could pop up for a quick look was not a good idea.

Jemeryl patted Tevi's back again. "Come on, sister. Let's walk for a little."

Aimless milling around was another acceptable form of behaviour for the distraught worshippers. Nobody paid Jemeryl any attention when she reached the rear of the hall and started drifting back and forth until she had the idol in its right alignment.

Jemeryl pulled Tevi into a one-armed sisterly embrace. "There. I think I was standing directly above this spot. Then Ci turned and went to the window a little to my right."

Tevi broke away and stared up, hands raised in a gesture of earnest appeal to the heavens. After a few seconds in this dramatic pose she again collapsed around Jemeryl's neck.

"We're too close. I can't see the windows. The balcony's in the way."

Jemeryl looked across the hall, running a line of sight from where she was through the idol, under the high point of an arch, to a rack of lighted candles on the far side.

"We should move on."

Tevi released her hold and nodded, the picture of inconsolable misery. Jemeryl was struck by the memory of how Tevi had been when they first met, so honest and guileless it was almost painful to watch. Back then, Jemeryl had been the one who enjoyed the games of subterfuge. Somewhere over the years, Tevi had become a competent actress. Had she corrupted her lover, Jemeryl wondered, or was the change due to Tevi's experience and maturity?

They continued shuffling around the perimeter of the hall, avoiding several people who were lying sobbing on the floor, and making a major detour around a group of flagellants, most of whom seemed to realise that they were supposed to be hitting themselves, although a couple did not appear quite so choosy.

At last they reached the rack of candles. Jemeryl looked across the crowded hall. From where they now stood, she had a clear view of the balcony and the row of arches that formed its outer wall, each one with a window.

Tevi was behind her and obviously making her own calculations. She wrapped her arms around Jemeryl's stomach, pulled her close, and whispered, "Was it the sixth or seventh window from the right?"

Jemeryl turned her head. "The sixth, I think. But just maybe the other one."

"Still cuts out a lot of angles." Tevi raised her voice. "I need some fresh air. We can come back soon."

"Of course, sister."

After the frenzied atmosphere of the temple, the streets felt calm, sane, and safe. Jemeryl had to remind herself that this was a dangerous illusion. Nowhere in Kradja was safe and violence could break out at any time. More than this, Sefriall's spies and informers would still be around. Inside the temple any sort of odd behaviour was acceptable. Out here, they needed to be more guarded in their actions, although with more space, they did not need to go to the same theatrical lengths to avoid being overheard.

Jemeryl looked at the outer wall of the great hall. After a few moments to orient herself, she identified the row of windows behind the balcony. "I can see the outside of the sixth arch, but not the actual window. So someone there couldn't see us."

Tevi nodded. "We'll just walk on a bit and see what sort of angle of vision the window does have."

"It would be a lot easier if I could go up to the balcony and look out."

"It would be even easier if Sefriall wandered up and handed me the emanator and a large hammer. When you're wishing for what you can't have there's no point in half-measures."

Jemeryl laughed. "True."

They soon discovered that the deeply inset window had a surprisingly restricted field of view. However, this still took in a large slice of Kradja, extending to the most distant houses on the outskirts of town.

Tevi pouted at the window. "So, we can cut the options down to a couple hundred houses."

"I think we can do a lot better than that."

"How?"

"Ciamon would have wanted the emanator near at hand. Regardless of whether he could do anything to protect it, knowing he could get to it within minutes would have made him feel safer."

"I'll take your word on it. You're the one who knew him."

Jemeryl stared sadly at the window, remembering Ciamon. Had he changed over the years? Had he truly been the same person as the one she had known? The boy she had once loved? Jemeryl lowered her gaze, pushing her thoughts on. Brooding about the past could wait.

The path leading to the front of the temple was lined with gardens and tranquil courtyards to impress the arriving pilgrims. The rear was the business side, where a number of support buildings stood. Sentinels patrolled the area, and Jemeryl was aware they were already attracting a few suspicious looks. The attention was not pointed enough to be worrying—many pilgrims would stop and gape in awe at the temple—but standing for too long in any one spot was unwise.

"Do you think we can wander around here without the sentinels stopping us?"

The deafening peal of the midday bell drowned out Tevi's first answer. She stared at the source for a few seconds and then lowered her mouth to Jemeryl's ear. "Possibly. There's enough ordinary tradesfolk around, but I've got a better idea."

Jemeryl followed Tevi's gaze upwards. The square bell tower soared above the surrounding buildings. The bell itself was just visible through the open windows at the top, swinging back and forth. A flock of agitated pigeons swirled around the red tiled roof, black dots against the blue sky, waiting for peace to return to their roost.

The final peal faded away as Tevi and Jemeryl approached the base of the tower and the door opened. Tevi hailed the departing bell ringer. "Please. We would beg a favour of you."

The woman's sour look was not promising. "What is it?"

"My sister wants to pray for the return of the god's blessing."

"Her and the rest of Kradja."

Tevi dropped her voice to a level appropriate to confidential entreaty. "She's got this idea if she can get closer to the blessed Ciamon, she stands more chance of her prayers being heard."

The bell ringer's expression implied that as far as stupid religious quirks went, this did not even have the virtue of being funny. "So?"

"You know he ascended into the sky?"

"Yeah."

"I just wondered if it'd be possible for us to climb up your bell tower."

"I don't—"

Tevi moved closer to the woman, dropping her voice still lower, so that Jemeryl could no longer make out what was said, but she saw a few coins change hands.

The bell ringer pocketed the money and gave Jemeryl a look, halfway between pity and a sneer. "May your prayers be answered. Shut the door when you've finished." She trudged away.

The inside of the bell tower was dank and smelly. The wooden ladder up was covered in pigeon droppings. Jemeryl peered at it dubiously. "Is it safe?"

Tevi knocked on a rung. "Seems sound enough."

"Do you want to go up and tell me what you can see?"

"Come on. Four eyes are better than two. You might spot something I miss."

"What about my broken arm?"

"Who's watching?"

Tevi scurried up the ladder. Jemeryl slipped the sling over her head to free her arm and followed on more cautiously, trying to ignore the squelchy ooze under her fingers.

A series of ladders and half landings, five in all, got Jemeryl to the top. The view surpassed even that from the roof of the Calequiral mansion, although it was a while before she could appreciate it. Her lungs were burning from the climb and the acrid air. She leaned her forehead against the balustrade, gasping. "You're doing this to me on purpose, aren't you?"

"What?"

"Getting me climbing up and down all over the place."

She felt Tevi pat her. "The exercise will do you good."

Once she had got her breath back, Jemeryl raised her head. The temple precinct was laid out below, making judging the angles easy. Seven, or possibly eight, buildings would have been visible from the window where Ciamon had been standing.

On the east side were three stone-built blocks. The two nearest the bell tower were both long and low with tiled colonnades along one side. The third was separated from the others by a patch of garden. Despite the heat, plumes of smoke trailed away from its multiple chimneys. It clearly had an association with another nearby building. A stream of people trotted back and forth between them. Given the smoking chimneys and the time of day, Jemeryl's bet was on these last two buildings being a kitchen and refectory.

A circular two-storey structure with a domed roof occupied the middle of the area. A ring of small windows ran around the top, but the sole opening on the ground floor was a wide double door. South of this stood a timber building that was clearly a stable. Jemeryl was sure it was the same one where she arrived as a prisoner with Gante and Taedias. Currently, two horses were tied to a post in its small central courtyard.

The largest building took up most of the western side of the area. Sentinels stood on guard outside the door, and as Jemeryl watched, a returning patrol marched in. The final possible building was behind it, but Jemeryl was doubtful whether it would have been visible to Ciamon from the window.

She pointed. "Do you think we need to worry about that one?"

Tevi wrinkled her nose in thought. "He might have been able to see a corner of it. But in that case, wouldn't he have gone to another window with a better view?"

"Probably. So there are what…seven buildings we need to think about?"

"Yes."

"Where do we start?"

Tevi pointed to one of the long buildings with the verandas. Even from the distance it was possible to see the carved bundle of wooden leaves hanging outside its door. "How about the infirmary?"

❖

Tevi staggered up to the door and pounded on it, weakly but with desperation. She was alone. The risk that healers might want to examine Jemeryl's supposedly broken arm was too much to chance. When there was no response, she slumped against the side of the entrance and then thumped the door again.

"What d'you want?" The voice from inside sounded hostile.

"My guts. I've eaten something bad. I need help." Tevi moaned the words.

"What do you think we can do about it?"

"You're healers, aren't you? I saw the sign."

The door opened a fraction, enough to show the face of a surly young man. "Magic don't work no more. The healers can't do nothing."

"Please. I think I'm gonna die."

"Are you deaf or stupid? The mag—"

"What is it, Esley?" The new voice was older and female.

"There's some woman here. Reckons she's sick and needs help. I've told her we can't do nothing," the young man, presumably named Esley, replied.

The door opened wider. Standing a little way back was an elderly woman dressed in the hooded brown gown of a follower of Perithalma, the god of healing magic.

Tevi appealed to her directly. "Please. I think it was a pie I ate yesterday. It didn't taste too good but it was cheap. But I've been throwing up all night, and my bowels, they... You don't want to know. Now my head feels like it's gonna explode. Please, can't you help?"

"As Esley said, my ability to work magic has gone, ever since Ciamon put his idol in the temple." The healer's distress and resentment were both clear.

"But herbs and potions. They still work, don't they? What'd you have given someone before? Can't you try that?"

The elderly healer hesitated and then stepped back. "Come in. I'll see what I can do."

Ignoring the resentful look from Esley, Tevi staggered after the healer down a hallway and into a small room.

"My name's Zorathe. I'm a healer. Or I used to be. I don't know what I..." The elderly woman was clearly ill at ease, almost to the point of tears. "I'll do what I can."

"Thanks. That's all I want."

Zorathe pressed the back of her hand on Tevi's forehead and then under her chin. "A temperature. Maybe." Her eyes darted randomly around the room, like a cat watching flies. "I can't see your aura. Can't see anyone's." Her fingers probed Tevi's throat. "Why do I bother? You might as well ask Esley. It's all..." She pulled down on Tevi's eyelid to examine the underside. Her face contorted in anguish and she backed off. "Why...I..."

Zorathe's state of agitation had been growing throughout the examination. Now it had shot through the roof. For an instant, it even looked as if she might run away. Her hands clasped each other in a writhing knot and then she wiped her face, as if trying to force herself back under control. "I'll get you a potion. It might help. I don't know anymore."

Zorathe fled the room. Had the loss of her powers undermined her sanity, or had she always been an emotional wreck? While waiting for her to return, Tevi took the chance for a quick scout around, but found nothing remotely matching Jemeryl's description of an emanator. Could she exploit Zorathe's unsteady mental state to conduct a wider search? How should she play it?

Tevi was still pondering this when Zorathe reappeared. The healer's composure was, if anything, even more fragile than on her departure. The cup in her hand shook so violently that the milky contents were in danger of being spilt as she passed it to Tevi.

"Drink this." Zorathe's voice was a squeak.

Tevi raised the cup to her lips, but then stopped. Ciamon's morphology was depriving the healer of not only her work, but also a part of herself—one of her senses. Zorathe was like someone struck suddenly blind or deaf. More than this, healing was not just a job, it was a calling. It was about saving lives, the most important work in the world.

Was it any wonder that Zorathe was taking the current situation so badly? And yet Tevi did wonder. Zorathe's reaction seemed misdirected, and contained more fear than anger. Jemeryl had lost far more of herself without being reduced to panicked apology. Somewhere, deep in her guts, Tevi felt a ripple of disquiet hardening. She looked at Zorathe. The healer was watching intently, but her eyes fixed on the cup where it touched Tevi's lips, and the expression on her face one of conflict, escalating into horror.

Tevi lowered the cup. "What's in this?"

Zorathe jerked back. The direction of her gaze lifted the few inches from Tevi's mouth to her eyes. Now there was no mistaking the anxiety, the dread, and the guilt. "It's...it's...I..." She took a step back and then her demeanour collapsed completely. Tears tumbled down her face. "You've taken everything already. I don't know any more than the others. I'm sorry. Oh, Perithalma forgive me. I'm sorry." Zorathe crumpled against the wall behind her. Her hands covered her face.

Tevi abandoned the pretence of food poisoning. She put down the cup and approached the sobbing healer. "Who's taken everything?"

"You sentinels. When you were here before."

"Why do you think I'm a sentinel?"

"You can't pre..." Zorathe was sobbing too hard to finish.

"I swear. I'm not a sentinel."

"The disguise. Dyeing your skin. I could tell. You haven't got your eyelids right."

So much for leaving Jemeryl and her fake splint behind. "If I was a sentinel, why would I need a disguise?"

"You're trying to trick me. To catch me out. But I can't tell you what you want to know."

Tevi hesitated, but Zorathe had seen through her disguise and knew she was not an ordinary pilgrim. "Calm down. I'm not a sentinel. In fact, I suspect we're on the same side."

Still quivering, Zorathe raised her head and peered at Tevi. "Who are you?"

"I'm working for the Coven. We want to destroy the morphology that stops magic working."

Zorathe's eyes widened as much as her swollen lids allowed. "Is that possible?"

"I wouldn't be here risking my neck if it wasn't." Tevi glanced at the cup. "You put poison in that, didn't you?"

"I'm sorry. I shouldn't have. I'm sworn to Perithalma to save life at all cost but...but...the sentinels..." Zorathe's sobs eased, although fresh tears rolled down her cheeks.

Tevi put a supportive arm around her. "What did they do?"

"They came here, took our supplies of herbs and potions. They wanted to know how they worked, how we know which ones to use. But all of us, we'd lost the ability to see what was needed. We tried to explain, but the sentinels accused us of not wanting to share our knowledge. They said we were deliberately holding out on them. They tried beating us into telling them. But we couldn't."

"They hurt you?"

"Not me. I was the oldest." Zorathe's distress increased. "But Gyde, Palry. Ronel died and the sentinels still didn't believe us. Finally Ciamon went. Ascended into heaven, so the story is. Sefriall took over at the temple and the sentinels lost interest in us. All the other healers grasped the chance to flee, but I couldn't desert Perithalma. Esley stayed to look after me. He's a good boy. But when you came and I... I'm sorry. I was frightened." Zorathe wiped her eyes.

"I understand. It's all right." Tevi spared only a glance for the cup of poison. Maybe, if she had drunk it, she might not be quite so forgiving, but Sefriall, not Zorathe, was her true enemy.

Zorathe's hands tightened on Tevi's arm. "Can you really bring the magic back?"

"I'm sure we can, but we need information."

"I don't know anything."

"You don't know what I'm after."

"I'm just—"

Tevi cut in. "For starters, did Ciamon leave anything here in the infirmary for you to take care of?"

Zorathe looked confused, then shook her head. "We wouldn't have done any service for the one who had reviled Perithalma."

"He might have made it seem like it was..." Tevi shrugged. "I don't know what he could have said. It mightn't have seemed important, but is there anything here that Ciamon sent?"

"No. Nothing."

"Good." Tevi smiled. "Believe me, this helps. It means we can ignore the whole infirmary. Now, what can you tell me about the other buildings around here?"

"You really want to know wh..." Zorathe's voice faded out.

Tevi nodded.

Zorathe frowned, before apparently deciding to take Tevi at her word. "To the north, that's the kitchen. We used to share the herb garden with them. But we've no use for the herbs. The cooks can have them all. The other building like this, over there"—she gestured—"with the veranda, that used to be a second ward of the infirmary."

"Nothing from Ciamon is stored there?"

"I don't know. I don't have anything to do with it now."

"Why not?"

"We don't need it. We aren't treating any patients. The sentinels have taken it over as barracks. Who knows what they've put in it?"

"When did they move in?"

"A month ago."

"So that was after Ciamon died?"

"Died?"

"You didn't believe the ascended into heaven story, did you?"

"You're sure?"

"He was murdered." In answer to the shocked look, Tevi added. "Not by me, or anyone with me, but I witnessed his death."

Zorathe looked pained. "Perithalma forgive me, but I feel no regret."

Tevi returned to her questions. "The other buildings. The circular one. What's that?"

"The basilica. It's where the convocation used to meet, but there's no convocation anymore. To the south of it is the stables. That's the one with the courtyard in the middle. The big block to the west is the original barracks. Once there was just a few ceremonial temple guards. Now Sefriall has them overflowing the place. There isn't enough space in the old barracks. I told you they've taken over our ward."

"Anywhere else?"

"Yes. They've moved into the junior acolytes quarters as well."

"Is that near here?"

"It's the square one on the other side of the basilica."

Tevi nodded as she positioned it on her mental map. It was the building she had already dismissed as being out of sight of the window. Only one more was left to account for. "The building next to the kitchen is the refectory, right?"

"Yes. It used to be for the priests. But it's another one the sentinels have taken over for their own use. Nobody else eats there now." Zorathe's frown returned. "Are you sure this helps?"

"More than you would think possible."

❖

The patrol of sentinels marched through the dusty square, ignoring Tevi and Jemeryl, sitting on the ground in the shade of a palm tree.

Jemeryl waited until they were well out of earshot. "Zorathe was very helpful."

"Once she'd stopped trying to poison me."

"I can't believe a healer would do that."

"It's understandable when you think what she'd been through with the sentinels."

Tevi's words sparked off an uncomfortable train of thought for Jemeryl. "I didn't mean..." Jemeryl chewed her lip. Healers were revered—the only magic users universally trusted. What sort of insanity would motivate anyone to assault them? "When I pushed Ci about medicine, I'd been trying to help. To get him to think. I didn't imagine it would end up like that. Not with people getting hurt…killed."

"You aren't the only one to have good intentions go awry."

"That doesn't make me feel any less guilty."

Tevi's arm slipped around Jemeryl's waist. "The blame doesn't lie with you. And even if it did, sitting here wailing won't help. Be positive. We're making progress."

"We know what the buildings are—or were."

"And we can discount most. The kitchens wouldn't be a safe place to leave something. Too chaotic and with too many casual workers trotting in and out. Anything left there would be at risk of being used as firewood or chucked out as rubbish."

"I guess the same applies for the refectory."

Tevi nodded. "And the stables. In fact, the only real candidate is the old barracks. The sentinels' discipline is awful. I'd be embarrassed to command them. But their barracks are guarded."

"They have more than one barrack block now." Jemeryl paused. "Although since the infirmary ward didn't become one until after Ci was dead, he can't have left the emanator there."

"Right. And the basilica was in disuse from the time he took over."

"I'm not sure we can dismiss it, but I agree the barracks is the place to start. Except getting in to look around won't be easy."

"It will be, if I disguise myself as a sentinel."

"You think you can just put a red cloak on and saunter in there?"

"Pretty much. No one will challenge me, because no one knows what's supposed to be happening. The sentinels haven't got a clue about being soldiers. You can tell from the way they stand guard. The way they react. The way they marched blindly through this square just now."

"Shame we didn't keep the helmets and cloaks we took before."

"Believe me, it won't be hard to get me fresh ones."

"And for me."

Tevi shook her head. "I'll go in alone."

"No, you won't."

"It's—"

"You've already had a healer trying to poison you. I'm not letting you face soldiers alone."

"Pretend soldiers."

"Pretend soldiers with real swords. I'm going in with you."

"You'll be too conspicuous with your arm in a splint."

"Soldiers get wounded. I thought it was an occupational risk."

"Wounded soldiers get noticed."

"Then I'll take the splint off. We'll find another way to hide my amulet."

Tevi sighed. "You're not going to give in on this, are you?"

"No."

Tevi leaned her head back against the tree trunk, clearly thinking. "What are you like at archery?"

"The last time I played with a bow I was about six years old."

"Really?" Tevi smiled. "I think that makes you perfectly qualified to be an archer in the sentinels."

❖

The bracer was the bulkiest one Tevi had been able to find, and the red tunic was designed for someone with considerably longer arms than Jemeryl's. Tevi folded back the sleeve and then fastened the bracer to hold it in place, covering Jemeryl's amulet. As a final touch she tugged out the material and adjusted the set of the folds to hide the outline. Tevi smiled. It ought to work.

Jemeryl frowned and then flicked the reinforced leather plate with her fingernails. "Shouldn't this shield bit be on the outside of my arm?"

"No."

"What's it supposed to achieve there?"

Tevi was amazed. "You really have never shot a proper bow, have you?"

"Why should I? Magic is far more effective if I want to flatten something at a distance."

"Right. Well, if you'd ever hit yourself on the wrist with a bowstring, you wouldn't have asked that question."

Jemeryl raised her arm as if holding an imaginary bow. Her frown grew. "Can you really hit yourself with the string?"

"Oh yes." Tevi grinned in amusement. "Although if you held your arm like that, the bracer would be no use."

"Why?"

"Because the string would hit your elbow first."

Jemeryl looked downcast. "I'm not very good at the part, am I?"

"Just keep the bow unstrung and you'll be fine."

Tevi picked up a helmet and placed it on Jemeryl's head. The cheek flaps hid her face, and the nose guard further distorted her appearance. The chances of them being recognised were comfortably slim.

In the end, acquiring the uniforms had proved even easier than Tevi anticipated. Not one of the sentinels sleeping by the bathing pool had stirred as she helped herself to the cloaks, helmets, and tunics. Admittedly, the sloppy soldiers had made a better effort to secure their swords, but since these were not standard issue, Tevi had been able to buy substitutes in the market, along with the bracer, bow, and quiver.

Tevi completed her own disguise, slipping the helmet on her head. "Ready to go?"

Jemeryl merely nodded in reply.

They were using a room in the infirmary to change clothes. With the return of magic at stake, Zorathe had willingly offered whatever assistance she could, including Esley's services in stealing the uniforms, although Tevi was pleased she had not needed him. Her conscience would not let her place more risk on the healer than she could help—not after the capture of the previous volunteers.

On the short march to the barracks Tevi was aware that she and Jemeryl were out of step, but given the training standards of the sentinels, it ought only to improve their masquerade. Certainly the sentries on duty showed not the faintest reaction as they entered.

Immediately inside the door was a large chamber spanning the width of the building. Stairs at the rear went up and down, and corridors led off on either side. Tevi suspected that originally the space had been a formal entrance foyer, but now it was more like a dosshouse, with straw-filled pallets covering most of the floor. Several clusters of off-duty sentinels were lounging around.

Tevi knew that to avoid a challenge, the main thing was never

JANE FLETCHER

to look confused or uncertain, but this did not mean they had to keep
moving. She dawdled to a stop and half faced Jemeryl. "I know it was
the Coven who sent them."

"Nah. It was those Nolians."

"How could Nolians hurt our idol? I tell you, the Coven's behind
it. It was magic."

"The Nolians can do magic."

"In their dreams."

Their voices were pitched just loud enough to be overheard, but
not so strident as to make it obvious this was their intention. As Tevi
had expected, the few heads that had turned on their arrival went back
to how they were before.

While keeping up the mock argument, Tevi studied the
surroundings. She did not need long to decide that nothing in the foyer
might be concealing the emanator. Jemeryl must have reached the same
conclusion. With a nod of her head, she wandered towards a corridor,
still debating the relative iniquities of the Coven and the Nolians.

Away from the entrance hall, the changes that had taken place
were even more apparent. Judging by the marks on the ceiling, interior
walls had been ripped out to make space for the expanding army. Every
square inch was being utilised. If the emanator had ever been here, it
would have been turfed out during the course of the restructuring.

The off-duty sentinels divided into two distinct groups. The devout
believers were reading or knelt in prayer. The others were gossiping or
playing dice. Tevi recognised the mark of opportunists who had signed
on hoping for another town to pillage. No one from either group showed
any interest in Tevi and Jemeryl until they had nearly completed their
circuit of the ground floor.

A solidly built woman blocked the passage. "You looking for
someone?"

The above-average amount of gold braid indicated an officer. Tevi
snapped a salute. "Yes ma'am. We have a message for Captain Lydian
from his mother."

"I've never heard of him."

"He transferred in from the Villenes reserves five days ago."

"I didn't know we had any." The woman shrugged. "Must be in
Eagle patrol."

"Have they moved?"

The woman pointed, still arrogant but no longer combative. "Nope. Still along there."

"Thank you, ma'am."

Their return to the entrance hall attracted even less notice than before. The emanator was definitely nowhere on the ground floor and Tevi suspected little would be achieved by continuing the search, but giving up was certain failure. She strolled to the rear of the room. The way up was blocked by a small group of officers, talking. Without missing a step, Tevi headed downstairs.

The low-roofed cellar was damp and dark, but the light was sufficient to see that it was piled with mounds of junk. Tevi assumed most of the original furniture and fittings of the barracks would have been thrown out or sold. The cellar must be the dumping spot for items that someone thought might still have a function. Would anyone have wanted to hang on to the emanator? If so, surely it would be here.

At her side, Jemeryl sighed loudly. "You know, it was really careless of Captain Lydian to lose his dagger."

Tevi grinned. "I don't rate our chances of finding it in all this."

"We're going to have to search, though."

As it turned out, the story of the lost dagger was not needed. Despite Tevi and Jemeryl spending over an hour rummaging through the entire cellar, nobody came to investigate what they were up to.

The last item of any interest was an iron-bound chest. Jemeryl knelt to examine the lock. "I don't supposed you'd know how to pick this."

"Nope."

"The emanator might be in it."

Tevi slid her fingers under the bottom of the chest and shook up and down. Something was rattling around inside. "That might be it."

Jemeryl broke out laughing. "No."

"How do you know?"

"Because if you bounced it around like that, you'd have knocked the transient vertices out of alignment."

"That would stop it working?"

"Yes. Definitely."

"I'll remember that." Tevi lowered the chest back to the ground.

Jemeryl plonked herself on the lid and sighed. "So, it's not here."

Tevi took a seat beside her. "It's still progress. Elimination will get us there in the end."

"Do we try eliminating the upper floor?"

"Why not?"

The top floor of the barracks was clearly the officers' quarters, noticeably different in atmosphere to the one below. The internal walls were still in place and no pallets or off-duty sentinels were in sight. A single corridor with numerous doors led left and right.

Hesitation was the thing to avoid. Tevi set off to the right, testing the doors as she went. A little to her surprise, they were all unlocked. Was it due to overconfidence that no thief would dare enter? Whatever the reason, the first four doors Tevi opened gave access to simple bedrooms. Even if Ciamon had thought it safe to place the emanator in living quarters, the austere furnishing offered little in the way of storage space. Each room was checked and dismissed in seconds. Unfortunately, the fourth room they tried was occupied.

The officer looked up from his desk. "What do you want?"

"Sorry sir, I thought this was Captain Lydian's room."

"Who?"

"Captain Lydian. He's just transferred in from the Villenes reserves."

The officer scowled. "Never heard of him. Try the other end."

"Thank you, sir." Tevi backed out and closed the door.

Was it worth pushing their luck further? However, Jemeryl had already set off to the other end of the corridor. She was the one who tried the door furthest from the stairs and then glanced over her shoulder.

"Locked." Jemeryl whispered the word.

The only locked room in the building. Was it significant? Tevi pressed her hands against the door. The dry desert air had sucked the life from the wood. The frame was old and warped, crumbling into powder when she rubbed. Tevi knew that she could force the door, but was it worth the risk? Then the memory of Darjain's gentle smile drifted through her head, followed by the image of him hanging from a gallows. Tevi grasped the handle and pressed hard.

The wood splintered with a sound like hot fat spitting. Tevi paused for a moment, but no sound came from within the room and no heads appeared along the corridor. She pushed the door open and stepped into yet another bedroom, although appreciably grander than the others. They had found the commander's quarters, larger and more luxurious than anyone else's, but still with a total absence of arcane magical devices.

Tevi sighed and looked at Jemeryl. "I don't think it's here."

"No."

"Shall we go?"

"Might as well." But rather than leave, Jemeryl crossed the room to a small table and picked up a small pouch lying on it. Coins jangled when she shook it. "If we give an obvious reason for the break-in, it might stop them looking for the not so obvious."

"True." Tevi smiled. "The drinks tonight are on you."

"Actually, I think they're on the commander."

CHAPTER THIRTEEN—THE JOURNEYMAN BLACKSMITH

Ciamon had turned away from the idol and gone to the window. Jemeryl clawed at the memory, trying to picture the exact expression on his face, his tone of voice, where his eyes had gone, but by now she had run through the scene so many times she knew she was in danger of rewriting it in her head.

"We can't be sure he was looking at where he'd put the emanator." Jemeryl voiced her doubts.

"True, but it's all we've got to work with. We need to rule out every building."

"Or get a better lead."

"That would be nice."

Dusk was approaching as they made their way back to the Calequiral mansion. Traders were closing their shops and workers were returning home, but there was no feeling of everyday routine to the town. Everyone was on edge, except for the manic preachers screeching their sermons at street corners. Their calls for mortal blood and divine vengeance made Jemeryl wince. The only good thing was that the general fear and suspicion made it unremarkable for her and Tevi to be walking along, heads together, whispering like conspirators.

At the infirmary, they had changed back into their scruffy pilgrim clothes and left, not wasting a second. Before long, someone would discover the broken door to the commander's quarters, if it had not happened already. They wanted to be well away before any trouble started, not least because they were both anxious to avoid endangering the healer. Nothing to link them to the infirmary had been left behind.

The stolen uniforms were in a bag over Tevi's shoulder, although they had not yet made up their minds whether it was worth the risk of hanging on to the clothes in case they were needed again, or if they should ditch them under a pile of rubbish.

Jemeryl turned her thoughts back to their problem. "Which building do you want to concentrate on next?"

"It's your turn to pick, since I was wrong about the barracks."

"I don't think I've got any better ideas. The barracks was the best hope. Ci would have wanted the emanator in a secure place."

"Certainly if it's as fragile as you say."

"I wouldn't go as far as fragile, but it couldn't take the thumping you were giving whatever was in the chest."

"Anyway. It has to rule out the stables. It's not the place to store anything you don't want kicked around by horses."

Jemeryl mentally ran through the list of buildings. "How about the basilica? It's no longer being used for the convocation. Why don't we ask Zorathe if she knows what's happening there now?"

"I'm guessing it's being used by the sentinels for something. They're short of space and I can't see them letting a building stand empty. If Ciamon had left the emanator in there, it would have been carted out ages ago."

"It'll do no harm to ask her."

"True. While we're at it, we could try searching the infirmary. Ciamon might have snuck something in without Zorathe knowing."

"I'm sure not. He hadn't even known there was an infirmary here, until I pushed him into asking Sefriall." Jemeryl winced, reminded again of what her questions had led to.

"He'd have known there was a kitchen."

"He'd also have known it wouldn't be a good spot to store something he didn't want disturbed. The refectory wouldn't be much better."

"Unless he disguised it as a lion's head and hung it on the wall." Tevi's tone made it clear she was not being totally serious.

"A more likely bet would be a quiet wine cellar."

"Or a locked storeroom." Tevi sighed. "I'd really thought we were onto something when we found the locked door in the barracks. Ciamon could have put the emanator in a room and then sealed it by magic. That would have been safe."

Jemeryl stopped dead in her tracks as Tevi's words sparked off a new memory.

Tevi looked at her. "What is it?"

"Something Larric said. He'd been talking to a blacksmith." Jemeryl frowned and carried on walking as she tried to recall Larric's exact words. "No. It was the blacksmith's apprentice."

"I don't remember him mentioning one."

"It was the day we all separated to hunt leads. He told us the story, but it might have been before you arrived back at the Four Winds."

"What did he say?"

"The master blacksmith had been called to the temple by Sefriall to open a locked door, but couldn't. Which would make sense if Ci had used magic on it. The apprentice told Larric how Sefriall had been getting angry and threatening to have them hanged."

"But it's not as if Sefriall knows what the emanator is, so she won't be trying to find it and wouldn't be able to do anything with it if she did."

"If she knows there's a room that was important to Ci, and now she can't get into it, you can bet that'll get her curiosity going."

"Maybe," Tevi conceded. "Do you remember any other details?"

"I don't think there were any. It wasn't the main point of the story, just the explanation of why the blacksmith and apprentice had come to be in the temple. The only reason Larric mentioned it was because they'd overheard a report given to Sefriall about the nomads."

"How about the apprentice? Did Larric give a name or a description?"

"I think it was a woman, but that's it." Jemeryl was angry with herself. "I should have paid more attention."

"Don't be so hard on yourself. Sefriall had a problem with a locked door, somewhere in the temple, and employed a blacksmith to fix it. It's hardly the sort of thing to jump out as vitally significant. It still might be nothing more than a lost key."

"A master blacksmith ought to be able to deal with a normal lock." Jemeryl looked at Tevi. "You said a better lead would be nice. I think this is it."

Tevi grimaced. "In that case, can I take back the word *nice*? Breaking into a magically locked room in the middle of the temple isn't going to be easy."

"That's our second problem. First, we need to track down the blacksmith. How many of them do you think there are in Kradja?"

"A town this size? Less than a dozen, I'd have thought."

"That's not too bad. But..." Jemeryl's mind was leaping forward.

"What?"

"Sefriall's running the town. She can pick whoever she wants. Cost won't be an issue."

Tevi nodded. "Especially since she wouldn't need to pay. I'm sure her sentinels could persuade any blacksmith to piously volunteer their services free of charge."

"She wouldn't have called on anyone but the best. We just need to find out who has the best reputation. And the easy way to do that is to ask." Jemeryl smiled and glanced over her shoulder. They had just passed a street porter trundling his empty handcart back to wherever empty carts go at the end of the working day. Jemeryl slowed her pace until he again drew level. "Excuse me."

"What?"

"I'm new in town and need some advice. The lock on my master's strongbox has jammed. It's been in his family for generations and he doesn't want it damaged by a ham-fisted blacksmith. He wants the best. Who'd you recommend? Price is no issue."

"Keliah."

"Where do I find Keliah's forge?"

"Third to last on the southern approach road to the market."

"Thank you."

The porter trundled away.

Jemeryl grinned at Tevi. "There you go, Keliah on the southern approach."

"As long as the porter isn't a friend of Keliah, or his brother."

"How about we separate, both ask ten people, and meet up at the mansion to compare notes?"

"Done."

❖

"I'll see you by that wall."

"Right. Good luck."

"You too." Tevi patted Jemeryl's shoulder and then watched her stroll away. Once she was lost from sight amid the traffic, Tevi turned towards her own goal.

The façade of Keliah's forge was double the size of any other shop on the street and well maintained. Smoke trailed away from an impressive set of chimneys. The wooden anvil hanging above the door had a fresh coat of paint on it and only the highest-quality goods were on display. Business was clearly going well for Keliah.

Of the twenty votes they had picked up the night before, nine had named Keliah as the best blacksmith in Kradja, while another seven had gone to a rival called Orasies. Two had claimed that Lysjani was every bit as good but only half the price of the others. However, in Tevi's experience, cheapest was seldom the best, and she was sure Sefriall would be every bit as sceptical as herself. One respondent had come straight out and recommended his sister's best friend. The final person had obviously suffered some bad experiences and had sworn there was not a single blacksmith in Kradja who could tell copper from cheese. Tevi had sympathised, even though the reply had not been very helpful.

With a clear choice between Keliah and Orasies, they had each taken one to investigate. Tevi squared her shoulders and marched through the doorway of her allotted blacksmith. The main room of the forge was at least thirty feet deep and twice that in width. The walls were hung with dozens of examples of metalwork, in various stages of completion—weapons, armour, tools, and ornaments. The range and complexity of the items made an impressive array, as was undoubtedly Keliah's intention.

In the middle of the rear wall stood a brick-built furnace where a boy in his early teens was methodically pumping the bellows. Presumably he was Keliah's apprentice, which was not promising if Jemeryl had been right about Larric's informant being female. A gaunt elderly man stood by a bench to one side. He had been squinting along the length of a contraption consisting of three parallel rods when Tevi entered. He put it down and scowled at her.

"Do you want something?"

"Are you the owner?"

"Yes. So what are you after?"

Tevi suspected her shabby clothes contributed to the lack of welcome in his voice. She did not look like someone who could afford Keliah's merchandise or services.

"My mistress has sent me. The clasp on this has broken and needs repairing." Tevi held out a small brooch.

Keliah wiped his hands on his apron and strode over, but at the sight of gold, his attitude softened from hostile to merely curt. "Give that here."

While he examined it, Tevi stood back demurely. She had bought two brooches from the market that morning, one for herself and one for Jemeryl. Now she had met Keliah, Tevi was grateful she had been able to afford something he would take seriously. He was clearly not the sort to chat with riff-raff.

"It happened on the journey here. We arrived late last night. My mistress sent me out, first thing this morning to find the best bl—"

Keliah cut through Tevi's words, shouting at his apprentice. "Daqui! What do you think you're doing? Don't stab at it."

"Sorry, sir." The boy's forehead knotted in concentration as he painstakingly worked the bellows.

The blacksmith turned back to Tevi. "Someone's been rough-handed with this."

Keliah's tone was sharp, making it sound as if he was accusing Tevi of damaging the brooch on purpose. Admittedly, this would have been absolutely correct, but it did not stop Tevi feeling irritated. Although she was playing the part of a servant, she was still a customer, and might expect a little civility from the blacksmith. However, getting into an argument would not help.

Tevi tried to look shamefaced. "I know. My mistress was very angry. It's not her best jewellery, but it has memories for her. That's why I came to you. I've heard yo—"

"I can look at it tomorrow."

"Thank you. I know my mistress will be happy to wait." Tevi spoke quickly, hoping to get to her point before she was interrupted again. "With your reputation you must be very busy. Before coming here I asked around town to find the best blacksmith, and everyone I spoke to was ver—"

"The price will be six florins."

Tevi's attempt had failed. Keliah's clearly had no interest in hearing flattery from a mere servant. From his expression, he was insulted that Tevi had even dared to ask questions about his workmanship.

"My mistress has only authorised me to pay up to four."

"Five."

"I cannot say, but if she's pleased when she picks it up, maybe. And I'm sure—"

"Daqui! I told you to go easy. I didn't tell you to fall asleep. Can't you see the colour of the coals?" Again, Tevi had lost the blacksmith's attention.

The boy ducked his head, as if fearing a blow. "Yes, sir. Sorry."

Tevi made one last attempt to steer the conversation. "I'm sure she'll be pleased. I've heard your work is good enough for the temple. Someone said Sefriall herself has called on your services. That must—"

"Tell your mistress she can pick it up the day after tomorrow."

Tevi gave up. "Thank you. I will."

She turned away. Keliah was clearly not about to tell her anything. Maybe, if Jemeryl came by to collect the brooch, dressed more expensively, she might have better luck. Or maybe Keliah was uniformly rude to everyone, regardless of status. Already he was back yelling at his apprentice.

"By Toqwani's balls, boy! Are you blind or stupid?" Keliah raised his voice yet louder. "Vorn. Come and take over from this imbecile."

Tevi paused at the doorway and glanced back. A young woman wearing a heavy leather apron and gloves appeared from a back room. Soot and oil darkened her face. She was a few years older than the unfortunate Daqui. Vorn must be either a journeyman or a second apprentice. Was this the person Larric had spoken to? Tevi studied the woman. How to find out? Tevi was quite sure Keliah would not let his employees stand around idly gossiping with customers.

Tevi left the forge, consoling herself with the idea that tracking down Vorn might prove unnecessary. With enough luck, Orasies would have turned out to be a cheerful chatterbox, who had not only told Jemeryl all about her trouble with Sefriall's mysterious locked door but had provided a detailed map of the way there, with all guard points and other hazards carefully noted.

In wishful thinking, there really was no point going for half-measures.

❖

When Jemeryl returned to their agreed rendezvous point, she was not surprised to see Tevi already there waiting. The visit to Orasies's forge had taken far more time than expected.

"Sorry I was so long."

"That's all right." Tevi's smile of greeting held a querying edge. "I'd been hoping it meant your blacksmith was bombarding you with more information than you knew what to do with, but judging by your face, it didn't work out that way."

Jemeryl sighed heavily. "No. Afraid not. How about you?"

"The only things Keliah would lower himself to tell me was how much the repair would cost and when I could pick it up. But I'm sure if I'd said I wanted to hang myself he'd have told me where I could find some rope."

"Not what you'd call friendly?"

"Hardly."

"Orasies wasn't so bad. Although she seemed to think she needed to use little words when she spoke to me. And she ignored me as soon as anyone else came in—which happened twice. That's why I took so long."

"It's the clothes. We don't look like their class of customer."

"Probably. But it meant I got to hear her full sales pitch two times, complete with name dropping. For what it's worth, she didn't brag about working for the High Priest at the temple."

"Maybe spending a couple of days being unable to open a door isn't something she wants to brag about."

"True. And Sefriall had been making nasty threats about gibbets and things. Orasies might be trying to push the whole thing from her mind."

Tevi tipped her head at the nearby forge. "From what I saw of Keliah, Sefriall could sell tickets in town when she had him hung. If I was his apprentice, I'd want to book a front-row place."

"Did you see the apprentice?"

"Yes."

"A young woman?"

"Nope. A boy, but there's an older girl working for Keliah as well. From her age, I'd have guessed she was a journeyman."

"I'm sure Larric said it was the blacksmith's apprentice who told him about the door."

"Maybe he doesn't appreciate the difference. Most sorcerers aren't too bothered about trade guilds and how they licence their members."

"Maybe. Though it's equally possible she wasn't the person he spoke to. But that's our next step, seeing if we can copy what he did and talk to people. Larric was making a round of the taverns and eating houses, trying to pick up gossip. If he spoke to any tradesfolk, it would most likely be during their lunch break. Which ought to be around about now."

"That's if Keliah lets his workers take time to eat."

"We'll see." Jemeryl pointed to a tavern. "That's midway between the two blacksmiths. Their employees might pop in for lunch. We could see if we overhear anything. If not, we can move on to another tavern."

Jemeryl started to walk away, but before she could take a step, Tevi grabbed her arm. "We can do better than that. Look. Do you see the woman who's just left Keliah's? That's the journeyman I saw there. She's cleaned herself up, and taken off her protective wear, but it's definitely her."

"Do you think she'll recognise you?"

"I doubt it. She never glanced my way."

"Great. Let's see where she goes."

The young woman hurried along the street. She went past the tavern and ducked into a narrow alley immediately after it. Jemeryl and Tevi sauntered in pursuit. They did not want their quarry to get too far ahead, but neither did they want to attract attention by running. Fortunately, they turned the corner just in time to see her disappear through a doorway a few dozen yards further along.

The rich smell of hot food filled the alley and Jemeryl was not surprised, when they reached the open door, to find a cheap eating house inside. She felt a surge of optimism. The place was noisy and crowded, exactly the sort of establishment she could imagine Larric visiting in the hunt for gossip. Three long tables were squeezed in with barely room for a walkway between. Already most seats were taken, but she and Tevi were able to find a free spot on a bench immediately behind the woman they had followed.

Despite the hubbub, Jemeryl was close enough to listen to the conversation behind her. The woman was clearly a regular and knew most of the people on her table. Within a minute, Jemeryl had learned that the young woman's name was short for Vorndashi, she had missed a good laugh the night before, her brother was due in later, her favourite parsnip bake was on the day's menu, and as Tevi had suspected, she would pay good money to see her boss dangling by his neck.

The food, when it arrived, was cheap and plentiful to the extent that Jemeryl could understand why the other patrons were willing to overlook the shortfalls in choice and quality, although for her own mind and stomach, the trade-off was not quite worth it. She and Tevi ate in silence, listening intently. However, no mention of the temple or locked doors cropped up. That would be too much to hope for.

Jemeryl had eaten as much as she could bring herself to swallow when there was a round of good-byes and the general sound of movement from the table behind. Jemeryl glanced over her shoulder. Most customers on the table were leaving, and although Vorn was still finishing her dinner, surely she would soon be gone. Keliah did not sound like someone who would tolerate leisurely lunch breaks. Yet Larric had engaged someone in conversation. Surely Vorn was the person he spoke to.

Making use of the drop in background noise, Jemeryl pitched her voice just loud enough for the woman behind to overhear. "It's not the magic that's gone. It's the ability to work it."

Tevi took the cue. "What's the difference?"

"Old spells keep on working."

"You're full of bullshit. What'd you know about it?"

"The healer told me. When I showed her my broken arm." Jemeryl waved the splint for emphasis. "She said she had a charm to speed up the knitting of bone, and all I'd need to do was to wear it on my wrist."

"Why didn't she give it to you then?"

"That's just it. It was in a box with a magic lock. Now the healer can't work any magic, she can't unlock it."

Tevi crowed. "And you fell for that? She was just stringing you along."

"She's a good woman. She wouldn't lie."

"My arse."

Jemeryl had to fight the urge not to punch the air when she felt a tap on her shoulder. She looked around, trying to appear surprised.

Vorn was leaning back to talk to her. "The healer most likely was telling you the truth."

"How would you know?" Tevi asked, keeping up her role as sceptic.

"I'm a journeyman, working for Keliah the blacksmith. About a month ago, we got called up to the temple by Sefriall herself. She had a door she couldn't unlock and she wanted him to sort it out. But he couldn't. He said it was magic, and he ought to know."

"How? He ain't a witch, is he?"

Vorn picked up the remains of her lunch and shunted herself over to their table. Clearly, she liked to chat, and from what Jemeryl had heard about her employer, she would not get much chance at work.

"Not quite. But Keliah used to have a bit of magical ability. Maybe not enough to count as a proper witch, but it was what made him such a good blacksmith. Since Ciamon made his idol, Keliah's lost all that. He always was a pain in the arse. Now he's just...phut." Vorn's face twisted in a grimace. "Soon as I can find another job, I'm leaving. It's Daqui the apprentice I feel sorry for. He's still indentured to the old bastard for another six years."

"Keliah was sure the lock was magical?" Jemeryl asked.

"He said it was an ordinary lock, but someone had put a spell on it. Even though he's lost his gift for magic, he knows how to spot things like that. But he had a hell of a job convincing Sefriall. I tell you, I was shitting myself. I thought we were both going to get strung up."

"You were at the temple with him, working on the door?"

"Yes. Except the door wasn't in the temple itself. It was on one of the buildings round the back."

Jemeryl's throat constricted with the effort to keep her voice sounding neutral as she asked, "Which one?"

"The old basilica. Where the convocation used to meet."

Tevi returned to her sceptical routine. "Who'd want to lock that by magic? What's in there to worry about anyway?"

"All the old idols from the temple. When Ciamon took over, he had them taken out and dumped in the basilica. He must have got someone to put the spell on it, as well. I can see why he wanted to keep the evil idols out of people's hands. Someone might try to bring the other gods back." Vorn frowned, clearly trying to think, although Jemeryl got the impression she was not very good at it. "But he was supposed to be the herald of the Cyclian gods. Why didn't he leave their idols out?"

"Who knows? But that'll be why Sefriall wanted the door open. She wants to get her old idols back in the temple," Jemeryl suggested.

"You could be right. The ones in there at the moment are a bit rough." Vorn mopped up the last of her meal with a piece of bread and then stood. "I've got to go. Nice talking to you." She turned and left.

Jemeryl stared at the unwanted food congealing on her plate and laughed softly as a sudden realisation struck her. Why had she not thought of it before?

"What is it?" Tevi asked.

"I told you Ciamon didn't like lying. He told the truth. He said the emanator was in the idol. He just didn't specify which idol."

❖

Tevi counted to twenty. She did not know whether to be pleased or despairing when the two sentinels reappeared, exactly on cue, in the patch of moonlight by the kitchen. The predictability would make her task so much easier, but it pained her professional sensibilities that the holy warriors had not grasped the concept of varying their patrol route. They also seemed to have no idea that the point of sentry duty was to be alert for potential trouble. Neither had spared a glance for the herb garden as they passed. Tevi shook her head. A dozen fighters could have been hiding in the deep shadow of the bushes, rather than just her and Jemeryl.

"Will you have time to climb in?" Jemeryl asked, once the sentinels had gone.

"No problem. I'll just wait until the other two cross behind the infirmary. You stay here until the first lot go by again, then I'll drop a rope to pull you up."

"Fine."

"And keep an eye out, just in case someone varies their route."

"What if I do see someone?"

"Here." Tevi picked up a dead branch and scratched it across the ground in three sharp bursts. "Make a signal exactly like that. If whoever you've spotted hears it, they'll just think it's a rat in the bushes."

"Supposing there's a real rat making a noise round here?"

"We only need worry about the rats that can count to three."

Right on cue, the second patrol marched into view, around the basilica. Both Tevi and Jemeryl became silent and motionless until the sound of the two sentinels' footsteps had faded behind the infirmary.

"Right. Here I go."

Tevi reached over and squeezed Jemeryl's hand, then scooted across the twenty yards of moonlit gravel between the herb garden and the basilica. The foot of the wall was in shadow. Tevi ducked into it and crouched with her back pressed against the stone, listening. No shouts, whistles or running footsteps. So far, so good.

Coiled over her shoulder was a length of rope with a grapple. Tevi shook it loose and stared up. The row of windows was twenty-five feet above her head. The basilica was an old building, in a plain architectural style. The windows were no more than small unglazed holes with an arched top. Getting through would be a tight fit, but she expected to manage it without difficulty, unless Ciamon had also thought to protect the windows against intrusion.

The idea of poison or fireball traps was worrying, although Tevi was sure that Ciamon lacked the imagination to think of entering by any way other than the door. Jemeryl had been equally certain he would never have used any malicious spells even if he had, but there was only one way to find out.

Tevi swung the iron grapple in a circle and launched it at the window opening directly overhead. Luck was with her and on the first attempt, the pointed tines caught on the lip and held firm. Tevi gave one sharp tug to test and then started to climb.

The rope creaked at the strain of her weight and a soft breeze sighed under the eaves. The only other sound was the rasp of her knees against the wall. The outside of the basilica had been painted with a rough limewash, plastered thickly enough to blur the grooves between the stones. Tevi was nearly at the window when she heard something else—three short bursts of rustling, like a rat burrowing through rubbish.

Tevi froze, aware that she would show up against the white wall, even though she was still in deep shadow. Who had Jemeryl spotted?

Had the sentinels changed their patrol routes? Which direction were they coming from and would they spot her? Was it better to wait and see, or to run now? Then Tevi heard the footsteps, but they were not those of soldiers on patrol. Someone was stumbling in her direction.

A few seconds passed and a figure appeared around the side of the basilica. The moonlight was just sufficient to show the red cloak. He was a sentinel, but not one on duty. The man was clearly blind drunk. His steps were making as much progress sideways as forwards. Presumably, he was on his way back to the barracks after a heavy night in a tavern or brothel—possibly both, although from the state he was in, he was most likely incapable of getting his money's worth in the latter.

His route would pass directly beneath where Tevi was suspended, but his difficulty getting the ground to stay under his feet was taking all his attention. His eyes were locked on the gravel and the only way he was going to look up was if he fell flat on his back. While this carried a higher likelihood than Tevi would have wished, she knew she was far safer staying where she was.

The drunken sentinel stumbled beneath her feet. He braced a hand against the wall to steady himself, and then lurched on. Tevi was just relaxing when she felt the rope jolt in her hands. She looked up as a second tremor ran through it. Her first thought was that the grapple was slipping, but then she saw the stone lip of the window shift and crumble. A chunk of masonry the size of her head broke away from the building, bringing the grapple and a shower of loose fragments with it.

Tevi's feet hit the cobbles a split second before the cascade of stones. The noise was enough to bring the drunken sentinel to a halt. However, he was not able to turn around quickly. Tevi grabbed the nearest large piece of stone and leapt forward. The sentinel was clearly trying to coordinate his knees for the about-face manœuvre when Tevi smashed the stone down on his head. His helmet would have absorbed most of the damage, but the blow was still hard enough to send him crashing to the ground, where he lay, unmoving.

At the sound of running feet, Tevi dropped into a defensive pose, ready to deal with more sentinels, but it was only Jemeryl, racing to her side.

Jemeryl skidded to a stop. "Have you killed him?"

Tevi shook her head. She could hear the soft groans coming from the man. "He'll be fine."

In confirmation of her words, the moans turned to snores. Even without being hit, he must have been close to passing out from the drink. Tevi caught hold of his ankles and pulled him back the short distance until he was lying directly beneath the cracked windowsill. She arranged the largest fragment of stone close by his head.

The next patrol to go by would find him. Would they believe it was an accident with falling masonry? The man himself would not be able to give any creditable account of what had happened. But regardless of whether the truth eventually came out, the patrol would waste several minutes questioning him before they raised an alarm. With any luck, it would be enough time for her and Jemeryl to get well clear of the area.

Tevi took Jemeryl's hand. "Come on, let's go. The patrol will be back soon."

Jemeryl pointed at the comatose figure. "Will he be all right?"

"Better than us if we don't get going."

Tevi led the way to the herb garden and from there under the infirmary colonnade and into the main part of town. The streets were quiet and deserted, but they were no place to hang around if you did not want to attract attention. Not until they were back in the Calequiral mansion did Tevi feel safe, and even that was a very relative term.

❖

Daylight confirmed what Tevi had suspected the night before. She studied the small fragment, white on one side, brown dust on the other, and then passed it to Jemeryl, who was sitting beside her on the roof of the mansion.

"What's this?"

"A bit of the basilica. I picked it up last night."

"This isn't stone. It's…" Jemeryl scratched at it with her nail. "Mud brick?"

"Yup. Very ancient mud brick. Newer stuff wouldn't crumble that way."

"The basilica looks like stone."

"That's the plaster coat and limewash. I'd guess it's been falling apart for some time, but rather than rebuild it properly, someone's gone for the cheap option of trying to cover things up."

"That's why it broke away?"

"Yes."

"It won't be worth going back tonight to try another window?"

"No. But if you don't mind waiting another couple of decades, I predict the roof will fall in and smash the emanator for us."

"That will be too late for the Coven. The world will belong to people like Bykoda."

"Ciamon really didn't think things through."

"I know. But we need a new plan."

Tevi grinned. "I've got one."

"What?"

Tevi reclaimed the fragment of mud brick and held it in her palm. "We didn't know the walls were so weak, so there's no way Ciamon would have."

"Right."

"He wasn't the most imaginative of people."

"He wasn't stupid."

"But he was linearly minded. He only considered the straightforward, head-on approach to problems."

"In some things."

"We're talking architecture."

"We are?" From her expression, Jemeryl was having trouble seeing where Tevi was going.

"Ciamon put a spell on the lock. What chance he'd have thought to put a spell on the hinges? Or strengthened the walls?"

Jemeryl took a few moments to weigh it up. "Not much, I'd have thought. Does that help us?"

"The lock won't matter if the doors are no longer standing."

"We've looked at them. They're huge and reinforced with iron."

"I'm thinking of what they're mounted on."

"All right. The walls will be the weak spot. But even you aren't strong enough to kick them down."

Tevi's smile broadened. "I think I know how to get some helpers."

CHAPTER FOURTEEN—FALSE IDOLS

Midafternoon in Kradja was blisteringly hot, when even the lizards and sand flies sought shade. Once it would have been a quiet point in the day, a chance to catch up on sleep or sit idly gossiping with friends. Now it added irritability and tiredness to the volatile mixture on the streets. As Jemeryl watched the crowd she saw someone clip someone else's elbow in passing. A trivial accident, yet clenched fists and spat curses followed. Only wariness averted a fight. For all either antagonist knew, the other might be one of Sefriall's spies. All around, eyes homed in on the brief conflict, eager for some excitement, only to glaze over again when the two parted with no more than a last muttered exchange of insults.

The dusty square was full of too many people with too much time on their hands. Three preachers were haranguing the crowds from positions around the square and another two crazed souls were writhing on the ground, spouting garbled prophesies of slaughter. A group of pilgrims stood chanting at one side. The crowds drifted from one to another, boredom battling the taut anticipation of a wild dog pack. What would they do if they scented blood?

Jemeryl viewed the scene anxiously. "Are you sure you can do this?"

Tevi grinned. "Just watch me."

"Supposing something goes wrong?"

"The worst that can happen is I'll get laughed at. And that's happened to me before."

Jemeryl tried not to let her fears show as she nodded and stepped back. She trusted Tevi utterly, and yet the mere thought of what was proposed made her guts turn to ice. Failure could be so much more dangerous than Tevi was suggesting. Anyone could see the Kradja mob was violent and unstable. Could Tevi really control it? Playing with fire was a child's game by comparison.

Jemeryl found a vantage point halfway up a short flight of steps, with a clear view over the heads. She spotted Tevi striding through the mob, to where one of the preachers had claimed the prime site. The high rectangular block of stone in the middle of the square must be the plinth for a statue. What was not so clear was whether the monument had been removed or if it was yet to arrive.

Without hesitation, Tevi vaulted onto the block. The resident preacher turned and glared at her, first in manifest surprise and then outrage. The man was tall and powerfully built, and was clearly not expecting to have his position challenged. From where she stood, Jemeryl could see that the threatened confrontation had immediately caught the mob's attention. People were turning in the direction of the block. A slow drift towards it had begun.

The preacher said something to Tevi, too indistinct for Jemeryl to make out. However, Tevi's reply was loud and clear enough to be heard across the square. "Because I've got something important to say and you haven't."

The preacher advanced, clearly intending to push Tevi off the plinth. Despite the man's greater height and weight, the unequal contest was only ever going to have one winner. The crowd cheered as the preacher tumbled over the edge and laughed at the unfortunates who were not able to dodge out of his way in time. Already, Tevi was commanding a bigger audience than anyone else in the square. Even some of the chanters broke off to watch.

People shuffled in tighter, awaiting her words. Instead Tevi said nothing. Arms crossed, she paced the block, staring down with the stern expression of a judge about to pass sentence. Silence rippled out across the mob, hushing voices and stilling movement. Yet more eyes were now on Tevi.

Jemeryl divided the crowd out in her mind. Some were intrigued, their curiosity caught by Tevi's unorthodox beginning. Some were sceptical, expecting yet more of the same. Some were avid. Were they hoping for further violence? The two remaining preachers screamed ever louder in an attempt to retain their audience until they too fell silent. Their faces showed confusion that Tevi's poise could so totally triumph over their volume. With each second, the sense of anticipation grew. Jemeryl did not need magic to recognise the collective shortening of breath and speeding pulse. All eyes were on Tevi, waiting.

At last she spoke. "Why are you here?"

The echoes died away. The crowd shuffled expectantly.

"Why are you here when our gods are being insulted? You stand in the very shadow of the temple. And not a stone's throw from here, the idols of the false gods are being protected and honoured. You know their names: Perithalma, Yalaish, Harretha, Nolius...Nolius." Tevi's voice rosed to a shout on the repetition. Several people standing closest to her flinched.

"You remember their idols, how they mocked the temple, claiming a place as if they belonged there. The blessed prophet Ciamon cleared them out, but he didn't go far enough. That job he left for us. Are you ready? Doesn't your heart burn to see them gone? Don't your feet itch to kick down the door they're hiding behind? Don't your hands ache to smash them into a thousand fragments?"

From where she stood, Jemeryl could see how Tevi's militant words sent a new wave of restlessness sweeping through the crowd. People were looking at their neighbours, judging the mood around them. The questions on their faces were easy to read. If safety lay in numbers, how did the numbers stack for this new preacher? Was it safe to join her crusade?

"You ask for Toqwani's blessing. Well, I ask you, what have you done to deserve it? You"—Tevi's arm shot out, pointing into the crowd—"standing there scratching your arse. Or you, with your finger up your nose. Are you searching for your brains? Why should the gods bless you?"

Heads craned to spot the unlucky individuals singled out. Jemeryl smiled. It was irrelevant whether or not Tevi had really noticed anyone in the crowd acting in the way she had claimed. People were standing straighter, fidgeting less, so as not to attract her ridicule. She had them jumping to her words.

Tevi lowered her voice. The crowd became utterly silent to hear her. "You remember the idols, the jewelled eyes, the gold and silver bedecking them. False tribute to false gods. Now they revel in the offerings their demented followers gave them. The honour. The riches. And you stand here, letting them keep the spoils their lies brought them. No wonder Toqwani has withdrawn his blessing. Don't you want to show him what you think of the false gods? Don't you want to treat their idols as they deserve?"

The first shouts of agreement rang out. Fists punched the air. Jemeryl watched the crowd falling for the twin lures of rioting and looting—the perfect cure for boredom.

"They sit in the old basilica, a convocation of wickedness. And here we are, five hundred strong." Jemeryl judged that Tevi exaggerated the numbers, but the added confidence could do no harm. "We can break down the doors. We can destroy the false idols. We can show Toqwani that we are worthy of his blessing. Who then will stand against us? We are the army of the true gods."

Jemeryl looked on, bemused. It was the sort of performance she had never before witnessed from her lover. Tevi massaged the crowd with her voice, inspiring, taunting, praising, castigating. Sometimes picking out individuals. Sometimes addressing the skies. Sometimes speaking so directly that it was as if she was talking to every single person present, face-to-face. The crowd responded, pressing in ever closer around the plinth. The smiles and cheers grew louder.

Tevi was taking charge of the mob. But was it really so surprising? Tevi had led Bykoda's conscripted soldiers into battle against trolls and other monsters. She had been responsible for a mercenary guild house. She had been raised to be a leader of a warrior clan. It stood to reason that along the way she would have learned something about crowd control and motivation. Jemeryl smiled, shaking her head. Why had she ever doubted Tevi?

Finally, as she had begun, Tevi fell silent and stood, arms folded, watching the crowd. A quizzical smile twisted her lips, her tone conversational. "So. What are you doing, standing here listening to me, when you could be doing something for your gods?" Tevi raised her voice to a shout. "Why are you still here?"

A roar answered her. The crowd had recognised the signal for the fun to begin. Tevi jumped down from the plinth, vanishing from view, but Jemeryl had no trouble knowing where she was. A tight knot formed around her, a hard core of bodies, pressing through the more loosely packed crowd and drawing it along after. People streamed from the square, shouting and laughing, heading for the basilica.

Jemeryl was caught up at the rear of the mob. By the time she arrived at the destination, the action was already under way. Tevi and a group of nine others had picked up a stone horse trough to use as a battering ram and were bearing down on the basilica.

The wooden door boomed under the impact. Timber screeched and plaster cracked. The echoes reverberated from the temple walls with a sound like thunder, incongruous under the cloudless blue sky. Yet the noise was almost lost amid the deafening whoops from the mob. Again, the battering ram pounded into the door.

Jemeryl wormed her way back to the straggling outskirts of the crowd, from where she could take stock of the area. Sentinels were tumbling from the doorway of their barracks, but their actions spoke mainly of confusion. Most did no more than stare and point, some milled around indecisively, a few ran back in, going to seek either instructions or reinforcements. Jemeryl knew the riot would not be allowed to continue unchecked. Someone would take charge of the sentinels. How long did they have?

The battering ram boomed again. Jemeryl looked back. Deep cracks were running through the plaster around the door. White flakes dropped, revealing the crumbling mud brick beneath. Another strike and the top of the door was wrenched loose from its hinges. It buckled, tilting at a drunken angle. Small stones rained down on those manning the stone trough, but it clearly served only to encourage. The cheers from the watchers reached a new crescendo. Another two thumping impacts and the doors fell in with a crash. The mob surged forward, trampling over the fallen timbers. Jemeryl followed on, one of the last to enter.

The interior of the basilica was a large open hall under the domed roof, sixty or so feet across. A ring of wooden columns around the edge supported an upper balcony. Worn and chipped clay tiles covered the floor, although not many were visible between the feet of the mob and the assembled ranks of idols.

The statues covered the entire ground floor. Jemeryl stared at the bewildering menagerie—dog-headed women, winged monkeys, three-headed snakes, pot-bellied men. How many gods had been worshipped at the temple? How many idols were stored in the basilica? And which one was the emanator inside?

Cheers, crashes, and laughter filled the air. Even as Jemeryl was looking around, she could see the number of idols decreasing. A shout and a thud sounded to her right. Jemeryl jumped back just in time as a toppled statue smashed to the ground beside her. A hundred marble shards exploded across the tiles. Looters descended on the wreckage, scouring for anything of value.

Jemeryl's splinted arm clearly counted as enough reason to explain her inaction. None of the mob paid her any attention as she stood, a bystander to the carnage. More crashes. More idols destroyed. Yet still the upper dimensions did not return. Soon the sentinels would arrive to stop the rampage. Would Tevi's rioters find the correct idol in time? Briefly, Jemeryl closed her eyes but then she opened them and looked up. Light from the windows shone over the balcony, revealing another ring of idols, sitting like an audience facing in, silently watching the performance below.

Jemeryl gave a wry smile. Yes, that was definitely Ciamon's style. He had sealed the door by magic, but he would then put the idol as far from the entrance as possible. Never mind that common sense would say if his adversaries were able to overcome his locking spell, forcing them to walk a few more yards was unlikely to prove much of a hindrance.

Where was Tevi? Jemeryl peered around the scene of chaos, eventually spotting her with some fellow rioters at the other side of the room. The group was in the process of toppling a huge metal statue of a child holding a fish. Jemeryl worked her way through the excited mob.

"Tevi." Jemeryl yelled to be heard above the tumult of shouts and the deafening clang as the idol hit the ground. The fallen copper statue did not shatter like stone, but the child and the fish parted company. An arm also came loose, which one resourceful rioter claimed to use as a club.

Tevi was moving on to the next idol, but she turned at her name. "What?"

"That's where he'd have put it." Jemeryl pointed upwards. She suspected her voice was drowned out, but Tevi's expression showed immediate understanding.

"How do we get up?" Tevi mimed the words.

"I don't know. I..." Jemeryl twisted, peering around the hall.

No stairs or ladders were visible, but a small door was set into the wall opposite the entrance. She tapped Tevi's arm. "There."

Jemeryl followed on as Tevi shoved her way across the hall, clearing a path. At the door, Tevi grabbed the handle and rattled it vigorously for a few seconds. She bent and shouted into Jemeryl's ear. "Locked. Do you think he'll have used magic again?"

"Count on it."

Tevi nodded and took a few steps back. She launched herself at the door. The wooden boards rattled in their frame, but did not crack. The noise attracted the attention of several nearby rioters and the uproar abated slightly.

"Get the trough. We need this door down. There are more idols up above." Tevi shouted the command.

A section of the mob started to obey, but at that moment, a fresh outcry erupted by the entrance. The difference in tone was unmistakable compared to what had gone before. Fear rather than excitement lay beneath the cries, and then Jemeryl heard the crisp orders, barked in military style. The sentinels had arrived.

All around her, the hall was emptying. The mob poured from the basilica, screaming, fighting, shoving. A few rioters, less prone to panic, still had their hand full of whatever loot they had gathered. Others had dropped everything and fled.

"We've got to go," Tevi said into Jemeryl's ear.

"Right."

"Just run and be ready to duck. The sentinels won't be looking for a prolonged fight, but they'll take a swipe at you as you go past."

"Doesn't sound too good."

"It'll be better than being caught standing here on our own when the sentinels came in. Come on." Tevi grabbed her hand and towed her through the fleeing mob.

Dozens of the red-cloaked warriors were drawn up in ranks outside the door. Most were doing no more than maintaining their intimidating stance, waiting for the mob to leave the basilica. A few were striking out at the fleeing rioters as they passed, using batons rather than swords. Their obvious aim, as Tevi had said, was to speed the crowd's dispersal, rather than get into a fight or inflict serious casualties—although they clearly felt there was no harm in applying a little extra deterrent for anyone who might be tempted to repeat the disturbance.

Jemeryl dodged one blow and saw Tevi fend off another. A man ahead of them stumbled, diverting the nearest sentinels' attention. Jemeryl sidestepped the obstruction and then pelted on, still holding Tevi's hand. The mass of runners in front was thinning out, and then suddenly there was open space, with nothing between her and the safety of the surrounding streets. Jemeryl would have kept on, following the path of the other fleeing rioters, but Tevi steered her down a deserted side alley. The shouts faded behind them but they did not stop until they had reached a quiet square, far from the basilica.

Tevi collapsed on a step in the sun, clearly trying to look an ordinary pilgrim and not a fleeing rioter. She grinned. "That was fun."

Jemeryl flopped down beside her. "I don't know about that, but I guess we made progress."

"One door down and only the idols on the upper floor left to deal with."

"We won't get away with the same tactic again."

"We may not need to. Sefriall isn't tolerant of other religions. I bet she'll destroy the other idols. If the emanator's in one, she'll do our job for us."

"We can't count on it, and she won't destroy the Cyclian idols. Ci might have put the emanator in one of those."

"In which case, Sefriall will move it into the temple." Tevi shrugged. "It's a public place. We can get at it there."

"Depends on how many Cyclian idols there are. If it's just one, we ought to be able to hit it before the sentinels on duty stop us. If there's five or six…" Jemeryl did not need to finish.

"So you think we should try to destroy it before she has a chance to move it from the basilica?"

"That would be nice. How long do you think we have?"

Tevi wrinkled her nose in thought. "I guess Sefriall will start with clearing out the wreckage. Given the mess we left, it will take her people the rest of today. Tomorrow, she'll break down the door to the balcony and retrieve any idols she finds up there."

"Then it has to be tonight. Do you think she'll set a guard on the basilica?"

"Probably." Tevi smiled. "So isn't it a good thing that we hung on to the sentinel uniforms?"

❖

Tevi and Jemeryl stomped around the corner of the infirmary. The lack of synchronisation in their footsteps would not allow Tevi to think of it as marching. It was the bleak hour before dawn. The wind gusting across the herb garden was cold enough to steal the heat from Tevi's bones. Off to the east, the sky was starting to pale, but not yet enough to show the rooftops of Kradja in silhouette. The setting moon was low on the horizon, washing the scene with pale blue.

The basilica stood crouched before them, a paler patch against the dark mass of the temple. One small yellow lantern shone over the sentinels on guard duty by its broken doors. Tevi and Jemeryl headed directly for them, without breaking step.

The two sentinels had been talking, huddled in the doorway out of the wind. They turned at the sound of boots hitting cobbles, but the sight of uniforms immediately put them at ease. They relaxed visibly and made no move until Tevi and Jemeryl had reached the doors.

"Right. We're here." Tevi delivered the announcement in an upbeat tone to imply that she was not merely stating the obvious.

The two sentinels exchanged a confused look. "Are you supposed to be?"

Tevi now mimicked their confusion. "Yeah. An hour before…" She glanced at Jemeryl as if seeking confirmation. "Yeah. We…er… definitely. We're on duty."

"I thought we were here till dawn."

"That's not what we were told."

"Who by?"

Jemeryl scowled and chimed in. "Shit. Do you mean I could have stayed in bed? It was warm there." She started to back away.

"Hang on." The sentinel clearly realised he was in danger of arguing himself into a longer stint in the cold. "You sure you're on duty now?"

"That's what my captain told me last night," Tevi said.

"Can't tell his arse from his elbow," Jemeryl muttered, still edging away.

"Someone's made a screw-up on the rota."

"Not the first time."

"So...er..."

The first sentinel's uncertainty was not shared by his comrade, who had been listening and watching with growing animation. She pushed in front of him. "But since you're here, you might as well..." Not bothering to finish the sentence, she turned and immediately marched away. The clear intention was to prevent Jemeryl's departure by beating her to it.

The remaining sentinel took a sharp breath, a decision made. "Right. Cheers. We'll be off." He hurried to catch up with the woman who was already well on her way to the barracks.

Tevi watched them go, shaking her head in disgust. "They don't know how lucky they are I'm not their commanding officer."

"The failings of one's enemies are cause for celebration, not complaint." Jemeryl grinned as she lifted the lantern off its hook by the door.

"Unless you're wanting excuses as to why you didn't win."

"Which we're not."

Tevi took one last look at the moonlit scene and then joined Jemeryl inside the basilica. All the wreckage from the afternoon's riot had gone. The ground floor was clear. Tevi walked to the rear door and pulled on the handle.

"Still locked," she called over her shoulder.

Jemeryl had turned the lantern wick up and was squinting at the dark balcony. "I can see the idols still there."

"Great." Tevi unwrapped the rope from her waist and swung the grapple. "Let's see if this works any better on the inside."

"Wood shouldn't crumble like mud brick."

"It might if it's rotten."

The grapple caught on the rail of the balcony and lodged firmly. Tevi gave an experimental tug and looked at Jemeryl. "Do you want to go first?"

"Climbing isn't my strong suit. You can pull me up."

"Have I told you that you need to take more exercise?"

"Yes. Have you forgotten my answer?"

By way of reply, Tevi blew a kiss.

The balcony quivered, bouncing Tevi gently as she hauled herself up the rope, hand over hand. However, the grapple held firm and there was no sound of splintering wood. Not until Tevi reached the top of the rope did the wood start to creak. The railing spindles were leaning out at a worrying angle and did not look overly secure in their mounting, but after a bit of tricky manoœuvring Tevi was able to get her toes onto the lip of the balcony floor and roll over the handrail.

The wooden planks of the balcony were old and worn. It was too dark to be sure, but from the rough texture under her hands, Tevi guessed they had been subject to insect attack. Fortunately, the structure still appeared sound. Tevi stood and looked around.

The balcony was five feet wide, running in an unbroken circle around the basilica hall. The light from the Jemeryl's lantern was just sufficient to pick out the ring of idols, staring out in silent witness. A darker patch of shadow, a short way to Tevi's right, looked to be an archway, doubtless the top of the stairs reached from the door below.

Tevi leaned over the railing. "Right, Jem. I'm good. Tie the rope under your arms and I'll pull you up."

"How many idols are there?"

"Loads."

"Any sign which one has the emanator?"

"Don't know. It's too dark to see if one has a big cross painted on it. Perhaps when you bring the lantern up."

Jemeryl pouted at Tevi and then laughed. "Right." She grabbed the dangling rope.

While waiting for Jemeryl to secure herself, Tevi stood, listening to the wind gust over the roof, the trill of grasshoppers and the distant screech of a night bird. Not much longer, and their mission would be over. She was eager to leave Kradja, eager for her and Jemeryl to be back living their lives together in mundane domesticity. Saving the world was an overrated pastime. With any luck, Alendy would have too much on his plate to bother them.

The wind dropped. In the resulting hush Tevi heard something else, faintly at first but rapidly getting louder—running footsteps, approaching the basilica.

"Jem. There's no time. Someone's coming. Just grab hold." Tevi spoke in an urgent whisper.

Jemeryl spared one sharp glance for the door. "Right. Pull."

Tevi hauled on the rope. The sounds of feet were louder and closer, pounding with the hard beat of soldiers' boots. There had to be at least a dozen sentinels. This was not a patrol returning to barracks on the double or some other unrelated group. The sentinels had urgent business at the basilica, and that could only mean one thing. The replaced sentries had not been quite so gullible as they seemed. Tevi clenched her teeth, pulling even more urgently.

Light flared from the floor of the basilica, bright enough to reach the rafters. Voices called out. "You, stop!"

"Quick. Archer."

Desperately, Tevi heaved again. Jemeryl's hands came into sight, above floor level, clasping the rope. One more pull and Tevi would be able to grab her.

A bowstring twanged. Jemeryl cried out and the rope went slack. At the sudden loss of tension, Tevi stumbled backwards, losing her balance and colliding with an idol.

"Jem!"

The answering chorus from below was jubilant. "Got her."

"It's the sorcerer."

Tevi scrambled back to the rail. She hung over, looking down on the group clustering around Jemeryl's crumpled body. Just in time, from the corner of her eye, Tevi saw the archer raise her bow. Tevi dived back. The arrow hit the wall above her head.

A new, authoritative voice spoke out. "Is she alive?"

Tevi flinched, recognising Sefriall.

"Yes ma'am."

"Bring her here."

Jemeryl was not dead, but the situation was desperate. Quickly, Tevi pulled the rope out of the sentinels' reach. For the moment, they could not get to the balcony, but the respite was temporary. Soon they would break down the door to the stairs, or get their own grapples. Tevi stared around wildly. The sentinels had brought more lanterns with them and the light was now strong enough to see the idols clearly. Twenty of them in a ring. Huge and heavy. She would not have the time to destroy them all. Which one was the emanator inside?

Tevi twirled around and latched on to the idol she had previously bumped into. Time was limited. Every second would count. She had to destroy the emanator. Her hands and eyes ran over the marble statue, hunting for some sign that it had been tampered with, some clue that Ciamon hidden his emanator inside.

"You up there," Sefriall called out.

"What?" Why not speak if it might buy a few moments more?

"Give yourself up."

"Why?" The idol appeared intact with no joins or removable parts. Tevi moved to the next.

"Are you a fool?"

"Maybe. My mum said so."

"You can't escape and we have your companion prisoner. If you don't surrender, I'll have her killed."

Tevi's hands clenched on the idol. She took a deep breath, forcing herself to think rationally. "Go on, then."

Judging by the silence, this had not been the expected response. Tevi tried to make herself continue, but she could do nothing until she knew whose bluff would win. As Sefriall had pointed out, she was trapped. The threat to Jemeryl was purely an attempt to save a little time and effort. If Sefriall had any use for Jemeryl alive, then she would not kill her. And if Sefriall did not, then she would kill Jemeryl, regardless of whether or not Tevi gave herself up.

Tevi scrunched her eyes shut. She knew all logic was on her side, and yet—

The only thing that would guarantee their safety was if she found the emanator and destroyed it. Tevi opened her eyes, unclenched her fists and continued her search.

"Let me put it another way." Sefriall's tone was angry. Clearly she was not used to being defied. "Give yourself up, or I'll make your companion wish that I would have her killed."

A scream, sharp, piercing, and agonised, filled the basilica, echoing off the rafters, striking at Tevi's gut. Jemeryl had made the sound. Tevi knew it. For a moment, Tevi could not move, could not speak.

"I'll kill her." Tevi whispered the words under her breath. "I'll rip her heart from her body and I'll…"

Again Jemeryl screamed. Tears filled Tevi's eyes.

"Give yourself up."

Tevi fought for control of her voice. "You're not making it sound inviting."

"I just want information."

"That's what they all say."

"This basilica. What's so important about it? Why are you so keen to get in here?"

"We're just nosy."

"I think not. This basilica meant something to Ciamon. I know that. I saw the way he watched it. I'd wondered what was in here."

"Idols."

"What are you intending to do with them? I know you're working for the Coven. My agents in the square recognised you this afternoon, but they couldn't get near you with the mob. But I guessed you'd be back. That's why I had a watch set."

Tevi clenched her teeth. Of course Sefriall had.

"I've questioned your associates, the ones we took prisoner after your depraved attack on Toqwani, but they've told me nothing except sacrilegious nonsense. I know you're planning on performing some dark ritual here. That much is obvious."

"There you go. If you know that, you don't need anything more from me."

"Which god do you serve?"

"Wouldn't you like to know?"

Sefriall's angry sigh was loud enough to be heard on the balcony, and then Jemeryl screamed again, longer and more harshly than before.

Tevi clamped her hand over her face, furious at both herself and Sefriall. She had allowed herself to become sidetracked and waste time she did not have. She had to move on to the next idol, but her hands were shaking and her vision was so blurred that if Ciamon truly had painted a large cross on the idol, she doubted she would have been able to see it. The search was pointless. Why not just pick an idol at random and heave it off the balcony? She stood one chance in twenty that it would be right.

The ringing clunk of metal on wood made Tevi flinch. A grapple had landed on the balcony to her right. A moment later and another followed. Sefriall had also been stalling for time. Now Tevi knew she had mere seconds left. The ropes went taut as sentinels started to climb.

Think. Tevi stabbed the order at herself.

On the way to the basilica, she and Jemeryl had been talking, light-heartedly running over the events of the afternoon. Jemeryl said she had known the emanator would be on the balcony because Ciamon would have put it as far from the door as possible. She had joked at the total lack of logic on his part, but she was right. It was the way Ciamon's mind had worked. Tevi raised her head. It also meant the emanator would be in the idol furthest from the way up.

Tevi jumped from her crouch and scrambled around the balcony. She squeezed past the fatter idols, heedless both of the shouts from below and the arrow that clattered into the wall behind her. The first sentinels were reaching the balcony. Two more were getting ready to follow. Tevi ignored them. The dark archway was now directly opposite where she stood. Two idols faced it, one on either side of her. Tevi stared at them. Which one contained the emanator?

On her right was the figure of something, half goat, half lizard, with a head encased in a sunburst. On her left was the statue of a six-armed man, naked except for a medallion hanging around his neck. Tevi shuttled between the two, hoping for some clue. Another arrow zipped passed her ear, hitting the man's medallion, drawing Tevi's gaze. Engraved on the disc was a crescent moon stamped with an eye. Tevi had seen the symbol before on a medallion worn by Botha, the Nolian priest.

Of course—Nolius, god of magic. That would have appealed to Ciamon's sense of what was fitting. On the hillside above Villenes, he had said that Nolius was playing an important role in his plans. Where else would Ciamon have put the emanator? Tevi tapped the statue. It resonated like a copper bell, metal and hollow, but also heavy. Would she have the strength to move it?

"Stop right there." The shout came from behind her.

Tevi glanced over her shoulder. More sentinels were on the balcony. This would be her last throw of the dice. The gap was just wide enough for Tevi to squeeze behind the idol. She braced her shoulders on the wall and pushed, but Nolius would not budge.

"There's no point hiding. We know where you are." The sentinel's voice was nearer.

Tevi scrambled up, a foot on the statue's calf, the other on his rump, and then onto his shoulders. Tevi's head was now pressed against the rafters of the roof. From her high viewpoint she saw there were six sentinels on the balcony. Five were coming towards her. The last was an archer, standing in front of the archway opposite, arrow on bowstring.

Tevi placed her feet on Nolius's shoulders and shoved with all her potion-enhanced strength, throwing the muscles of her legs and torso into the effort. Slowly the statue tilted forward. Tevi let up for a moment. The statue rocked back, and then Tevi pushed again, building on the momentum. For a heartbeat, the idol teetered in a precarious balance and then Nolius toppled, crashing through the weak wooden railing and over the edge of the balcony. Tevi almost followed, but she managed to fling her arm around the neck of the other idol and stop herself falling. Surprised shouts of warning and yelps of fear came from below.

The nearest sentinel was only a few steps away, sword drawn, but he was no longer looking at her. His attention was on the floor of the basilica and the damage the fallen idol had caused.

"Whatever you were aiming at, you missed," Sefriall shouted defiantly.

"Really? I was aiming at the ground." But had she succeeded? Had she destroyed the emanator?

Arrow! Duck! A familiar voice shouted in her head. Tevi obeyed on instinct, her reactions trained by years of experience. Only when she saw the arrow hit the wall did she recognise what she had heard. The voice of her prescience, her one weak sense in the upper dimensions. The voice that plucked warnings from the second dimension of time. The morphology had gone and magic had returned.

Even as the thought went through Tevi's head, she was aware of a growing disturbance below. Screams, shouts, and frantic motion. The light in the basilica increased, blazingly, blindingly.

The sword-wielding sentinel stopped, frozen in his tracks. He had his hand up, shielding his eyes, trying to see what was happening on the ground. Now he turned back to Tevi, hefting his sword. "What sort of trick—"

"No trick."

"What is it?"

"You can't guess?" Tevi grinned. "That, my friend, is one of the Coven's best sorcerers, in full possession of all her ability to work magic. And given what's been happening, I'd guess that she's more than a little pissed off at you and your mates. If I was you, I'd run."

A fireball shot into the air and exploded, showering sparks. The screams from below intensified. The sentinel threw away his sword and fled, leaping off the balcony without bothering about the rope. Tevi collected his discarded weapon, then moved to a secure section of railing and looked down.

In the middle of the basilica stood a figure that looked mostly like Jemeryl, except it was ten feet tall and encased in white fire. The only other people visible were a couple of sentinels who could not leave the building quickly enough. They either had not noticed the absence of bodies so far or were not trusting that events would continue this way, but Tevi could have told them that Jemeryl would only kill as a last resort. Currently, her light show was inducing all the terror she needed to disperse her opponents.

A few seconds more and the last couple of sentinels were gone. Jemeryl sent a final fireball after them and then shrank back to her normal size and appearance.

She looked up. "Are you all right?"

"Yes. How about you?"

"I got an arrow in my leg." Jemeryl sounded furious. "It damn well hurts."

"I know. They do." Tevi swung over the balcony railing, hung briefly, then dropped and rolled. She reached Jemeryl, who sank into her arms. "Are you sure you're all right?"

"I am now. But Sefriall was…" Jemeryl shuddered convulsively. "She's nasty."

"She is."

Jemeryl pulled back and looked into Tevi's face. "You told her to go ahead and kill me."

"I knew she was bluffing."

"You hoped."

Tevi held Jemeryl tightly, remembering the dread she had felt. "True. Quite desperately. But I knew the only way to save us both was to destroy the emanator."

"And you succeeded."

"It was close."

Jemeryl pulled Tevi down into a long slow kiss and then looked into her eyes. "So now do we find Larric and Ashkinet and get out of town?"

"Sounds like a good plan to me."

CHAPTER FIFTEEN—LEGACY OF EVIL

The horse trough used as a battering ram during the riot had been put back in place and refilled. Tevi collected water from it, using her helmet as a bowl. All around, birdsong greeted the dawn that was breaking blood-red on the horizon. The only other sound was shouting, coming from the sentinels' barracks. News was clearly spreading, but nobody was approaching Tevi, either in challenge or solidarity.

Jemeryl was waiting back in the basilica. Tevi knelt beside her and started to rinse the blood from her wound but stopped, hearing a sharp intake of breath.

"Sorry. Did I hurt you?" Tevi had been careful to avoid touching the arrow.

"No. It wasn't you. The water was colder than I expected. Silly of me."

"You're sure?"

Jemeryl nodded.

Once most of the blood was gone, Tevi examined the damage. The arrow lodged in Jemeryl's thigh was clear of bone, ligaments, or major arteries, but the edge of the wound was torn and gaping in a way Tevi would not have expected for a simple arrow puncture. It confirmed her suspicions about what Sefriall had done to make Jemeryl scream. Tevi clenched her jaw, fighting to get her anger under control. She would need steady hands. Revenge could wait.

"Right. I'm going to take the arrow out. Try not to move."

"I'll be fine. I've got it under control and can't feel a thing."

"Whether it hurts or not, it's only natural to react. I want to pull it straight and not do any damage to the surrounding tissue."

"You mean, more than Sefriall has already done?"

The anger again kicked at Tevi's gut. She met Jemeryl's eyes. "I'm going to kill her."

"No, you're not." Jemeryl's answer was immediate. "It doesn't matter. We've ruined her game of taking over the world. That's enough of a payback for me."

Tevi took a deep breath, trying to calm her emotions. The arguments over what to do about Sefriall could also wait. Tevi carefully grasped the arrow shaft and pulled. Jemeryl flinched but showed no other reaction. Fresh blood began flowing as soon as the arrow came free, but stopped, even before Tevi could press her hand over the wound to stanch it.

"I can control the bleeding." Jemeryl's voice was tight but not pained.

"Can you wiggle your toes? Nerve damage can be—"

Jemeryl's toes duly wiggled. "I'll be fine. It wouldn't hurt to have a trained healer look at it, though. Medicinal magic was always my weak spot."

"We're right by the infirmary. I'll carry you."

Jemeryl gave a soft laugh. "No need to rush. I'm not quite that incompetent. We'll find Larric and Ashkinet. They might need some attention too. Sefriall can be—" Jemeryl broke off. "We can all see Zorathe together."

Tevi hesitated, wanting to argue, but Jemeryl was the best judge of her injury. Even so, Tevi cut a strip off the red cloak she had been wearing and tied it around Jemeryl's thigh, ignoring her protest. "Humour me. It can't do any harm."

Jemeryl's words died in an affectionate smile that made Tevi's chest constrict.

Wounds never hurt in the rush of battle. Not until the pace slowed afterwards would they burn. Blood was merely red liquid when the sword struck. Only in the cold aftermath did it gain the ability to turn Tevi's stomach. Tevi had been desperate when Jemeryl had fallen and screamed, but the urgent need to act had kept her focused. Now Tevi had time to think, and remember.

How could she forget that Sefriall had deliberately caused Jemeryl pain? Had threatened her life? Tevi put her hand on her lover's leg, feeling the warm pliant texture of skin. This touch was necessary for

Tevi's existence. Words were inadequate to express how very precious Jemeryl was to her. Tevi wrapped Jemeryl in a hug and buried her face in Jemeryl's neck, smelling the familiar body scent. Tears burned Tevi's eyes at the thought of ever losing her.

Jemeryl rubbed the back of Tevi's head. "Honest. I'm all right." Her tone was soft with reassurance.

Tevi nodded, shoving away the fears. "Shall we go?"

They paused at the doorway of the basilica. The tumult of birdsong was still in full spate over the rooftops of Kradja. A last few stars still glinted but the sky had lightened to pale blue. In the streets bordering the temple, townsfolk were emerging from their houses. Fear and caution were the norm in Kradja, making it hard to judge whether the people were more reticent that usual. However, the absence of sentinels was conspicuous. How would events go once the news spread of the return of magic? Sefriall's plans for holy war would be curtailed. Would she still be able to keep control of the town and temple?

Jemeryl was cautiously testing her weight on her injured leg. Tevi saw her shiver. They had both been wearing loose leggings under their tunics against the night chill, but Tevi had needed to cut Jemeryl's off before removing the arrow.

"Are you cold? Do you want to borrow my—" Tevi reached for her waistband as she spoke.

Jemeryl stopped her, catching hold of her wrist. "I'm fine. The day will heat up soon enough, and walking will help. Let's go."

The temple did not open for worshippers until dawn and the main hall was deserted except for a half dozen sentinels standing vigil over the idol. Now the glamour was gone, the sentry duty did not carry the same incentive and Tevi suspected volunteers would be harder to come by. Certainly, the sentinels' body posture showed they were cold and bored. The bowed heads spoke more of tiredness than piety. At the sound of footsteps, a couple glanced up. The uniforms Tevi and Jemeryl were wearing muted any immediate reaction but the discord with their causal stroll clearly caused confusion. Sentinels were supposed to make some attempt to march.

"What are you doing here?" The officer barked the question.

"We're looking for our friends," Tevi replied.

"What?" The officer's voice became yet more strident. "Which battalion are you with?"

"Oh, we're not sentinels. We stole these uniforms."

"Are you a fool?"

"Do you know, you're the second person to ask me that today, and it's not even breakfast time yet."

"I don't know what you think you're doing here, but you've made a mistake."

Tevi smiled. "You're either very brave, or behind with the news. Either way, the mistake is all yours."

The officer turned to his subordinates. "They match the descriptions we've been given. Take them down to the cellar, and then find out what's happened to the sentries on the door."

"You might want to think about doing that the other way around."

The officer had clearly had enough of talking and ignored Tevi's advice. "Don't just stand there. Get them."

Jemeryl waved her hand idly, like someone trailing her fingers through water. A stream of sparks spun away, dancing in the dim light. The mere sight was enough to stop the advancing sentinels, although they did no more than watch in bewilderment until the sparks struck them. The soldiers in the lead jerked back and yelped, as if stung by hornets. The others were still fumbling for their swords when the sparks reached them also.

"That looks like it hurts," Tevi observed, grinning.

"No worse than getting an arrow in your leg."

Suddenly, Jemeryl moved in a faster, punching gesture. An archer on the stairs had shot at them. The arrow exploded midair, showering burning splinters of wood and feathers on the floor.

The sentinels did not hang around to see more. Tevi watched them flee. "It might be an idea to keep one to question."

"Any preference?"

"In theory, the officer should be the best informed, but who knows with the sentinels? It's obvious nobody thought to let them in here know about what's been happening outside."

"He's still as good a pick as any."

Jemeryl pulled her clenched fist towards her. As if the officer had been a puppet on strings, he tripped over nothing and crashed to the ground. He was still frantically feeling his legs as Tevi reached him. His face was twisted in panic.

"Don't. Please. Oh, my legs."

Tevi crouched beside him. "We just want a few answers, and then you can go."

"I'm not—"

Tevi cut through his babbling. "You may have spotted that the ability to work magic has returned. My companion is a Coven sorcerer and Sefriall has just been rather nasty to her, so she's not in a good mood. You really don't want to waste her time."

The officer's eyes locked on Jemeryl's black amulet and his mouth clamped shut.

Tevi continued. "There are two other Coven sorcerers Sefriall has got prisoner. We're here to find them. It'll be a lot easier all round if you tell us where they are. Three elderly priests were captured at the same time. I wouldn't mind a chat with them either."

"They're…they're…" The man's voice was a high-pitched squeak. "I've not been involved with them. But…in the cellar. That's where they were taken. But I don't know anything about it."

"This cellar you know nothing about?"

The officer nodded.

"Would that be the same one you ordered your men to take us to?"

"I…I…yes."

"So you can give me directions on how to get there?"

He held out an arm, pointing. "Through the arch there. A corridor. The last room on the right. The stairs down are in the corner."

Tevi patted his cheek. "Thanks." She stood and faced Jemeryl. "You can let him go now."

The officer scrambled away.

News was definitely spreading. Shouts and banging doors echoed from all around as Tevi and Jemeryl left the great hall. When they were halfway along the corridor, a sentinel burst through a doorway ahead, still struggling to pull her shirt down over her head. Her face emerged from the cloth. The sudden expression of shock was extreme enough to be comical. The half-dressed soldier skidded to a stop, turned and fled in the opposite direction. Tevi and Jemeryl followed sedately.

The room they reached showed signs of being hastily vacated. Chairs were overturned and the rear door was ajar. Tevi led the way to the stairs.

"I remember this," Jemeryl said. "It's where I was put when I was first brought to the temple."

"How long were you kept here?"

"Only a few minutes. Sefriall rescued us. It's funny, looking back. I was so pleased to see her."

"I wouldn't mind seeing her as well at the moment, but it wouldn't be funny." Tevi could feel the anger still seething inside.

"We're here to get Larric and Ashkinet, not revenge."

"That's if they're still here. If they're awake they'll most likely have—"

The underground room at the bottom of the stairs was too dark to see, but this was not the reason Tevi's words had died in her mouth. The stench of blood, excrement, and death assailed her, recalling foul memories. There was only one place that smelt this way. She heard Jemeryl snap her fingers and a light sprang into existence, confirming what her nose had already told her. Tevi tasted bile, rising in her throat.

Bloodstains splattered the flagstones of the floor. To one side stood a heavy table, scattered with implements Tevi took only the quickest peek at. Stained leather straps hung off the corners. She did not need to see more. Crude partitions at the rear divided part of the cellar into two cells. Moans were coming from the one at the right, turning to whimpers of fear as the light increased.

"It's all right. We've come to rescue you. We're not the..." Tevi bit back the words. "We're not the people who've done this."

The whimpering did not stop. Why should it? Charades of rescue were a common trick played by torturers. The victims needed to see her face. Maybe then they would believe their ordeal was over.

The door was locked. Tevi could not be bothered with finding the key. She kicked hard, splintering the flimsy wood. The cell was too dark to make out details, although Tevi was sure more than one person was inside. Tevi looked over her shoulder. Jemeryl was still standing at the bottom of the stairs, staring around in horror.

"Jem. I need some light here."

"I ca..." Jemeryl swallowed visibly, grimacing as if fighting down nausea, before stumbling over to join Tevi.

Two filthy, naked figures were huddled in the cell, one male, one female. The man lay unmoving, curled on his side. The other shrank into the corner, knees up and face buried in her hands. Neither was young enough to be one of the Coven sorcerers.

Tevi knelt beside the woman and gently placed a hand on her shoulder. She was the one who had been whimpering. "I don't know if you know me. But my name's Tevi. I'm here to rescue you."

The woman let her hands fall. It was Botha, the priest of Nolius. A stab of guilt cut through to Tevi's heart. She had led Botha here, with promises of victory, and then abandoned her to this. The sudden expression of joy that flooded Botha's face only twisted the knife.

"You're really...oh...thank you." Tears flowed from the old woman's eyes. She clumsily grasped Tevi's hand.

Tevi could not speak as she tallied up the bruises and burns, the missing and mangled fingertips, the raw, open cuts on the old woman's body.

Jemeryl was by the other figure. "It's Darjain."

"Is he alive?"

"Yes. Just. He's been—" Jemeryl was breathing hard, clearly struggling with her self-control. "I'll find some clothes. And check the other cell."

"Leave us some light."

"Yes. Sure." Jemeryl backed away.

Botha was curled sobbing over Tevi's hands, still clutching them like a lifeline, though her grip was weak. Tevi stroked her hair. "Why did Sefriall do this? What was she after?"

"She thought we knew where you were. That we were all working for the Coven. She wanted to know your plans. She wouldn't believe... she wouldn't..." Botha's sobs drowned out her words.

A soft cry came from Jemeryl in the next cell. Tevi had not heard her enter. Presumably the sorcerer had used magic rather than her foot to open the door.

"What is it?"

"Larric. Ashkin..." Jemeryl could not finish.

"How are they?"

"Dead. Both of them."

"Sefriall started with them," Botha whispered. "They told her about the morphology and the idol, but it made no sense to her...the skein, perceptual bars, things like that. Sefriall was convinced the Coven was planing a profane ritual to get its power back. She wanted to know how to stop it and how to undo the magic spell they'd cast on the idol."

"But you and Darjain? You wouldn't have known anything."

"Darjain was leader of the priests. She thought he'd be the one in contact with the gods, and Yalaish was the god who worried her most. She wouldn't believe him. But me..." Botha shuddered. "Me, she didn't care about. That's why she left me to last. That's why I'm still..."

"Alkoan?"

"He was a Cyclian priest. One of hers. She didn't think he'd have anything to do with Yalaish so she had him hanged the morning after we were captured."

Jemeryl returned to the cell. "There's nothing in here I'd want to touch. I'll look upstairs. There'll be clean robes in the temple, even if I have to take them off a priest's back."

Tevi nodded. "I'll meet you in the room above." She looked at Botha. "Do you think you can walk?"

"If I lean on you."

Tevi shuffled over to Darjain. He appeared unconscious, but as she cradled him in her arms his face contorted in pain. "Jem. Can you do something? He's awake."

Jemeryl had been leaving. Now she returned. "I can make sure he sleeps."

"Do it."

Darjain patted Tevi's arm. "Who...who is it?"

Tevi knew he could not see her. He would never see anything again. Both his eyes were missing. "It's Tevi. I'm taking you to the infirmary. The magic has returned. The healer will be able to help you."

Jemeryl held her hand over his forehead. Her fingers moved in an intricate dance.

"It's too late. But I know...I know..." Darjain's voice was fading, although his lips still moved. He wanted to say something.

Tevi lowered her head. "What is it?"

"I know why Yalaish weeps."

❖

In their twelve years together, Jemeryl had never seen Tevi so crazed with anger. After leaving the two tortured priests in Zorathe's care, Tevi stormed straight back to the temple. Jemeryl struggled along behind, trying to keep up, although for her part, she would have chosen never to set foot in the building again. The remembered horror of the cellar made her feel physically sick.

In fact, going anywhere would not have ranked high among Jemeryl's choice of activities. She knew she was walking with a pronounced limp. The arrow wound was not quite as trivial as she had tried to make out. Despite her best efforts, she could not totally block the dull ache or the tingling darts up her thigh. Yet the discomfort did not bother her as much as the fact that Tevi seemed not to notice, or care. None of her requests to slow down were answered.

By the time they reached the balcony at the rear of the great hall, Jemeryl could take no more. She locked the exit using magic. Tevi tugged violently at the handle and then backed up, as if preparing to kick the door down. The delay gave Jemeryl the opportunity to put a hand on Tevi's arm and claim her attention.

"Tevi. What are you going to do?"

"I'm going to find Sefriall and I'm going to kill her."

"Just like that? In cold blood?"

"My blood is plenty hot enough."

"What will it achieve?"

Tevi's face furrowed in disbelief. "You ask that? You saw Darjain and Botha."

"How will killing Sefriall help them?"

"It'll make sure she never does the same to anyone else."

"She did it because she was in power and she thought they might stop her plans. Now the morphology has gone, so has her power. Her plans are ruined. She'll never have to do anything like that again."

"You think she had to do it this time? And who knows what she'll think is necessary in the future?" Tevi scowled. "A sword in her heart will make sure of it."

"There's been too much violence already. More won't make anything better," Jemeryl pleaded.

Tevi's face was implacable. Without answering, she turned back to the door. "Is it you, keeping the door shut?"

"Yes. I'm…I just wanted to talk, and you wouldn't wait." Jemeryl released the door. Regardless of how much she disagreed with Tevi, Jemeryl would not use magic to stop her. They could argue with each other, but the use of force, either physical or magical, would attack the bedrock of trust in their relationship.

Tevi wrenched the door open and marched on, single-minded. Priests, servants, and sentinels scattered before her. Jemeryl caught the whispered comments as they passed.

"The Coven is here. A hundred sorcerers."

"They're going to destroy the town."

"Why have the gods deserted us?"

For all the notice Tevi gave them, they might not have been there. Only the lone brave sentinel who tried to stop her entering the High Priest's quarters got her attention, and that was merely for the two seconds it took Tevi to knock him senseless. Jemeryl hesitated by the crumpled form. Should she find someone to carry him to the infirmary? Screams from the inside the door made up her mind. She might not be able to affect Tevi's actions, but she had to try.

Panic-stricken servants fled from Tevi's angry advance through the High Priest's quarters. Jemeryl hobbled after as quickly as she could and caught up in the bedroom. Four servants were cornered there. Jemeryl entered just in time to see Tevi grab the nearest one by the front of her tunic and slam her against a wall.

"Where's Sefriall?"

"She's gone."

"Where?"

"I don't know." The girl's eyes were stretched wide in fear.

Tevi again slammed the servant against the wall. "Where?"

"Tevi!" Jemeryl shouted. "That's a housemaid, not a soldier. Think about what you're doing."

"Ma'am." The girl's eyes turned to Jemeryl in desperate appeal. "I don't know where Sefriall's gone. An hour ago, she was in and out in a flash. No one's seen her since. She said the Coven sorcerers were coming to get her."

Tevi released the servant's tunic. The girl darted aside and escaped. Tevi glared after her but made no further move to give chase. Jemeryl collapsed in a chair and watched as Tevi prowled around the room, slamming her fist on walls and kicking cabinets as she passed. Maybe if Tevi took her anger out on the furniture it would help her calm down.

"What now?"

"Now?" Tevi stalked to a chest and threw open the lid. "I'm going to search the room and see if I can find any clues about where the bitch has gone."

Jemeryl nodded, feeling relieved. The more time Tevi took, the more chance her rage would subside and she would start thinking rationally. The methodical act of searching might also help clear her head.

It seemed to work. By the time Tevi was halfway around the room, the insane fury had left her face. She no longer looked like someone who would assault domestic staff. Tevi opened another chest. This time, the hint of a surprised smile touched her face. "Hey. Look what I've found."

"What?"

Tevi pulled out a bundle. "These belong to us. Do you remember our stuff that Ciamon confiscated? Sefriall hung on to them. Here's my rune-sword and your staff."

Jemeryl started to get to her feet, but her leg had seized while she had been sitting. She hissed at the pain and sank back down. Before she could boost the numbing spell, Tevi was at her side.

"Jem. Are you all right?"

"My leg. It's—"

"You should have stayed at the infirmary and had Zorathe look at it."

"And let you rampage through the temple on your own, terrorising housemaids?"

A guilty expression crossed Tevi's face. "That wasn't too good of me."

"True."

"Come on. I'll take you back to the infirmary."

"You'll forget about killing Sefriall?"

"No. Not after what she did. I can't let it drop. Darjain and Botha were caught and hurt because they followed me. I owe it to them." The blind, uncontrollable anger had gone from Tevi's face, but the grim resolve that had replaced it was no less frightening. "I'll track her down, to the end of the earth if need be. And I'll make her pay."

❖

Tevi paced in the shade of the colonnade outside the infirmary. Gravel crunched under her feet. The afternoon heat was such that sitting still would have been more sensible, but the coiled tension inside her needed release. The search of Sefriall's rooms had turned up no clues, nor had Tevi been able to find anyone who would admit to knowing anything.

Could she have forced one of the sentinels or priests to speak? The idea made Tevi uncomfortable. If she had, it would have made her no better than Sefriall. As it was, she felt ashamed, knowing how out of control she had been that morning, and morality aside, forcing a lie from an ignorant bystander would only lead to a wild goose chase. However, Tevi was not about to give up. Sefriall would die for what she had done.

On a nearby ledge, Jemeryl was seated, watching her pace. Tevi was aware of the reproach in her lover's eyes, and while she was willing to concede that attacking the housemaid had been wrong, Tevi could not understand the ethical standpoint Jemeryl was taking. They had both seen the cellar. Jemeryl knew what had happened there. How could she back away as if it were nothing to do with her?

Tevi stopped pacing. "How can you let Sefriall get away with what she did? Don't you feel any responsibility for making her pay?"

"I would in the Protectorate, but I don't have any authority to administer the law here."

"I'm not talking about law. I'm talking about what you feel in your gut."

"My gut says it's for the people of Kradja to deal with Sefriall."

"It was our friends she tortured and murdered."

"The people of Kradja have been her main victims. It's up to them to decide what they want to do. I don't have the right to use magic to force my ideas or morals on them."

"The people of Kradja knew what they wanted. They had a nice temple and some decent priests. They made a good living from travellers. Then a Coven sorcerer screwed it up. Don't you owe them for that?"

"What I owe them is what Ci took away—the right to sort out their own lives."

"So why were you here at all? Why not let them keep the emanator?"

"Don't be stupid. The morphology it induced would have destroyed the Coven. That was why we were here. To remove the threat to the Protectorate. Now it's gone, we should stop interfering."

"Ciamon interfered. He released a monster in this town. We can't wash our hands of it. We have to undo as much of the harm he caused as we can."

Jemeryl sighed. "I agree. Ci was the root cause of it all. If he'd never come here, Sefriall wouldn't have had the chance to do what she did. She'd have stayed an ordinary priest. She wasn't responsible for the situation she ended up in."

"She's responsible for what she did when she got there."

"The world is full of people who'd have done the same if they'd been put in her place. She's just unlucky that she was put in a position that brought out the worst in her."

"Unlucky!"

"Maybe that's not quite the right word, but Ci was the one who overturned all the social structures that kept her in check. He was responsible for what Sefriall became, and he's paid for it."

Tevi felt a new flare of anger, this time directed at Jemeryl. "What you mean is Sefriall is a poor ungifted victim of magic. Only sorcerers can control all the dimensions. Everyone else is at the mercy of circumstance, so they can't be fully held to account, like children, or animals."

Jemeryl also showed signs of irritation. "No. I don't mean that. But how about you? How much is this because it's a woman who's harmed a man? Because men are vulnerable and women ought to protect them. Would you be so eager to avenge a woman? Or would you feel she ought to be left to avenge herself?"

Tevi hesitated. Was there a shadow of truth in what Jemeryl said? Did it matter if there was? "I don't know. I'd like to think I hold everyone equally to account for their actions. None of us get to choose the conditions of our lives, but we can choose how we react. Sefriall chose to do what she did. And I won't choose to walk away. I must act in accordance with my conscience."

A polite cough interrupted Tevi. Esley stood in the nearby doorway. The infirmary porter ducked his head in a nervous bow while casting sideways looks at Jemeryl. The presence of a sorcerer clearly made him ill at ease.

"Please, ma'am. Zorathe sent me with a message."

"What is it?"

"She thought you'd want to know Darjain died a few minutes ago."

Tevi spun away, unable to speak. She stared at the temple, but the scene smeared as her eyes filled with tears. That was where Darjain had worshipped the god he had loved. He had cared about people. He had harmed no one. He had deserved a better end.

Esley continued. "She wanted you to know it was probably for the best, what with the state he was in. He hadn't woken up again after you brought him here, so he didn't suffer any more."

"How about Botha?" Jemeryl asked the question.

"She'll be all right…mostly."

"Thank you."

Tevi heard Esley's footsteps fade and then Jemeryl's, getting closer.

"Tevi? Are you all right?" Jemeryl's hand rested on her arm.

"I…er…no. Not really." Tevi wiped her eyes. "I feel to blame."

"You did all you could."

"Like leading him into Sefriall's hands and then abandoning him?"

"You're not being fair on yourself. Remember, you tried to talk him out of it."

"I should have tried harder. If nothing else, I owe him justice now. I can't fail him twice."

"Then you're setting yourself up to fail. Sefriall's gone and we don't know how to find her."

Tevi clenched her jaw. There had to be something she could do—defeat would be too bitter—and then a new thought struck. "Parrash. He'll know where Sefriall has gone."

"Yes, and most likely he'll have gone there with her." Jemeryl's voice was unsympathetic.

"Maybe, maybe not. Either way, his sister will know how to find him."

"Do you know how to find the sister?"

"I know where her bakery is." Tevi turned her head.

Jemeryl's eyes searched her face. "Tevi. Can't you let it go?"

"No. I've got to try. Will you come with me or wait here?"

"I want nothing to do with your quest for vengeance. I'm not going to kill anyone."

"I'm not asking you to. But will you stand in my way?"

Jemeryl sank her face into her hands. Tevi stood waiting for her answer. At last Jemeryl looked up again. "Never."

Sefriall had been wise to flee before news got out. The market was in chaos, with ex-pilgrims literally fighting for a place on any transport leaving Kradja. So far, the weapons were fists, not blades, but it could change at any moment. Hysteria was taking over. With each hour, the rumours got more lurid. By now, the approaching sorcerers were riding dragons and griffins. Jemeryl made sure her black amulet was invisible. She did not want to find out what sort of panic would erupt if it was spotted.

Tevi led the way down a side street. Jemeryl trailed after, battling with misgivings. Should she have kept out of it? She could have waited at the infirmary for Tevi's return. She did not want to play any part in hunting down Sefriall, so why was she there? But the turmoil on the streets provided her answer. Supposing Tevi did not return? For Jemeryl to say she would never forgive herself was the most absurd understatement.

One on one, Tevi was more than equal to any warrior in Kradja. Even odds of two to one would present little challenge, but Tevi was not invincible. She could not fight a mob single-handed. She could be stabbed in the back. Jemeryl looked at her lover walking in front of her. No matter how events might turn out, Jemeryl knew that she was there, and always would be, to watch Tevi's back.

The streets they passed through had been getting both shabbier and quieter. Before long, the buildings were made of simple mud brick with foul-smelling refuse piled in corners. The activity had gone from frenzied to nothing. When they turned the next corner, the only living things in sight were a stray dog sniffing at rubbish and three white birds perched on a rooftop. However, the quiet conveyed no air of safety. It was the false stillness before an ambush. Jemeryl could feel eyes tracking them from windows.

Tevi stopped by a door and thumped on it. There was no answer. She thumped again. "Open the door, or I'll smash it down."

When this produced no response, Tevi took three steps back and then charged the door with her shoulder. The frame shook and Jemeryl heard the sound of snapping wood. Before Tevi could take another run, the door opened a crack.

"The shop's closed. Ain't you heard? The Cov—"

The speaker got no further. Tevi kicked the door fully open and strode in. Jemeryl followed more cautiously. The shop was clearly a bakery. The smell of yeast and flour was unmistakable, and a few unsold loaves were on the table. A teenage boy lay on the floor, scrabbling away from Tevi, who stood with her arms folded. He had clearly fallen when the door was forced open and not yet regained his feet.

The boy reached a wall and started to lever himself up. "What do you want?"

"The owner of this place. Her name, is it Ashla, Aslie, Aisel… something like that?"

"Aslie."

"Right. I want to talk to Aslie."

"She's not here."

"Really? Well, I'll just have a look around." Tevi moved towards a passage at the rear.

"Why do you want to see her?"

"I've got a few questions to ask."

"She's n—" The boy stopped, then took a deep breath and raised his voice. "Aunt Aslie, there's someone who wants to talk to you."

After a few seconds of silence, Jemeryl heard the sound of footsteps descending stairs. A woman appeared in the passageway. She was in early middle age, plump, with the deeply tanned skin of the local townsfolk. "What is it?"

Tevi's smile held no trace of friendliness. "Your brother Parrash. I want to find him."

"How should I know where he is?"

"Because you and him work together. That's why you let him use your cellar to infiltrate the old priests. They're mostly dead now." Tevi's expression wavered. "Darjain died a short while ago. He was a good man, a friend of mine, and you helped betray him to Sefriall. I want revenge."

"I wouldn't have done nothing against Darjain. He's…" Aslie's eyes darted between Tevi and Jemeryl.

"You played your part, but Sefriall's the guilty one. It's her I most want to find. Unfortunately, she's skipped town. I think your brother is either with her, or he knows where she's gone. I also think he'd have called by here first, or sent a note. After all, he owes you, after you got your business ruined helping him."

"I don't know where he is." Aslie's assertion was too quick and too bland. Jemeryl did not need magic to know she was lying.

"You sure?" Judging by Tevi's cynical tone, she was equally unconvinced.

Resting against the corner behind Tevi was one of the long-handled iron shovels used for taking bread from the ovens. Tevi picked it up and hefted it thoughtfully. The threat of violence was clear. Aslie's eyes widened although she said nothing.

Tevi held the shovel horizontally in both hands, like a quarterstaff. "I'd have to say I don't believe you."

Aslie cowered back, but Tevi made no move to strike her. Instead, without any sign of effort, Tevi bent the thick metal pole into a knot. The display of unnatural strength produced an immediate response.

Aslie's mouth sagged open. "You're sorcerers."

"My friend is. I'm something else."

Up until now, both Aslie and the boy had ignored Jemeryl. Now their heads simultaneously jerked in her direction. At their terror-stricken expressions, Jemeryl felt obliged to offer reassurance. "I'm not here to hurt you. Ignore the rumours. No sorcerers are on their way. Why should there be? The Coven has no interest in Kradja now it's not threatening the Protectorate."

Neither looked to be taking any comfort from her words. Aslie retreated towards the passage.

Tevi stepped forward, blocking her exit. "Come on now. You know you can't run away."

"Please, I don't…"

Tevi slipped the largest loop of the mangled shovel handle over Aslie's head, as if it were an oversized necklace. "What Jem said is quite true. The Coven has no interest in hurting anyone in Kradja. But I've got a personal score to settle with Sefriall. So, if you know where she is, why don't you tell me? Then we'll go. Or you can tell me where your brother is. If he answers me nicely, I won't even hurt him." As she spoke, Tevi pulled on the handle, tightening the loop.

Aslie's eyes bulged in terror. "Sefriall wanted him to go with her, but he knew the Coven would be after her. He thought he'd do better on his own. He came by here this morning, to pick up some things he'd need. Now he's hiding."

"Where?"

"Some friends of his. They own the Wayfarer House, on the east side of town. They've got a secret room in their attic. He's there."

CHAPTER SIXTEEN—THE LAST TEAR

The Wayfarer Inn obviously catered for a wealthier class of traveller than the Four Winds House. The two-storey stone building had glazed windows and a paved forecourt. The tops of palm trees peeking over the tiled roof indicated that there was an enclosed garden courtyard for the guests' use. The owners also had the money to protect their property in times of trouble. A pair of surly-looking guards stood outside the door.

Jemeryl eyed them anxiously, anticipating a confrontation. She and Tevi had changed out of their stolen uniforms at the infirmary, but this meant they were now dressed like destitute pilgrims. She could not imagine the guards would let them enter without a challenge.

She was right.

"Where do you think you're going?" One of the guards moved to block the entrance when they were still some way off, but clearly did not take them seriously enough to tighten her grip on the cudgel. She merely tapped it gently against her calf, just to remind them it was there.

Tevi did not falter. "We're going to start by talking to the owner."

"Clear off."

"Get out of my way."

"I'm warning you."

"Same here." Tevi was less than ten yards from the door, still striding forward.

Jemeryl was a few steps behind. Although she could not see directly, from the way Tevi's arms and shoulders moved, she deduced that Tevi was pulling back her outer robe and reaching inside. The guards had been watching with belligerent disdain, which shaded into surprise when their attempts at intimidation had so little effect. Now they responded with shock.

"Shit. She's got a sword."

Both raised their cudgels. The woman held hers in a defensive block, but the man lunged out, swinging wildly. Presumably, his intention was to get to Tevi before she had a chance to draw her sword. In this, he was successful, but it did not help him. Tevi ducked under the poorly timed swipe and kneed the man in the stomach with enough force that his feet left the ground. He stumbled back into his companion, who was then too busy fending him off to duck the punch Tevi threw at her jaw. The two guards hit first the wall and then the ground.

"I did warn you." Tevi stepped over their feet.

Jemeryl paused in the entrance. The lobby was cool and dark. Marble statues of nymphs and satyrs stood in the corners. Doors opened on both sides and an archway at the end gave access to a central courtyard where bright sunlight fell on a lush display of exotic plants.

Tevi stood in the middle of the tiled mosaic floor, looking around, clearly deliberating about where to start her search. However, sounds of the brief scuffle had not gone unnoticed. A pair of elderly, well-dressed women appeared in the archway, dithering nervously, and then a younger man spilled through a doorway on the right.

"What's going on? Where's—"

Tevi cut him off. "Are you the owner?"

"Who are you?"

"I asked first."

The man turned towards the entrance. "Trai? Zenis? What are you doing?"

"If they're your doormen, I've just flattened them. I'll do the same to you if you don't answer me. Are you the owner?"

He looked back at Tevi. "What do you want?"

"Some answers. Don't make me ask again."

The man drew himself up. "Yes. I'm one of the owners. I don't know what y—"

"I want to talk to Parrash."

"Who? There's no one of that name staying here."

"His sister told me he was in your attic."

Jemeryl heard moans and the sounds of movement behind her. The two guards would soon be back on their feet. Would they try to tackle Tevi again? Jemeryl shifted away from the door to get out of their path. She would only intervene if Tevi looked to be in danger. The owner glanced in her direction, as if noticing her for the first time, and then turned back to Tevi.

"I don't know anything about the woman who told you that, but she's lying."

Tevi sighed. "I don't have time for this."

She walked to the nearest statue, put her foot on the nymph's thigh, and gave a hard shove. The marble hit the tiles and cracked in two at the waist. The nymph also lost an arm and her nose. At the same moment, the bloodied guards stumbled in, breathing heavily. Anyone could see that they had just been on the losing side of a fight. The two women, presumably guests, had been watching with increasing agitation. They retreated into the courtyard and disappeared amidst the foliage.

The innkeeper's eyes were shifting in disbelief between the smashed statue and his battered employees. Finally he fixed on Tevi. "You can't—"

"I can." Tevi reached into her robes and drew her sword. "Take me to Parrash."

"The sentinels will—"

"The sentinels are currently having some problems, but I think, once the dust has settled, what's left of them will be very interested to know Parrash is hiding here. Do you really want to get them involved?"

The innkeeper took a half-step towards his guards, but they were clearly in a poor state to eject an intruder, especially one who had already defeated them. Abruptly, the fight left the innkeeper. He signalled for the guards to go, then pointed at the door he had arrived by. "This way."

The room they reached, at the top of the inn, had to be the servants' quarters. Even with the current state of overcrowding in Kradja, Jemeryl was certain guests who could afford the Wayfarer Inn would not be sleeping on straw-stuffed pallets, six to a room. Clothes and other personal effects were scattered around, but nobody, including Parrash, was currently in the room.

"Where is he?" Tevi was implacable.

"In here." The innkeeper pulled on a wall-mounted candleholder. Jemeryl heard a faint click and saw movement. A waist-high section of wall swung open.

"What is it, Kas?" a voice called from inside.

"Some people want to talk to you. I'm sorry. They were…they knew you were here. Your sister told them."

"Who—"

The voice died as Tevi ducked under the opening. She glanced back at the innkeeper. "You can go." Her tone made it clear this was not just a suggestion.

"I'm sorry, Pash." The innkeeper retreated.

Jemeryl followed Tevi into the secret chamber. Parrash was backed in a corner, staring at them in terror.

Tevi advanced until she was standing over him. "I suspect you haven't heard the news. Darjain died an hour ago."

"I…I didn't know." Parrash's voice cracked in panic. "I didn't do anything. I wouldn't have hurt Darjain. He was a good man."

"You betrayed him, and the rest of your colleagues, to Sefriall. You've been working for her."

"I haven't."

"Do you want to deny putting the poison in the wine as well and framing me?"

"I'm sorry about that. I was just trying to kill Ciamon."

"On Sefriall's orders. I bet she had plans to get called away so she wouldn't drink the wine."

"I wasn't working for her."

"How about Ciamon? Do you know anything about what happened to him?"

"No. I wasn't—"

Tevi's hand shot out. She grabbed a fistful of his hair and pulled his face to within inches of her own. "You're lying. I was there, right under your feet. We'd been hiding under the steps when you rode in with the sentinels. I saw you standing by Sefriall as she stuck the knife in his heart. I heard what she said to you. Every single word of it."

"It was Sefriall. She's mad. She'd have killed me if I ha—"

Tevi shoved him away. "You haven't been formally introduced to my partner, have you?"

Jemeryl frowned, certain that social etiquette was not Tevi's intent. Parrash merely stared.

"But with your spying at peepholes, you must know she's a Coven sorcerer. You've probably heard the ability to work magic has returned."

His eyes opened wider.

"I don't want to waste time with more lies. So there are two ways we can do this. Either you answer all my questions as fully and as truthfully as you know how, or Jem will go through your head with her spells and rip the information from your thoughts. You'll be insane by the end..." Tevi shrugged. "But it's your choice."

Jemeryl opened her mouth, about to assert that she would do nothing of the sort. However, Parrash did not give her the chance to speak. "Anything. I'll tell you anything."

Tevi gave a grim smile. "Good. First question. The big one. Where's Sefriall gone?"

Parrash swallowed, breathing deeply. "South. She's heading for Lijoni. There's another big Cyclian temple there."

"How many people has she got with her?"

"Just a few. No more than three." Parrash licked his lips, and then the words tumbled out in a rush. "She wanted to get away as quickly as she could. She wasn't going to wait to get everything together. She left that for me. I'm supposed to get sentinels, supplies, and things and meet her at Qualeisi Oasis. But I'm not going to. That's why I'm hiding here. I've had enough. Like I said, she's mad. The Coven will be after her and I don't want—"

"You don't want to be anywhere near her when the hundred sorcerers turn up, riding on dragons?" Tevi suggested. "You're a coward and you've run out on her when she not winning anymore. You know, strange to say, but I find that totally believable."

Parrash clamped his mouth shut and swallowed nervously, his eyes still locked on Tevi.

"This Qualeisi Oasis, where is it?"

"Southwest. It's easy to find without a guide. That's why she picked it to meet at. It's the furthest south of the oases, the last tear of Yalaish."

"How do I find it?"

"Go due south out of Kradja until you see a line of mountains on the horizon. It's about a day and a half. When you see the mountains, bear west, towards the tallest one. There's a long gorge, like a dried-up river valley. It cuts across your path. You can't miss it. Get to the bottom and head south again. After another day, the valley drops down and the oasis is at the bottom. Takes about three days in all."

"Three days. Is that on foot? On horseback? With a wagon?"

"Horse or mule."

Tevi took a step back and crossed her arms. "Anything else you'd like to tell me?"

Parrash shook his head.

"You wouldn't be so stupid as to lie, would you? Because we'll both be very annoyed if we go all the way to Qualeisi and Sefriall isn't there. You know you can't hide from a Coven sorcerer. We'll find you again, if we need to. Count on it."

"It's true. I swear. She'll be there, waiting for me."

"I'll pass on your best wishes." Tevi turned away. "Come on, Jem. We need to find some horses."

On the stairs down, Jemeryl caught Tevi's shoulder and pulled her around. "Even if I approved of this hunt, there's no way I'd have used magic to probe his mind."

"I know that, but he didn't. People are always ready to believe the worst of sorcerers."

Tevi's grin only increased Jemeryl's irritation. "It doesn't help when we're used for making wild threats."

"You're annoyed?"

"I want no part in this. I'm just tagging along to make sure you don't get hurt."

Tevi's lips tightened in a thin line, but then softened. "I'm sorry. I'll leave you out of it from now on."

Jemeryl released her grip. "Where are you going to get horses?"

"I'm sure there'll be a few in the stable here."

"They aren't ours."

"We've got enough gold to buy ten dozen. Someone will sell."

The innkeeper was loitering in the lobby when they returned. Tevi marched over to him. "Your stables, where are they?"

"Parrash?" He said the name as a question.

"He's fine. He may have pissed himself, but it's nothing that can't be fixed with a good wash. Now, your stables."

"Why?"

"I'm fond of horses." Tevi gave him a shove. "No questions. Just show me the way."

Over half the stalls in the stable were empty. Jemeryl was surprised, given the overcrowding in Kradja. Had so many guests fled already? Two more were making ready to depart as they entered.

Tevi, in the lead, had already seen them and was homing in. "Hey, you!"

The two guests were a man and a woman, both in early middle age and dressed in soft leather travelling gear. Jemeryl guessed they were well-off traders. The horses were healthy, clean-limbed animals, and not cheap. A third pack mount was nearby, loaded with supplies.

The man looked around, his expression somewhere between irritation and alarm. "What?"

"I want to buy your horses."

"You can't afford them." The assumption was not surprising, given Tevi's shabby appearance.

"Name your price."

"They're not for sale."

"I think they are."

Jemeryl slipped to the side of the stable, where she could watch everyone, without getting in the way. The trader's eyes brushed over her briefly and then moved on to the innkeeper, who was wavering by the entrance. "Master Kastani. Who is this person and what's she doing here? I don't expect this sort of thing in your inn."

"She's not—"

Tevi cut in. "I'm not someone you should mess about with. I want your horses, but I'm ready to pay. So name your price."

"No." The woman trader now spoke. "I know why you want them. The gods have forsaken Kradja. The power to work magic has returned and the Coven are on their way to destroy the town. Of course you want our horses. Everyone wants to get away. But you can't have them. The High Priest was nothing to do with us, and we're not going to stay here and be killed."

"Then I've got some very good news for you." Jemeryl could not see Tevi's face, but she could hear the smile in her voice. "I can tell you with absolute certainty that the Coven sorcerers aren't on their way here and they aren't going to kill anyone. You can sit in this nice inn, take it easy, and wait for all the fuss to die down. But I've to get somewhere fast, so I need horses. Yours will do fine."

"You can't have them."

"Don't make me take them by force."

"You're a thief." The woman backed away, while her gaze shifted to the innkeeper. "Kastani, where are your people? I thought you had guards."

"I've already dealt with them. They're currently bandaging their cuts and bruises. Luckily for them, the healers are in business again." Tevi stepped forward and grabbed the reins of the nearest horse. "Jem. Take the other one and let's go."

The metallic ring of a sword being drawn sliced through the stable. Tevi jerked around and faced the male trader, who now had a curved scimitar in his hand. In an instant, the woman had also pulled out a pair of long knives. She flourished them dramatically, diverting Jemeryl's attention so that she missed the man's attack. Fortunately, Tevi was more alert. The first Jemeryl was aware of it was the sudden burst of movement when Tevi dodged the thrust, and ripped out her own sword.

Jemeryl watch in dismay. What should she do? Would Tevi be able to defeat the two opponents at once? Jemeryl pressed her hand to her mouth, torn. She would not stand by and see Tevi injured, but the two traders were guilty of nothing. Supposing Tevi hurt them?

The woman was circling, clearly intending to get Tevi caught between her and her partner so they could attack from both sides simultaneously. However, Tevi was not about to let that happen. In a move so quick that it caught the traders, and Jemeryl, by surprise, she dropped onto her hands, twisted, and rolled. Tevi's legs swung in a wide arc, hitting the woman on her ankles and knocking her feet from under her. The woman landed heavily on the floor, her head hitting the ground hard enough for Jemeryl to hear the crack.

Meanwhile Tevi had risen in a fluid action and before the man had time to react, she was surging forward. At the last moment, the trader brought his scimitar across to parry. The two blades met. With a normal opponent, he might have done well enough, but not against

Tevi's strength. The scimitar was stripped from his hand and he was spun around by the impact. Tevi's follow-up kick sent him flying face first into the wall.

At the other side of the stable, the woman was struggling to get back up, but was no further than her knees. Tevi charged back across the stable and stood over her, raising her sword for a downward swing. The women looked up, her dazed expression turning to hopeless panic. She had no time to mount a defence.

"Stop."

Jemeryl would watch no more. She reached through the sixth dimension, grabbed a knot of tensors, and ripped it loose. The released energy erupted in harsh light, etching the scene starkly in raw black and white. Cries rang out from those dazzled. Jemeryl released the tensors and then diverted the flow, sucking heat from metal. Tevi and the trader dropped the weapons that had turned to ice in their hands. The man was on his knees, fumbling for his scimitar. He also jerked back.

"Enough." Jemeryl looked at the traders. "Don't worry. We won't steal your horses."

Shocked silence filled the stable, broken only by the woman scuttling crablike to her partner's side. Not until she was behind him did she get the nerve to stand fully upright. She put her hand on his shoulder, shaking visibly. The fear on her face when Tevi had stood over her was as nothing compared to the dread written there now.

The man was equally cowed. "I'm sorry. We didn't know."

"It's all right. We don't—" Jemeryl did not get to finish.

"Please. You can take the horses."

"They're yours." Neither trader was listening to her.

Tevi bent down and retrieved her sword, using a fold of her robe to shield her hand from the cold. "You heard them, Jem. Let's go."

Jemeryl stood still. She had intervened, and her magic had been used to deprive innocent traders of their rightful property. Anger boiled up at Tevi for putting her in that position. Jemeryl had known the hunt for Sefriall would cause only harm.

Tevi was already mounted on one of the horses. "Jem, are you coming?"

Jemeryl was tempted to say no, but she knew she would regret it. Within a few hours she would have changed her mind and be chasing after Tevi. Why make her life more difficult than need be?

Before they rode out, Tevi took a purse from her belt and threw it to the traders who were still huddled in a corner. It landed on the straw by their feet. "Here. That's about five times what the horses are worth. Buy yourself some new ones when everyone stops acting crazy."

Jemeryl waited until they were clear of the stable before giving vent to her feelings. "Are you pleased with what you did?"

"Yes. We know where Sefriall is, and nobody got badly hurt."

"Only because I was there." Jemeryl's outrage overflowed. "You nearly murdered them."

"They started the fighting."

"Aren't they allowed to defend themselves from thieves?"

"I wasn't trying to steal."

"What do you call taking something when the owner says no?"

"You're angry at me."

"Aren't you angry at yourself?"

Tevi did not answer for a while. They were riding side by side. Jemeryl turned her head to look at Tevi's face in profile. Tevi was staring ahead, frowning, while her jaw worked. Was this the first hint that Tevi might be having doubts? Even so, she was clearly not yet ready to change course.

"We didn't have any option. You saw the market. We wouldn't be able to buy any horses there, and the traders don't need to get away. We know the Coven isn't going to attack Kradja."

"We did have an option. We could have stayed here."

"We have to find Sefriall."

"There's no *have to* about it. We could let it go."

"I can't." Tevi's expression wavered briefly. "I know you feel differently. Do you want to go back and wait in Kradja for me?"

"Yes." Jemeryl hung her head. It was good they so rarely disagreed, because she was just as stubborn as Tevi. "But I'm not going to."

❖

Although its overall direction continued due south, the gorge twisted and turned, rarely allowing them to see more than a furlong ahead. All the while, the bottom dropped and the walls on either side rose higher. Tevi would have been happier with more advance warning of what lay ahead, but as Parrash had said, there was little chance of getting lost.

The dust-filled air was stifling in the midafternoon heat. Tevi could feel sweat trickling down her back. The horse was a local animal, bred for the desert conditions, but its head was drooping. Tevi considered stopping for a break, but Qualeisi Oasis had to be very close. Once they had dealt with Sefriall, they could rest by the water.

Tevi's hopes were confirmed when they turned the next bend. The first hint of green showed in tufts of grass. Another half mile and the huge cacti had been replaced by palm trees and spindly shoulder high bushes.

"Tevi," Jemeryl said.

"What?"

Since leaving Kradja, their conversation had been limited to the trivial—the practicalities of food and sleep, observations on the scenery and wildlife, the state of Jemeryl's leg and gossip about people they knew. Nothing had been said of their destination, or Tevi's plans for when they got there.

"We're being watched."

"How many?"

"Five."

"Are they doing anything?"

"Just tracking us."

Tevi looked around. Whoever it was knew their business. "They're well hidden."

"Not in the fifth dimension."

"Parrash said Sefriall only had three sentinels with her."

"He must have lied."

"Or they're somebody else."

"Who?"

Jemeryl's question was answered when they turned the next bend. The valley floor was filled with vegetation. At the heart of it, open water glinted between the trunks of palm trees. They had reached the oasis. Still there were no humans in sight, but a herd of piebald goats foraged nearby.

Tevi reined in her horse. "Looks like I might not get to kill Sefriall after all. If the nomads have captured her they'll have beaten me to it. Would that make you happy?"

"No. Relieved, maybe." Jemeryl's voice was tight. "What do you want to do?"

"We might as well go and find out for sure if she was here. And the horses need a rest. This will be better than out in the desert." Tevi glanced around. "Plus it wouldn't be a bad idea to let them know who we are." She urged her horse forward.

As they approached, armed figures emerged from concealment amid the greenery. Tevi stopped her horse a dozen yards from the old woman standing prominently in the middle and walked the final distance on foot.

"Who are you?" The elder issued the challenge in a thick nomad accent.

"A friend."

"Whose friend?"

"A lot of people. At the moment I'm here for Darjain. I want to avenge his death." A stir rippled among the listeners as several translated Tevi's words.

"I didn't know he had died. I'm sorry. He was a true servant of Yalaish."

"He was a good man."

"You say his death calls for avenging?"

"Yes. Sefriall murdered him."

The nomad elder nodded. "Then I'm even more grateful Yalaish delivered her into my hands here."

"You've killed Sefriall?"

"Not yet."

"I want to talk to her."

"No. We're dealing with the blasphemer. You should go."

"Our horses need rest. And I want to see her." Tevi was happy for the nomads to take their revenge. They had also respected Darjain, and had suffered their own loses at Sefriall's hands, but she had to be sure. She had to look on her enemy.

"You can stay here and rest. We'll bring water for your horses. Then you must go."

"I'll go after I've talked to Sefriall."

The warriors on either side tensed. Weapons that had been lowered were raised again. The elder waited a few seconds before speaking—a pause possibly intended to give Tevi time to assess the situation. "We do not allow that."

"I bear you no ill will. But I will see her."

Tevi stepped forward, knowing that Jemeryl would back her up. She was grateful there was no longer a reason for conflict between them. Had she been on her way to kill Sefriall she could not have taken her lover so much for granted. Of course, Jemeryl would still have protected her, but at a cost to the mutual trust between them.

A bowstring twanged. An instant later, Tevi heard a snap and the crackle of flame. She did not bother to turn her head. She was now within arm's reach of the elder, but the woman was no longer looking at her. Her eyes were fixed over Tevi's shoulder at where Jemeryl was standing. Blue and green light played over the nomad's weathered face. Tevi guessed Jemeryl was indulging in a few daytime pyrotechnics—harmless, but effective at getting the point across. Surprised cries came from the warriors.

Tevi tilted her head. "You have numbers on your side. We have magic." She walked past.

The nomads exchanged hissed comments among themselves, but no one challenged Tevi as she followed the narrow winding track through the shoulder-high grass. Presumably Sefriall would be held somewhere near the centre of the oasis. Footsteps and the play of coloured light on the leaves let Tevi know that Jemeryl was following close behind.

A bird took off as she passed beneath, its wings whirring loudly. The only other sounds were the soft lapping of water from ahead and the buzz of insects. Then Tevi heard a bestial growl, guttural, soft and low. She pushed through the last clump of sprouting fronds and emerged onto a sandy tract leading down to the waterside.

More nomads were here, twenty or thirty in number. Those who were standing nearest backed away, revealing a black shape spreadeagled on the ground. The outline was humanoid, but it was lacking in detail and seemed to ripple. Tevi approached, even as her suspicions grew.

The body had to be Sefriall. Tevi reached the conclusion by deduction rather than recognition. Who else would the nomads treat this way? Three red-clad corpses hung from nearby trees. These would be the sentinel guards, summarily dealt with. The High Priest herself had been stripped and staked to the ground. Tevi guessed that honey or some similar attraction had been smeared over her. Huge desert ants now covered her in a living blanket, dissecting her bite by bite. A dark moving trail led off and disappeared under the bushes. That way must lie their nest.

"Oh that's…that's…" Jemeryl's voice at her shoulder was sick with disgust.

Tevi reached out and took her hand.

The sand beneath Sefriall was stained red. More glimpses of raw flesh peeked through ebbs in the flowing black mass. Tevi also saw white on her fingers where the ants had already eaten down to the bone.

A larger movement shuddered through the form and again Tevi heard the guttural, inhuman moan. Sefriall was not yet dead—not quite, but she no longer had the strength to scream. Tevi's guts twisted in a spasm and Jemeryl's grip tightened painfully. Carefully, Tevi extricated her fingers and advanced to Sefriall's side. Ants ran over Tevi's feet, but with the feast on offer, they paid no more attention than if she had been a rock.

In a swift motion, Tevi pulled her sword from its scabbard and held it, point down over Sefriall's chest.

"Tevi. You don't need to do that. She'll be dead soon. There's no hope for her."

"I know, but no one deserves to die like this. Not even her."

Tevi plunged the sword down into Sefriall's heart. The air was forced from the priest's lungs in a final gasp. Tension in her arms and legs was released and her body sank lifeless on the sand. The ants carried on with their scavenging, unabated. Tevi pulled her sword free and turned around.

The elder had followed them and now stood, surrounded by her followers. "She defiled *Yalaish si liarajali.* She poisoned the holy water of the first tear shed by Yalaish. It was fitting that she should die here, by the last."

"I hope your god is pleased with you."

Tevi doubted whether the bitter irony in her words would get through, but she did not have the stomach to stay and say more. She pushed by the cluster of nomads, returning to her horse. The animal would have to go a little further before she could let it rest. She would make it up to the horse somehow, but Tevi would not stay by the oasis a moment longer.

After all the deaths Sefriall had instigated, after all the misery she had caused, after scheming to impose her dogma on the world, it made a mockery of her victims' suffering that she should be killed for the damage she had inflicted on water.

❖

"Damned silver balls. I'm a magpie, not a stupid budgie." Klara's voice was even more scornful than normal.

"Magpies are supposed to collect shiny things. I'm sure Thaldo thought you'd like them." Jemeryl stroked the magpie's back. It was good to be in contact with her familiar. She had summoned Klara to meet her as soon as she was close enough to do it in safety.

"He thought I was going to play with them. Don't know what sort of game he had in mind."

"Football?"

"Do I look like a magpie who'd be daft enough to kick something made of metal?"

"He meant well."

"They're the worst sort."

Jemeryl leaned back in her chair and turned her head. Outside, autumn rain was falling on the streets of Lyremouth. Through the tavern window, she watched porters pushing handcarts, their collars turned up against the drizzle, and children splashing through the puddles. Friends were calling to each other from the shelter of awnings, while a pair of new lovers, immune to the elements, stood kissing on the street corner. The scene was so safe and ordinary, and one random act might set off a chain of events that could destroy it.

"The murdered child, the gardener's daughter. Do you know if the person responsible was ever caught?" Tevi's thoughts were clearly running in a similar vein.

"No. I could try to find out."

"Whoever it was has more to answer for than they know."

"They weren't really to blame for what happened in Kradja. They only murdered one child…" Jemeryl stopped and shook her head. "I can't believe I just said that."

"I guess, in their favour, they wouldn't have tried pretending they were doing it for a noble cause, and right was on their side."

"I know what you mean. Somehow it makes it worse that Ci and Ralieu were both wanting to make the world a better place. A few more good intentions and the entire world could have been at the slaughter."

"They were just inanely naïve. I was thinking more about Sefriall." Tevi's face twisted in a frown. "I wish I'd got to talk to her. Did she see her actions as evil? Did she care? Had she convinced herself she was doing what her gods wanted?"

Jemeryl looked at her. "Does that mean you've changed your mind about her?"

"Softened a little. Seeing someone eaten alive can do that."

"If she was walking around now, safe and well, would you still try to kill her?"

"I don't know. The nomads, they're decent people, and seeing what…" Tevi sighed. "I think I've gone off the idea of revenge a bit."

"That's good."

"I'm not so sure. I may have gone off the whole idea of people. The citizens out there"—Tevi pointed at the window—"they seem all nice and sensible. One deranged sorcerer and they'd be a bloodthirsty, rampaging mob."

"I think that's…"

"What?"

"I've been trying to work out why I didn't want to help you hunt down Sefriall. I mean, Larric and Ashkinet were my friends too. And I was just as appalled by what happened to them. But…" Jemeryl chewed her lip, trying to get her thoughts in order. "Ci wasn't even a very good sorcerer. If I get things wrong, I could do so much more harm than he did."

"Is that a good reason to do nothing?"

Jemeryl drummed her fingers on the table. "It sounds like I'm abdicating all moral responsibility, but perhaps I should. I'm a sorcerer. It's not fair I have so much more power than ordinary people, but that's how it is, and I can't pretend differently. So maybe I should just focus on practical problems, sort out what has to be sorted, here and now, and then let it go. If I get serious about morals, it could get out of hand. Striving for absolute ideals is a luxury I can't afford, because I have to know when to stop."

"You think the world is better when it's ruled by unprincipled opportunists?"

"I think it's safer. Maybe that's why the Coven works so well. Rather than letting sorcerers try to create our vision of paradise, we're too busy competing with each other to get a better seat in the refectory and rubbishing each other's work and dealing with squabbles between guilds."

"And patronising magpies with silver balls," Klara added.

"And worrying about who's taken up with an undesirable lover?" Tevi carefully repositioned her tankard on the table, which Jemeryl interpreted as displacement activity masking her concern. "Do you think Alendy will try to separate us again? You're meeting with him tomorrow afternoon to discuss your plans for the future, aren't you?"

"Yes. But I shouldn't think he'd dare. The last thing he wants is more trouble, and if he tries to send me away from you, that's exactly what he'll get. Plus, after the way we've just hauled his arse out of the fire, I think I ought to be able to name my job."

"Do you want to go back to Horzt?"

Jemeryl scrunched her nose. "I'm not bothered. A change of scenery would be nice, and Thaldo ought to be settled there by now."

"With his silver balls." Klara was not to be deflected from her complaints.

Jemeryl prodded the magpie with her forefinger, raising an indignant squawk, and then looked at Tevi. "Where would you like to go?"

"Somewhere where I don't have to meet many people. Like I said, I've gone off them a bit at the moment."

"There might be a village up on Whitfell Spur that needs a witch."

"With just the occasional basilisk?"

"Or two." Jemeryl smiled. "Do you really want to become a hermit?"

"No. But I'd like to spend a bit of time without seeing anyone die."

Klara bobbed her head. "I'd have to question whether you're in the right profession as a member of the guild of Mercenary Warriors."

Tevi sank down in her chair, frowning. "Do you think you could get a post in Lyremouth?"

"I think I stand a very good chance. As I said, Alendy owes us a big favour."

"Even if it meant having you and me here together under his nose?"

"He's got people breathing down his neck over his handling of Ralieu. I can't see we're going to be a major priority for him." Jemeryl looked at Tevi. "What would you do here?"

"I ought to be able to get work training new members at the guildhall. I've had enough of seeing people hurt. I'd like to spend a few years helping people stay unhurt."

Jemeryl nodded. "I'll see what I can do."

"But would you be happy here?"

Jemeryl again stared out at Lyremouth—or the small part of it on view—struck by the irony. When she had finished her apprenticeship and been sent far from Lyremouth, her sole ambition had been to return. The dream of advancing the study of magic while rising up the Coven hierarchy had been her only goal.

"You know, there was a time when if you'd asked me that, I'd have laughed."

"Why?"

"Because back then, it was the only thing in life I wanted."

"What changed?"

Jemeryl looked back and smiled. "I met you."

APPENDIX

THE LEGEND OF MORFULAJI AND
THE AVATAR OF YALAISH

As told by the desert nomads around Kradja

Long, long ago, a spectre named Morfulaji escaped from the nightmare realms of chaos to unleash its carnage on the world. The undead fiend took the form of a monstrous bear, using dark magics to give itself the appearance of life. Such was the spectre's power that it assailed even the god-home and for a while it seemed that the gods would be overthrown and chaos would claim all creation.

Only mighty Haith, god of hunters, was not dismayed. She pursued the bear across the planes of existence until at last she confronted Morfulaji. Long and ferocious was the battle. All heaven rang with the sound of the conflict. But Haith proved victorious. She slew the spectral bear and flayed its carcass. The hide she then presented to her mother, Yalaish, as a trophy.

But this offering gave Yalaish fresh reasons to be troubled. Although the threat from Morfulaji was over, Yalaish knew Morfulaji's skin was possessed of great power. She feared it would be a cause of strife among her turbulent children were it kept in the god-home. So she secretly put it in the keeping of a human wise-woman called Ralieu. Yet even here it was not safe.

Of all her children, the triplet gods were always the greatest source of grief to their mother, the first to stir up trouble, the last to bow to her commands. Thus it was now. By devious means, Toqwani, god of destruction, found out where the skin of the spectral bear had been entrusted. The god descended to earth and took a human avatar. Calling himself Ciamon he infiltrated Ralieu's household as a servant and when he saw the chance, he stole the magical skin.

Toqwani returned to the god-home and summoned his cyclian

siblings. He showed them his prize and said, "See what I have. Join with me. With its power, we need no longer be subservient to our mother."

The hermaphrodite Rashem would take no part in it. "Put this thing aside, brother, for I predict you will have little joy from such an evil source. While I share your desire for supremacy, nothing can be built on foundations of chaos."

Koneath, though, was delighted and immediately joined her brother in rebellion. She also took a human avatar, assuming the name of Sefriall. Together, the two cyclian gods went to the town of Kradja and occupied the temple, claiming it solely for themselves. They cast out the priests of all other gods, and stripped their altars.

In the great hall of the temple, they constructed a golden idol and sealed the skin of the spectral bear inside. Great magic did they weave around the idol, infusing it with their godhead. Once their spells were complete, they harnessed the monstrous power of Morfulaji's skin, casting a sphere of protection, a thousand miles across.

The idol's power was such that, in the region it covered, none but Koneath and Toqwani could work magic. Healers could not cure sickness, sorcerers could not cast spells, seers could not foretell the future. The gods themselves were not immune. Not even their mother could assail them with her full power, while they were under Morfulaji's protection.

The rebellious siblings drew on the skin still more. They summoned an army of red demons from the realms of chaos, and then finally they inflicted a madness on the people of Kradja, so that they would worship no god other than the cyclian triplets. All other holy places were usurped or desecrated.

Only we, the desert people, were immune to the madness. We held true to Yalaish and many of us fell in battle with the red demons, trying to defend the holy places. For the cyclian siblings were keen to show their contempt of their mother, and sites dedicated to her were savagely attacked. Most grievous of all, the first tear of Yalaish was overrun by the red demons and its sacred water poisoned. Bitter indeed was that day. A thousand generations will pass before we forget.

Yet in their action, the siblings showed a lack of wisdom. For in desecrating her sacred oasis, they alerted their mother to the mischief they were about, and once she saw what her children were doing, Yalaish would not let them continue unchecked. However, the power of

Morfulaji's skin was such that even the all-mother could not challenge her rebellious children directly. Guile was to be her first weapon, and in this, Yalaish was not lacking.

She also now took a human avatar and descended to earth. In the form of a common mercenary warrior, she made her way to Kradja, travelling unheralded and in secret. None knew who she was. Her presence on earth might have gone forever unrecognised were it not for a minor incident on the way.

One member of the party she travelled with was Siashe of Jeqwai's kin. He had no idea that the female warrior was more than she seemed. Yet one night, when all others lay sleeping, Siashe awoke from a dream. In the moonlight he saw Yalaish walking through the campsite. One of the wagons was stopped with its wheel on her backpack. As Siashe watched in amazement, he saw the lone woman lift the wagon to retrieve a blanket. Ten men could not have picked up the wagon, and so near Morfulaji's skin, no witch or sorcerer could have moved it by magic. Thus Siashe knew only the avatar of a god could have performed the feat.

We can but wonder why Yalaish revealed herself in this way. Had she truly been unaware she was observed? Did she want her devout followers to know she had not abandoned us in our need, and ever she would protect us? Or did she anticipate needing our support? Speculating on the motives of a god is at best foolish, but whatever Yalaish's intentions, in this manner was the divine nature of her avatar revealed.

Once Yalaish arrived in Kradja, she set about gaining the ear of her defiant children. In this she was soon successful. Neither Koneath or Toqwani recognised their mother. Although they must have been on their guard, anticipating Yalaish to move against them, undoubtedly they were not looking for her to come alone and in such a humble guise. But for her part, Yalaish well knew the nature of her children, and how to charm them, mixing wisdom with flattery. Before long she was their most trusted adviser.

Yalaish plied them with honeyed words, saying, "Great is your power. All the world should bow before you. Yet you hold your hand. Why do you not demand the coven sorcerers of Lyremouth do you homage?"

In this, Yalaish was feigning innocence, for well she knew that

Lyremouth lay beyond the reach of Morfulaji's power. Her intent was to coax her children into overreaching themselves, appealing to their arrogance and pride.

"The sorcerers have great magic at their command," Koneath said.

"They also have great arrogance and show you contempt. Why do you not punish them? Surely even the sorcerers cannot hold off the army of red demons at your command," Yalaish said, knowing the demons from the realms of chaos were not dependent on Morfulaji's skin for their power, and could lay siege to Lyremouth with hope of victory. Her words were thus a trap, luring the rebellious gods into attempting an assault on Lyremouth, and Toqwani took the bait.

With their army of red demons, the siblings set off across the desert, and Yalaish went with them. Meanwhile in Lyremouth, the sorcerers received the news with concern. However, the army never got as far as the shores of the Middle Seas.

As Yalaish had known, the demons were as formidable as before, even when beyond the reach of Morfulaji's skin. But Koneath and Toqwani were now vulnerable and Yalaish was able to move directly against them. Toqwani, god of destruction, was the first to fall under the spell his mother laid on him. Toqwani's fierce nature was inflamed, so he was overwhelmed by blood madness and the urge to tear down all around him. Unable to master his fury, he charged into the nearby town of Villenes, followed by the red demons, bringing death and ruin with him.

Many innocent people died at his hands and great was the devastation he wrought. Yet at his most harmful he was also at his most exposed. Relentlessly, Yalaish pursued him through the ruined town, and at last found him alone and undefended, with none of the red demons to aid him. Still Toqwani thought to defy his mother, for the avatar of a god may not easily be slain. But in her hand, Yalaish held a sanctified blade—a weapon had the power to destroy the god's mortal form. This she thrust into the heart of Toqwani's avatar, cutting through the bonds of magic that held his godhead on earth. The release of power was so intense that his mortal body was incinerated, crumpling into ash, and his divine spirit was carried back to the god-home on a shaft of light.

However, his sister, Koneath, did not succumb to the blood

madness. Although she felt the lure, it was not in her nature to respond. The weakness of the god of builders lay elsewhere. Realising their mother had beguiled her and her brother and their downfall was at hand, she pulled herself back from the brink. So Koneath was able to flee back to Kradja, taking most of the army of demons with her.

Yalaish had thus dismissed one of her rebellious children from the mortal world, but her victory was not complete. Furthermore, she knew her daughter would not fall to the same trick again. Flattery and false counsel would no longer serve, but neither was a direct onslaught likely to succeed. Before an army got within a hundred miles of Kradja it would be spotted and engaged. No matter how formidable a force Yalaish raised, its chances would be slim against the red demons as long as Morfulaji's skin limited her power.

A show of force was surely what Koneath would be expecting, and her scouts would be on the lookout for a large army. Thus, while Koneath's eyes were focused on the horizon, a small band might avoid her gaze and pass into the heart of Kradja without drawing notice Yalaish set about gathering a band of heroes, few in numbers yet potent enough to destroy the idol containing Morfulaji's skin.

The number of heroes Yalaish enlisted was three times three. First she went to Lyremouth and appealed to the leaders of the coven. The army of demons advancing on Lyremouth had dismayed them and they speedily agreed. Three of their best sorcerers, most skilled in the arcane arts, volunteered for the task. Secondly, Yalaish went to the priests. The devout Darjain was also quick to offer his support, and two other priests joined him in lending their wisdom and their piety to the cause.

Finally, Yalaish came to us, the desert people, her most faithful followers. Although she still appeared no more than a common warrior, from the testimony of Siashe, many suspected her true nature. Great was the honour of serving her and all who could yet stand and hold a weapon begged to be allowed to follow her. From our number, she selected three of our bravest warriors; Gaithon the quick, fleetest of foot; Waljed the strong, unbeaten in battle; and Lianthe the deft, whose arrows never missed their target.

Meanwhile, Koneath was desperate, anticipating her mother's attack, and became ever crueler seeking out those she thought might oppose her. Yet she still envisioned that Yalaish would move against her in force, so she was not on her guard for the small band of heroes who slipped through her defences. With Yalaish to lead them, the band crossed the desert unseen. They stole through the streets of Kradja with none to note their passing. Finally they stood inside the great hall of the temple, within sight of the golden idol itself. And all this while, Koneath was blind to the threat, unaware that retribution for her disobedience was at hand.

Yalaish unleashed her band of heroes. Too late did Koneath realise her error. In panic she recalled her red demons from the outskirts of her land. They descended on the temple, flowing in like a river of evil. But Yalaish had chosen her heroes well. Such was their might and their skill and their wisdom that they withstood the horde of demons long enough for Yalaish to complete her task. The idol was cast down and destroyed, and once again Yalaish reclaimed the skin of the spectral bear. Now its power was hers.

At her command, the red demons faded and slid back to the realms of chaos. Alas, their numbers had been overwhelming and they had taken their toll on the band of heroes. On that day died Darjain and another priest and also two of the sorcerers. Also fell Gaithon, who would never again run across the desert sands, and Waljed, with his legendary strength. Never again would Lianthe loose arrows at her foes. Yet their names will live forever in our hearts, for with their sacrifice they erased our shame from the defilement of the first tear.

The losses were grievous, but the idol had been destroyed, and with it, Koneath's power was broken. The red demons were gone and the people of Kradja awakened as if from a nightmare and remembered the gods of their ancestors. Also the gift of magic returned. Healers, witches, seers, and sorcerers could again work their spells. All that remained was to destroy Koneath's mortal body and return her spirit to the god-home.

Yalaish went out into the market square and leapt onto a plinth. From there she addressed the gathered townsfolk. "People of Kradja. You have been beguiled by mischievous gods who have led you into acts of great impiety. Now is your chance to show your repentance. Join with me and wipe this sacrilege from the temple."

Dismay rose in the hearts of all who heard her words, knowing what they had done under the spell of Morfulaji's skin. The people followed Yalaish, storming the temple and sweeping the remnants of Koneath's rule aside.

Koneath fled, her plans in ruins, but still she was unwilling to return to the god-home, fearing her mother's rightful anger. With only a handful of supporters she escaped across the desert, seeking some place to hide. Yalaish followed on in close pursuit, hunting down her defiant daughter. For many long days the chase continued. Ever Koneath kept in the lead, hoping to delay the inevitable reckoning.

In the midst of the desert, Koneath thought to rest at a small oasis, not knowing that one of our tribes was gathered there. At once, our people recognised the woman who had ordered the desecration of the tears of Yalaish and who had persecuted our people. They knew her as Sefriall, a priest, and were unaware that she was really an avatar of Koneath. Our people took her prisoner and tried to end her life in retribution for the harm she had inflicted. However, the avatar of a god may not be killed by mortal hand. Despite all they did, Koneath's spirit still inhabited her human body.

The people wondered what sort of monster they held, but then Yalaish caught up with them. Still she had the sacred weapon that could destroy a god's avatar. While the people looked on in awe, Yalaish drove the blade into Koneath's mortal heart. The divine spirit left the avatar and ascended to the god-home and the human body was swallowed by the sands. Yalaish then left the oasis and departed across the desert as quietly as she had arrived.

Although none can say how Yalaish dealt with her rebellious children after she returned to the god-home, for us on earth the matter of Morfulaji's skin finally resolved, and the time of upheaval was over. Of the band of heroes, the one surviving sorcerer returned to the Lyremouth with news of what had passed, and the priest, Botha, became leader of the temple, healing the damage caused by Toqwani and Koneath.

And none but we, the desert people, noted that the avatar of Yalaish, in the form of a lone mercenary warrior, had vanished from the mortal earth, her work done.

About the Author

Jane Fletcher is a GCLS Award–winning writer and has also been short-listed for the Gaylactic Spectrum and Lambda Literary awards. She is author of two ongoing sets of fantasy/romance novels: the Celaeno series—*The Walls of Westernfort, Rangers at Roadsend, The Temple at Landfall, Dynasty of Rogues*, and *Shadow of the Knife*; and the Lyremouth Chronicles—*The Exile and The Sorcerer, The Traitor and The Chalice, The Empress and The Acolyte*, and *The High Priest and the Idol*.

Her love of fantasy began at the age of seven when she encountered Greek mythology. This was compounded by a childhood spent clambering over every example of ancient masonry she could find (medieval castles, megalithic monuments, Roman villas). Her resolute ambition was to become an archaeologist when she grew up, so it was something of a surprise when she became a software engineer instead.

Born in Greenwich, London in 1956, she now lives in southwest England where she keeps herself busy writing both computer software and fiction, although generally not at the same time.

Visit her Web site: www.janefletcher.co.uk.

Books Available From Bold Strokes Books

The High Priest and the Idol by Jane Fletcher. Jemeryl and Tevi's relationship is put to the test when the Guardian sends Jemeryl on a mission that puts her not only in harm's way, but back into the sights of a previous lover. (978-1-60282-085-2)

Point of Ignition by Erin Dutton. Amid a blaze that threatens to consume them both, firefighter Kate Chambers and property owner Alexi Clark redefine love and trust. (978-1-60282-084-5)

Secrets in the Stone by Radclyffe. Reclusive sculptor Rooke Tyler suddenly finds herself the object of two very different women's affections, and choosing between them will change her life forever. (978-1-60282-083-8)

Dark Garden by Jennifer Fulton. Vienna Blake and Mason Cavender are sworn enemies—who can't resist each other. Something has to give. (978-1-60282-036-4)

Late in the Season by Felice Picano. Set on Fire Island, this is the story of an unlikely pair of friends—a gay composer in his late thirties and an eighteen-year-old schoolgirl. (978-1-60282-082-1)

Punishment with Kisses by Diane Anderson-Minshall. Will Megan find the answers she seeks about her sister Ashley's murder or will her growing relationship with one of Ash's exes blind her to the real truth? (978-1-60282-081-4)

September Canvas by Gun Brooke. When Deanna Moore meets TV personality Faythe she is reluctantly attracted to her, but will Faythe side with the people spreading rumors about Deanna? (978-1-60282-080-7)

No Leavin' Love by Larkin Rose. Beautiful, successful Mercedes Miller thinks she can resume her affair with ranch foreman Sydney Campbell, but the rules have changed. (978-1-60282-079-1)

Between the Lines by Bobbi Marolt. When romance writer Gail Prescott meets actress Tannen Albright, she develops feelings that she usually only experiences through her characters. (978-1-60282-078-4)

Blue Skies by Ali Vali. Commander Berkley Levine leads an elite group of pilots on missions ordered by her ex-lover Captain Aidan Sullivan and everything is on the line—including love. (978-1-60282-077-7)

The Lure by Felice Picano. When Noel Cummings is recruited by the police to go undercover to find a killer, his life will never be the same. (978-1-60282-076-0)

Death of a Dying Man by J.M. Redmann. Mickey Knight, Private Eye and partner of Dr. Cordelia James, doesn't need a drop-dead gorgeous assistant—not until nature steps in. (978-1-60282-075-3)

Justice for All by Radclyffe. Dell Mitchell goes undercover to expose a human traffic ring and ends up in the middle of an even deadlier conspiracy. (978-1-60282-074-6)

Sanctuary by I. Beacham. Cate Canton faces one major obstacle to her goal of crushing her business rival, Dita Newton—her uncontrollable attraction to Dita. (978-1-60282-055-5)

The Sublime and Spirited Voyage of Original Sin by Colette Moody. Pirate Gayle Malvern finds the presence of an abducted seamstress, Celia Pierce, a welcome distraction until the captive comes to mean more to her than is wise. (978-1-60282-054-8)

Suspect Passions by VK Powell. Can two women, a city attorney and a beat cop, put aside their differences long enough to see that they're perfect for each other? (978-1-60282-053-1)

Just Business by Julie Cannon. Two women who come together—each for her own selfish needs—discover that love can never be as simple as a business transaction. (978-1-60282-052-4)

Sistine Heresy by Justine Saracen. Adrianna Borgia, survivor of the Borgia court, presents Michelangelo with the greatest temptations of his life while struggling with soul-threatening desires for the painter Raphaela. (978-1-60282-051-7)

Radical Encounters by Radclyffe. An out-of-bounds, outside-the-lines collection of provocative, superheated erotica by award-winning romance and erotica author Radclyffe. (978-1-60282-050-0)

Thief of Always by Kim Baldwin & Xenia Alexiou. Stealing a diamond to save the world should be easy for Elite Operative Mishael Taylor, but she didn't figure on love getting in the way. (978-1-60282-049-4)

X by JD Glass. When X-hacker Charlie Riven is framed for a crime she didn't commit, she accepts help from an unlikely source—sexy Treasury Agent Elaine Harper. (978-1-60282-048-7)

The Middle of Somewhere by Clifford Henderson. Eadie T. Pratt sets out on a road trip in search of a new life and ends up in the middle of somewhere she never expected. (978-1-60282-047-0)

Paybacks by Gabrielle Goldsby. Cameron Howard wants to avoid her old nemesis Mackenzie Brandt but their high school reunion brings up more than just memories. (978-1-60282-046-3)

Uncross My Heart by Andrews & Austin. When a radio talk show diva sets out to interview a female priest, the two women end up at odds and neither heaven nor earth is safe from their feelings. (978-1-60282-045-6)

Fireside by Cate Culpepper. Mac, a therapist, and Abby, a nurse, fall in love against the backdrop of friendship, healing, and defending one's own within the Fireside shelter. (978-1-60282-044-9)

A Pirate's Heart by Catherine Friend. When rare book librarian Emma Boyd searches for a long-lost treasure map, she learns the hard way that pirates still exist in today's world—some modern pirates steal maps, others steal hearts. (978-1-60282-040-1)

Trails Merge by Rachel Spangler. Parker Riley escapes the high-powered world of politics to Campbell Carson's ski resort—and their mutual attraction produces anything but smooth running. (978-1-60282-039-5)

Dreams of Bali by C.J. Harte. Madison Barnes worships work, power, and success, and she's never allowed anyone to interfere—that is, until she runs into Karlie Henderson Stockard. Aeros EBook (978-1-60282-070-8)

The Limits of Justice by John Morgan Wilson. Benjamin Justice and reporter Alexandra Templeton search for a killer in a mysterious compound in the remote California desert. (978-1-60282-060-9)

Designed for Love by Erin Dutton. Jillian Sealy and Wil Johnson don't much like each other, but they do have to work together—and what they desire most is not what either of them had planned. (978-1-60282-038-8)

Calling the Dead by Ali Vali. Six months after Hurricane Katrina, NOLA Detective Sept Savoie is a cop who thinks making a relationship work is harder than catching a serial killer—but her current case may prove her wrong. (978-1-60282-037-1)

Shots Fired by MJ Williamz. Kyla and Echo seem to have the perfect relationship and the perfect life until someone shoots at Kyla—and Echo is the most likely suspect. (978-1-60282-035-7)

truelesbianlove.com by Carsen Taite. Mackenzie Lewis and Dr. Jordan Wagner have very different ideas about love, but they discover that truelesbianlove is closer than a click away. Aeros EBook (978-1-60282-069-2)

Justice at Risk by John Morgan Wilson. Benjamin Justice's blind date leads to a rare opportunity for legitimate work, but a reckless risk changes his life forever. (978-1-60282-059-3)

Run to Me by Lisa Girolami. Burned by the four-letter word called love, the only thing Beth Standish wants to do is run for—or maybe from—her life. (978-1-60282-034-0)

Split the Aces by Jove Belle. In the neon glare of Sin City, two women ride a wave of passion that threatens to consume them in a world of fast money and fast times. (978-1-60282-033-3)

Uncharted Passage by Julie Cannon. Two women on a vacation that turns deadly face down one of nature's most ruthless killers—and find themselves falling in love. (978-1-60282-032-6)

Night Call by Radclyffe. All medevac helicopter pilot Jett McNally wants to do is fly and forget about the horror and heartbreak she left behind in the Middle East, but anesthesiologist Tristan Holmes has other plans. (978-1-60282-031-9)

Lake Effect Snow by C.P. Rowlands. News correspondent Annie T. Booker and FBI Agent Sarah Moore struggle to stay one step ahead of disaster as Annie's life becomes the war zone she once reported on. Aeros EBook (978-1-60282-068-5)

I Dare You by Larkin Rose. Stripper by night, corporate raider by day, Kelsey's only looking for sex and power, until she meets a woman who stirs her heart and her body. (978-1-60282-030-2)

Truth Behind the Mask by Lesley Davis. Erith Baylor is drawn to Sentinel Pagan Osborne's quiet strength, but the secrets between them strain duty and family ties. (978-1-60282-029-6)

Cooper's Deale by KI Thompson. Two would-be lovers and a decidedly inopportune murder spell trouble for Addy Cooper, no matter which way the cards fall. (978-1-60282-028-9)